PRAISE FOR *SISTERS ONE, TWO, THREE*

"Delightful, heart-wrenching, and honest, this book is a lovely examination of memory, the past, and how, despite flaws, the strength of family ties remains throughout years of tumult and misunderstanding."

—*Publishers Weekly*

"An emotionally gripping portrait of a family's secrets and confessions . . . Star brings all the members of the Tangle clan to life—these are multifaceted, complex characters with remarkable depth and nuance. Readers will enjoy seeing childhood quirks resurface in the Tangle adults, and fans of Jamie Brenner and Elizabeth Kelly will adore this compelling multigenerational story."

—*Booklist*

"A consistently compelling and entertaining read from cover to cover, *Sisters One, Two, Three* clearly showcases author Nancy Star's genuine flair for deftly created characters and original storytelling."

—*Midwest Book Review*

"An extraordinarily moving, beautifully written novel, *Sisters One, Two, Three* is a searing portrait of a family haunted by tragedy and fractured by the toxic power of secrets. As the story progresses, we grow to know and love the fierce and eccentric Tangles, a family at once familiar and like no other. I was riveted from the first page."

—Christina Baker Kline, #1 *New York Times* bestselling author of *Orphan Train*

"Witty, compelling, and wise, *Sisters One, Two, Three* is the kind of novel I always crave but rarely find. Glory Tangle's relationship with her children, both as kids and as grown-ups, is as real as it gets. She's a fantastic character, a match for the surprises to be found in the perfectly evoked island setting of Martha's Vineyard. I really loved each of the three sisters, too, and was very nervous for all of them! Nancy Star, thank you so much for the hours I spent in these pages."

—Alice Elliott Dark, author of *In the Gloaming* and *Think of England*

"Nancy Star's gripping novel of mothers and daughters and sisters shows us how we can never escape our families—and why that may be our salvation. Full of surprising twists and deep emotional insights, *Sisters One, Two, Three* will keep you glued to your beach chair, casting worried glances at those little clouds threatening to gather into a storm. This book will transform the way you see your own family's past and its future along with the way you experience the power of now."

—Pamela Redmond Satran, author of *Younger*

"With delightful wit and the prowess of an expert storyteller, Star offers profound insight into the maternal heart in this deftly braided tale of the utterly original Tangles. *Sisters One, Two, Three* begs to be read in one big gulp—and will leave you with a lasting understanding of the treacherous balance between love and autonomy."

—Lisa Gornick, author of *The Peacock Feast* and *Louise Meets Bear*

"What is it that fascinates us about the bonds between sisters? There have been many great stories about that special bond, and this is no exception. Enter the Tangle sisters, held together by love, common experience, and a web of secrets. From cautious Ginger to adventurous Callie to busy bee Mimi, you won't be able to help seeing yourself in this family, the things that pull it apart and ultimately tie it back together. Set some time aside to read this gem; you won't regret it."

—Catherine McKenzie, bestselling author of *Hidden* and *Fractured*

RULES
FOR
MOVING

RULES

FOR

MOVING

NANCY STAR

LAKE UNION
PUBLISHING

Text copyright © 2020 by Nancy Star

Published by Lake Union Publishing, Seattle

www.apub.com

Amazon, the Amazon logo, and Lake Union Publishing are trademarks of Amazon.com, Inc., or its affiliates.

ISBN-13: 9781542006378
ISBN-10: 1542006376

Cover design by David Drummond

Printed in the United States of America

for Larry

By an established custom, the houses are let from this day [May 1st] for the term of one year certain; and, as the inhabitants in general love variety, and seldom reside in the same house for two consecutive years, those who have to change, which appears to be nearly the whole city, must be all removed together. Hence, from the peep of day till twilight, may be seen carts which go at a rate of speed astonishingly rapid, laden with furniture of every kind, racing up and down the city, as if its inhabitants were flying from a pestilence, pursued by death with his broad scythe just ready to mow them into eternity.

—*Felton,* American Life: A Narrative of Two Years' City and Country Residence in the United States, 1843

PROLOGUE
SPRING 2018

What a headache. It had never crossed her mind that the house on Applegate Road—her neighbor's house—would end up to be one of those listings that kept her awake at night. A stubborn house that just wouldn't sell. A gem of a place where everything went wrong. Today's problem, a pregnant woman. Dana had nothing against pregnant women. She'd happily led five perfectly normal pregnant women up and down these stairs this month alone. But this woman was so pregnant—nine months at least, possibly ten—she could barely move. Dana could feel it coming; the prospective buyer's water was going to break right there, on the recently recleaned round rug that sat in the center of the once-again-spotless foyer. She took a breath and reminded herself that she had a fully stocked *Realtor's Secret Kit* in the trunk of her car. While it was true that so far the kit had only been put to the test on ink, coffee, and blood, she was confident—pretty confident—that it would be up to the challenge of amniotic fluid, if it came to that.

The woman's husband, who'd already made two jokes about how it wasn't his idea to move, was sluggish until he got to the basement. There, as if woken from hibernation, he charged into the utility room.

A moment later he slumped. There was nothing in Dana's secret kit to fix this. Sellers could scrub till their muscles were sore but a clean boiler still wasn't pretty. Basements were so often like that, disappointing.

She hustled him out and guided them both to the main downstairs space. "Here's what I love. A blank slate. Waiting to be transformed. You see bare walls. I see magical playroom."

Two stony faces stared back at her. Normally she could connect with anyone. Her husband said she could connect with a corpse. But these two? Nothing. It was the house. It made her nervous. Like it was judging her. "So!" She brightened her smile. "Ready to go up and see the kitchen? You are going to be over the moon when you see the kitchen."

"Could use an update," she allowed as she watched them scan the maple cabinets, doors askew. "But the beauty of that is you get to do it how you want." She saw the man glance at the one chipped terra-cotta floor tile. "What counts is the bones. Floors you can change. If the bones are bad, nothing you can do."

The air felt flat. She leaned toward the woman. "Can I tell you a secret? This is my block. Trust me, I don't show this house to anyone I wouldn't want on my block." The woman's spine seemed to stiffen. "Don't worry. I'm a very respectful neighbor. I never pry. Come. Let me show you the best part." She whisked them to the large window at the back of the living room. "Look how big the yard is. And how private. There's so much you could do with that space. Put in an outdoor kitchen. Bluestone patio. Farmhouse table. Tea lights on the bushes. Oh my god, I want to come over to your house for dinner and you haven't even said if you like it."

"I like it," the woman said.

Dana smiled. "I knew you would. You remind me a little of Lane. She's the woman who used to live here, with her son, Henry. Precious boy. Six years old. Face of an angel. Dark curly hair. Huge eyes. Sweetest thing you ever met. Even though he didn't talk."

The woman placed a protective hand over her belly. "Didn't talk?"

"But smart as a whip," Dana quickly added. "And very talented. His drawings were deep. Not surprising. His mom was deep. She used to write the *Ask Roxie* column. Ever read it?"

The woman shrugged. What did that mean? Did she not know the column? Did she not like the column? That would be a surprise. Even people who didn't like Lane liked her column. "Lane rented the house from my neighbor Nathan. He was one of my favorite neighbors. This was his divorce house. A totally amicable divorce. I guess the house started to feel too big for him, living alone. Or maybe he just needed a change. Like I said, I never pry. All I know is one day, out of the blue, he tells me he's moving and renting the place out. I was the one who showed Lane the house. Nathan was supposed to, but there was an emergency at his job. He's had a lot of jobs. He's a voice actor now. For a video game. How cool is that? I don't know what kind of emergencies they have in video games but an emergency is an emergency. Nathan tried to reach Lane to reschedule but she was already in the Lincoln Tunnel, on her way, and the call didn't go through. So he called me. Everybody calls me. Because they know I love to help. Lane fell for the house the minute she saw it. A lot of people were interested in renting it, but Nathan is a mensch so he rented it to her. Which thank god, because you would not believe what Lane had just been through. It was . . ." Dana caught herself. "Icing on the cake, the two of them hit it off like you wouldn't believe. It was *bashert*. You know what *bashert* means?" They didn't. "Meant to be. Soul mates. Very unusual people: a voice actor and an advice columnist. People tell me I should write an advice column. Which if I did? My advice to you? This is your house."

The woman crossed her arms. Full defensive position. All eye contact over.

It was because of her stupid comment about Henry. Why did she tell a pregnant woman about a boy who didn't talk? "You know what? I misspoke. It's not that Henry didn't talk. He was a chatterbox with his mom. He just didn't talk to *me*. Which if you think about it, was smart. Because once you get me going, you can't shut me up. I wish you could meet them. Great people. Salt of the earth. Like you. They're at Nathan's summer place now. On the Cape. Or Martha's Vineyard. Or maybe Maine. I don't know. I don't pry. A beautiful place is the point. This place is beautiful too." Stop talking. Move them along. "Shall we step outside?"

Outside Dana directed their diminishing attention to the newly installed top-of-the-line roof. "Looks like slate but it isn't, which means you don't have to take out a mortgage every time you need to replace a shingle." She pointed toward the stone below the clapboard. "One hundred percent Manhattan Schist. Forget insulation. Nothing gets through Manhattan Schist."

A mailbox door creaked open. Their heads swiveled toward the house next door. A woman scooped out her mail and disappeared inside. "That's Rory. My dentist. I know she doesn't look like a dentist. She looks like a model. But she's a dentist. What a doll. Last month I had a toothache in the middle of the night and she met me at her office. In her nightgown. That's the kind of block it is. Best block in town. Best people. Best kids. The colleges the kids end up at? Amazing. I can get you a list." She was a moron. Parents didn't think about college until after the baby was born. What was wrong with her?

What was wrong with her was this house. Selling houses wasn't hard for her. She was a positive person who saw the best in everything. All she had to do, all she ever did, was tell it like she saw it. But showing this house? It was like sciatica. One wrong move and everything went out of whack. What kind of idiot tells a pregnant woman, *The boy who used to live here didn't speak.* She took a silent breath and went in for the close.

"You know how they say, if the walls could talk? Well these walls do. They talk to me. And what they're saying is, this is the house for you."

The woman thanked her and told her they'd think about what they'd seen and the man said he'd get back to her, which was a bad sign because nine times out of ten, when there was good news, it was the woman who called.

Dana got in her car, checked her phone and zoomed off to her next showing.

The house on Applegate Road—a road with neither gates nor apples—was left alone with its memories of the people who'd lived there before: the man who did voices, the woman who gave advice, and the child, with the face of an angel, who didn't speak.

PART ONE

NEW YORK CITY

WINTER 2017

January 15, 2017

Ask Roxie!

Roxie Reader Good News Alert!

Do you wish you could send Roxie a question and get your answer in *real time*?

Now you can! Roxie's first ever online Live-Chat Wednesday is coming soon!

This is a bonus for Guild-Plus Members only! Subscribe today so you don't miss out!

Dear Roxie,

My maid of honor just told me I'm a psychopath. Talk about psychopaths!

It's because we had a fight. Because she's not coming to the bridal party dress fitting. Because it conflicts with her boyfriend's grandmother's ninety-fifth birthday party. Choosing her boyfriend over me is so high school! Not to mention we made the plan two months ago. Aren't plans supposed to be honored? Why does she think they call it maid of honor anyway?

As far as her boyfriend's grandmother's birthday, that's just an excuse. The real reason she's getting her dress fitted another day? She doesn't like how she looks in it. Which I'm sorry, but I didn't pick it. The bridal party voted. Twelve bridesmaids love it. Because it's one of those dresses where no matter how tall or short you are, it looks super great on you.

To be honest, it doesn't look super great on her. But it's not her wedding. Who's going to be looking at her? And seriously, if she wanted to, she could do something about her weight. It's not like she has a "condition." If I could stop smoking for my wedding, she could lose ten pounds. All right, fifteen. All right, twenty.

I am a person who values friendship. So in the spirit of friendship, I told her what I thought—about her responsibility as my maid of honor and about the dress and her weight. She didn't even bother to pretend to listen. When I asked her if she was listening is when she called me a psychopath.

Since when is it a crime to say the truth?

Yours,
Very Disappointed Bride

Dear Very Disappointed,

Congratulations on your upcoming wedding! Be sure to try and take it all in. Weddings go by so fast. And congratulations on your talent for reading minds! What? You can't read minds? Then how do you know the "real reason" your maid of honor won't come to the fitting?

Let's take a breath and consider this: a maid of honor who hates her dress won't ruin your wedding. A maid of honor who hates her bride will.

Her dress is not the problem. She agreed to get it fitted, just not on the day you picked, which sounds rough and hurtful for sure until you consider there is no way her boyfriend's grandmother's ninety-fifth birthday party will be rescheduled for your fitting. You know that, right? Good.

Now let's talk about the psychopath in the room. Crazy as it sounds, honesty is probably not the best policy for you. I'm sure you didn't mean to piss off your friend, but you did and—incoming wedding alert—that's a problem. Luckily it's a problem you can fix. Here's how:

First, apologize. Don't wait. Don't waffle. Don't put it on her. *I'm sorry you're so hypersensitive about your weight* is not a good apology even if it's true. What's called for here is a simple, heartfelt, *Sorry. That was hurtful. I shouldn't have said it.* Next, offer to come to her fitting.

Given what you say, she probably could use some moral support when she puts on that dress.

Like you, I can't read minds. But I'm going to make an educated guess:

If you're big about this—apologize, offer to go to her fitting, forever stop mocking her weight—your maid of honor will be your most devoted attendant on your big day.

Go for it! Be big. Be happy. And congrats!

Yours forever, or at least for now,
Roxie

1

Done. Lane Meckler hit the *Send* key and her email to the reader known to her only as Lost Soul disappeared from her screen. With luck, her email would get to Lost Soul before it was too late. With more luck, Lost Soul would follow her advice and immediately call the hotline number she'd included so he could get help fast. More than that was out of her control. She closed her laptop and heard herself let out a long breath. She hadn't realized she was concentrating so hard that she'd forgotten to breathe. Blinking her bleary eyes, she looked around. Where was everyone?

Lane's thirty-six-inch swath of desk was at the most distant work-table in the office. Farthest from reception, bathrooms, kitchen, private phone pods, it sat adjacent to a wall of windows made of special textured glass that managed to prevent anyone from looking out, but did nothing to stop glare from coming in. Most of the Guild workers assigned to Lane's long table quickly asked to be relocated anywhere else. But there was a self-sorting bunch who were happy with this spot, people who preferred glare on screens and distance from food to being in the center of activity. Lane was one of those people.

She stood up and scanned the room. Except for Jem, who sat next to her, hunched over, earbuds in and typing fast, everyone was gone. She checked the time. Five o'clock. Too early for the office to empty out, even on a Friday.

Jem looked up and took out an earbud. "They're at the party. You really don't hear anything when you're concentrating, do you?"

"That is true." Also true was that she had completely forgotten tonight was the annual office event she never went to. This year it was a skating party. Ice-skating with the folks in her office was not Lane's idea of a good time. Okay, any kind of party with any group of people was not her idea of a good time. Last year it was an indoor pool party—the invite promising a four-hour tropical escape from the harsh New York City winter—and Lane skipped that, even though she was a dedicated swimmer. She did not swim to socialize. She did not socialize. "What about you?" she asked Jem. "No ice-skating?"

Jem gave a quick shake of the head. Jem did not socialize either.

Lane didn't press it. She scooped up the leavings of her day, Post-it notes with itemized lists of tasks not yet done, scrap paper with phone numbers of social workers and lawyers she had not yet called, a bag of nuts she'd bought, opened and then forgot to eat. "Don't work too late, okay?"

Jem smiled. "Thank you, Roxie."

Lane smiled back and quickly cruised down the empty corridor. She wouldn't have said that—*Don't work too late*—if there had been anyone else around. While it was true she was a professional advice columnist, Lane worked hard to make sure her colleagues did not mistake her for a twenty-four-hour help desk. As deeply committed as she was to helping her *Ask Roxie* readers with their problems, she was equally committed to trying to get through her day otherwise left alone. Except for her son. And Jem. Jem was what Lane thought of as a perimeter person. She had a soft spot for people like Jem, those who made their way through the world trying not to take up too much space.

She dropped her food garbage in the designated bin and was almost at the exit to the reception area when she heard a sound. She stopped. The sound stopped. A head bobbed up over a nearby desk partition and then disappeared. She heard another noise. Sniffles. She held her breath and listened hard. Was someone crying?

Okay. No thanks. Not now. Her column was online only. She was off duty, unavailable, not interested in getting sucked into a conversation with an unhappy stranger. She took another step toward the exit and stopped. What if it wasn't an unhappy stranger? What if it was someone who'd fallen down or taken ill? She let out a sigh and switched direction.

The origin of the noise was a very young woman—was she even old enough to work here?—sitting at a desk, trembling as she cried.

"Aw honey," Lane said. "What's wrong?"

The young woman's mouth was working hard to contain her emotion. "I went to the bathroom because I was upset about—it doesn't matter. It's just I stayed there for a really long time and when I came back everyone was gone. And I don't know why. Was the building evacuated? Did something awful happen?"

"No. It's nothing like that. Everyone's at the party." Lane saw the confusion on the young woman's face. "When did you start working here?"

The young woman sniffled. "Yesterday."

"Okay." Lane took out her phone and searched her email. "It's in here somewhere. There's a party every January. For team building. Ah. Here it is." She asked the young woman—her name was Alyssa—for her phone number and texted her the address for the skating rink. "I'm Lane, by the way. You should go. You'll have a good time."

"I wasn't invited. Anyway it's too late."

"Everyone's invited. And it's not too late. These things go on forever. When it's over the party just moves to a bar. You should go," Lane repeated. "You'll meet people. You'll make friends." Alyssa hesitated. "I would go with you, but I have to get home. My son, Henry, is waiting for me. Want to walk to the elevator together?"

"Okay." Alyssa gathered her things. "Thank you. For being so nice."

"I'm not that nice," Lane told her and smiled. "Come on. Let's go."

As they waited for the elevator in the empty reception area, Alyssa glanced at the wall and noticed the large poster of Lane's face. "That's you? You're Roxie?"

Lane glanced at the image and turned away. The shoot for the poster had been slow and painful even though Lane did her best to cooperate. She didn't fight the stylist who told her she had to—absolutely must—change into a blue blouse to bring out her eyes. She didn't argue with the hair guy who, after saying he was in love with her natural curls, proceeded to blow-dry her hair so that it hung straight as a sheet. The problem was the photographer who, despite being full of compliments—he adored her big eyes and long lashes; he could not believe her perfect skin—got annoyed that Lane was unable to fix her expression.

"Can't you give me a more approachable face?" he asked.

"Probably not," Lane told him.

"Too tense," he'd grumbled an hour later, as if telling someone they were too tense had ever made anyone relax.

"Sorry you have to see that," Lane told Alyssa. "They put those up everywhere. To promote *Roxie's Live-Chat*. I don't know who decided it was a good idea to paste my face on walls and buses. I mean, would you want to talk to that face?"

"Yes," Alyssa said with what sounded like reverence. "You look super friendly."

Lane took a quick glance. She could see nothing friendly in the face on the poster, but she didn't want to contradict Alyssa, who had finally stopped sniffling. "Thanks," she said instead.

They rode down in the elevator in silence. In the lobby, Lane said, "Have fun," and then stopped to check her phone, while Alyssa continued out of the building, alone.

She'd missed three texts on her phone, all of them from Aaron. Her husband never texted. Her eyes went to the earliest in the thread.

Just got out of the cab!!! Took Henry to Milo's!!!!

So much for claims that it was hard to tell tone in a text. Turned out if you knew someone well enough, punctuation did the trick. Genial Aaron was never exclamatory except in an ironic way, when he was what she thought of as *drunk annoyed*. She let that sink in, that at five o'clock Aaron was already drunk annoyed.

She knew immediately what had annoyed him, in the way that couples who fought all the time did, their arguments so repetitive by now that they each could play both sides with perfect pitch. Aaron was annoyed that Lane hadn't been home in time to take Henry to his friend Milo's for his first ever *late-over*.

Neither of them had heard of a *late-over* until Henry told them about it. "It's like a sleepover," he explained, "except you don't sleep. You get in your pajamas and you brush your teeth, but at bedtime your parents come and take you home." He told them the next part purely as a matter of fact: "Everyone in my class has gone on one except for me."

Naturally Aaron could not let that stand, his son being behind in something, even though Lane tried to get him to see that rushing to arrange a late-over might not be teaching Henry the right lesson. Maybe it wasn't a bad thing, she'd said, for Henry to be in the back of the herd when it came to his social life. Aaron had listened, annoyed—he never did take advice well from her—and then proceeded to pick up his phone and make the date.

Now, because Aaron had unilaterally decided to take Henry over to Milo's half an hour earlier than their plan, he thought she was late. She wasn't late. In truth, she probably would have come home earlier if she hadn't gotten held up by that letter from Lost Soul. But it was not reasonable to stop in the middle of dealing with a letter from a reader who'd come to the conclusion that ending his life would be a gift to his family, just because Aaron might have a bout of anticipatory annoyance at her hypothetical tardiness.

Caring about desperate people did not make her an irresponsible parent. She was clear about her priorities. Henry always came first. Tonight's choice was not between Henry and work. It was between coming home early so Aaron wouldn't get agitated and helping someone in crisis.

Next text, **Showering**. No exclamation points.

Showering? She and Aaron had never been overcommunicators. By now they were barely communicating at all. Why would he text, *Showering*? Was the next text going to be, *Drying off*?

The next text was, **Where are you????**

Wait. Now she remembered. There was a dinner. A work dinner. Aaron had a work dinner tonight somewhere on Long Island. Port Jefferson? Port Washington? It was definitely a port but she couldn't remember which one because she really hadn't been listening because she wasn't going. He'd asked her to go and she said no.

Wait. Had she said no? She definitely meant to say no.

Why would she have to say no? How could he think she would agree to go to a business dinner. Yes, it was true: as far as the world knew they weren't getting divorced. They weren't even separated yet, officially. No one besides the two of them knew. Well the marriage counselor knew. And their lawyers. And maybe Brielle.

Brielle was Aaron's "drinking partner" and though Aaron insisted Brielle didn't know any details about their marriage, he also insisted she was *only* his drinking partner. The first time Lane asked Aaron what a drinking partner was, she got an eye roll. The second time she asked, he got a shot of bourbon. After that time, she stopped asking.

The decision to keep their plan to divorce private until they told Henry was mutual. But according to Aaron it was never the right time to tell Henry. There was always something pulling him away. Even after she'd enlisted the aid of a therapist and her lawyer and his lawyer and their marriage counselor, Aaron still found reasons to delay. "Bad time for me," he'd tell her and then sometimes, to mix things up, "Bad time for Henry."

Just because no one knew they were getting divorced did not mean Lane was going to go with Aaron to some business dinner party and be all wifey. She didn't like to do that when things were good. When were things good? She couldn't remember.

She texted back—On my way—and hurried home, scarf wrapped over her mouth to keep out the wind, cold wet air turning her cheeks raw. She spent most of the walk home—it was thirty minutes door to door—trying to get Aaron's voice out of her head. Their last argument had been brutal, Aaron's anger exploding in a battery of name-calling: she was cold as ice, hard as granite, dreary as dust. Actual spit had come out of his mouth when he said, *dust*. The word had stuck like an earworm. It was that complaint—not *cold* or *hard* but *dust*—that hurt the most.

Their building came into view and she stopped. If it weren't for Henry she wouldn't go in. She'd walk away. Turn right, turn left—either direction was fine. But leaving now was not an option. She pulled up the collar of her coat and, head to the wind, walked inside.

Their apartment was near Lincoln Center in a tall building on a high floor, with sparkling views of the city and the nonstop backdrop of sirens racing down Columbus and up Amsterdam. In the city, someone was always having an emergency.

They could afford the place because of a below-market rental-rate perk, offered by Aaron's boss, who owned the building. The small one-bedroom was perfect for them until Henry was born. Now Henry was six and they were still there. When people asked them why they hadn't moved yet, they either said it was because they were too busy to figure out where to go next, which was true, or because they'd gotten used to the solution: giving Henry, who went to bed early, the bedroom, while they slept on the living room pullout couch. That was also true, for a while.

Being privy to what went on in strangers' lives was a hazard or a privilege of Lane's job, depending on the day. Either way she knew when a marriage went south it was not unusual for one partner to be banished for some amount of time to a couch. New York City real estate being what it was, she and Aaron ended up banished there together.

The doorman gave her a wide smile, which she answered with a milder version of her own. She avoided conversations with the doormen, who were replaced roughly every six months—theirs was a building of complainers—because she'd never been good with names. To compensate, she'd mastered a genial expression that suggested she really would love to chat if only she had more time. The doormen didn't care. To them she was the introverted wife of Aaron Dash, a man who was friendly enough for both of them.

As a neighbor, Aaron had many appealing qualities. In the elevator he was quick to offer to hold a leash, a baby, a package. Whenever a sign went up announcing a new committee, it was almost always Aaron's name that topped the list. He loved meetings of all kinds, except AA. He refused to go to one of those.

For Lane, meetings were like social gatherings: to be avoided. As for the elevators in her building, she dreaded them. It wasn't that she was claustrophobic; she actually liked small spaces. Rather it was because Aaron too often boasted to their neighbors about her job, which meant Lane sometimes found herself cornered in the elevator by someone whose name she couldn't remember, asking, at times urgently, for advice. As if she could solve anyone's problem in the time it took to get from the lobby to the eleventh floor.

She didn't bother with her key. When Aaron drank he left the door unlocked. As soon as she put her bag down on the console table in the small foyer, she saw him sitting on the marital pullout. He was wearing a sports jacket, slacks, and shoes with no socks. She could not explain why it bothered her so much, this latest affectation, even in the winter, no socks.

The TV was off, his phone wasn't in sight, no newspaper, magazine or book was at hand. He saw the question on her face and answered it. "I've been waiting." A moment passed. "Luckily," he said, and Lane tipped her head, wondering what could possibly come out of his mouth next, "Milo's mother graciously agreed to turn their late-over into a sleepover. Since obviously you forgot to get a babysitter to pick Henry up."

"Did you ask Henry if he wants to have a sleepover?" Their apartment had never felt big but now that they hated each other and had to pretend they didn't, it felt like a closet. "Wait. Why do we need a babysitter to pick him up?"

"Because of the dinner party."

"Why would I go with you to a dinner party?"

"Because it's for work. Because it's important. Because you said you would."

Had she? It was possible. "I'm not going. I'm calling you a Lyft." She found his phone on the kitchen counter next to the bottle of bourbon. "What's the address?"

Usually a question like that—these days any question—would be enough to trigger a rat-tat-tat of protests. *I drive better drunk than you do sober. You don't trust me because you don't trust anyone.* But tonight Aaron didn't protest. Maybe he was too drunk to protest. He called out the address. She plugged it in his phone.

It would be expensive, Aaron taking a car from the city to Port Somewhere on Long Island. But he was too drunk to drive. She didn't have any protective feelings for him, per se—by now she was up to about 30 percent disinterest, 70 percent disgust—but he was Henry's father.

"The car will be here in four minutes. You better go down."

And just like that, he did.

When she called Milo's mother to apologize—there'd been a mix-up, she would come get Henry at bedtime as first planned—the mother let out a disappointed, "Oh." The boys were so excited their late-over turned into a sleepover, she told Lane. They weren't going to be happy to hear the plan had changed again. Would Lane reconsider and let Henry stay the night? Of course Lane agreed. It would be better, Henry not seeing her like this, in a funk. He could read her face like a book.

She made herself eggs and after she cleaned up, opened her email to scan for a *Roxie* letter into which she might disappear. She hadn't yet settled on one when the doorbell rang.

Their building had a front desk staff to announce visitors, but it wasn't unusual for a neighbor to stop over to have a word with Aaron in the evening, reporting trouble on the committee that decided Christmas tips, or needing help developing a list of Best Practices for Owners of Big Dogs. But tonight when she opened the door, a uniformed policeman was standing there.

His eyes looked sad. She paled and held her breath.

"May I come in? It's about your husband."

She put her hands to her chest and said, "Thank god."

He didn't flinch. He was one of those cops who looked as if he'd seen it all.

She quickly explained, "I was afraid it was going to be about my son."

He didn't care. He asked her if she wanted to sit down and she told him she was fine and stayed where she was. She was fine except for her heart, which was beating so hard she was sure he could hear it.

He got to the point. Her husband had hit a car, crashed into a concrete barrier on the Henry Hudson Parkway, and perished.

She was repeating the word, *perished*, when it occurred to her. "He wasn't on the Henry Hudson. He went to Long Island. He would have taken the L.I.E. and—" She stopped. Aaron didn't drive to his dinner. She hadn't let him drive. She leaned against the wall and let out what felt like all the air in the world. "It wasn't Aaron. He took a Lyft. I called it for him. I'm sorry for whoever it was, but it wasn't my husband."

The policeman took out his notes. "Driver's license said *Aaron Dash*." He looked up. Lane nodded. He proceeded to read the make and color of their car and then their license plate. "That yours?" She nodded again. "You know the name of the passenger?"

"Pardon?"

"The woman he was with didn't have ID."

"Brielle?" She ran through the facts in her head. Aaron had blown off the Lyft she called him. Then he called Brielle. Then he blew off the dinner in Port Somewhere to go somewhere else. She noticed that the policeman had jotted down *Brielle*. "Is Brielle dead?"

"There were six fatalities. Your husband, his companion, and the passengers of the other car." He ignored her widening eyes and continued, "A family. Must have been coming home from a ski trip. Snowboards stopped traffic in both directions." He paused. "Brielle's last name?"

"I have no idea." Lane didn't faint, exactly. It was more of a sliding down unexpectedly, so that one moment she was standing and the next moment she was sitting on the herringbone wood floor in the small foyer of the apartment she'd been planning to leave.

She remained numb for the rest of the night, moving without feeling, talking without thinking, soldiering on through the necessary tasks, each call pointing the way to the next. When she told the grim news to her sister, Shelley said, "Did you ring Mom and Dad?" When she called her parents, they asked if Aaron's brother knew. When she called Aaron's brother, he asked for the name of the funeral home. The man at the funeral home wanted to know if she'd been to the hospital yet. At the hospital Lane was ushered into a small room where another woman was waiting. The woman introduced herself as Brielle's mother. Lane had no idea how she managed to say, "Sorry for your loss," to the woman who was the mother of Aaron's girlfriend, but she did.

It was only when she finally laid her head on her pillow and positioned her body at the very edge of her side of the pullout that it occurred to her: she'd been lucky about one thing; Henry was at Milo's. She didn't know how she would have gotten through the night with Henry watching, first the policeman, then the phone calls, then the trip to the hospital. She felt a second wave of relief when she realized she didn't have to go through the motions of Henry's bedtime ritual, Tell Me That Story. Henry loved the tradition, which Aaron started, of bedtime stories about his parents. Aaron's stories were usually more exciting than Lane's, because even though they started with a nugget of truth, by the end he often spun that nugget into fantasy. Perhaps she should have paid more attention to that, she thought now, how much Aaron enjoyed burnishing the truth.

Whichever one of them was telling the story, the routine began the same way: by giving Henry a choice. *Want to hear the one about the day I tried out for Little League? Want to hear the one about the day Dad and I got married?*

At some point Henry would pick. "That one. Tell me that story."

What story worth telling could Lane have possibly come up with on the night Henry's father died?

24

In the morning, when she picked him up at Milo's, Henry didn't ask why they were taking a taxi home instead of the subway like they usually did, or why, when they got to their building, she kept her hand on his shoulder and briskly steered him toward the elevator.

News was spreading fast. She could see it in the eyes of the neighbors coming out of the package room.

Inside the apartment, Lane waited until after Henry put his backpack on the hook, until after he took off his sneakers and placed them, toes facing out, under the console table in the hall, before telling him they needed to have a talk. Her hands back on his shoulders, she guided him to the couch. She could feel him sensing it, that something big was about to happen.

To avoid confusion, she made sure to speak slowly. "I have very sad news. Dad was in a car accident last night and he died. Do you understand what that means?" Henry looked at his feet and nodded. She put her hand on his cheek and felt his warmth. His skin was still baby soft. "It's very sad. It's okay to cry."

He didn't, at first. His tears came later and when they did, Lane felt them in her chest; it was as if her heart—not a figurative heart but the actual organ—was bruised from seeing Henry so sad, bruised from imagining the family that never made it home from their ski vacation. About Aaron, all she felt was a blank space.

Once the official note was posted in the mail room with the special font they always used to announce that someone had passed away, the news blasted through the building. People who'd never spoken to her before stopped her on her way in, out, up, and down. She didn't know their names. To her they were the knit-browed young mother who wouldn't put down her tantrummy toddler, and the young couple who, always in a rush, banged on the elevator button as if that would make it come faster, and the old man who twirled his wedding ring when he met her eyes. All of them were sorry for her and sorrier for Henry. He was, like his father, everyone's favorite. Affection for him was passed from one doorman to the next. They called him the mayor of the building, shouting, "Morning, Mayor," every day when he left for school and, "How are things at city hall?" every day when he came home.

Not very good, he would have said if anyone dared ask now.

No one did, but Lane knew they would. It was only a matter of time.

2

At the graveside service, Lane felt boxed in by a wall of unfamiliar bodies with faces set in identical grim expressions. She could count on one hand the people she knew. Aside from Henry, none of them were family. Aaron's brother—whom he never saw—turned out to be too ill to make the trip. Lane's sister, Shelley, who lived in a London suburb, and her parents, Sylvie and Marshall, who lived in southwestern Florida, had competing ill-timed emergencies. For Shelley it was something to do with her mother-in-law. For her parents it was something to do with her uncle. She wasn't sure of the details because after she heard the important part, they weren't coming, she'd stopped listening. Their absence was not really a surprise.

There was another group of mourners she could tell she was supposed to know by how their faces brightened when she met their eyes. Nothing was required of her—the grief everyone assumed she felt gave her a temporary pass—but she didn't want to appear unkind to people whom she'd met and then forgotten, so she returned nod with nod, hug with hug, sigh with sigh.

As for the army of Aaron's grief-stricken friends whom she'd never met, the ones now shooting curious, furtive glances in her direction, she averted her eyes, tightened her grip on Henry's hand, stared into the hole in the ground and waited for the next instruction.

When it was time, the rabbi, whom she'd been introduced to half an hour before the service, guided her to the pile of freshly dug earth beside the grave and gestured for her to pick up the shovel that stuck out straight up. *Like a vampire's stake,* was what she thought.

The shovel resisted at first and then came out so quickly her body swerved and the mourners gasped. As she shoved the scoop back in the dirt, she reminded herself what the rabbi had told her during their brief meeting. The rituals she performed today were to honor her husband in front of those who loved him. Lane hadn't said anything to the rabbi about how she felt toward Aaron—Henry had been sitting right beside her—but she suspected he had seen something flicker across her face because when he said that, about honoring Aaron in front of those who loved him, his eyes drilled into hers as if with a secret message. Now he touched her arm. She stopped midscoop.

"Tradition tells us," he explained as he guided her hand so that she rotated the handle, flat end of the scoop now on top, "to lift the dirt on the back of the shovel. This shows our reluctance."

Lane nodded and did her best to lift the earth that smelled like worms onto the back side of the shovel. She walked gingerly—shovel, earth, herself—to the grave. It seemed to her that she'd hardly gotten any dirt to stay on the back of the shovel, but when the loamy earth hit the coffin, the thud was loud enough to make her recoil.

The rabbi pointed her toward where the shovel had been. "We do not pass the shovel from one to the next," he explained, not just to her. "We return it instead to the mound." He waited while Lane jammed the shovel back into the wormy earth. "Thus allowing each mourner a chance to have their own moment of anguish."

Lane went through the motions of sticking the shovel where the rabbi indicated it belonged, but she didn't hear the rest of what he said. Her focus was now on scanning the crowd for Henry. She found him standing in front of Jem, her friend from work, whose hands were gently resting on his shoulders. She swiftly moved beside him and took his hand.

The rabbi continued to explain customs to those who were, and those who were not, still listening. Lane didn't realize the service had ended until she saw a line had formed, Aaron's bolder friends snaking their way toward her. They stopped, in turn, to clasp her hand in theirs, or to kiss her cheek, sometimes on one side, sometimes on the other, sometimes on both, whichever it was, she got it wrong. It was during this dance of kisses, hugs and murmured condolences that the full weight of Lane's dilemma hit her. How was she supposed to act toward people eager to help her in her time of grief, when these same people would have treated her with disdain if Aaron had lived long enough for her to leave him. There was no way she was going to share the details of her failed marriage with strangers, or confide to acquaintances how exhausting it had been to live with a man whom everyone else adored. Even if she had been a person who shared, she wouldn't share that now. There was no need for Henry to hear it. Not now. Not ever.

Avoidance was a fickle friend. The doorbell rang at all hours, as hard to ignore as the heavy odors that now infused their hallway, a mash-up of comfort food smells: butter, noodles, stew.

Sometimes at night when she was in bed with Henry, who didn't want to sleep alone in his room anymore, he would tell her he heard a tapping, someone lightly tapping at their door. When she investigated, first with a suspicious glimpse through the peephole, then with a swift swing of the door, as if that might be enough to scare away an intruder, there was never anyone there. There was just food. A breakfast casserole. A baked zucchini. A mac and cheese. Aluminum foil tins pressing one against the other so that everything would fit on the doormat, as if there were an acknowledged edict against tin touching floor.

No one seemed to ask themselves where this food would be stored or who would eat it, meals cooked to serve six or eight or twelve. She wondered if people didn't know how to divide the quantity in a recipe or if they'd decided, en masse, that it would look too pitiful, a meatloaf for two.

She reminded herself daily that each meal was an act of kindness. But the cumulative power of the kindness—she really wasn't used to kindness—made it hard to breathe.

It didn't take long for her small refrigerator and freezer to become jammed and for the food to turn. Getting rid of the food posed its own set of problems. One night she carried a bag of spoiled chili to the incinerator room, only to find the chili cook holding the garbage chute open.

"Hey Lane," the chili cook greeted her. "Look at this. Second time in a week. Pizza box. Stuck."

Lane tried to remember her neighbor's name. Was it Ann? Amy? Emily? She had no idea. All she knew was that she'd been introduced and reintroduced to the woman who brought her the chili too many times to ask her name now. The woman's nostrils flared as she picked up the scent of something familiar.

"Oh. Sorry." Lane backed out of the room. "I just remembered—" She moved the Hefty bag behind her, the lump of uneaten chili visible, like a ghost, through the white plastic. "I have to get back because—" Because why? When she couldn't think of a single reason, she said, "Good night!" Her voice came out giddy. As she hurried down the hall, she could feel the bewildered chili cook trying to puzzle out her strange behavior.

In the apartment, she found Henry sitting up in bed waiting. "I'm sorry," he said. "I won't do it anymore. I'm not crying now. See?" He offered her a smile so fake she felt it like a punch to the gut.

She had no idea he'd been crying. "Aw buddy, you can cry. Cry whenever you want. It's good to cry. Otherwise your feelings can get all stopped up."

It was during one of her long intervals of wakefulness—in those hours of the night when it seemed as if the night itself decided how long a minute would be, how long an hour—when Lane resolved that in the morning, she would call Miss Mary, the school student assistance counselor. After the call, she would go for a swim. She could feel it in her bones when she fell out of her routine. Now more than ever, she needed to disappear into the meditative state she found when swimming laps.

Miss Mary said it was perfect timing. Her weekly Loss Circle was meeting today, at lunch. With that organized, Lane headed to the new gym she'd joined in Midtown West.

This gym was ten minutes closer to her office than her old one, which meant she'd get in ten more minutes of swim time. It also meant she wouldn't have to deal with the hypercompetitive culture of her old gym. She'd gotten two reprimands in the past month; one for swimming too slow, one for stopping midlap to hang on the wall. That she'd stopped because of a foot cramp and only needed to hang for a moment till it passed did not matter to the pool's overzealous self-appointed monitor.

The new pool was a much better fit. As she tucked her shoulder-length hair into her cap, she felt her body relax. At her old pool, the cranky monitor hadn't been entirely wrong about Lane's swimming speed. She always started out slow, taking a lap or two to let her worries cycle through and then out of her mind. But by the end of the second lap she'd accelerate with a sudden switch in speed that she experienced as if a hand were at her back giving her a push. She didn't require a swimming monitor to push her to get on with it. She was quite used to giving a push to herself.

Today she ruminated about Henry: wondering whether the Loss Circle would help him, wondering whether she should have asked exactly what happened in a Loss Circle, wondering if, whatever happened, Henry would like it. He did like Miss Mary. She liked her too. Maybe she'd call Miss Mary later and ask for some tips on things to do at home to help Henry work through his grief. There was nothing she wouldn't do.

At the end of her second lap, she arrived at her destination: empty-brained peace.

It was three weeks to the day after Aaron's death that Lane opened the door—Henry was getting dressed for school when he told her he heard someone tapping again—and found a woman in the midst of placing a lasagna on her doormat.

The fact that there were, at that moment, three lasagnas in her refrigerator and one in her freezer was no excuse for her reaction. Nor was the fact that this particular lasagna was so large it made the doormat beneath it look like a dirty sisal trivet. Still, she should have said, "Thank you," and taken the food inside.

The woman was one of several ladies in the building who had confusing faces. Smooth, shiny foreheads, high-placed puffy cheeks, mouths permanently fixed in odd smiles. Only their hands—Lane noticed them when they pressed the elevator buttons—showed their age. Upper eighties was her guess but nineties was not out of the question.

The ladies adored Aaron and why wouldn't they? He always took the time to stop and talk, asking after their health, complimenting them on their hair, listening to their problems and then pointing them to Lane for professional advice. They'd cornered her several times in the elevator asking her opinion: what to do when friends died and no one called to tell them; what to do about children who didn't send thank-you notes when they got a check; what to do about restaurants that seated them in the back, near the toilets. Lane would shrug off their questions with a weak smile and they'd respond with an icy silence. She didn't mind. She was fine with any kind of silence.

None of this excused her reaction. The only thing wrong with the woman was her timing. Hers happened to be the lasagna that broke Lane's filter.

"I was going to divorce him," Lane told the woman.

"What?"

"Aaron. We were going to get divorced. He was a drunk. You probably didn't know that. He was very good at hiding it. I was going to leave him. With Henry. I'm very sad for Henry. But for me, it's really a relief."

The woman stood, blinking, in the dim hallway.

Okay, that was a mistake. "Sorry." She picked up the huge foil tray, which felt like deadweight in her arms. "I'm overwhelmed. I'm sure you can understand. You're so kind to bring over a meal." Her filter malfunctioned again. "It's very big."

"Poor boy." The woman grabbed her lasagna. "Loses his father." Her deep-set eyes narrowed and her gaze locked on to Lane's. "Ends up with you." She turned and, kitten heels clicking, hurried to the elevator.

Lane stood, stunned. Henry called out, "Mom?"

"Coming." She shook off the woman's words and locked the door behind her.

That night as they lay side by side in bed, Henry shimmied closer to the wall and said, "We have a small family now, right?"

"Yes." Lane twirled one of Henry's dark curls.

"But that's okay because families come in all sizes."

She nodded and smiled. This must have been something Miss Mary had told him.

"And now we have something in common." Henry grinned.

Lane felt herself relax at the sight of his smile. "What's that?"

"I don't have a dad and you don't have a dad."

Her body went heavy as stone. "Aw buddy. I have a dad. Remember Grandpa Marshall? Remember when we visited him in Florida? He's my dad. And Grandma Sylvie is my mom."

"I forgot." He flipped onto his back and closed his eyes. "Sorry."

She saw a tear escape down his cheek. "It's not your fault you forgot. They weren't at the funeral. It's understandable you assumed—" She stopped. "They wanted to come but there was a—" She stopped again. "It's my fault. It's been too long since we've seen them."

He squeezed his closed eyes tighter. "Why?"

How could she explain? It wasn't anything she'd planned. It happened so slowly she'd barely noticed. She hardly visited them, then she never visited them. She called them less and less; they called her less and less. Everyone seemed content with the arrangement. How had she missed the flaw in this? Aaron's parents had died when he was young. Hers were the only grandparents Henry had.

"You know what?" Lane said. "We should visit them. What do you think?" Henry didn't answer. His breathing was soft. He was finally asleep. She started to get up, slowly, so as not to wake him.

His eyes opened into slits. "Did someone knock? I think I heard someone . . ." His voice trailed off. His eyelids fell. His lips parted.

Lane listened to the soft click of his little-boy snore. Had someone knocked? She slipped out of bed, tucked in the blanket around him and padded to the peephole. As usual there was no one outside. She opened the door slowly, so it wouldn't make any noise. There was a basket on the welcome mat. It was the biggest one yet, even bigger than the huge overfilled corporate gift basket the Guild sent over, the one filled with muffins, bagels, coffee beans, mugs, kitchen towels, scented candles and a giant teddy bear.

This basket—it made no sense—had a puppy in it. Not a stuffed puppy, a live one. For a moment she thought, *Okay, a stray puppy hopped into a food basket and ate all the food.* But it wasn't a food basket. There was a cushion at the bottom, with a pattern of tiny dog bones. It was a puppy basket. Someone had left a puppy on their doormat.

She stared at the small white ball of fur that stared back at her. What was she supposed to do with a puppy? She had no puppy food in the house, no puppy bowls, no puppy crate or puppy pads. Whoever left the puppy hadn't even left a leash. She sighed and told the puppy, "Wait right there."

The puppy's wagging tail drummed a beat against the side of the basket. He started scrambling to get out.

"Okay," she told him as she scooped him up. "I'll bring you with me if you promise not to wake up Henry." The puppy answered by licking her face. She held him tight, ducked inside, grabbed her phone, and hurried back out to the hall.

The man on duty at the front desk in the lobby picked up on the first ring. She explained the situation: someone had left a puppy on her doormat, by mistake. "Can you come up and get him? With a leash if you have one. I would come down," she added, "but I don't want to leave Henry alone."

Henry's name worked like magic. The front-desk man said he'd be right up. Lane put the puppy back in the basket. She didn't want to pet him, but she did. When he moved his little head so that she would rub behind his ears, she didn't want to do that either, but she did. When she heard the elevator door open and saw the front-desk man walking down the hall with a leash, she leaned down and whispered to the puppy, "It's for the best. The only pet I ever had was a turtle and it died after three days. You can do better than me." Against her will, she kissed the top of the puppy's warm head and whispered, "Be good."

As the front-desk man briskly attached leash to collar, Lane asked if he would mind not telling Henry about this. He nodded in agreement and left without saying a word.

Inside she washed up, got into pajamas, and slipped into bed. She laid her arm across Henry's chest and once she was sure he was still sleeping, pulled him close and held him tight.

In the morning Lane told Henry the good news. Next week, instead of school, they were going on a trip. "On a plane. To Florida. To visit Grandpa Marshall and Grandma Sylvie. Isn't that great? I'll still have to work, but not all day. And maybe this time we can convince Grandma and Grandpa to go to the beach. That would be amazing, right?" She heard the fake cheer in her voice and stopped. She'd said enough. When it came to her parents, the less said the better.

An hour later, when they left for school, Lane noticed one of the doormen from their building standing in front of the building next door. He was chatting with the super while her puppy did its business on a tree. *Not my puppy,* she reminded herself and quickly swiveled Henry in the opposite direction, to catch a cab that had just discharged its fare.

3

Henry snuck open his eyes. His mother's legs were now uncrossed. When she first got into bed with him, she was on her back and her legs were crossed tight, like scissors. Now she was on her side and one of her knees was touching his leg.

Before What Happened, it was against the rules for her to stay in bed with him all night because if she did that, he would never learn how to sleep by himself. Sleeping by yourself was something everyone had to learn in order to be called a grown-up. But now that they were in what his mom called the New Norman, it was okay for her to stay in bed all the way till morning.

Probably the reason she made her legs go uncrossed was to be comfier. But what if that wasn't the reason. What if her legs got uncrossed because she was dead?

Sometimes his breathing made a loud drum sound in his head and he couldn't hear quiet things—like was his mom comfy or dead—so he held his breath to listen. But he still couldn't hear. Probably if he poked her he would know the answer—he guessed, *comfy*—but then he'd have to tell why he poked her and her face would get Mad.

Some people yelled a lot when they got Mad and some people yelled never and she was the one who yelled never. The way he could tell she was Mad was her voice got stricter and a vein came out on her forehead.

Worse than Mad was Disappointed. She hardly ever got Mad but she got Disappointed a lot. Disappointed was when her voice went quiet.

The first time he asked his mom if she was going to be dead soon, her eyes got Poppy-Out Big, which meant, Surprised. When her eyes went back to normal she asked him if he wanted to talk about his feelings. She said, "It's good to talk about your feelings because if you don't they can get all stopped up." She waited for him to say something back and when he didn't, she asked if he knew what *All stopped up* meant. He said, "Yes." *All stopped up* was what happened the day he used too much toilet paper. His mom smiled. Then she told him a memory she had about that day. Her memory was, she asked him to run and get the plunger and he said okay and ran all around the house looking everywhere and then he came back and said, "What's a plunger?"

Remembering that made her laugh. Laughing was his favorite face. After she laughed he stopped thinking about, *Would she be dead soon too?*

The next time he asked his mom if she was going to be dead soon she said, "No," in her strictest voice ever and the vein on her forehead came out faster so, Very Mad.

Sometimes her Mad face made him cry. Sometimes when he cried he made his eyes go Poppy-Out Big so his tears wouldn't dribble down his face, but usually that didn't work. When his mom saw his tears she always got quiet. Disappointed.

He decided not to ask her about being dead anymore.

Holding his breath made his chest hurt so now instead of thinking, *Is my mom comfy or dead?* he was thinking, *If my chest keeps hurting will I start to cry?*

His mom sighed and blew warm air on his face. He sighed too, even though he didn't want to. His sigh wasn't as loud as hers, but she heard it.

"You okay, buddy?"

He wanted to pretend he was sleeping, but she could always tell when he was faking so he nodded. She moved her knee so it wasn't touching him anymore but his eyes were still closed so he didn't know if they went back to scissors or not.

"You feeling sad?"

He shook his head and said, "Happy," and squeezed his closed eyes tighter so she couldn't see it was a lie.

"You don't sound happy."

He didn't know how to sound happy when he wasn't. Probably when he was a grown-up he would know. His mom knew. Sometimes when he stared at her to see how she was feeling her words said, *Don't worry. I'm fine,* but her face said, Sad.

The first time he met with Miss Mary alone, she gave him crayons and paper and asked if he would be a *deer* and draw a picture of his mom. He didn't know how to be a deer but he did know how to draw, so he did that. For his drawing he made his mom have a smiling face and he made her eyes sparkly with droplets on her eyelashes. When Miss Mary asked why he drew his mom with a smile but made her eyelashes have tears, he told her that sometimes his mom said she was happy but her eyelashes said something else.

Miss Mary told him he was smart to notice grown-ups' words didn't always match their faces. She said it would be better if everyone noticed that, but what can you do.

So far Miss Mary's words and face always matched. When she liked what he said, she smiled with her mouth open so wide he could see cavities. The first time he saw her cavities he didn't know what they were and he wasn't sure if it was okay to ask, so he didn't. She saw him staring at her mouth though, and it made her forehead go crinkled so, Worried.

Miss Mary used her most serious voice and said there was a rule in her room that he could ask any question he wanted. That was the main thing about her room. Safe for questions.

The question he asked was, "Why do some of your teeth have silver in them?"

That made her laugh with her mouth open even more, so he got to see even more silver. After she laughed she told him the silver was for cavities she got from drinking too much soda when she was little. When she finished telling him about that, she handed him a new sheet of paper and a bigger box of crayons.

There were a lot of crayons missing from the box and when he asked her why, Miss Mary said it was because some colors got used up faster than others. When he asked her why again, she said maybe they could talk about that later because she wanted to talk about something else now, which was, could he draw his family?

Drawing his family used to mean drawing his mom and his dad and him. Now he wasn't sure what it meant. Maybe he was still supposed to draw his dad. Maybe he wasn't.

Because he got quiet, Miss Mary asked him what he was thinking about. He told her he was thinking, "Was it okay for a person who liked to draw to not feel like drawing?"

Her forehead went crinkly again. "Of course. No one should draw if they don't want to."

She took a few crayons out of the box and asked if he would mind if she drew animals. She said, "Animals are good to draw when you want to *relapse*." When Miss Mary was finished he worried that she might ask if he could tell what kind of animal she drew. If she asked that, the answer that was true would be, "No," which might make her Sad. She wasn't a very good *drawrer*. But she didn't ask that. All she ever asked after she made a drawing was, "Do you like it?" and it was easy to give a true answer to that. "Yes."

The night his mom asked if he wanted to give a try at sleeping alone, her face looked like she wanted him to say, "Not yet," so that's what he said. He was pretty sure there were two reasons she still slept in his bed. One was, he didn't want to sleep alone. The other was, she didn't want to sleep alone either.

After he said, "Not yet," a big whoosh of air came out of her mouth, like the kind of whoosh that happens when you hold your breath for a hundred and a hundred minutes. That meant, right answer.

The most Disappointed his mom ever got was when he forgot about Grandpa Marshall. Even though she said, *It's okay. Don't feel bad. It's not your fault,* he could tell. Disappointed. The day after that was when she told him they were going on a trip to Florida to visit Grandpa Marshall and Grandma Sylvie.

That day her words said, "I've got good news," but her face said, "I'm sorry we have to go."

4

As she'd promised, Lane handed Henry his bag of airplane surprises as soon as he buckled up. She watched as he rummaged through the offerings—a new sketch pad, a pack of twelve twistable crayons, two Henry and Mudge chapter books, a travel LEGO set—and pulled out the art supplies.

She closed her eyes and tried to convince herself this trip was not a mistake, that it wouldn't be a repeat of the last time they came, when Henry was two and Aaron stayed behind because of a work conflict and she felt relieved. That was the year something shifted in their marriage, when, like Aaron's bourbon and for no discernible reason, it went from straight up to on the rocks.

There was one wonderful surprise on that trip: Shelley flew in from London, their taxis pulling up at the same time, one behind the other, in front of their parents' house.

When Sylvie opened the door and saw not one but both daughters standing there, her eyes went wide with surprise.

"Look who's here," Lane said to fill up the silence. "Look, it's Shelley."

"Your mother knows who she is, Turtle," her father said, suddenly appearing behind his wife. "Why do you always have to make a big megillah out of everything?"

Sylvie said, "Oh well." She didn't say more than that for the rest of the day; she just sat on the living room love seat looking vaguely uneasy.

Marshall, meanwhile, followed his daughters around like an over-eager puppy.

"Don't you have anything else to do?" Shelley asked him.

"I'm visiting," Marshall said. "Isn't that why you came? To visit?"

"Yes," Lane answered when it became clear that her sister—mouth closed, jaws mashing—was not going to. To Lane it felt as if she'd accidentally wandered into the middle of an argument she knew nothing about. This feeling wasn't unusual; in the Meckler family she often felt one link short of being in the loop.

The airplane loudspeaker crackled. The captain's voice broke through her reverie. "Sorry we weren't able to give you that great Manhattan skyline view but apparently the weather had other ideas. We do hope to make up the delay. Please sit back and enjoy the rest of your flight."

They hadn't been aloft for long when the captain's voice returned. "We're going to be coming into a bit of turbulence ahead. We should get through it fairly quickly but we do need everyone to please stay in your seats with your seat belts fastened."

The flight attendant walking the aisle stopped at Henry. "You buckled, sweetheart? You're not worried about a little turbulence are you? You look pretty brave to me."

Henry said, "Thank you," which is what his mother taught him to say whenever adults paid him a compliment or asked him a question he didn't understand. As soon as the flight attendant moved on, he turned to his mother. "What's turbulence?"

Lane shared a smile with the man at the window. "That's what they call it when it gets a little bumpy."

"Cabin crew, please be seated."

The turbulence hit. The ride got bumpy. Henry held on to the armrests and grinned.

When it was over, the flight attendant stopped by on her way to the galley. "Hey, sweetheart, how'd you do?"

"Good. I like turbulence."

She laughed and asked Lane if she could borrow Henry for a sec, to give him something special. Henry looked at his mother and nodded so she'd nod too, which of course she did.

Several minutes later he returned to his seat with his chest arched so Lane couldn't miss the wings pin now attached to his shirt. Eyes wide, he told her that after the lady pinned on the wings he had to move because the captain was coming out of the cockpit.

"No one is allowed to stand near the captain when he comes out," Henry explained. "But he looked at me. And he saw my pin. And he did this." Henry saluted his mother to show her and then scrambled over her legs to his seat. "I like this vacation."

The man at the window smiled again but this time Lane pretended not to notice. There was no way she was going to share with a stranger what Henry didn't know, that their time here on the bumpy plane might be as good as this vacation got.

It was as if the turbulence had uncorked in Henry a sudden thirst for information. Lane didn't blame him for having questions about the grandparents he didn't remember. It was the answers that were the problem.

His opener: "Will Grandpa like me?"

"Of course. He already likes you." Was that true? "He loves you." That had to be true.

"Is he nice?"

Another hard one. "Usually. Unless he sits around for too long. He gets grumpy doing nothing. When he's grumpy, we leave him alone. But he never stays grumpy for long. He's very excited to see you." She closed her eyes for a moment and tried to picture her father being excited to see Henry but she was unable to conjure any image at all.

"What about Uncle Albie? Is he nice?"

"Yes. Quiet but nice."

Henry moved from question to question with barely a breath in between. It felt to her as if he'd been hoarding them, just waiting for the right moment to present itself so he could give her a family quiz. Unfortunately for her, the right moment was now.

Will Grandpa play with me? I hope so. *Will Uncle Albie play with me?* I doubt it. *Why not?* He likes to be alone. *Why?* Some people prefer to be alone. *Is that why Grandpa calls you Turtle? Because you like to be alone?* I don't like to be alone. I like to be with you. *So why does he call you Turtle?* He started doing that when I got a turtle as a pet.

She left it there. No point sharing the rest, how her father had teased her about the turtle. "You're two of a kind," he'd said. "You on your bed. Him on his rock. Both of you sitting alone, staring into space while the world whizzes by."

He wasn't wrong about the turtle, which didn't do anything except for dying several days after she got it. Unlike the turtle, which expired quickly, her nickname lived on. Years later, when she told Aaron how much she hated being called Turtle, he invented a new nickname for her and made a stab at getting her father to switch.

"Call her Duck," he told Marshall. "That's what I call her. My sweet little odd duck."

Lane had never been and still was not a fan of nicknames.

"Can I call you *Turtle* like Grandpa does?" Henry asked. "Or *Duck* like dad used to?"

She noted, but didn't comment on, his use of the past tense. "Absolutely not. You can call me Mom." She leaned over and kissed the top of Henry's head. "I'm going to close my eyes for a minute. Get a little rest. Want to try and rest with me?"

Henry said he would, but when Lane opened her eyes a moment later, he was staring at her, waiting to ask another question: "Did Uncle Albie always live with you?"

"No." Lane's memory for the details of her nomadic childhood was spotty, but some things, like when her uncle moved in, were clear. Before he moved in she had her own room. After, she shared with Shelley. Before he moved in, they would sit around the dinner table when her father came home and talk over each other, everyone vying to be the first to say what happened while he was away. After, they ate in silence. "He moved in when I was your age."

"You're lucky. I wish Aunt Shelley would move in with us."

"Me too. But she has her own family. Uncle Quinn and Melinda. And they live in England. You remember that, right?" He nodded. She closed her eyes.

It was sweet, Henry wishing his aunt lived with them. There'd been no sweetness when her uncle moved in. No explanation, either. Just her father's curt announcement, followed by a warning: "Uncle Albie lives with us now. Don't bother him. Your uncle isn't me."

Lane and Shelley had to work hard not to laugh at that. Their father wasn't someone anyone would choose to bother.

The call bell dinged from somewhere at the back of the plane. She opened her eyes.

Henry was staring at her again. "How come Uncle Albie didn't live with his own family?"

There was no way she was going to answer that. "Some things are hard to explain." She shrugged. "Oh well." And there it was, the evasive vagueness of Sylvie Meckler, living inside her. "We should try and rest. So we'll have lots of energy when we get off the plane."

Henry nodded and settled down. Lane closed her eyes and let the muffled buzz of the airplane rock her into a dreamy state. Her thoughts drifted back to the last time they'd visited her parents. She could still picture their dinner the night she arrived. It was the usual Meckler spread of mashed potatoes, skinless chicken breasts, and some kind of vegetable hidden beneath a camel-colored sauce. The kind of meal, Lane later learned, most people would eat only when they were getting over a stomach bug.

They sat in the kitchen on wood stools around a rickety folding table. After several minutes of eating in silence, Sylvie abruptly stood up and started clearing.

Marshall put his napkin on his plate and stood up too. "Excellent meal, Sylvie. Now if you'll excuse me, I have to use the washroom."

"Washroom?" Shelley repeated as soon as he was gone. "Who says, *washroom?*"

"I don't know why you two are so hard on him," Sylvie said, even though Lane hadn't uttered a word. "It hasn't been easy." She turned and saw her daughters' puzzled expressions. "I suppose you should know. Uncle Albie's ill. That's why he didn't join us for dinner."

"He never joins us for dinner," Shelley said. "Uncle Albie is always ill."

"Not always." Sylvie scrubbed the inside of the saucepan and then the bottom and then the handle.

"Almost always," Lane offered. No one could legitimately argue with that. For as long as he'd lived with them something had been wrong. When he first moved in there'd been a menu of explanations for his absence at dinner. He was under the weather. Getting over a virus. Feeling run-down. Running a low fever. Finally their mother settled on the blahs.

"Nothing you can do about it," she would say. "The blahs are the blahs." If their father was home he'd chime in with, "The miseries are the miseries."

Oblivious to the suds still coating the handle, Sylvie placed the saucepan on the drying rack. "It's no one's fault," she said, meeting Lane's eyes. "Your uncle has—"

"The blahs," Shelley said. "We know. He has the blahs. The blahs are the blahs."

Their father walked in and nodded. "The miseries are the miseries."

Shelley shook her head. "Whatever you say."

"What is that supposed to mean?" Marshall asked.

"It means," Shelley said, "you'd think with all the doctors you've taken him to, something would have worked. I think Uncle Albie likes being sick."

"No one likes being sick," Sylvie snapped. "Anyway, this time it's different. He's not himself."

"He's exactly himself," Shelley said. She'd never had any patience for Uncle Albie.

Henry's fingers slipped out of her hand and Lane opened her eyes. He was finally asleep, head tipped to the side, small hands neatly folded on top of his seat belt. She checked the time—an hour to go—and closed her eyes again.

On their last trip to Florida Henry had one tantrum—he was, after all, two years old—and then gave up. Lane could tell that he sensed her discomfort, even if he didn't understand it. And why would he? He had no way to know that his grandfather was more ornery than usual or that his grandmother didn't always look as faded as a photograph left out in the sun. He had no clue that it wasn't normal for grandparents to fail to make a single accommodation to a grandchild's visit; there were no toys or games or children's books anywhere in the house. When Lane finally turned on the TV hoping for the Cartoon Network—really anything would do—the knob came off in her hand.

Eventually her mother dug up a pile of paper and a couple of pens and Henry occupied himself with that. His pictures were mostly scribbles but even then, at two, drawing seemed to soothe him.

Lane and Shelley did their best to try to organize an outing but Marshall shot down every idea. The circus museum was being renovated. The animal sanctuary was under investigation. The beach would be too cold.

It would definitely not be too cold for Henry, so the sisters decided to take him to the beach on their own. They proceeded to deal with the obstacles as they arose. No umbrella? They had hats. No beach chairs or blanket? Towels would do.

"You're just going to go?" Marshall asked them. "And leave your mother here?"

That was it for Shelley. She led Lane into the kitchen and said, "They're impossible. I don't know what I was thinking. I'm rebooking my flight for tomorrow. You should do the same. It won't get any better. It never does."

"It's not that bad," Lane said.

"It's totally that bad." Without consulting her, Shelley returned to where their parents were sitting—side by side, as if glued together, on the love seat—and announced the change of plans. "I just heard from Quinn," she reported. "He has to go on a business trip so I have to go home. And Lane just got a call from Aaron. He isn't feeling well. She has to leave too."

Later, when they were upstairs packing, Shelley told Lane to stop feeling bad that they lied to cut the trip short. "Did they ask a single question? No. Did they say, 'Where is Quinn going?' or, 'What exactly is wrong with Aaron?' No. Believe me, they're as relieved as we are."

In the morning when they all left for the airport it was more getaway than departure, the sisters hurrying Henry into the taxi, arms waving, kisses blown from tense mouths and in the cab, two long sighs of relief on either side of an oblivious boy.

Once they got past airport security, Shelley turned to Lane. "Next time, you come visit me. I can't do this anymore. I hate to fly. Feel how clammy my hands are." She laid her sticky hands on Lane's cheeks. "And that's after taking a Klonopin." She squatted in front of Henry and looked him in the eye. "These trips are killing me. Will you come to London? Melinda is desperate to meet you in real life."

Henry didn't know how to answer so Lane answered for him. "Thank you."

"All right then. Time for Aunt Shelley to go find a bar near her gate." Shelley grabbed Lane in a tight hug. "I wish we had time to talk." She held fast. "On the count of three. One, two—" She stepped away. That was Shelley, always leaving before Lane was ready.

As she watched her sister disappear into the crowd, Lane felt a wave of grief that made her gasp. "Tickle in my throat," she told Henry, who'd looked up to see why she'd made a noise.

He remembered none of this. His cousin, Melinda, was now sixteen and though the two of them had spoken on screens of many sizes, they'd still never met in real life.

Sylvie must have been looking out the window when they arrived because by the time they got out of the taxi she was standing on the front walk, waving. "Look at you."

Since their last visit her mother had turned from slim to frail. When Lane hugged her she felt bones.

"Look at you," Sylvie repeated. She turned to Henry. "Look at *you.*"

Since her mother didn't move, Lane pulled Henry close and gave him a hug by proxy.

"It's all right," her mother said. "It's all right."

"What's all right?" Lane asked.

Henry tugged at his mother's sleeve. "Can I see the pool?"

Sylvie's face turned pink and Henry seemed to shrink as he belatedly remembered his mother's warning. His grandparents had a pool in a room they called the lanai. A sliding door connected the lanai to the living room but the door would be locked and the pool off-limits. Pool closed. House rules. Uncle Albie never learned to swim.

When Henry looked up at Lane, his eyes were wet. "I'm sorry I forgot."

"That's okay," she told him and drew him closer.

"Turtle?" Lane's father came barreling out of the house and Sylvie stepped aside to make way. "There she is. Turtle." He gave Lane a one-armed hug and extended his hand to Henry. Lane braced herself, unsure if Henry's handshake would pass muster.

"Excellent," Marshall said, and Lane felt her shoulders drop a notch. "Very strong. Did your dad teach you that? To shake hands?"

"Oh," Sylvie said.

"It's okay." Lane put a hand on her mother's shoulder and felt a tiny shudder. "Henry and I talk about Aaron all the time. It's good to talk about him. We don't avoid it. And yes, Aaron had a good strong shake. Like Henry's."

"Don't just stand there," her father boomed. "Come in."

Lane felt herself slide into a state of high alert. She glanced at Henry, whose eyes were tracking her, studying her movements to figure out what to feel. She put on a smile and led him inside.

Henry sat down in the foyer to take off his shoes. At least he'd remembered the rule about that. It took some tugging; his feet grew surprisingly fast. Some days it seemed the shoes that fit in the morning were tight by the afternoon. The sneaker on his right foot wasn't a problem but when he yanked off the left one it flew out of his hand and skittered across the floor. He froze and Lane readied herself to defend him from the inevitable scolding.

Her father let out a booming, full-bodied laugh. "What an arm! Have you tried out for baseball yet? With an arm like that you should.

I had quite an arm when I was your age. Your mother did not. Some kind of hand-eye coordination issue. But you don't have any issues at all, do you?"

Henry looked at his mother, unsure of whether he had any issues and if he did, unsure of what they were. Lane mouthed, *Thank you*, and Henry echoed the words out loud. It was only after she heard him let out a quiet sigh that she realized both of them had been holding their breath.

The house was more furnished than the last time Lane visited, which wasn't saying much. The last time there had been only the essentials. A love seat in the living room. Stools and a folding table in the kitchen. A dresser and a bed in each bedroom. Now, there was a dark wood table with matching chairs in the dining alcove, and the shelves in the living area were finally filled with books. Somehow, despite the additions, the house retained a just-moved-in look that belied the five years her parents had been there.

Five years in one place was the Meckler family record, if they didn't count Shelley. Shelley broke the record in a big way when she married Quinn and moved into the Wimbledon home his family had occupied for three generations. It was Lane's opinion that the existence of that family home was what attracted Shelley to Quinn in the first place.

That her parents had taken little with them to Florida was not a surprise. Take Only What You Love was the first item on Sylvie's Rules for Moving, a list Lane and Shelley were made to memorize and recite every time they packed up house, which they did every three to five years while Marshall hopscotched from job to job and state to state, Nutley to San Diego, Rochester to St. Louis, rising up the ranks of various pharma companies, first sales rep, then district manager, then regional manager, then a job in headquarters that didn't last long because—well,

Lane didn't really know why. Something about her father didn't like being on the inside. What followed were several months of unemployment and a move back to New Jersey for a job at a lower rung on the ladder and when that didn't work out, a rapid slide downhill, one less appealing job to the next, none as good as the last, until, unexpectedly, early retirement.

The Florida house was supposed to be their last move. "Only way I'm leaving this place is on a stretcher," her father joked, and then got annoyed when no one laughed. Their place was now no more or less furnished than any other the Mecklers had lived in, but it was missing the single sign of settling in that Sylvie allowed: a crewel embroidery saying that she would stitch, have framed, and hang on the wall herself.

Another of her mother's routines: she left behind the old sayings and hung up a new one shortly after moving into each new house. Sometimes there would be only one; sometimes there were a few. In one house, Lane remembered, Sylvie bought so many crewel kits that their living room wall ended up covered with squares and rectangles of sayings. The sayings themselves made no sense to Lane. *Today is a good day for a good day. All you need is love and a little rain.*

When Shelley asked what that one meant—*All you need is love and a little rain*—their mother looked flummoxed, as if before that moment, she'd never given a thought to what her needlework said; she just bought what was in stock at whatever store she'd managed to find.

Lane was wondering about what the absence of an embroidered saying meant—could her mother be less gung ho about their final move than her father claimed?—when she heard the clatter of feet. She turned and saw Henry with his face pressed against the sliding door to the lanai.

"Is that the pool? I could teach Uncle Albie to swim. I could teach him the back float. The back float is easy."

His grandfather winced. "No one's swimming." He stepped over their bags. "I'll bring those up later, Turtle. I'm in the middle of organizing the garage. Been putting it off for years. Here's some advice for you, Henry: Don't put things off. If you do, it just makes things worse."

"Thank you," Henry said.

"Finally," Marshall muttered. "A polite one."

The door from the kitchen to the garage groaned open and slammed shut.

Sylvie turned to Henry. "Would you like to go out and play now, dear?"

Lane couldn't imagine what her mother thought Henry would do outside. "How about you show us around?" Her nose picked up the chemical tang of new carpet. The walls smelled of fresh paint. "Did you just redecorate?"

Sylvie shrugged. "Who can say? Time flies. This is our living room area. Love seat. Chair." She walked a few steps and stopped. "This is our kitchen area. Fridge. Yellow cabinets."

"Speckled countertop," Henry offered, thinking this was a game.

Sylvie smiled and led them up the stairs. She stopped in the hall. "That room is Grandpa Marshall's and mine." She pointed. "That room is Uncle Albie's."

Henry bent down to look through the slit between the closed door and the floor. "Is he there?"

"I'm afraid not, dear. He's away on a little vacation."

"Is that what we're calling it now?" Marshall bellowed from the foot of the stairs. He let out a sound of disgust. "Where's my level, Sylvie? It's not where I left it. Did you move it?"

"I'll be right there." She hurried to finish the tour. "Bathroom. Guest room."

Lane was stuck on Uncle Albie. "On vacation where? With who?" Her mother stayed silent. "With Aunt Beadie?" Lane shook off the chill of a memory she didn't want to have.

The color drained from her mother's face. "I didn't think you remembered her."

"I only met her that once, but her face—it scared me." Lane wasn't sure why she'd chosen this moment to admit that. In true Meckler style, they had never spoken of that night. What she remembered about her aunt was the stuff of dreams, bad dreams. A woman with slick, oily cheeks and eyes that peeked out of tiny slits. She understood now that what she saw that night was a woman slayed by grief. But at the time it had looked to her like Aunt Beadie's features were melting off her face. To get away from her, she ran upstairs and Shelley followed and they hid in what they would soon be told was their shared bedroom. It was through the closed door of that room that they heard yelling and sobbing. And it was in that room where Shelley made up a game called *Guess Who's Crying Now?* that Lane didn't want to play.

Marshall's voice cut through Lane's reverie. "Sylvie," he boomed from downstairs. "Are you ignoring me because you're trying to annoy me? If you are, it's working."

"I have to help your father find his level. I'll be back with the bedding."

While Sylvie made her way downstairs, Henry and Lane walked into the guest room.

Henry asked the obvious question. "Where's the bed?" There had definitely been a bed the last time they visited. Now there was a couch covered in delivery plastic. Henry sniffed the air. "What's that smell?"

Lane sniffed and smelled smoke. Had someone been smoking? She sniffed again. It didn't smell like cigarettes. "Smells like someone burned toast." She cracked open the window and set to work, with Henry's help, tearing off the thick casing. When they were done, she lifted up the cushion. "A pullout. Like in our apartment."

"What's that noise?" Henry asked.

Lane stopped and listened. "Uncle Albie's TV. He watches a lot of TV."

Sylvie walked in, her eyes just visible above the bedding piled in her arms. "Here we go."

"Uncle Albie's back," Henry reported. "We can hear his TV. Can I watch with him?"

"That's my TV," Sylvie said. "Did you know there's a channel where *Law & Order* is on all day? Would you like to watch *Law & Order* with me?" she asked Henry.

"Mom—that is not appropriate for a six-year-old."

"Why is the window open? The air-conditioning is on." Sylvie closed the window. "Would you like to go out and play now, dear?"

Her mother was not making sense. "What is there for Henry to do outside? It's hot. The pool is off-limits. Do you even have a ball for him to kick around?"

"No." Her mother's face went flat.

Lane regretted her harsh tone. Why did it always go like this? "You know what might be fun? A sprinkler. Would you like to do that, Henry? Run around under a sprinkler?"

"No sprinkler," Sylvie said quietly. "Underground irrigation." She stopped to think. "I know. You can help your grandfather. He's got lots of tools. Hammers and drills. Would you like to watch him drill?"

"Can I?" Henry asked Lane.

She did not have a good feeling about this but Henry looked so excited.

"Didn't you tell me you were going to have to do some work while you're here?" Sylvie asked. "You don't want to keep your *Roxie* readers waiting."

Was that sarcasm? No. It was her father who made fun of her column. Her mother was a fan. And she was right; there was no vacation from email. "It's fine with me if it's fine with Grandpa," Lane told Henry. "But ask first. Don't assume."

"It's always better to be outside, don't you think?" Sylvie asked Henry as she guided him down the stairs. "Nothing like fresh air."

"I thought you were taking him to help Dad in the garage?" Lane called. No answer. She checked her watch and laughed when she realized she wasn't checking to see what time it was; she was checking to see how much time was left before they could leave.

5

Organizing the garage made no sense to Lane. For starters, she couldn't see the point. Aside from the empty cartons stacked in the corners and the rusty implements hanging from the hooks, the garage was empty. Other than throwing away a rake and a push broom laced with cobwebs that suggested it hadn't been disturbed in a while, what was it he needed to organize? Even if what Lane's father claimed was true—*Just because you can't see a mess doesn't mean it isn't there*—why now, this week, the one week she was visiting, to tackle a project he said himself he'd been putting off for years?

"You've got to admit it's a beauty," Marshall said, tapping the large squat box that sat on the melting macadam. "Shipped overnight. The things they can do. Maybe I should have added you two to the order. Could have saved you a bucket of nickels. You think that would have been more fun, Henry? Coming by box?" He started to push the box up the sloping driveway. "Is no one going to help me?"

"Ridiculous," Lane muttered, but she helped anyway. So did her mother, both of them pulling the box from the front while Marshall and Henry pushed from the back. It was slow going, but shimmy by shimmy they got the dumb box—that's how she thought of it now—into the garage.

"Bravo!" Marshall applauded. "Henry, let me see those muscles." Henry flexed his imaginary muscles and his grandfather clapped again. "You are going to be a strong one. Now watch carefully." He pulled a box cutter out of his back pocket. "This is important." He saw Lane scowling. "Someone's got to teach the boy things like this now." He lined up the cutter with the seam of the box. "Okay, son, number one rule for all jobs: Choose the Right Tool." He sliced easily through the tape. "Number two rule: Give Your Team Specific Directions. Don't leave it to chance. Take it from me. Chance doesn't work."

Lane and Henry's specific directions were to hold the box steady. Sylvie had moved back to stand against the wall, as if in protest, so she didn't get any directions. Marshall put himself in charge of lifting the contents out of the box. When he was done he admired the pile of metal on the floor. "This is their premium model. Extra-large capacity. Extra-strong security." He picked up a steel leg. "Talk about heft. Talk about heavy-gauge construction."

Why talk about that? Why express love for what Lane could read on the side of the box was a SEVENTY-EIGHT-INCH-HIGH STEEL CABINET WITH LOCK. What about expressing love to the boy who'd just lost his father? The boy who, despite his original excitement at the chance to help his grandfather with his tools, was now struggling not to cry. There really was no predicting when grief would hit.

"Fine, I'll read the manual," Marshall said, as if someone had been haranguing him. He read slowly, first the cautions, then the contents, then the step-by-step assembly. "See how simple? Screw. Plug. Tighten. Done."

Lane turned at the sound of Henry sniffing and saw a single tear escape from his wide-open eyes. She moved closer and took his hand. "Come on, buddy. Let's go inside."

As Marshall continued to admire the dumb box and even dumber cabinet, Sylvie slowly circled the pile of hinges, legs and posts and asked, "Why do we need this?"

"Why?" Marshall heaved an exasperated sigh and then noticed Lane and Henry heading toward the kitchen door. "Shouldn't leave a job half-done," he called to Henry. "Things slip away if you don't make an effort." He turned to Sylvie. "Storage. Remember? We decided. Storage."

In the morning when Lane and Henry came down for breakfast, Marshall was back in the garage.

"Can't that wait until we leave?" she asked her mother. "Is it going to be the end of the world if he doesn't organize the garage this week?"

"Maybe yes, maybe no." Sylvie's eyes darted to the clock. "How did it get to be so late? I haven't made Albie his tray."

Lane followed her mother's glance, first to the clock, then to the stairs. "Is Uncle Albie back?"

"Oh." Sylvie sat down. "No. I forgot."

"Are you okay?" Lane asked her.

"I'm fine," her mother said. And quickly added, "Why wouldn't I be?" She looked at Henry. "How are you, dear? What interesting thing would you like to do today?"

Unsure of how to respond, Henry looked to his mother for help.

"First things first," Lane told him. "You have some schoolwork to get done."

After breakfast, Lane helped get Henry settled on the sofa with a pencil and the math packet his teacher had given him to work on while he was away; combining and comparing was the lesson. When she returned to the kitchen, her mother was gone and her father was in her place.

"Is Mom okay?" Lane asked him.

"You're the expert. You tell me."

"I don't know. That's why I'm asking."

"Maybe you should write a letter to Roxie and see what she thinks." He grumbled the rest. "People asking strangers for advice. Might as well use a Ouija board. That's what you are."

"I'm a Ouija board?"

"A stranger."

"Not everyone has someone to ask."

Her father grunted. "People need to learn how to make do for themselves. To try hard and if that doesn't work, to try harder. You're not dumb, Turtle, but you don't know everything."

For a brief moment Lane let herself wonder what Roxie would say if she got a letter about Marshall or Sylvie or any of it—but Henry walked in, so she let the thought go. She was grateful for the interruption; nothing good would come from thinking about that.

In his hand, Henry held a worksheet that had a tear in the center of the page and a trail of pink eraser crumbs flaking off, like dandruff. He'd been struggling. "Got a problem there, buddy?"

"If you want advice from your mother," Marshall said, "you better get in line."

Henry looked around the kitchen to see where the line was.

"That was a joke," Lane explained. "Which was hard to tell, because it wasn't funny. May I see?" Henry handed over his paper and Lane read the instructions aloud. "Ring the right answer."

"Are they still telling children to do that?" Sylvie asked as she came into the kitchen. "Why on earth they don't just say *circle the right answer* I'll never know. Generations of children have been scurrying about looking for a bell to ring and for—" She stopped. "Did you hear that? Is that the van?" She looked at the clock and then at her husband. "It's much too soon for Albie to be back, isn't it?" Marshall threw up his hands as if in surrender and left the room. "Your father gets so ornery," she told Lane. "It's because he's alone too much," she explained to Henry and then asked, "Would you like to help him again, dear? You did a wonderful job of cheering him up yesterday."

Henry looked at his mother, who said, "Only if you want to."

"Why wouldn't he want to?" Sylvie asked. "Come, Henry. Let's go see what he's up to now." She put out a hand and Henry took it and followed her to the door that led from the kitchen to the garage.

"You don't have to," Lane called after him, but he kept walking.

"He *wants* to," her mother insisted. "Go do your work. Lunch is at noon."

At noon, Lane came down from the guest room where she'd been working and found her father at the coffeepot pouring a refill and her mother staring into a glass bowl on the counter. There was a mound of chopped celery at the bottom of the bowl and a bag of frozen corn on the counter. Lunch preparation—if that was what it was—seemed to have come to a halt.

"What's going on?" Lane asked.

"Here she comes," Marshall said. "Ready to make a big megillah out of nothing."

"Where's Henry?" Lane asked.

Marshall glanced around. "I don't know."

"I thought he was with you. Henry?" Lane called. "Henry?"

When Henry didn't answer, Marshall went out to see if he was in the garage and Lane raced upstairs to check the bedrooms.

"Not in the garage or the lanai," her father reported when they met up in the foyer.

Lane felt a wave of dread. "The pool."

"Door's locked," Marshall said. "Pool's covered."

"He must have gone outside is all," Sylvie said. "To play."

Lane ran out to the backyard but Henry wasn't there. And why would he be there? The yard was nothing more than a square of patchy brown grass so forlorn even the worms had abandoned it. "Henry?" she called anyway. "Henry?"

She was standing on the sidewalk in front of the house, on the edge of panic, when she saw a garbage truck up the street parked at a strange angle. The motor was on and rumbling loud. The running lights stared like a pair of oversize eyes. The front grill was set in what looked like a toothy smirk. The driver was slowly heading toward her. His limp was what she noticed first. That he was carrying something was what she noticed next. It was Henry. Henry had his arms wrapped around the man's neck. She watched as the man stopped, said something, and put Henry down.

Henry ran fast. He ran right into her, threw his arms around her waist, and closed his eyes.

"Aw buddy, what happened?"

"He's okay," the garbage man called. He had a barrel chest and wide shoulders but his steps were small. His left leg dragged. "He's okay now," he added. When they were finally face-to-face, he told Lane what happened: how he stopped his truck in front of her parents' house, hoisted the giant box in the back, and drove away; how he assumed the box was heavy because of packing material, until he heard a noise; how he quickly pulled over and got out to inspect the cargo. That's when he saw there was a boy—her son—curled up in the bottom of the box, like a cat.

At some point Lane dropped to her knees but she didn't let go of Henry, she just pulled him closer, so close there wasn't room for air between them. "It's okay," she told him and kept repeating it, to him and to herself. "It's going to be okay."

At first she didn't notice that a crowd had gathered. Like lint to fleece, by texts and calls, news had rippled up and down the block. People pressed in, voices rising in a jumble of words. "It's all right now."

"The boy's okay." Someone took out their phone and then others followed. Soon all faces were obscured. It was as if by silent and unanimous decision, and without any clear reason, that they all began to film the encounter.

Snippets of conversation reached her. "Look how upset—" "He can't even imagine—" A chant started. "Hug. Hug. Hug." And then, "Hug it out. Hug it out. Hug it out."

In the end, Lane did hug the driver, an awkward, self-conscious hug in which her body stayed rigid, as far away from his as possible. To her it felt as if they'd been cajoled into putting on a show, egged on by a crowd that, once they got what they wanted—a tidy and happy resolution to a near tragedy—applauded and retreated to their respective homes.

Finally it was just them, Lane, Henry, the driver and Marshall, who had come outside to see what all the fuss was about and now stood awkwardly, unsure of what to do next. The driver—Lane read the metal name tag affixed to his shirt pocket—Reggie, made the first move: he walked over to Henry and, with a grimace, kneeled down on his bum knee so he could see him eye to eye. He extended his hand.

Henry, ashen faced and silent, remained perfectly still. As far as Lane could tell, he hadn't blinked since the driver set him down. Shock, she realized. All of them were in shock. She gave Henry a nudge. He stretched out his arm and his small hand disappeared into Reggie's fleshy palm.

"Tell him thank you," Lane whispered, but Henry wouldn't so she said it instead. "Say goodbye," she prompted, but Henry wouldn't say that either. "Do you want to come in for a minute?" she asked the driver.

"No." It was Marshall who answered. He stood behind her, his body stiff as a plank, tipped back.

She swung around to face him. "No?"

"Your mother isn't feeling very—"

"Come inside," she told Reggie, ignoring her father. "Have a glass of water. Catch your breath."

Her father objected again. "I really don't think that's—"

"Dad." Lane cut him off.

"It's okay," Reggie said. "No need to be cross. Your dad's just shook up. Right, Grandpa? Who wouldn't be shook up?" He looked at Henry. "You're shook up too. I can see that. Look, son, I've got six grandkids and they do all kinds of things when they get bored. Comes with the territory. You think you're the first boy who ever climbed into a box and fell asleep? I can tell you, you are not. You didn't mean any harm. And no harm done. Right, Grandpa?"

It took a moment for Marshall to answer. "Right."

"You know what I think?" Reggie said to Henry. "I think, start the day over. Get back into bed, hop out, give yourself a stretch, brush your teeth. Like it's a new day. That's the way to do it. Right, Mom? Go home and start over?"

Lane nodded. He was right. They needed to go home. Where was home?

"Better get back to my route." Reggie looked down the block toward his vehicle. He didn't seem eager to move on. "Y'all take care now."

Lane thanked him again and watched Reggie limp, slowly, back to his truck.

That lunch was a chicken-salad-and-corn sandwich with a side of pudding barely made it into her consciousness. Whatever relief she'd felt was gone. What was left was numb exhaustion. She ate without tasting.

"Doesn't Henry like pudding?" her mother asked.

Lane looked over at Henry's plate. He hadn't taken a bite of anything. "Not hungry?"

Henry shook his head.

"Aw buddy," Lane said. "Remember what the driver told you? No harm done. It wasn't your fault." She turned to her father. "Tell him it wasn't his fault."

Her father begrudgingly complied. "Not your fault." He turned to Lane. "Not *my* fault."

"Oh well," Sylvie said.

Marshall crossed his arms over his chest. Her mother used the tip of her index finger to pick up some toast crumbs from the table.

"Would you like to draw?" Lane asked Henry. He nodded. "Want me to get your markers?"

He shook his head and got up to get them himself.

"What's that smell?" Sylvie said as Henry walked past. "Smells like garbage."

Lane stared at her father. "You didn't tell Mom what happened?"

"Nothing happened." Marshall marched to the garage and slammed the door.

Lane turned to her mother. "Remember when Dad asked Henry if he thought it would have been more fun to come here by box than plane?" Sylvie thought about it and nodded. "Well guess what? While Dad was supposedly watching Henry, Henry was climbing into that box at the curb. What was Dad thinking, saying something like that to him and then putting the box out at the curb, like an invitation?" She wasn't mad at Henry for climbing into the box. And she didn't blame him for falling asleep there either. They'd hardly gotten any sleep at all the night before, both of them woken multiple times by thumps and bangs and the thrum of her father bickering with her mother, just the one voice, just his. On top of that, there were multiple trips to the bathroom. Lane took Henry twice; the third time he asked if he could go alone to show her he was brave. Of course she said okay. She fell asleep that time, waking only when he climbed back into bed and whispered, "Mom?"

She'd answered, "I'm here," and he'd snuggled close and asked if he could tell her something and she'd said, "Of course." And the next thing she knew it was morning and sunlight was sneaking in through the slats of the gray vertical blinds and Henry was on his back, asleep and pale. So pale she went hunting for a thermometer. She woke him to take his temperature, which was about the only thing in the house that was normal.

Her anger now shifted to her mother. "Why did you let him go outside alone?"

"He didn't go outside. I walked with him to the garage so he could help your father."

"Who didn't notice that he wandered off and fell asleep in a box."

"He's a curious boy," Sylvie said, as if that would make things better.

"He fell asleep," Lane reminded her. "In a box. Like a stray cat."

"Oh well," Sylvie said.

"A garbage truck picking up Henry in a box is not an *Oh well* story."

"A recycling truck," her mother corrected her. "Tuesday is recycling."

"What's the difference." Lane felt her face heating up. "Do you understand what could have happened? Reggie said it's loud in his truck. So loud he can't think. But for some reason he heard something and he pulled over and he got out to look. Imagine what would have happened if the garbage man hadn't heard Henry call out."

"Recycling man." Marshall had come in. "Monday is garbage."

To avoid screaming, Lane let out a slow stream of air and counted down from ten. "It doesn't matter," she told them when she got to eight. "What matters is, the driver somehow managed to hoist himself up onto the back of the truck even though he has a bad leg. What matters is, he followed the sound and saw Henry's hair." Her parents were finally still. "Reggie said if it hadn't been so early in the run he would have started the—" She stopped, closed her eyes, composed herself and continued, "Compactor. That's what he does when he gets a big box that someone should have broken down. He starts—" She paused and took another breath. "The crusher."

"Here we go," her father said. "My fault."

Lane ignored him. "Reggie said the miracle is your house is early on his run." She dropped her voice to a whisper. "If it wasn't, Henry could have been . . ."

"Could have been," her mother repeated. Her lips flattened into a line. She reached out her hand to press it against Lane's cheek and then seemed to think better of it.

Her father let out a disgusted sigh at the display of emotion and left.

"Is Henry with you?" her mother called to him. "Where's Henry?"

"Getting his markers," Lane said. But he should have been back by now. She took the steps two at a time and found Henry in the guest room curled up in a fetal position on the open pullout. "Aw buddy." She rubbed his arm.

He rolled onto his back. "I want to go home."

She told her mother first. "We're going to leave tomorrow."

This time when her mother said, "Oh well," she sounded sad.

Her father was back in the garage; the morning's near disaster hadn't diminished his urge to organize.

"We're leaving," she told him.

"See you later."

"No, I mean really leaving. Back to the city."

He put down his drill. "You shouldn't have scared your mother like that. Telling her the boy could have been crushed. Hasn't she had enough to deal with?" He picked up the drill. "He shouldn't have climbed inside that box."

"What does Mom have to deal with other than you?"

He turned on the drill. Its scream was his answer. She went in to rebook the flight. When the representative told her there'd be a penalty for the change she asked if it could be waived and then explained about

Aaron dying and how she felt it was important for Henry to visit his grandparents. It wasn't like her to say any of this.

None of it mattered. "We no longer offer bereavement fares," the woman told her. "But based on what you're telling me, you wouldn't have qualified anyway."

Sylvie was on the sofa watching TV when Lane told her, "I got us on a noon flight tomorrow. We'll leave at ten."

Her mother nodded, half listening. "You look lovely." She turned to Lane, who was staring at her, dumbfounded. "Don't look at me. Look at you." She pointed to the television. There she was, Lane hugging Reggie, on the news. "I wish you smiled while they were filming you. You have such a lovely smile."

"You realize you're watching a news story about me being a neglectful mother."

Her mother gave her a dismissive wave. "Oh well."

In the morning on the way to the airport, Henry didn't speak. He said nothing on the plane, nothing in the taxi, nothing to the doorman, nothing to the dog walker in the elevator, nothing to the dog. Lane realized this in retrospect. In the moment, things seemed normal. The New Normal.

A blast of stuffy air greeted them when she opened the door to their apartment. She pulled their bags inside. Henry asked what they were having for dinner. It was as if everything that happened in Florida was already forgotten. They decided on Chinese. As usual, Henry chose the dishes and Lane called in the order.

For the rest of the night and in the morning he was his normal sweet and chatty self with her, so she had no idea until she got the call from school the next day that her son had gone completely silent everywhere else.

February 15, 2017

Ask Roxie!

Hey Roxie Readers! Roxie's online Live-Chat
Wednesdays are almost here!

Remember, Live-Chat Wednesdays will be available
for Guild-Plus Subscribers only!

If you love Roxie's column, subscribe today so you
don't miss out!

Dear Roxie,

I'm sorry if I'm wasting your time. I know my problem
isn't the end of the world but it's keeping me up at night.
I hope you can tell me what's the right thing to do.

The problem is my daughter's finger. Everyone tells
me, calm down, it's just a finger. But when it comes to
children, is there such a thing as "just"? Doesn't everything matter?

It's because of what happened last month when we visited my brother-in-law in Wichita. He was recovering from a heart attack, is why we went. We were at his house when my daughter's finger got slammed in a door.

Her brother slammed the door, is how it happened. He claims it was an accident. I wasn't there so I don't know. All I know is her finger got smashed and I nearly fainted when I saw it.

At the emergency room they took an X-ray and told us the finger wasn't broken, which, thank God. But I cannot describe how horrible it looked. It had a dent near the top and the tip was squashed flat like a pancake.

The doctor started bandaging it up—like everything was over—so I asked, very nicely, don't you think she needs to see a plastic surgeon before you put the bandage on?

The doctor started shouting at me. Did I even know what the word *need* meant. Did I understand that no one *needs* to have a plastic surgeon for a tiny bruise on a little pinky. It wasn't a tiny bruise, by the way, and it wasn't on her pinky. It was on her pointer.

Maybe the doctor was having a bad day.

Back home, when our trip was over and it was time to take off the bandage, I couldn't believe what I saw. Her finger looks bizarre. You can't help but notice it's not normal. I can't stop staring at it.

Luckily I happen to have a neighbor who's a plastic surgeon who's done tons of work on kids in the neighborhood. So I figured, why not ask him to take a look? Except when I told this to my husband—who is truly stubborn as a mule—he said, "Absolutely not. Her finger's fine. It works like it's supposed to. If she's not bothered, why are you?"

Why I'm bothered is kids are mean. Girls especially. Twelve-year-old girls, worst of all. My daughter goes to a sleepaway camp in the summer where the girls are merciless. At camp you can't hide anything. I know because I went to camp and I got teased. If you're teased at camp, it's over. News gets out. I don't know how, but the kids at home always hear. Starts out you have no friends at camp. Ends up you have no friends, period.

I don't see why my daughter should end up lonely and depressed over something we could fix if my husband didn't put his big foot down.

Last night I got a brainstorm. If I take a photograph of her finger while she's sleeping, and pop over to my neighbor's house with it, I could ask him what he thinks and no one would be the wiser. Technically it wouldn't be a consultation. My question is, being that I'm just dropping by the doctor's house, neighbor to neighbor, would I be covered by patient-client confidentiality? I'm sorry to bother you with something so small but my husband cannot know. He is stubborn as a goat.

Yours,
Weirded Out

Dear Weirded Out,

Wow. There's a lot to unpack here.

Let's start with this: nothing is harder than seeing a child in harm's way. I can imagine how scary that was, seeing your daughter's smashed finger. It must have really hurt! (I'm talking about her.)

Now it's time for some tough love. You're spinning out of control. You started out in reality—you have a child with a slightly odd-looking finger—which, may I point out, might not be completely healed yet. But then you leap to fantasyland where your daughter has grown up and, after years of teasing, turned into a depressed loner. That is a nightmare! Time to wake up!

Good morning! Now that you've joined me back in reality, let's talk.

Number one: Stop looking at your daughter's finger! Right now! I mean it! If you feel an urge to stare at a finger, stare at your own.

I hate to admit it but I agree with your husband on this one point: if your daughter's finger works and she's fine with it, you have to be fine with it too.

I would be remiss if I didn't stop here to point out that you appear to have some unfinished business. Your daughter isn't being teased but once upon a time you were. It is clear you are still feeling hurt about this.

73

That's understandable. Being teased is painful. But given how long ago that occurred, it's probably time for you to take a look at that pain. If you don't, you risk confusing your pain with your daughter's and that's going to end up painful for both of you.

Number two: Stop taking orders from your husband! Right now! I mean it! The next time he tells you he's putting his foot down, tell him he can put his foot wherever he wants but just because his foot is bigger doesn't mean he gets to decide everything.

Marriages are full of disagreements but no partner gets to have the final word every time. You describe your husband as stubborn. Is that all he is? Do you and your husband have a fair and equal partnership? If not, alarm bell! Time to get up and go to counseling. If he won't go, no problem. You're a grown-up. Go yourself.

Number three: Have you paid any attention to your son lately? Because you need to. Right now! I mean it! A kid who hurts his sibling can feel awful, whether he meant to do it or not. You say it was an accident but you qualify it with "he claims." Do you not believe him? *Was* it an accident? It's worth asking. And it's worth listening with a kind heart to his answer.

Speaking of hearts, how's your brother-in-law feeling? I hope he's healing well.

The only person in your family who sounds like they're doing great is your daughter. You should be proud of her. You've raised a kid who doesn't care that her finger looks funny.

And if someday your daughter asks what you think about that finger, don't hustle her off to a plastic surgeon. Tell her everyone's body gets dinged along the way. Tell her our dings hold the stories of our lives. And if she doesn't remember the story of her ding, tell her once upon a time in Wichita, her finger got caught in a door and she was brave.

Yours forever, or at least for now,
Roxie

6

When the Guild offices were first redesigned—polished concrete walls and floors, long gray steel worktables, orange-splash-of-color desk partitions—everyone complained. The open plan's promise to foster free-flowing energy and collaboration turned out, in reality, to be a call-center aesthetic where the only things flowing freely were distractions.

The first solution was noise-canceling headphones, which Hugo the receptionist was charged with handing out and keeping clean. The second solution was to install the messaging platform Eeze. After Eeze was installed, all communication switched to virtual.

As an independent contractor, it wasn't mandatory for Lane to be on Eeze—she was an island unto herself—and to no one's surprise, she opted out. Being part of a group online was as unappealing to her as being part of a group offline. But she could still observe the effect Eeze had on the office. Guilders now tapped away all day messaging colleagues who might be in the DC office, or in LA, or in London, or sitting right beside them. No one ever knew. Silence was the new noise.

Today Lane was grateful for the office culture of silence, because today was her first day back after a short bereavement leave and the last thing she wanted to do was talk about what happened. Of course Sam, her managing editor, knew, as did Jem, her desk mate. Jem had been a heroic and unexpected helper, so kind to Henry at the funeral service, so thoughtful afterward, twice showing up at the apartment with offerings, crayons and jelly donuts for Henry, dark chocolate and a small bunch of dried lavender for Lane.

Lane had been direct with both Jem and Sam: she did not want people at work to know about Aaron's death. She did not want to re-create the awkwardness she felt in her apartment building at work. At work she wanted to work. The only way to avoid getting stacks of cards and consolation cake, the only way to get out of having people tell her she would get over the loss soon, or she would never get over the loss, was to not share the news.

"Can we keep this private?" she'd asked them both.

They gave the same answer: they couldn't guarantee it would be private, but they wouldn't be the ones to share.

Now all she had to do was get through the reception area. She wished she could hustle past Hugo like everyone else, but she couldn't. She'd seen it happen too many times, Guilders rushing past him as if he were a potted plant, music playing through their earbuds so they wouldn't hear him say hello, eyes averted so they wouldn't see him smile or nod. She saw the effect this had on Hugo, how each slight made him slump a little more. How after each slight he'd get even more eager, sound ever more desperate for connection. So Lane always said hello to Hugo, always with a smile and when he waved her over, as he did today, she always came.

"Color me surprised," Hugo said when she stepped out of the elevator. "How come you cut your trip short?"

What had he heard? Lane proceeded with caution. "Happy to be back."

"You came back because you missed me, right? Being away from me is torture."

"Exactly." She smiled and headed for the double doors that led into the main office space. The doors were controlled by an electric eye, which blinked twice and then stopped.

"It's on the fritz," Hugo called over. "Been doing that for days. Only sees some people. No one knows why. Maybe it's because you're all in black. Try waving your arms."

Lane waved her arms. The red eye flashed. The doors opened. A hidden diffuser shot a puff of fragrance at the back of her head.

Hugo stood up. "Sorry! I should have warned you! I guess everything went on the fritz while you were gone. Someone's coming up to fix that now. Do you need a paper towel?"

"I'm fine." The electric eye blinked again. "Thank you," she said, and hurried through.

Join Us. That was the name of the scent that now hung on her like a cloak. Developed by a lab specializing in bespoke fragrances, it was a mix of fifteen oils and elixirs, which seemed like a lot considering it smelled like nothing more or less than grapefruit. According to its creators, Join Us provided a *homeopathic sensory boost* that would increase both energy and joy of community. From what Lane observed, the only obvious uptick was in office pranks. Coming to work and finding your desk grapefruited—a dozen grapefruits on a desk was not unusual but even one did the trick—was a weekly occurrence. To her relief, Lane had never been grapefruited. Turned out you needed to be an insider to get pranked.

She moved at a brisk pace, quickly winding her way past rows of Guilders working in silence, like mourners in a funeral home. Actually, Aaron's funeral hadn't been at all silent. On top of the steady hum of his friends bartering details to get clear on what happened—*Who was in the car with him? Where had they been going? Why wasn't Lane going to that?*—there was a persistent car alarm that went off when one mourner's car bumped into another's. The rabbi had to resort to a two-finger whistle to get everyone's attention. Lane wouldn't have cared about any of it, if she hadn't been with Henry. She'd had to work hard to resist an impulse to put her hands over his ears to protect him from the noise. He was such a little soldier that day, eyes facing forward, mouth a straight line, and silent.

She turned down the aisle that led to Sam's office. The hush here was so complete she found herself stepping lightly to avoid detection.

It didn't work. She heard her name and turned to see a woman hurrying toward her. It was the new hire she'd found crying the night Aaron . . . She stopped herself. She did not want to think about that night. She tried to remember the young woman's name. Louisa? Selina? Joanna? She had no idea.

"Hi Lane. Remember me? Alyssa?"

"Of course. How are you, Alyssa? How was the party?"

"So great. Thanks for making me go. I met so many people." She whispered the next. "I made friends."

"I'm so glad," Lane whispered back. "I knew you would." She pointed toward Sam's office. "I have to go. Meeting with Sam."

"Sorry," Alyssa said. She hesitated for a moment and then quickly moved in and gave Lane a hug. "Thank you."

"Thank *you*," Lane said, and hurried on.

Lane knocked on the glass wall and walked in. The bite of Mentho-Lyptus in the air stopped her. She knew before she saw him that Sam already had a visitor. The Guild CFO, Bert, was sitting in the guest chair that was just out of sight from the doorway. Bert, the bad cop to Sam's good, was addicted to sucking on cough drops because, he claimed, Mentho-Lyptus improved his clarity.

He popped up from the guest chair. "Hello, Lane-Roxie-Lane."

Sam gave her a sympathetic smile. He knew she did not enjoy the nickname. She did not enjoy anything about Bert.

Bert extended his arm, which Lane thought meant he wanted to shake her hand. He did not. What he wanted was to give her a cough drop; Bert thought everyone could use a little extra clarity.

She slipped the cough drop in her pocket. "For later," she told him. "When I'm writing."

He nodded and pointed his finger at her like a gun. "Clickety click." He turned his hands into fists and popped his two thumbs up. "You're doing great, Lane-Roxie-Lane."

Okay. This meant clicks and eyeballs were up on her column. But Bert being a fan meant nothing. He had no favorites. He had numbers. If her clicks were up, he liked her. If they were down, she was deadweight. She would not have stopped by if she knew he was there.

"Sam," Lane said, "do you have time for a quick chat after the Monday meeting?"

Sam nodded. Bert looked dubious.

"Clickety clickety," Lane said.

"Clickety clickety," Bert echoed, impressed.

While most of the office was composed of extremely well-groomed young women and very skinny, scruffly young men, the universe at Lane's worktable was populated by a less uniform crowd. The doughy, the mottle-skinned, the old, the odd.

Lane's friend Jem sat on her right. Jem was a perfect seatmate: razor-sharp focus on tasks at hand, no interest in breaking for chitchat, all food snacks and hair products were odor-free. To Lane's left was an older man. Older folks were rare at the Guild. Lane and Hugo, in their forties, were outliers. This man looked to be on the upper edge of his fifties. Maybe that was why he kept his head down. Literally down and hunched over. He rarely raised his basset-hound eyes, not even to say hello to Lane or Jem. He worked in a monk-like trance, completely still except for the movement of his stubby fingers on his keyboard. Lane didn't know his name, he didn't know hers, and they both found this to be a satisfying relationship.

Except today when she pulled out her chair to sit down, he stopped typing and sat up straight. She had never seen him sit up straight.

"Hi Roxie," he said. "I mean Lane. I don't really know what I'm supposed to call you. Either way, I'm sorry for your loss."

Lane was temporarily speechless but Jem asked the question she was thinking.

"Who told you? And her name is Lane. You're supposed to call her Lane."

"You can call me whatever you want," Lane told the man. "I answer to anything. And thank you."

He nodded and returned to his keyboard hunch.

"I didn't tell him," Jem said quietly. "Maybe it was on Eeze. I hate Eeze."

"Why would it be on Eeze?"

"There's all kinds of crazy groups on Eeze now," Jem told her. "This morning I saw one about Hugo called, 'What Does Hugo Do All Day?' But don't worry. Eeze is going away soon. The powers that be finally realized there's hardly any project collaboration going on there anymore. It's all gossip and complaints. Apparently the over-forties group is claiming the under-thirties group ruined it for everyone." Jem studied Lane's expression. "Do you want me to check and see if there's a group about you? I'm sure there's not. Forget I said that. Don't even think about it. Can you do that?"

"Yes. I'm very good at not thinking about things."

Jem smiled and went back to work. Lane opened her laptop and silently acknowledged to herself that today was going to be tough. Then again, every day had been tough at work, now that her face, blown up extra large with a huge and fake-looking smile, was all over the Guild website and on the reception area wall. There was probably no one left at the Guild who didn't recognize her. She wished she could tell them, all the identical-looking scruffly young men and well-groomed young women whose names she didn't know, that she hadn't volunteered to be on those posters. To the contrary, she'd argued hard against both the Live-Chat—she wasn't going to be any good live, even if in this case *live* meant being alone in a room, typing answers to readers' questions in real time—and the publicity blitz that went along with it. Head down, eyes on the screen, that was the answer. She got to work dropping virtual letters into the four virtual folders on her desktop: NEXT, SOONER, LATER, NEVER.

Sorting took a lot of time but Lane found it relaxing, once she got going. When she first started at the Guild the column came with an intern who did the sorting for her, but that didn't work out. Judgment was so personal. The intern had a good eye for what made a compelling letter but she wasn't inside Lane's head. She couldn't figure out all of Lane's quirks. Neither could Lane. Sometimes she got worked up about a letter that she never would have expected to hit a nerve. She was fairly disconnected from her nerves.

The sounds of people chatting broke through her concentration. She looked up and saw a parade of Guilders heading toward the Super Zone for the Monday meeting. Closing her laptop, she joined the march.

The *Ask Roxie* column was never on the agenda at the *What do we have? What do we want? What do we need?* Monday meetings. In the rare event that there was a change planned for the column—Bert's idea for the Live-Chat, for example—they discussed it in the quasi privacy of Sam's glass-walled office. When she complained about the meetings to Aaron, he'd always ask her why she bothered to go. The same question could be asked of everyone who went. From what she observed, no one was really there. Yes, people walked in and sat down in chairs around a long table, but they weren't really present. She could see it on the screens they didn't bother to hide. They scrolled from Twitter to Instagram to Everlane and read Eeze messages that popped up at the top of their screens and then disappeared like tiny explosions. Everyone had developed a talent for listening with scant attention for the sound of their own name. If they heard it, they'd sit up on full alert. Otherwise, words passed over tipped heads like vapor.

The reason she went to the Monday meetings was the same reason everyone did: to put in real-life face time. At the Guild that wasn't optional. The employee handbook did have a section on working remotely but it was short. One sentence was all it took to say, *Zero-Tolerance Policy.*

Questions about real-life face time were among the most common ones asked by the new hires who stopped by her desk. She was used to this by now, that for some reason certain nervous new hires gravitated toward her instead of to the robustly informative HR woman whose actual job it was to orient them. They'd approach on light feet and wait for her to notice them before whisper-asking, *Where's the bathroom?* or, *Is it okay to go outside for lunch?* or, *Are we allowed to work remotely?* She'd gently point them to the appropriate resource and assure them that they were going to figure this all out fast and they always did. Within a week they'd find their peers and Lane's help would no longer be needed. She was basically a stopgap measure, which she didn't mind. Being a stopgap was the perfect amount of interaction.

It was a remote working situation that was what Lane wanted to discuss today with Sam. The zero-tolerance policy would be a hurdle, but as an outside contractor who reported directly to him, it would not be a wall. Sam had been her champion from the start. Discovering new talent was the part of his job he loved best. Lane was one of many on a long list of people Sam was proud of having found.

When they first met, Lane was a freelancer in high demand. Her reputation was as a fast, sharp, meticulous writer who juggled assignments for digital and print, wrote long-form and short, and could move with agility between the worlds of reported pieces and service features. She was usually overbooked and sometimes overwhelmed, but she never missed a deadline.

Lane had long been a fan of the *Ask Roxie* column. It was a rare diversion that she and her mother shared, a perfect topic of conversation for when there was nothing safe to talk about, which was almost always the case. This was back when the column was written by the original Roxie, Roxie One, a woman named Gabby Curtis, who lost the gig after her very public breakdown.

Gabby's decline had played out in real time and in plain sight, her columns getting more and more off base as the months went by. The answer that got under Lane's skin was to a reader worried that her son was using drugs. In Lane's opinion, Roxie One's response was cruel and bullying. To her dismay, her mother came to Gabby's defense.

"Things aren't always black-and-white. Sometimes a person has to do what a person has to do."

In a stew of annoyance that was partly in response to her mother's reaction, and partly in response to what Roxie One had said—Lane got so riled up that she was moved, for the first time in her life, to post a comment online. She wrote it in a thunder of indignation and when she was done, she felt surprisingly great. It was the first time she'd ever dared express her rage.

What happened next was as much a surprise to her as it was to everyone else. Hundreds of *Roxie* readers clicked the *Like* button on Lane's post. Dozens more commented on it. She was hooked. Expressing her opinion about Roxie One's increasingly tone-deaf answers—always careful to keep below the limit of fifteen hundred characters—became how Lane began her day.

What Lane didn't know was that while she was writing snappy comments to Roxie One's answers, Roxie One had segued from writing insensitive replies to making up *Ask Roxie* letters of her own. It was an oft-told story at the Guild, a cautionary tale. First Gabby created fake letters, then she ran out of ideas for fake letters, then she turned to poaching letters from the archives of her competitors. If she had taken the time to paraphrase the letters, it's possible no one would have been the wiser, but all she changed were the pronouns. It didn't take long before an eagle-eyed reader noticed it and called her out. And just like that, Roxie One was gone.

Credit where it was due, it was Sam's assistant, Chloe, who flagged Lane during the search for Roxie's replacement. Chloe had given up on reading Gabby's answers altogether—they'd gotten too weird—and went straight to Lane's comments instead. She wasn't alone. As Bert would soon confirm with a spreadsheet, the number of readers who currently commented on Gabby's answer was a fraction of the number who commented on Lane's.

For Lane, getting the *Roxie* gig was like winning a lottery she'd never even thought to enter. Writing the column allowed her to pour out all the emotions she would never express in real life. And the column brought her the perfect kind of friends: virtual. The gig was a perfect match she got through a lucky break.

But getting approval to work remotely was not something she could afford to leave to luck. Her strategy was a two-pronged appeal to Sam: first as the trusted mentor who'd always championed her, next as someone who'd recently suffered a loss. Sam's wife passed away a year ago. Unlike her marriage, theirs had been a grand love story. Lane wasn't planning to lie to Sam about her relationship with Aaron, but if he assumed, based on his own experience, that she was devastated by grief, she wasn't going to correct him.

❧

When Patty Petronacci, the *Life and Death* editor, sat down next to her, Lane tensed. Had Patty heard too? But the editor didn't offer condolences. She just waved the air and said, "Good luck getting that off."

"Pardon?"

"I don't know what they put in that diffuser but last week it got me." She raised her arm to her nose. "It's gone now. Took forever. I tried soap, vinegar, lemon, lavender. Nothing worked. Just time."

"Morning, everyone." Sam walked in with Bert trailing behind. "Before we get started, Bert wants to say a few words."

Bert stood behind his chair. "Who are we?" The mood in the room shifted. "People used to say the Guild was a place for innovators." Earbuds came out. "The Guild always looked beyond the present moment. Now?" He snapped his fingers but no one spoke up. "Are we still connecting the dots or are we regurgitating the garbage?" Everyone was on high alert. This was not how Bert usually spoke, so many words, none of them *click*. "Things move fast out there." He tipped his head toward the window. "Those who don't adapt don't survive." Even the noisy breathers were now holding their breath. "I'm here to tell you change is coming. Big change. Sam is leaving us."

At the sound of gasps, Sam stood up. "Okay, Bert. I'll take it from here."

Bert sat down, lips pressed together, hands in fists, knuckles white.

"I'm not leaving anyone," Sam said. "I'm relocating, temporarily, for the Guild-Europe start-up. You folks, right here in this room, are still my first priority. This is the best team the Guild has ever had." Faces brightened.

From behind him Bert said, "But—"

"But," Sam continued, "none of us can pretend the landscape hasn't changed. As most of you know, our friends across town decided they're going to shut down their in-house podcast division. The good news is we're going to take advantage of that. Over the next few months a crew of podcast producers will be coming over here to work on what was our webcast team. Unfortunately there will be redundancies."

A well-groomed young woman raised her hand. "So, if all these podcast producers are coming on the webcast team, what does that mean for our webcasts? Are you saying video is over?"

Lane went on alert. Bert had been leaning on her to do a *Roxie* webcast for months. The only reason she'd agreed to do the online Live-Chat was to get out of doing that.

Bert took the answer. "Let's just say that's not a profitable avenue for us at this time."

"Could we back up?" asked a scruffly young man. "When you say redundancies, are you talking about a couple of people losing their jobs? Or are you talking about a full-on BuzzFeed-style fifteen percent staff slash that—"

A commotion of sidebars drowned him out, most of it about the latest gossip on which company's digital writing staff was talking about joining which union.

Another scruffly young man, this one angry, broke through the scrum to call out his question to Sam, who was standing patiently but looking unhappy. "Word on the street is that the Guild is considering cutting its news division."

A wide-eyed young woman across from Lane looked at her and mouthed, *Is that true?*

Lane shrugged. She wasn't a person who would know anything about words on the street.

"The word on the street is wrong," Sam said. "Our news division is the beating heart of this organization. Folks, no one here is talking about massive layoffs. We're talking about adjustments. Small adjustments. The Guild has always done things differently. Being different is one of our core values. That's not changing. We will work through this together and we will find the path of least pain." He turned to Bert. "Agreed?"

"Clickety click."

"Okay," Sam said. "Since the Earth, as far as we know, is still turning, what do we have? What do we want? What do we need?"

The meeting proceeded. As always, the editor of the *Crime* column was last to report. When she finished her update Sam stood up. "Go forth and write well."

It took half an hour for Sam to finish up with all the people who wanted a quick word. When he was done he slid into the seat next to Lane, who'd been answering email while she waited. "The hordes have been placated for now. I'm all yours."

Bert slid in beside him. "Lane-Roxie-Lane, you have hit a new and inspiring high with that Crazy Bride column. Which you then topped with the Weird-Finger Mom. The people have spoken. They love it when you're mean."

"I'm not mean."

"Call it whatever you want. But do yourself a favor. Give a rest to the depressed. That guy who wanted to . . ." He shook his head. "Click-a-cide. Earnest is over. Stick to snark."

"I need a minute alone here, Bert," Sam said.

"Sure." Bert smiled. "Snark yourself out."

As soon as Bert left, Sam's face softened. "How you doing? You have good people around you? That was key for me."

"I do. Thanks."

He looked relieved. "I know how hard this is. It's going to be hard for a while. I'm sorry I'm leaving town, but I'm just a call away. You need anything, you say the word."

"I need to work from home." There. She got it out. "I realize the timing's terrible."

Sam nodded. "Bert won't like it. But—okay. I'll handle him. You keep doing what you're doing. Maybe throw him a crumb. Go a little heavy on the snark for a bit. Can you?"

She nodded. "And I can't do the Live-Chat." She hadn't planned to bring that up.

Sam winced. "Oh Lanie. We've been promoting the hell out of that. Why not?"

"I'm not good live."

"You'll be great. And it's not in-person live. It's online. You can do it in your pajamas."

"I'm not kidding."

"Okay. I hear you. But Bert really wants the Chat. The only thing he wants more is a podcast. Can you give him a podcast? He's got some big idea about a podcast with you and—"

"No. A podcast is worse. I can't. I'm sorry. It's just right now—"

"You don't have to explain. I get it. I've been there." He drummed his fingers on the table. "Okay. Here's what we'll do. You work remotely. We table the podcast. I'll come up with a workaround to make you more comfortable with the Chat. I feel for you, Lanie. It was rough, those first weeks after Hannah died. It stayed rough for a while."

"Thanks. I really appreciate your help. I'm going to be fine. I just need to keep my focus on Henry right now. Henry and the column." She saw Sam waiting. "And the Live-Chat."

Back at her desk Lane blew off the troubling thought that despite Sam's assurances, her job was on precarious footing. She had definitely made a tactical error when she stopped talking to her magazine contacts. There were half a dozen of them, editors she'd worked for over the years. Not friends—at least she didn't think of them as friends. Work people. After she started at the Guild, most of them had reached out for a drink or a meal but she put them off. She put them off as many times as it took for them to give up. That was a mistake. She seemed to go from mistake to mistake.

Losing her job was not an option. Her plate was full and her expenses were on the rise. Her rent had just gone up—the landlord had slipped a note under her door about the increase. She needed to find a therapist for Henry. She and Shelley had to figure something out for their parents. Something was not right with them. Either they needed to move closer or someone needed to check on them more often. Not her. It was Shelley's turn for that. Except Shelley would never agree because . . . She took a breath and stopped. She didn't have time to solve this problem now.

Laptop open. *Roxie* in-box open. Most recent letter open. A man was troubled by his difficult decision to turn down his ne'er-do-well brother's request for his kidney:

> I have a family of my own. Three beautiful boys. My wife's pregnant with our fourth. What if one day one of my kids gets sick or in an accident and—perish the thought—they need my kidney. Which I no longer have because I gave it to my brother who doesn't take care of himself. I swear I'm not sure he'll even be alive in five years. My mother says I'm a monster to think that. My mother says family sticks together no matter what. But I'm turning him down because of family. My family. My boys and the baby I don't know yet. My mother says I'm hard-hearted and selfish and cruel. I'm worried she's right. What do you think?
>
> Yours,
> Donor Do or Donor Don't

Finally—disappearing into someone else's life—Lane could breathe.

"Dear Donor," she wrote. "Not hard-hearted. Not selfish. Not cruel."

On her way out, Hugo gave her a smile so big it looked like it hurt. She flashed back to Jem telling her about the latest group on Eeze, "What Does Hugo Do All Day?" He had no idea he was the butt of so many jokes.

She stopped at his desk. "Have you ever thought about working somewhere else?"

"What did you hear?"

"Nothing." She hadn't thought this through. Telling Hugo he was the subject of an Eeze group would crush him. She wasn't herself. "I didn't hear anything."

"What *didn't* you hear?"

"Nothing. I was just thinking about how you're so friendly and full of energy and good at your job. Any place would be lucky to have you."

The elevator doors opened. She said, "G'night," and disappeared inside.

As soon as the doors closed, she escaped into her thoughts about the letter from the brother with the kidney. She liked what she wrote at the beginning of her answer, but she was worried about the ending, which wasn't at all snarky. She'd tried to be snarky, but it felt wrong. Maybe it was the letter. Some letters were just too heartbreaking to have fun with. Or maybe it was her. Maybe she was losing her snark.

The elevator landed. The doors opened. She walked out into the night and headed home. It took her three blocks before she realized she was heading in the wrong direction.

7

Lane had just figured out how to turn off the TV in the small waiting room when Henry ran in, followed by the therapist.

"Hey buddy. How'd it go?"

Henry gave her a big hug and said nothing.

Doctor Bruce stood behind him, face inscrutable, which worried her until a moment later when Henry gave her a spirited double thumbs-up. What a relief.

"Two thumbs up for me too," Doctor Bruce said. "Also two toes-up but you'll have to trust me on that. I never take off my shoes at work. Smelly feet," he confided to Henry.

Lane thought the therapist looked like he might actually have smelly feet. His rust-colored shoes were scuffed and had taken on the shape of his toes. His pants were creased across the thigh. His shirt was a shade of gray that looked like it may have started out white. None of that mattered to Henry, who was now smiling up at him.

"Mom and I are going to have a little talk," Doctor Bruce told him. "You can stay here and watch TV, or do a puzzle, or draw—"

"Henry loves to draw," Lane interrupted. "Sorry. You probably know that already."

"No. Thanks for sharing that. I offered Henry paper and he shook his head and I assumed drawing wasn't something he liked to do. Always a bad idea, to assume." He turned to Henry. "You probably weren't in the mood to draw." Henry nodded. "Are you in the mood now?" Henry nodded again. "Great. I'll show Henry where to find markers and paper," he told Lane. "I'll meet you over at my desk."

As Lane made her way around the perimeter of the playroom adjacent to Doctor Bruce's office she wondered if Henry had been playing. The cardboard containers of play food in the wooden kitchen cabinet were lined up on the shelves in tidy order. Open plastic tubs filled with blocks, LEGOs, stuffed animals and toy dinosaurs all looked undisturbed. She spotted the small puppet theater in a corner; a family of puppets of assorted ethnicities, ages and genders lay collapsed on the stage like victims in a murder scene. Was Henry responsible for that? Or had he been sitting in the reading nook?

There were two foam chairs there, close together, one red and one blue. Both had white piping around the edges. Cartoon chairs, she thought, which made her laugh. She felt a presence and turned around. Doctor Bruce had joined her.

"I'm laughing because of the chairs," she explained.

He nodded. "You should see how it looks when I sit there. The children seem to enjoy that, me sitting in a chair that's way too small."

Lane tipped her head and read the title of the book that lay on the seat of the blue chair. *Where Did My Dog Go?* Did Henry know she sent away a puppy? Did Doctor Bruce know? "We don't have a dog," she told him. "Should we have a dog?"

"If you want a dog." He shelved the book and gestured toward the small office. Lane took a seat in the visitor's chair and the therapist sat behind his desk. He swiveled for a moment as if centering himself. "How are you?"

"Fine, thank you."

"Henry is delightful."

"Thanks. Did he speak to you?"

"No. I didn't expect him to. We played. Best way to learn is from play."

"Did you learn anything helpful?"

"Everything's helpful." He smiled. He had a kind smile but its effects were undone by his beard.

How could he not know that his patchy beard was distracting. Not everyone looked good in that kind of beard. Now he was staring at her. Waiting for her. He'd said something she'd missed and he was waiting for her reply. "Pardon?"

"I was asking about siblings."

"One. A sister. She lives in London. We don't see her much. She doesn't like to fly."

He seemed confused and then smiled. "I meant does Henry have siblings?"

"No." She wondered if it would be helpful if he did. What could she do about that?

"You said no pets."

"Right. I don't have anything against pets. It's just, Henry's never asked for one and I work full-time and now, being a single mom, it doesn't seem to make sense."

He wrote something down. "Anyone else live with you?"

"No. Why? Did Henry say someone did?"

"Henry didn't say anything."

"Right."

He took more notes. "And his father?"

94

"Died." How could he forget that? "I told you. On the phone."

"Yes, but not the circumstances."

Lane filled him in on the basics: date, time, cause.

He was scribbling faster now. "How did Henry hear about it?"

Lane would have preferred never to think about that day again but she was here for Henry so she recounted the details: How Henry had been at Milo's. How in retrospect it was a blessing, what with all the phone calls and the trip to the hospital.

"And while you were at the hospital and making phone calls, what was Henry doing?"

"Having dinner? Watching TV?"

"Are you asking me?"

"Sorry. He went out to dinner and he watched TV. Milo has a big TV."

"So you told him in the morning when you picked him up."

"No. Not at Milo's. Because, Milo."

"So as soon as you left?"

"No. Because we got in a taxi so, the driver."

"Okay, so in the taxi did you chat or were you silent?"

"We chatted." Was that the right answer? Was there a right answer? It was clear she'd handled it wrong.

"Chatted about . . . ?"

"Taxi talk. What Henry ate for dinner. What I ate for dinner. I couldn't remember what I ate so Henry tried to guess. Was it Chinese food? Was it Indian? We do a lot of takeout. You think it's awful that I don't cook."

"Not at all. I'm just trying to get a full picture. We're on the same side."

She didn't want to be defensive. He was trying to help. "We went into our building and the doorman waved, but he didn't say anything. Usually when the doormen see Henry they say, 'Welcome back, Mayor.' They call him Mayor because he's so friendly. He used to be friendly. But that night the doorman didn't say anything so I just hurried Henry to the elevator. There was an old couple in the elevator. Very fond of Henry. Like everyone. I was worried they were going to offer us their condolences, but they didn't." She stopped. "This doesn't matter, does it?"

The therapist smiled. "I'm just listening."

She nodded. "And then we went inside the apartment and I closed the door and locked it and Henry took off his shoes and hung up his backpack on the hook on the wall and I told him we had to have a talk." Doctor Bruce probably wouldn't understand why she'd waited until Henry hung up his backpack before she told him. He probably lived in a huge apartment with a big hall closet where you could just toss in your shoes and backpack, willy-nilly. In their tiny apartment if everything didn't get put in its proper place— She stopped. Okay. She was avoiding the next part. She forced herself to go on. "I walked him to the living room and I told him I had some very bad news and that it was very sad and that it was okay if he cried. And we sat down on the couch and I told him. I said, 'Your father was in a car accident last night and he died.'"

The therapist handed her a tissue box. She accepted it and put it down on the desk.

He clicked his pen. "What did Henry say after you told him?"

"Nothing. He got very quiet and he went to his room."

"What did he do there?"

"Not sure. I figured he wanted to be alone. He came into the kitchen later while I was making dinner. I was peeling carrots. He was crying. We went to the couch and sat down and I held him and he stopped crying and told me he was tired and could we watch a movie and I said sure." She hoped Doctor Bruce wouldn't ask what movie it was because she couldn't remember. She also couldn't remember what they had for dinner besides carrots. Her memory of that day was like her memory of many days, like the electric eye at the Guild, sometimes lit up bright, sometimes off. Blinky. She glanced up and saw the doctor looking at her, expectantly. "Henry asked if I would sleep in his room with him and I said yes. Aaron and I used to sleep on the pullout."

The therapist had nothing to say about that.

"And in the morning—this is going to sound strange—he acted as if nothing happened. And that was that."

"Doesn't sound strange at all. Do you have anything you want to ask me?"

"Yes. Is it normal? For a child to stop speaking when they lose a parent?"

"Normal is not a helpful construct." He put down his pen. "There's things we know and things we don't know. What do we know? Your son is grieving. And he's anxious. Not surprising considering his father died unexpectedly."

"He said he's anxious?"

"He didn't say anything. But we know this, young children who experience the loss of a parent can be anxious for a time. They wonder— I'm speaking as Henry now—Why did my father die? Was it something I did? Is my mother going to die now? What can I do to prevent that? Of course we know he didn't cause it and we know he can't prevent it. But he doesn't know that. Not for sure. And then we have the other piece. How he found out."

"What's wrong with how he found out?" There it was again. Defensiveness.

"It's not a matter of right or wrong. But imagine it from his point of view. His mom was her regular self when she picked him up at his friend's house even though his father had just died. She was her regular self in the taxi, in the lobby of the building, in the elevator."

Did he think she should have told Henry in the elevator in front of the neighbors? In the taxi in front of the driver? In front of Milo? Was that horrid woman right? Had the wrong parent died? She slumped in her seat.

". . . how acting as if nothing was wrong," the therapist was saying, "could be confusing."

Wait. He had it wrong. "Henry was okay after Aaron died," Lane told him. "He cried—an appropriate amount. And then he went to school and he spoke to his teachers. We went together. I told them the news and they asked him how he was doing and he said he was doing okay. I hung around for a while to make sure he really *was* doing okay and he was. I saw him talk to his friends. And when we went to Florida he spoke on the plane. And when we visited my parents he spoke to them."

Why did she bring that up? The last thing she wanted to do was to tell the therapist what happened in Florida, that her father left out a box, and Henry climbed in it, and— Is that why Henry stopped speaking? Because he got tossed out in a box? She didn't want to bring up the box. If she told Doctor Bruce about the box, she'd have to tell him about her father and her mother and everything that went with it, and— No. She was not going to get into that now.

"Something else I should know?" he asked.

"No." She slumped again. She had to tell him. At least the part about the box. For Henry's sake. "Something happened in Florida. A crazy thing. Henry was playing in a big box and he fell asleep and the box got picked up by a recycling truck, which was terrifying, for him and for me. He's okay, obviously, but—could that be why he's not speaking? Because he got"—it was hard to say—"accidentally thrown away?"

Doctor Bruce smiled. He had a very gentle smile. "There's a saying we use in medicine: *When you hear the sound of hooves think horse not zebra.* The box is the zebra. Grief is the horse. Your son's had a terrible loss. Why is it that first he spoke and then he stopped?" He shrugged. "Why does any child stop speaking one second and start another? We don't always find out. But I've seen this before and I'm confident Henry will speak again. What you need to concern yourself with—what we both need to concern ourselves with—is what to do now. This time, now, the time between when he stopped and when he starts, it's important. Are you ready to make a plan to help him?"

Of course she was ready.

In their plan, Henry would see Doctor Bruce once a week after school. Lane was to avoid putting any pressure on him to speak. She would set up a meeting with his teacher and the school resource team to make sure no one at school put pressure on him either. The school resource team was to provide adaptations that would help Henry communicate without making him feel ostracized. And lesson learned: Lane would never keep anything important from Henry again.

She broke her promise the next day, but what choice did she have? There was nothing to be gained by telling Henry that a woman in the elevator had kicked her in the shin.

It happened when she got back from bringing him to school. She wasn't thrilled to see the lasagna lady standing in the elevator when she got in, but she met the woman's eyes and forced a smile on her face and asked her how she was doing. She even admitted she'd forgotten her name. It wasn't an easy thing to admit, that even though they'd seen each other regularly for years, she couldn't remember her name. When people admitted to Lane that they forgot *her* name, she thanked them. She saw the admission as a sign of courage. But the lasagna lady did not seem to share that view.

It happened fast. The lady, who never did offer her name, seemed to shake from the force of holding in her fury and then her leg jerked out—it seemed involuntary but it was clear she meant it—and she kicked Lane's shin with the pointy toe of her black kitten heels.

"It's nine o'clock in the morning," Lane told her, as if time had anything to do with it, as if it would have made more sense to be kicked in the evening. "What's wrong with you?"

"What's wrong with me? What's wrong with you?"

The door closed and the elevator gave its little jolt and began its slow rise. The two women stood facing the door, Lane stunned, her shin throbbing, the lasagna lady's eyes fixed on the small rectangle above the door where the floor numbers, made up of tiny dots, flashed on a screen. Second floor. Third floor. Fourth floor. Surely no elevator in the world had ever moved this slowly.

"Your husband needed you," the woman blurted out as they passed the fifth floor. "Aaron needed your help."

Disoriented by the woman's words, Lane found she had none of her own. "Help," she echoed.

"You need help? Give me a break. Because an old lady gave you a little kick? Don't pretend that's not how you see me. Old. Past my *use-by* date. Aaron was never like that. To him I was a person. I know how you see us, Little Miss Uppity. We all know."

Lane felt like she had cotton in her ears. "We? We know what?"

The elevator door opened on Lane's floor but she didn't get off because her feet suddenly felt like they were stuck in concrete. The door closed and the elevator resumed its climb. When the door opened again they were on the penthouse floor. The lasagna lady gave Lane a narrow stare and stepped out. The door closed.

Lane's shin burned. She lifted up the bottom of her pants and saw the red mark on her shin. She dropped her pants leg and stood motionless, like a fool, wondering why the elevator hadn't moved. It didn't occur to her the reason was that she'd forgotten to press the button.

She heard a sigh. The lasagna lady on the other side of the door was waiting for the elevator to go down too. Another moment passed. The bell dinged. The door opened. The lasagna lady reached inside and pressed the button for Lane's floor.

"I wish you would just go away," the lady hissed as the door slowly closed.

Henry was silent on the way home from school but as soon as he stepped inside, he asked if he could have hot chocolate. He sounded positively cheerful, now that he was home.

Lane warmed the milk in a saucepan on the stove. With Aaron gone, their small galley kitchen felt like it had doubled in size. The apartment was now plenty big enough. But they couldn't stay. And the rent increase wasn't the only reason. It was exhausting to be there. If Aaron hadn't been everyone's best friend it might have been different but he *was* everyone's best friend. People were still upset. Some, like the lady in the elevator, were upset with her, as if his death had been her fault. She had to face it. She was living in what would forever be Aaron's apartment in a building forever filled with Aaron's friends.

"Here you go, buddy." She put the mug of cocoa on the tiny kitchen table that faced a small dark courtyard with a view of the kitchens in the building across the way. In the spring, when the window was open, the sounds from those apartments were amplified so that they heard everything. A woman stirring coffee. A man clearing his throat.

"You ever think about what it would be like to live in a house?" she asked Henry.

"Isn't this a house?"

"This is an apartment house. I mean an actual house, with a backyard."

"Like Milo's?"

Milo lived on the ground floor of a brownstone that had a tiny brick patio in the back where his mother grew herbs in pots. "Not like that. A separate house. With bedrooms upstairs and a big backyard and a basement with toys and a garage where you could store your bike, which you could ride to school. When I was a kid, no matter where I lived, I always wanted to ride my bike to school." That was true. What she left out was the part about how she rarely did because of the rule: she could only ride to school if Shelley was riding with her. And Shelley rarely rode her bike because she always had a gang of friends who preferred to walk. "I bet you would like living in a house and biking to school. What do you think?"

Henry drained the last of his cocoa, showed off his chocolate milk moustache and said, "Good!"

And like that, it was decided.

8

Lane hesitated before she dropped one and then another letter into the newest folder on her desktop: BERT-BANNED. The first letter was from a mother struggling to get over a decades-old loss of a child. The second was from a distraught high school senior whose dad had gotten scary mad when he heard that his daughter went behind his back to ask her grandparents for help with college tuition. Both letters took her breath away. Both letters deserved to be answered. But not now. In his most recent email to her, Bert had been clear.

"To be clear," his email began, "the world is depressing enough without *Roxie* making it worse. The numbers don't lie. Earnest and sad are over. As is this conversation."

She dropped ten more letters, all too earnest and sad for Bert, into the BERT-BANNED folder. The next two went into the folder marked SOONER. These were letters she would answer after consulting with an expert. She had many experts on deck—psychiatrists, psychologists, social workers— but the ones she reached out to most often were lawyers. A woman specializing in housing disputes. A guy who handled workplace issues. An inheritance guru. An authority on sexual assault. A fraud hotshot.

On second thought, the letters she dropped into the SOONER folder were also too earnest and sad for Bert. She dragged them out and dumped them into BERT-BANNED. She was back to none. No letters. She needed a letter. It didn't have to be great. Okay was fine. Just not earnest and sad.

But for some reason every letter she read today was earnest and sad. Where were all the over-the-top nitpickers, the laughably annoying whiners? All she needed was one irritated know-it-all and she could get on with the important task of her day: finding a house.

Next letter: "Dear Roxie, My sister just got arrested for drugs. She's not a saint but—"

No. She dumped the letter into LATER. Today was not a good day for drugs. Today did not seem to be a good day for anything, including finding a house. Finding a house should have been easy for her. So why was it that after quickly settling on the town they were going to move to, she'd lost confidence about moving. Moving was the normal state of being for the Meckler family. Deciding to move, planning to move, being in the process of moving, having recently moved, was what the Mecklers did best.

Except Henry had never moved before. What if he turned out to be unhappy in their new place? She shook off the worry. Jem—who'd introduced her to the New Jersey town where Lane was now looking for a house—had given her the names of several people who'd grown up there. People who'd moved away to college and then moved back to start families of their own. Lane had dutifully reached out by email to each of them and they all emailed back, eager to share how much they loved where they lived. It was a great family town, they told her. An easy commute, midsize, with an art museum and dozens of restaurants. The schools, Lane was happy to hear, were well known for being diverse. There was no good reason for her hesitation.

She opened the next letter. It was her least favorite type of letter, a Referee Letter. The people who wrote Referee Letters didn't want advice. They wanted to be anointed the winner of an argument. She dropped the letter into the NEVER file. Okay. She'd use the next one. Whatever it said, she'd find a way to write an engaging answer. She opened the next letter and read it.

"Dear Roxie, My husband cheated on me—"

Come on! This wasn't fair, getting a cheater letter now, less than a month after Aaron and Brielle took their final ride to nowhere. She'd known all along that a *drinking partner* wasn't a thing but she'd never really allowed herself to think of what that meant—Brielle was Aaron's girlfriend—until the day she met the girlfriend's mother in the hospital. All things were clear that night.

If the universe were a kinder place, a person whose husband had recently died in his car with his girlfriend would not have to answer an advice letter about a cheater. In fact, in a kinder universe there would be a permanent cheater-letter hiatus. A moratorium on marital discord. If not forever, at least for a few months. And not just for her benefit. It was for everyone involved. For all the readers—the cheated upon and, yes, the cheaters too. Because truly, there was no way she could be helpful on this subject. It was too close to home, too soon, too personal, too humiliating. If she answered this letter now, she would probably say something completely inappropriate like, *You think you have it bad, buster? You want to know what happened to me?*

Bert would love a letter like that. Angry, snarky, full of rage. Maybe she ought to read the cheater letter all the way through before she trashed it. She squinted—her eyes seemed to be physically objecting—and read on.

"Dear Roxie, My husband cheated on me. It was a one-night stand a long time ago. He says he regretted it immediately, but he didn't tell me for years. His reason: he was terrified I would kick him out."

Okay. She could do it. She could answer this one. It didn't sound anything like what happened to her. It was straightforward. A no-brainer, really. Which was perfect considering it appeared very little of her brain was working at the moment.

"Mom?"

How long had Henry been standing there? "Hey buddy. You okay?"

"Yes. Can I ask you something?"

"Of course. You can ask me anything. Come on in."

Henry slowly tiptoed into the large closet that she'd turned into an office. He looked like a cartoon cat burglar, hands like paws, paused midair.

Lane laughed. "You don't have to tiptoe. I'm not working now. What's going on?"

"Are we moving soon?" His hands curled into fists and dropped to his sides. He looked worried.

Lane felt her stomach dip. Okay. The good news here was that he felt safe enough to ask. She'd never felt like she could ever ask her mother about their moves. Instead she'd waited for clues. Boxes that would suddenly appear in the front hall. Her mother at the kitchen table, Yellow Pages open, narrating her search as she circled synagogues, churches, homeless shelters—any organization that advertised, "We Pick Up Junk for Free."

She remembered what that felt like so she'd been careful to keep Henry apprised of every step. As soon as she found the town, she told him about it. After she made an appointment with the real estate agent, she told him that too.

"We can wait, if you feel like you don't want to move yet," she told him now. "We don't have to move right away."

"*Can* we move right away?" He hid his thumbs in his fists. "Can we move tomorrow?"

"Aw buddy. It takes more time than that to move, even for me. We have to find a house first. And we have to get rid of all the stuff we don't want to take."

"The day after tomorrow?"

"Did something happen?"

Henry shook his head, hard, and in case that wasn't clear he added, "No."

"But you want to move soon, like the day after tomorrow?"

"Yes," Henry said. "Can it be bedtime now please?" He pulled his lips in.

Her chest felt tight with worry, but his pulled-in lips made her next step clear. "Of course," she told her little button-lipped soldier-son. "Let's go."

For Tell Me That Story Lane offered three choices, all of them random moments from her day. She really wasn't any good at Tell Me That Story. That had been Aaron's specialty. It really wasn't fair that he invented a routine that only he could do and then— Okay. None of it was fair.

Henry shook his head at each of her suggestions and she didn't blame him. They weren't very good. "How about if tonight we read a book instead?"

"Maybe you could tell me the story of how you and Dad really wanted a baby and you had to wait and wait and wait and then you gave up and then I came?"

Lane did not know that Aaron had told Henry that story.

"Or the story about how you and Dad lived in an apartment on Number Eleven Street which only had one room that was so small you could put one hand on the bathroom sink and the other hand on the kitchen sink but you didn't care because you said one room is enough, who needs a closet? But Dad wanted more than one room so people could come over for dinner so you moved to the apartment where we live now. And then I came and you and Dad had to sleep on the pullout couch but you didn't care because you're a good sport."

"Sounds like Dad told you all the stories. You know them better than I do."

"Not all of them," Henry said. "What about a story from when you and Aunt Shelley were little? I don't know any of those stories. Maybe one about when you went camping. Like when we went camping and there were loons on the lake and Dad and I slept outside so we could see shooting stars but you stayed in the tent."

"I don't have any stories like that from when I grew up. We didn't go on vacation when I was little."

"What did you do? Did you draw? Did you play games?"

Games. Games was safe. "There was one game Aunt Shelley and I played. With Grandma. But I was terrible at it."

"Tell me that story. About the game you were terrible at."

"Okay. The game is called mahjong. It's like a card game that you play with tiles, like domino tiles. And Grandma Sylvie loved it. Only she didn't have anyone to play with because you need four people."

"Why?"

"That's the rule. Four people."

"I mean why didn't Grandma have anyone to play with?"

"Because we moved so much." Lane saw the flaw in her explanation immediately. Her sister moved the same amount and she always had friends. Luckily Henry didn't challenge her. "Then one day Grandma got the idea that she could play mahjong if she taught me and Aunt Shelley how to play." Henry started counting on his fingers. "You're right. That's only three people and the rules say four. But Grandma Sylvie came up with an idea for a new rule, which was that the fourth player would be make-believe." Henry looked puzzled. "The first time we played she told me to get my favorite doll and put her in the empty chair."

"Was your doll always the pretend fourth player?"

"No." Lane closed her eyes and saw it happen, first Sylvie coming up with the idea that Lane's Cabbage Patch doll Delilah would sit in as their imaginary fourth, then Shelley spitting out the news.

"Delilah isn't here. Lane left her behind. Because you said she had to. Since she hardly played with her anymore. I guess Delilah is living in a garbage dump in San—"

Sylvie cut her off. "We'll try something else. Pick a name, Shelley. Any name."

And so it was that on some days they played mahjong with an imaginary guest player named Tina Turner and on some days with Prince and on some days with E.T.

Lane shared none of this with Henry.

"Why were you terrible at the game?" he asked.

"I didn't understand the rules." That was only partly true. The other part was that she realized from the start that as long as she went through the motions, as long as she paused long enough to look as if she were carefully choosing her hand, or considered her tiles before discarding, no one could tell if she was paying attention or not. For her those games were a chance to daydream. Playing mahjong turned out to be another iteration of being alone.

"I can play with you if you want," Henry told her. "I don't care if I lose. I'm good at losing. I'm a loser."

"Why would you say that?"

Henry closed his eyes and pulled the blanket up over his face.

"Henry?" The blanket shifted. "Did something happen at school today?"

Blanket down. "Nope." Blanket up.

"Are you sure? You seem . . ." She stroked the blanket where his hair would be. "Out of sorts."

Blanket down. Eyes open. "I have lots of sorts." Blanket up. Muffled voice. "You can go."

From her perch in the corner of the couch, Lane scrolled through her email to see if anyone from Henry's school—his teacher, Miss Mary, the nurse—had reached out through the parent portal, but no one had. She debated calling Doctor Bruce for guidance on what to do if Henry was upset and wouldn't say why, but Doctor Bruce had been very specific when they worked out their plan. If there was an emergency, she was to call him without hesitation. If it wasn't an emergency, she was to write down any questions she had in the log she was dutifully keeping to track Henry's progress and they would discuss it at their next appointment. Her gut was clear—something was bothering Henry. But she knew a lot about emergencies and this wasn't one.

Now that she thought about it, she didn't have to talk to Doctor Bruce to know what he would say. He gave her the same advice every session. It was the same advice Miss Mary gave. Lane's job was not to try and read Henry's mind when he was silent. Her job was to pay close attention to what he said and follow his lead.

What Henry said was clear. He wanted to move. The sooner the better.

Tomorrow she'd escalate the search for a new place.

Now on to the cheating wife.

March 15, 2017

Ask Roxie!

Dear Roxie,

My husband cheated on me. It was a one-night stand a long time ago. He says he regretted it immediately, but he didn't tell me for years. His reason: he was terrified I would kick him out.

Which I did. I kicked him out. I felt I had no choice. I was crushed by what he did. I felt I could never trust him again. I couldn't trust anyone again. And I couldn't forgive him. So I got a divorce.

In the ten years that have passed since our divorce not a day has gone by when I haven't felt regret. I still love my husband and I believe he is a good man. I believe that what he told me then is true: he had one affair, one time, never again. And I forgive him.

The problem is the trust part. I want to trust him but I'm struggling. I'm not sure how one goes about recovering from the loss of trust. My friends have given me lots of advice. Take one day a time. Be patient. All things come to those who wait. But I'm beginning to suspect it's possible that with a betrayal like mine, trust is a pipe dream, out of my reach forever.

My question for you: Do you think there can be a second chance for a marriage that's gone bad?

Yours,
Torn

Dear Torn,

If you're a regular reader of this column, you know I am no fan of cheaters. But based on your description of your husband's behavior, it doesn't sound like that's his thing. A single one-night stand gives him at least a shot at being included in the crowded category of humans who've made one terrible mistake.

But boy did he compound that mistake by not telling you for years!

It's not easy to keep a secret. It takes a lot of energy to keep things hidden. A secret can act like a tornado, scooping everything within its vicinity into its vortex, and then spitting it out like so much trash. Some people become consumed by their secrets. Others shove them down so deep, it's as if they've turned off a piece of their brain. For those people, it might truly feel as if the thing they want to forget never happened. They would swear to it. They're that sure. My guess is that's what happened with your husband.

Don't get me wrong. As a survival strategy, it works. But it comes at a cost. The cost in your marriage? After that one-night stand, it's possible your husband was never fully present in your marriage again. It's possible some part of him was always otherwise occupied, busy policing his secret to make sure it stayed tucked away.

But we need to shift the conversation. Move the spotlight off your cheating ex—you refer to him as your husband but let's be clear: he's your ex—and on to you. Why the delayed regret? Why take ten years to write to me?

It's time to take a long hard look at yourself and at what's happening in your life right now. What is happening? Do you have a job? Do you do any meaningful work? Do you have children? Friends? A hobby? Since all you've mentioned is your ex-husband, I'm concerned that he's taking up too much space in your thoughts.

To your question, do I think there can be a second chance for your marriage, my answer is no. You don't have a marriage. Your marriage ended a decade ago.

But don't despair. I have good news! Just because your marriage is over doesn't mean your life is over! Your life is just waiting for you to be in it. I don't know anything about you other than the one thing you've shared, regret, so if these suggestions are off base, my apologies. I hope you can accept them in the spirit in which they are offered. Pick one, pick many, pick all:

Apply for a job, if you don't have one. If you do, offer yourself up for a challenging new project. Look in on an elderly neighbor. Get involved in politics. Volunteer at a school, or an animal shelter, or a place of worship. Take up a sport. Take a class. Teach a class. Paint. Plant. Read. You need to put meaning back in your life. The key is in your hands.

But you have to be in it to live it.

Ready or not, off you go!

Yours forever, or at least for now,
Roxie

9

Marshall closed the door and stood still, listening to the noisy engine of the old ambulance as it rumbled up their block.

"No siren," Sylvie observed.

Marshall nodded. "No need to rush when your passenger is a corpse."

Sylvie made a noise of disgust and Marshall moved away from her, taking long strides to the reading chair, where he collapsed, bumping his head on the lamp as he sat.

"You all right?" Sylvie asked. "You need ice?"

"No and no." He rubbed his head for a moment and then let his hand drop to his lap. "I suppose that's it."

"I suppose it is." Sylvie looked around. Everything looked the same even though nothing was. "I suppose you should call Beadie. I think she'd want to know he's gone, don't you?"

"Pass," Marshall said.

"You can't pass. I can't call her. She hates me. I have no idea why."

Marshall gave her a look.

"It's not that. She hated me from day one. I used to keep track of all the times I'd call to make plans and she'd say they were busy. Took some time but I got the drift. They were always busy. There were always other plans. Because any plan was better than seeing me. Did you know he had to sneak out of his house the day he came here? Sneak out the back door of his own house to visit his sister. All to keep a promise we made when we were children. He was so proud of himself that he remembered. I could see it, soon as I opened the door. His cheeks were pink and his eyes were bright and he flashed that big smile that showed off the little gap between his front teeth. And he yelled out, 'Surprise! Here I am. Come to watch the eclipse with my favorite sister. Like I said I would. Like we always will. No matter what.' No matter what," she repeated. She noticed her husband's expression. "I've told you this already."

"Dozens or possibly hundreds of times."

"Beadie could not bear to share him. Not with me."

"I'd say you made up for it in the end, Sylvie, wouldn't you?"

"I wouldn't say that at all. I'm talking about Albie before. You didn't really know my brother before. He was so sweet. So funny. Always upbeat."

"Hah! Good one."

"He was. He was funny, upbeat, kind. Always, always kind. Even after Beadie threw him out like he was a piece of rotten garbage, he never said one word against her." She shook her head. "I can't call her."

"She doesn't need a call. She doesn't care. She's probably been wishing him dead for years." He drummed his fingers on the arms of the chair. "She wouldn't be the only one."

"Marshall." She crossed her arms and sat up straighter.

"It took its toll, Sylvie, having him here. You can pretend it didn't, but it did. People aren't meant to live in a state of emergency for half their lives."

"More than half," she admitted. "Honestly, to think that after all the times he tried . . ." She shook her head thinking about what she wouldn't say. "For him to go this way. Peaceful. In his sleep. Who would have thought? Makes you wonder, doesn't it?"

"No."

"Makes *me* wonder." She looked over at her husband. He closed his eyes. He wasn't interested in what she wondered but she wondered it anyway. "What do you think our lives would have been like if . . . ?" She didn't complete the thought. "Do you think we would have stayed in that house?"

"Not playing this game. What happened, happened. We dealt with it. The end."

"I think we would have stayed. It was such a lovely house. Of course you would have gotten job offers but you wouldn't have had to take them."

"I never had to take them."

She studied her husband. Nothing to do. No one to hate. "It's just us now, Marshall. You don't have to go blustering about the house trying to distract everyone. Albie's gone. The girls are gone. Oh no." Her shoulders sank. "The girls. Who's going to tell them?"

"Pass."

"I'm not sure Turtle can handle it. Another death. And Albie of all people."

"Don't tell her." Marshall heaved himself out of his chair and walked to the window. "At least the neighbors won't be knocking on our door to complain now."

"No one's going to be knocking on our door at all." Sylvie glanced at her watch. It was later than she thought. Time to make Albie his tray. Then she remembered, Albie wasn't going to need a tray. Not today. Not any day. A few minutes passed. She checked her watch again. The medical transport should be bringing him back soon. Then she remembered,

Albie wasn't coming back. Not today. Not any day. She blotted her eyes with her sleeve. "May his memory be a blessing."

"What did you say?"

"Nothing." Was this how it was going to be from now on? Forgetting and remembering and forgetting again? She took a deep breath. "Oh well. I'll call Shelley. I'll ask her to tell Turtle."

"That's your worst idea yet. The last thing we need is to have those two going on a trip down memory lane."

"They need to know their uncle passed away."

"You're not making any sense. You're the one who's always telling me Turtle isn't like the rest of us. She doesn't want to know. She wants to *not* know. Now all of a sudden you think it's a good idea for Shelley to fill her in?"

Sylvie stood up and started out of the room.

"I'm talking to you."

"I'm going to make us tea." She disappeared into the kitchen. After the kettle whistled, she came back and handed Marshall his mug. "Careful. It's hot."

He took a sip and burned his tongue. "Too hot." He handed it back.

She took it and put it down and glanced over at the stairs that led to the room where her brother no longer slept. She shook her head. "This is not how I imagined our lives."

"We did the best we could."

She didn't agree. But when Marshall wasn't in the mood to listen, he didn't. So she said, "Oh well," and left it at that, for now.

10

Gathering cartons to move. Sylvie's habits came to Lane like muscle memory, carrying with them the echo of her words. Grocery stores were where her mother got her boxes. *We're doing them a favor, taking away their garbage for no charge.* As her mother saw it, there was no other acceptable choice. Mecklers didn't buy boxes. *Only a fool would pay for an empty box.* Liquor store cartons were out of the question. *The neighbors have quite enough to gossip about as it is.*

As was often the case with her mother, the more that was said, the less Lane understood. Until the comment about the neighbors, Lane had no idea their neighbors were gossiping, and no idea what they were gossiping about.

Now, so many years later, here she was, taking a one-block detour on her way home from dropping off Henry at school, to stop at the grocer's for boxes. Like her mother, Lane bypassed the liquor store—which was closer—but not for fear of gossip. Rather it was with the knowledge that if she went inside, the shopkeeper would ask after Aaron and Lane would end up having to comfort him after presenting the shocking news that his favorite customer was dead.

Another of Sylvie's packing quirks: start slowly, with just a couple of boxes, and begin as soon as you know you're going to move; no need to wait until a new place is found. "Makes it easier to leave is why," Sylvie explained even though Lane never asked.

By the time Henry got home from school, an empty Bounty carton was waiting for him at the foot of his bed. The Dole carton that Lane picked up, which still held a trace scent of pineapple, was parked in front of the pullout. The pullout, which hadn't been opened in six weeks, was on the long list of items Lane was going to donate. A pullout might be handy to have in a house with multiple bedrooms, but she was not going to take this one, the pullout on which her marriage had died.

"First Rule of Moving," Lane reminded Henry after a snack of graham crackers and milk. "Take Only What You Love. Let's start with your books. Pick out the ones you love. We'll donate the rest."

For her mother's seventieth birthday, Lane had considered buying her a copy of Marie Kondo's tidying book. Sylvie Meckler had been ahead of her time, a professional tidier before that was a thing. In the end she didn't buy the book because she knew her mother would have donated it without cracking the spine. If Lane ever turned into a person who made a list of rules to live by, one of her rules would be Don't Bother Buying Sylvie Meckler Gifts.

"What if it's a book I like," Henry said, "but I don't love?"

This was as close to happy as Lane got, seeing Henry unafraid to ask her anything. He made it look so natural. It was natural, she realized. Just not for her. She turned away from her thoughts and smiled. "That's not a problem at all. Like is plenty good enough."

Her cell phone rang. Shelley. Lane felt a wave of relief. Ever since she'd complained to her sister about calling too early and disturbing Henry's sleep, Shelley had stopped calling. That wasn't the result Lane wanted. What she wanted—which she'd told Shelley the last time they spoke—was for her sister to call every day, but at a reasonable hour.

It was a waste of words, telling Shelley what she wanted. Her sister called on her own schedule; like the moon, it went in phases. She'd called weekly, or every other Tuesday, or on the first of the month. At least she called, was how Lane thought about it.

As for Lane calling Shelley, she didn't bother. Her sister never answered her phone. It was basically the equivalent of a jail phone, outgoing only. That had been okay—Lane could get used to anything—until the night Aaron died and Lane had to call continuously for over an hour before her sister picked up. To avoid a repeat of that, Shelley proposed a special signal. Next time Lane called three times in a row, her sister would know that someone had died.

"How are you?" Shelley asked her now.

"Good." Lane covered the phone and asked Henry if he would mind looking through his books while she talked to her sister. She moved to the small kitchen. "How are you?"

"Good." Shelley ran through the usual rotation of topics. The dismal English weather. Quinn's upcoming business trip. Melinda's latest accomplishments in orchestra, maths and sport.

Even when Lane was only half listening, she found the sound of her sister's voice calming. Maybe that was why, at Shelley's first pause, her defenses slipped and she shared what she hadn't even realized was on her mind. "I think it was my fault."

"It was not your fault. You have to let it go. It's way past time."

"Way past what time?" Lane asked. "What do you think I'm talking about?"

"That's what I wanted to ask you," Shelley countered.

Her sister could be so confounding. But Lane didn't want to risk an argument. "What I'm talking about is, maybe it was my fault Aaron drank. Maybe I drove him to drink."

"Stop it. He was an adult. He made his own choices. He made his own mistakes. You have to stop blaming yourself for everything that goes wrong in the world."

Lane didn't respond but she took note that her sister hadn't asked the obvious question: What did Lane think she'd done to drive Aaron to drink? She and Shelley really were a perfect team. Tethered by the phone, they stayed silent on two continents until Lane, ever a good Meckler, changed the subject. "We're moving to New Jersey."

"What? That's a terrible idea. Nothing good happened when we lived there. Either time."

Her sister was half right. The first time they lived in New Jersey, when Lane was Henry's age, things did not go well. But the second time was fine. It was true that the reason they'd moved back was her father's career had hit bottom. And when Shelley first left for college, Lane was lonely. But the high school wasn't too bad. It was big, for one thing, so the fact that no one paid attention to her was barely noticeable.

In fact New Jersey ended up being her answer when, in college, people asked her where she was from. At least that's what she said once she figured out that *Where are you from?* was a census question and not an invitation for a disquisition on the meaning of home, which is what happened the first time she'd answered with the truth: *I'm not really from anywhere.*

"We can't stay here," she told Shelley now. "I can't afford the city. And you wouldn't believe the pitying looks I get from people in the building." She didn't share that the lasagna lady kicked her or that Henry had stopped speaking in school. Like their parents, Shelley was quick to assume Lane's life was on the brink of disaster and Lane didn't want to give her any evidence that this assumption was true. "I found a great little town. Henry and I went there for lunch yesterday. He liked it a lot, so that clinched it. Team Henry is on the move."

"Do they have Widow and Widowers in the States? The dating app?"

"I'm not interested in dating. I'm fine with Team Henry being a two-person team."

"Do you really think it's wise to make a big decision in the midst of a traumatic event?"

"I'm not in the *midst* of a traumatic event. And since when is moving a big decision?"

Shelley cleared her throat, a nervous tic she'd had for as long as Lane could remember. "Take a leave of absence. Come here. Move here. Quinn has a friend who's perfect for you. He's called Patrick. If I weren't married, I'd marry Patrick."

It was nothing new, Shelley trying to convince Lane to move to England. In Lane's opinion it was because her sister had never stopped feeling guilty about leaving her behind.

"No thank you," Lane said. "Not taking a leave. Not moving to England. Not marrying Patrick." She waited. "Shelley?"

"I'm here." Shelley cleared her throat again. "Turtle?"

"I'm here."

Neither of them had anything more to say. Neither of them wanted to be the one to end the call. But Henry was waiting. "I have to go," Lane said.

"Okay. On the count of one—" Her sister hung up. Shelley always hated to say goodbye.

The day they tackled the kitchen, Henry stood on a stool, reached up high and carefully took down two tumblers. "One for you. One for me."

"I don't know, buddy. Maybe it would be a good idea to take a few more. For when you have friends over. You know you're going to make a lot of new friends, right?"

"Are you going to make a lot of new friends?" Henry waited. She nodded. He reached for two more. "Okay, four. One friend for you. One friend for me. One friend is all we need."

Had she told him that her mother always said that, one friend is all you need? It was dizzying hearing her mother's words come out of Henry's mouth. "I think you're going to make way more than one new friend. What about if we take six glasses?"

"Six glasses we love?"

Another wave of dizziness. She knew he wasn't intentionally challenging her mother's rules. It was more like he was holding up a mirror that made her see the rules made no sense.

No. This was not a good time to think about that. She needed to stay focused on Henry. The school counselor and the therapist agreed. Her only mission was to listen and respond to whatever he said.

"We don't have to love our glasses," she told him. "Liking them is good enough. And you know what? Let's take eight. I think you're going to end up with a lot of friends."

After Henry fell asleep, Lane went back to culling the kitchen cabinets, sorting as she went. Donate donate keep. Donate donate throw. As her hands worked, her mind flicked through a slideshow of moving days past.

The day they moved out of New Jersey—the first time they lived there—Shelley overheard an argument between their parents. "It think it's about whether or not Uncle Albie is moving with us," she reported to Lane. "I say he's not. What do you say?" Lane said nothing. She had no idea.

Later that day when it was time to go, after their parents got into the front of the car and Lane and Shelley got in the back, Shelley leaned over and whispered to Lane, "See? He's not coming. I'm right. I win."

But her victory ended a moment later when their mother turned around and said, "Scoot over. Don't make your uncle sit in the middle. It's a long drive."

There was a kerfuffle when they moved into the house in Rochester, their father calling them into the living room that first night to chastise them for leaving the front door open.

"Your uncle got out again," he said. "Is it that hard to close a door?"

As usual, it was left to Shelley to explain the details to Lane once their father left the room. Shortly after their arrival in Rochester, Uncle Albie had left the house without telling anyone where he was going. Lane knew this had happened once before, in New Jersey. That time Uncle Albie went out in the morning and didn't come back till night.

"Remember how worried Mom was last time he did that?" Shelley asked and Lane nodded. "Remember how when he finally showed up his face was red as an apple and he was all out of breath?"

Lane nodded and then repeated what Shelley had told her that time. "Because he got chased by a dog. A dog with a foaming mouth. Probably rabies."

"Correct," Shelley said even though she had deduced this on her own with no parental corroboration.

In Rochester, Sylvie solved the problem of Uncle Albie disappearing without telling her by hiring a locksmith to come and put in a double-keyed lock for the front door, in addition to the window guards she had him install in the upstairs bedrooms.

The locksmith had grumbled about the double-keyed lock. "I'm doing it but it's a bad idea. You need to be able to get out fast in an emergency. You don't want to be running around looking for a key."

"This is to prevent an emergency," Sylvie told him curtly. "And the key will be right there." She pointed to the narrow drawer of the small half-moon table that sat against the wall, one of the few pieces of furniture that came with them no matter where they moved.

It was on arrival day in the St. Louis house that Shelley got the idea to spy. Her inspiration came in the shape of a large hickory tree that stood in the side yard, adjacent to the bedroom assigned to their uncle.

"All we have to do is climb up to the first elbow," Shelley explained when they finished unpacking the boxes in their bedroom. "And we can look right in."

It didn't sound like a good idea to Lane. "I don't know."

"Aren't you interested in what Uncle Albie does in his room all day?" Shelley asked.

Lane admitted she was and several days later they executed the plan. Lane got lookout duty while Shelley climbed. As soon as she got into position, she shared what she saw.

"He's sitting in the La-Z-Boy," she called down. "His feet are up. He's wearing slippers. He's watching TV. Wait. No. He's sleeping. Wait. No. He's getting up. He's going to bed. He's in his bed. He's watching TV. Wait. No. He fell asleep. This is—" She stopped and the rest came out in a rush. "Mom just walked in, with a tray. She's watching him sleep. She's putting his tray down. There's a glass, and a bottle of Coke, and some crackers and—" She stopped again.

"What is it?" Lane called. "What's happening?"

Shelley scurried down to a low branch and dropped to the ground. "She saw me. I thought you were on lookout." Lane started to defend herself but Shelley said, "Forget it," and marched into the house to take her punishment, whatever it was.

There was no punishment for her or for Lane. But the next morning a truck arrived with MANNY'S TREE SERVICE written in big green letters on the side, and three men wearing helmets and gloves hopped out. With goggles on, they affixed ropes and cables and set up a bucket lift and the side yard screamed with the sound of chain saws until, several hours later, the giant hickory was a stump and their careers as spies were over.

It was in the fourth grade, while doing a math project, that Lane learned most families didn't move as frequently as hers. The math project was meant to teach the difference between mean, median and mode. The students were to interview their parents—Shelley helped with that part—about how many houses they'd lived in since they were married and for how long. After that, they were to make a graph. Lane did the graph herself.

The next day, the teacher pooled everyone's statistics and guided them to figure out the mean. As it turned out, the three-year average for the Meckler family threw off the average for the class.

When the teacher saw this, she clapped her hands. "Fantastic! This is a perfect example of why the median and mode are much more helpful than the mean."

The difference between mean, median and mode didn't stick, but Lane did learn a lesson that she later shared with Shelley. "In order for Mrs. Goldschlager to figure out what's normal, the data from our family has to be dropped."

Shelley's conclusion: "I guess we're even weirder than we thought."

They were packing up the closet in Henry's room—the one that used to be Lane and Aaron's—when Lane found a large wooden box tucked at the back of the top shelf. It was the kind of box Aaron used to send gifts to clients. Sometimes a bottle of spirits and a set of whiskey glasses. Sometimes a bottle of spirits and cigars. She sniffed. It wasn't cigars. She sat down on Henry's bed. "I guess Dad was going to send this to someone."

"We can leave it behind," Henry said.

"We could. Or we could send it to the person he meant it for. If there's a card inside." She slid back the cover. "There is." She took out an envelope. "It's addressed to you."

"That's the letter about the baseball Dad gave me," Henry said. "You were there when he read it to me. It's about how the baseball for real used to belong to Hank Aaron. Remember? You said, *Don't believe everything you read.* The baseball's in there too."

Lane looked inside the box. There was the baseball. Underneath it were three small flashlights. "Where did those come from?"

"Dad gave them to me. One of them came by mail in a box addressed to Mayor Henry Dash. It was in care of the doorman, from city hall. It wasn't really from city hall. It was from Dad. He was pretending. He was with me when it came. The doorman popped out of his standing place to give it to me. He said it was important." Henry leaned in to confess the next. "The doorman thought it was for real from city hall. Is it bad we never told him that it wasn't?"

"No." Lane stroked Henry's hair. "Not at all bad. A hundred percent not bad." She looked in the box. "Why did Dad give you flashlights?"

"I like to use them under my blanket. I collect them. I mean I used to collect them."

Lane blinked hard at the realization that Henry already had a *used to*.

"But I don't love them," Henry added. "I don't love Hank Aaron's baseball either."

Lane put the envelope back in the box and handed the box to Henry. "You might love them someday. Take it just in case."

It didn't take long for Lane to see she had not inherited Sylvie's single-mindedness when it came to packing. Her mother used to say that given her druthers she would have left everything behind. As a child Lane wondered if that meant one day her mother might leave her since she seemed as unattached to people as she was to things.

It was in college that Lane really learned what a ruthless curator her mother had been. The things the other students brought with them: frayed childhood blankets, ratty stuffed animals. She'd arrived with a single small suitcase and even that wasn't full. When her roommate asked where the rest of her things were, she noted the tone and went with, "It's coming." She always was a quick study. Saying, *It's coming,* was safer than saying the truth: *This is it. This will always be it.*

Aaron had asked the same question the first night he came into her room but there was something different when he asked. He was curious without judgment. This had surprised her. Then again, everything that happened with Aaron in those days was a surprise. That he was interested in her, for starters, the girl who always stayed in her room.

Of course she knew who he was. Everyone knew Aaron. He was the tall, lanky sandy-haired boy from the other side of the floor who was often in the common area making people laugh. There was always a crowd around Aaron in those days, always a girl at his side. A succession of girls. Party girls.

It was Aaron's roommate who pointed Lane out to him. The roommate was Lane's study partner in a class where having a partner wasn't optional. The roommate told Aaron that the girl down the hall, who never came out of her room because she was shy, was a good listener and super smart. Aaron was intrigued.

Later he admitted his own surprise that what started as a challenge—could he get the girl who was always alone in her room to laugh?—quickly became something else. He'd never been with someone like her before, someone quiet. "Every girl I ever dated was a yakker," he told her. "I never got a word in edgewise. Minute I started telling a story, they would tell one louder. But with you," he confessed to her, "I feel like there's more air in the air. I can hear myself think for once. I can talk without shouting."

As for Lane, she'd never been pursued before, much less by someone like Aaron. It took her a while to believe that the charismatic boy on her floor who everyone wanted as a friend had chosen her. He was her first and only boyfriend and, as it turned out, he had no problem making her laugh, back then.

It was the first night in her room when he'd asked her, "Where's the rest of your stuff?"

She surprised herself by telling the truth. "This is it. I don't need much. We moved a lot when I was growing up."

"Military?"

"Pharmaceutical." She then performed her single party trick, reciting the names of the drugs her father had been in charge of marketing when she and Shelley were teenagers. They'd decided to memorize them one day when their father accused them of not being serious about anything. They ended up turning them into a song, which they then sang to their father until he yelled at them to stop. Instead of stopping, they took to singing it quietly to each other in their room, whenever their father annoyed them. Lane still caught herself now and then, humming the tune they'd made up to go with the words. The words themselves were always right there, in the front of her brain: *Amoxapine and Trimipramine, you take them every day. Fluoxetine and Sertraline will send you on your way.*

The landlord, who was supposed to meet her at his house, got waylaid. A neighbor—Dana from down the block—who happened to be a real estate agent, greeted her instead.

"This is my very favorite house," Dana told her as they walked through the living room for the second time. "Some houses are so dark, I pray for a sunny day. But here . . ." She pointed to the windows. "The sun isn't out and look how bright? I mean, how can that even be?"

It was true. The house was full of light.

"My house used to have the same layout," Dana continued. "But I bumped out the kitchen. I don't even know why I bothered. This is perfect. Great for entertaining. Cozy for staying in. And the cherry on top? Best block. I'm over the moon that you found us."

"So am I," Lane said because she wanted the words to be true.

"I'm not supposed to have favorites," Dana confided. "You won't tell anyone will you?"

"No."

"I knew I could trust you. I have a good eye for good people. You'll fit right in on this block. You have a kid, right? I'm pretty sure Nathan told me you have a kid."

She nodded. "A six-year-old son."

"Perfect. There's dozens of kids on this block. Always playing outside, having good old-fashioned fun." She stopped herself. "But it's not an old-fashioned suburb. Honestly, it gets more like Brooklyn every day. Brooklyn with space." She seemed unsure again. "But not obnoxious Brooklyn. The perfect amount of Brooklyn." She smiled and walked to the window that looked out onto the street. "I love everyone on this block. There's not a single person I don't love. Sounds crazy but it's true. Everyone is great. Except for me. I talk too much. Which—professionally speaking?—not a good idea. Except in this situation, what's bad to say? I love the block. I love the house. I can totally see you living here. Come and see the playroom downstairs. There's so much space there you could invite the entire school to your son's birthday. By the way, the schools here are the best. The kids turn out so interesting."

The playroom convinced her. It wasn't set up as a playroom yet, but with some paint and a colorful rug, Lane could imagine it: a birthday party for Henry's whole class. Henry talking to everyone. "It's perfect," she said.

The neighbor smiled and then got serious. "One possible hiccup. Not a lot of rentals like this come on the market. You're going to have to move fast. I heard there are three families interested. If you're motivated, if you really want this house, which I hope you do, you need to tell Nathan immediately. Can your husband come by tonight to look?"

"My husband's dead." Lane saw the shock on the neighbor's face. "I am so sorry. I should not have said that. It's nothing to joke about. I mean it's true, but I shouldn't have said it like that. I haven't been myself."

"Of course you haven't." Dana put her hands to her heart. "I'm the one who's sorry." She patted Lane's arm. "Don't you worry. I'm going to call Nathan as soon as I get home and tell him he has to rent this house to you. And he will. Nathan is a total mensch."

Her sister listened quietly while Lane told her about the house she'd rented. When Lane was done describing it, Shelley said, "I'm happy for you. Really. I am." She was silent for a moment and then her voice got serious. "Listen, Lane, I talked it over with Quinn and Melinda and they agree. You don't have to worry anymore. About . . . if."

"If what?"

"You know." Shelley waited for Lane to understand. "You're kidding. You're going to make me say it?"

"I guess so."

"If something happens to you. I'm not saying it will. A person can only have so much bad luck. I know right now you're a happy little Team of Two. But a Team of Two needs a plan B for if it ends up a Team of One. So now there's a plan. Henry will come here. Melinda is totally on board. The fact that she even heard what I suggested is a shocker. You don't have a teenager so you have no idea."

Lane didn't know what to say to that, so she said nothing.

"Come on, Turtle. Don't get that way. I'm trying to help. I know you don't like to talk about bad things and I know you worry. So now, you don't have to. God forbid something happens, we'll take care of Henry here."

Lane had not yet let herself think about that particular bad thing. But okay. Now she didn't have to. Her sister had it covered. "Thank you. I appreciate it. I have to go pack."

"Remember: Take Only What You Love. Moving Forward Means Never Looking Back. If You Hold the Door Open for Dragonflies, Dragons Will Come In Too. Tread Lightly So You—"

"I know the rules."

"Okay. We'll hang up on three. One, two—" And Shelley was gone.

That night Lane lay awake for several sleepless hours, going through the list of catastrophes as they presented themselves. Some, but not all, were theoretical. In the end the thought that cycled through her mind in a loop was that her sister might be right. A Team of Two was probably not enough.

On their last night in the apartment, Henry asked Lane if she thought he'd like their new house.

"Definitely. But if you don't, there's always Grandma Sylvie's Fourth Rule for Moving. Tread Lightly So You Don't Leave Tracks. That means if you don't like where we move, we can always move again. Deal?"

"Deal."

In the morning when the movers came, they said what movers always said when they came to move the Mecklers. "This all you have?"

Lane heard her mother's voice as she replied, "This is all we have. This is all we need."

PART TWO
ESSEX COUNTY, NEW JERSEY
SPRING 2017

April 15, 2017

Ask Roxie!

Roxie Reader Alert! Do you love reading Roxie's columns?

Are you eager for her Live-Chat Wednesdays to begin?

Would you jump at the chance to listen to a Roxie podcast?

We want to know! Click here to tell us what kind of Roxie you want

and get a chance to win a one-year subscription to Guild-Plus for free!

Dear Roxie,

My eight-year-old daughter has a new friend who is very quiet and polite, which is great because my daughter is a loudmouth except for when this friend comes over and then I don't hear a peep. They like to go down to the basement and make projects. Collages, decoupages, puppets, clay thingies. They're very creative and not only that, they clean up. It used to be when my daughter's friends came over something always got broken. A lamp. A tooth. A toe. There were always tears and whatever they did they made a mess. With this girl, it's peaceful and clean and I love it.

My only complaint is about the girl's father. I have a very bad feeling about him. Don't get me wrong. He hasn't done anything bad. But every time he picks her up, she looks scared. Also, he's very big. An intimidating kind of big. And he's unfriendly. He never comes inside. He just stands on the front steps and waits. He looks angry waiting even though he never has to wait for long. His daughter always comes right away, which I don't think is normal. When I used to pick up my daughter from her friends' houses, I would wait twenty minutes, minimum, for her to stroll to the door. I say "used to" because with this new friend they only play here, at our house.

I have no proof the dad has done anything wrong. It's just my gut talking. Which I would ignore except this morning the girl's mother, who I've never set eyes on, called to invite my daughter for a sleepover. Mind you, my daughter has never stepped foot in this girl's house.

Maybe it's not reasonable, but I don't want my daughter to go on the sleepover. Except how am I supposed to explain that? Can I say she can't go when I don't have a good reason? On the one hand I think I should make up an excuse. Maybe we'll go to her grandparents that day. They're always happy to see her. On the other hand I think I should ignore my gut. Because probably he's fine. I should say yes and hope for the best. Probably nothing will happen.

No choice seems good. What do you think I should do?

Yours,
Queasy

Dear Queasy,

It's official! You've got a dilemma on your hands.

Let's talk for a minute about your gut. If you're a regular reader of my column you already know I'm a big fan of guts. Guts are smart. The biggest problem with them is that sometimes they're so quiet we don't hear them. But not yours. Your gut is screaming. Why ignore that? Why do any of us ignore our screaming guts?

Mostly it's because we worry, what if our gut isn't right? What if we accuse someone of something and we're wrong? Mistakes happen. Misunderstandings abound.

Take this dad. You think he's unfriendly. Maybe he is. Or maybe he's painfully shy and self-conscious about his size. Could the reason he stays outside on your doorstep be that he knows his size makes him look threatening?

Take the girl. You think she looks scared. Maybe she is. Or maybe before she came over to your house and was all quiet and helpful, she was rude to her mother and neglected her chores. Could she look scared because she knows when her dad comes to pick her up, she's in for a talking-to?

You admit you don't have proof of bad behavior. You can't be sure your suspicions are warranted. Maybe the fair thing to do is to give the dad the benefit of the doubt. Here's the rub: when it comes to our kids, doubt is not okay. When it comes to our kids, we can't afford to take chances.

Ask yourself this: Which would you regret more: that you offended an innocent stranger or that you put a child at risk so you could appear nice?

What should you do? Here are a few suggestions.

Make a rule: No sleepovers if you don't know the family. Then get to know the family! Invite them to dinner. You might learn something you didn't expect. Maybe you'll learn that once he's comfortable, the father is hilarious. Or maybe you'll learn the family is new to town and you are the only person who's reached out to them. Maybe this dinner will change their lives.

What do you do if they decline your invitation? Wait a week and try again. If after three times, they still say no, that's it. Tell your daughter you tried. The ball's in their court. The rule holds.

What do you do if they accept your invitation and over dinner your gut is even more insistent that something is amiss? Wait till they leave and tell your daughter you're very sorry but she can't sleep there. Tell her the truth: that you can't put your finger on it but your gut is telling you something isn't right. Use this as an opportunity to teach your daughter the importance of listening to your gut.

But wait, there's more! The next time this girl comes over, let her know that if she ever needs an adult to talk to, she can talk to you. Be prepared though; if she shares something that makes you think she's in danger, you're going to have to do something about it. I'm sure you don't want this to be how it plays out, but to protect a child, you have to be ready. Get the number for Child Services now.

One last thing: I would be remiss if I didn't caution you about throwing around words like *odd* or *weird*. People come in many flavors. What's weird to you might be wonderful to me. It takes a village.

Yours forever, or at least for now,
Roxie

11

Lane caught the scent of it in the kitchen: rising damp. If that was the worst of it, a hint of mildew, it would be fine. It was a fact of life she learned when she was young: most houses held smells. Some were easier to live with than others. The tang of ammonia from the old plaster walls in St. Louis was better than the trace of rot in the bedroom of the woman who died in her house in San Diego, a week before they moved in.

"Why do you have to let everything bother you?" Marshall grumbled when she gagged at the smell in the San Diego house. "Don't breathe so hard. You'll be fine."

Compared to that smell, which still made her gag to remember, mildew was nothing. Bleach and vinegar would handle that. She added those items to the shopping list on her phone and turned around to look for Henry. He had been right there, behind her. Circling back, she found him in the foyer, waiting.

"Am I supposed to take my shoes off here?"

Of course he'd ask that. In their apartment they always took off their shoes in the front hall so as not to track in city grime; now Henry wanted to know if city grime was a problem here as well. Another reminder of how different life was in the Meckler household, where the rules, once made, were never rescinded. A No Shoes rule that was made in the house with the cream-colored carpet remained in effect in the next house, which was carpet-free. And when Lane and Shelley took to skating in their socks across the shiny wood floors in the carpet-free house, Sylvie made a new rule: No Shoes *and now* No Socks. From that house they moved to the one where the wood floors sat on a concrete slab. With nothing below to warm the floors above, the floors were always cold. But freezing feet did nothing to change the No Shoes, No Socks rule.

"Don't come near me with those ice-cube toes," was Marshall's theme song in the frigid-floor house, the same way, "Don't breathe so hard," was his theme song in San Diego.

Whether or not a house would have a theme song was not something Lane knew right away. Things like that took time to know.

"Shoes can be on or off," she told Henry now. "Whichever way you want."

After an hour of waiting for the movers, Henry started to worry that they weren't coming.

"Why wouldn't they come?" Lane asked.

"Because maybe they stole our things. Like in the letter you got from *Ripped Off*."

"You remember that?" While it was true that on occasion Lane read a *Roxie* letter aloud to Aaron, she didn't do it when Henry was listening. Except maybe Henry was always listening.

"I remember *Ripped Off* wrote that when she moved to her new house the movers never came because they stole all her things. And you said, 'Probably you had too many things anyway.' And everyone got mad at you."

That was pretty close. As Lane remembered it, the specific advice Roxie gave was, "Look on the bright side. Now you can start fresh!" Either way, the end was the same. Readers grumbled. One accused her of being both clueless and cruel. She objected to cruel—she was never cruel—but being clueless about how most people felt toward their possessions? Guilty.

The problem with that letter was she never should have picked it in the first place. It hit too close to home. "Off to a fresh start," was what her mother said every time they moved and while the rest of her family seemed to believe this was good news, for Lane all a fresh start meant was a new place in which she would not feel at home.

"You should try acting like you belong," her sister would counsel when it was time to start a new school. "Try and look worth knowing."

Shelley was full of advice like that, the kind that sounded good until Lane thought about it. How exactly would a person go about looking worth knowing?

"You're too quick to settle," her sister complained one day after seeing Lane eating lunch with an awkward companion. "Don't glom on to the first person who shows an interest. Wait a week to pick who your friends are."

In Lane's experience, picking friends was not an option open to her. But she just smiled gamely and thought about anything else. That seemed the best route to surviving in a family where advice was freely given and always conflicting. The same day her sister counseled her to be pickier about her friends, her mother countered with, "Having friends is overrated," and "It's not your fault. They're not our kind."

Lane spent hours parsing what that meant, *not our kind*. What was their kind? People who moved a lot? People who were Jewish? People who had an uncle living with them who sometimes got lost just walking around the block? She didn't ask. Her mother made it clear with sighs and *oh wells* and talk about the weather; questions like that were not welcome.

Invisibility was the ticket. Bland clothes, unremarkable shoes, plain-Jane haircut. So long as Lane could manage those things she could pass for normal. Normal enough.

Shelley's advice took a hiatus when she left for college and while Lane didn't miss the advice, she did miss the adviser. To her disappointment, it was the day after Shelley graduated from college that she broke the news that she was moving away. She said this in the small bathroom of their second New Jersey house where she dragged Lane and then, like a character in a spy movie afraid of wiretaps, turned on the faucets before quietly sharing. She was going to England to live with Quinn, the young Brit she'd met on her semester abroad. She made Lane swear not to tell their parents her plan: "I'm going to marry Quinn. I'm never coming back."

It was a surprise to everyone that Shelley, the Meckler who most thrived on change, was voluntarily joining a family where change was not a thing. On the street where Shelley now lived, in a tony London suburb, the neighbors who'd moved in two generations ago were considered newcomers. There really was no predicting how a life would go.

"If the movers are robbers," Henry said now, "at least I still have my sketch pad." He drew it closer to his chest. "And you have your phone."

"I'm sure they're not robbers," Lane reassured him. "They probably got held up in traffic." She shouldn't have read that letter to Aaron while Henry was in the next room. "I guarantee they'll be here soon." She shouldn't make guarantees to someone who'd learned the hard way, nothing was guaranteed. "Let's go upstairs. You can pick out your room."

Lane had decided to let Henry choose his own room so that he'd have the feeling of agency. But now she regretted it. The room she wanted him to pick wasn't the room he chose.

"Don't you think this one would be better?" she asked, pointing to the room facing the backyard. "The bathroom is so close. Right across the hall."

He walked into the room and pointed to the panels on the wall. "What are those things?"

"That's for sound absorption. Doesn't it feel extra quiet in here?" She waited for Henry to notice. He shrugged. "The owner of the house is a voice actor. For video games. He used this room as a studio, so he could record at home. How cool is that?" She was repeating what the real estate agent had told her, mirroring the agent's enthusiasm, but Henry remained unimpressed. Soundproofing was not a perk to a six-year-old. Nor was proximity to a toilet.

"I choose the other room."

Lane followed him into the room facing the street. The one she didn't want him to choose. She had to get over it. It wasn't reasonable for her to feel uncomfortable in this room. "Okay. This is your room."

The afternoon light streamed in, turning Henry's small frame into a string bean of a shadow on the floor. The shadow followed him as he walked to the window to examine the bars. He'd noticed the bars as soon as they pulled up in front of the house, and asked why it was that all the front windows on the second floor of their house had them.

"They're window guards," Lane explained when they got out of the car. "We had them in our apartment in the city. In the city, it's the law."

"Is it the law here?" Henry scanned the houses across the street, none of which had window guards. "Why are we the only ones who have them?"

It would have been nice to have a lie at hand. But Lane had promised herself and Doctor Bruce that she would be diligent about sticking to the truth. Truth, he said, was what would make Henry feel secure. "I'm not sure if it's the law. I had them installed."

"Why?"

"So there wouldn't be an accident." Wrong word. Accident was what happened to his father. "Want to go downstairs and wait for the movers?"

It was too late. He'd seen something flicker across her face. "What kind of accident?"

Speak truth. Speak plainly. Follow Henry's lead. Doctor Bruce hadn't criticized her for her delay in telling Henry his father died. He understood there were no good choices that day. He acknowledged that telling Henry the next day was only one of a host of things that could have triggered her son's acute anxiety. But it was the one thing in her control to change. Speaking truth would help make Henry feel safe.

"The good news is," Doctor Bruce had explained, "the brain is wonderfully plastic. The pathways to trust can be rebuilt. You will get other chances. When Henry's ready, he'll test you. To see whether he can trust you and the world."

"How will I know when he's ready?" she'd asked.

"Imagine there's a door of trust between you. It used to be wide open. Now it's lightly shut. When he's ready, he's going to knock on the door. The trick is, you have to be listening. The knock could be quiet. Quiet enough to miss. So listen hard for a knock."

"Did you have an accident with a window?" Henry asked her now.

Was this it? Henry knocking?

"No." She took in a quick breath and let it out. "But my cousin, Ivy, did. Uncle Albie was her father."

"Why isn't he her father now? What happened?"

"Ivy went out the window and fell." She stopped. She'd spoken the truth, plainly.

"Tell me that story."

"Aw buddy, I don't think it's a good idea. It's a very sad story."

"How old are you in this story?"

"Six. Like you. Ivy was seven."

"Did Cousin Ivy live with you?"

"No. Uncle Albie didn't live with us then. I only met her twice and the first time I was too little to remember. The second time was when it happened."

"Is the What Happened to Ivy the same as the What Happened to Dad?"

"The ending is the same." She glanced out the window. The sky was sheet-metal gray.

"How did Ivy fall out?"

"She didn't fall out. She went out." Henry looked confused. "Our house had a porch in the front. And the roof to the porch was outside my window. Aunt Shelley used to call my window a magic door because"—Was she really going to say this?—"she liked to climb out the window and sit on the roof. The roof was almost flat." She raised her forearm to show the most gentle of inclines. "But still dangerous. Not allowed. She shouldn't have done it."

"Did Aunt Shelley fall off the roof?"

"No." Lane shook her head. "Just Ivy."

"Because, no window guards?"

Lane nodded and closed her eyes. And just like that there she was, in her bedroom with Ivy and Shelley, the three of them standing in size order, Shelley telling them they could see the eclipse from the roof. The shag carpet was the color of dead leaves, the same color as Ivy's hair. Ivy was a head taller than Lane and she wore her hair in braids that had little bits sticking out, dark-red and brown bits that looked as if they'd escaped. Braids that were pulled too tight on either side of Ivy's moon-shaped face.

Was Lane supposed to tell Henry that part, about the moon?

"Mom? Are you sad?"

Be honest. "Yes. It still makes me sad to think about it." This conversation was a mistake. She shouldn't have said anything about Ivy or the roof. She shouldn't have given Henry a choice about the rooms. She hadn't expected to feel this way in his room.

Henry walked over and stroked her arm. "It's good we have window guards. And we don't have a front porch. So, double safe. And I will never go on a roof. I promise. And promises are meant to be kept or else so double safe times two times two." He tiptoed to the window, his little hunchbacked cat-burglar tiptoe, and peered out. Was he afraid of windows now? "If I ever go to a house where there's a front porch and someone asks me to go out the window and sit on the roof I will say, *Double no. No Way.*"

"I don't think anyone will ask you to do that, but that sounds smart."

"And if they go on the roof and say it's a secret and I mustn't tell, I will still tell. Because some things you should never tell but some things you should tell no matter what, right?"

He worried about everything. "Right." Lane gave him a hug. "So where am I sleeping tonight?"

"Is it the New Norman in this house?"

"If you want it to be. It's your choice. I can sleep in your bed, or you can sleep alone."

"I choose you sleep with me."

The doorbell rang. The movers had arrived. The flurry of activity didn't last long. Hauling in boxes and setting up furniture was a quick job when a Meckler was moving. As soon as the movers were gone, Lane ordered a pizza. By the time the pizza was delivered, she and Henry had found and cleaned their dishes, cups and cutlery.

When it was time to wash up for bed, Henry asked Lane if she could stand outside the bathroom. "Just while I brush my teeth. So no monsters come in."

As far as Lane knew, Henry had never been afraid of monsters before. "Attention all monsters," Lane yelled from her spot in front of the door. "This is a no-monsters house. I repeat. No monsters are permitted here. Any monsters present must leave immediately." She poked her head in. "They're gone. Good?"

Henry smiled. "Good."

❦

The plan was that Lane would drive Henry on his first day in his new school. On the second day, he would take the bus. As requested, they met the resource room teacher in her office. Her name was Mrs. Lindsey. A tiny Tinker Bell of a woman with a kind face and fluttery hands, she explained to Henry that he would spend one period each day in her room and the rest of the day he'd be in his regular first-grade class with Miss Fiske.

"But you can come see me anytime you want," Mrs. Lindsey explained. "Even if it's just to drop by for five minutes. All you need is this." She handed Henry a rectangle of oaktag. "This is a pass to see me. It's like a magic carpet. Just show this to Miss Fiske and she'll let you come. Okay?" Henry nodded. "Okay. Now let's go on a tour so you can learn where everything is. Wait till you see the gym."

The tour ended at Miss Fiske's first-grade classroom.

"He'll be fine," Miss Fiske said to Lane at the doorway even though she couldn't possibly have any idea. Henry gamely waved goodbye and Lane watched as Miss Fiske gently shut the door.

For a moment Lane debated whether she ought to open the door a crack. Henry might feel more comfortable with the door open. She looked down the hall. All the doors of the classrooms were closed. She looked into his room through the small window. He was standing behind a chair at a desk and smiling as children, one by one, lined up to shake his hand. The teacher was smiling too until she glanced over and saw her face in the window. Lane waved and quickly left.

The Welcome Brigade lady was standing on the sidewalk when Lane pulled into the driveway. She'd heard about these women a few months ago when a flurry of letters complaining about them arrived in her *Roxie* mailbox. Sometimes it happened like that, questions multiplying like bad cells, everyone suddenly irritated about the same problem at the same time. What she learned for the column she wrote on the subject was that they worked for a company that targeted new homeowners. The women, masquerading as neighbors, were dispatched with fake smiles, baskets of swag, and the goal of getting inside the house to preach with zeal about the local businesses who were the company's clients. The worst *Ask Roxie* complaint Lane got was about a bad actor who used the job to worm her way into a house, where she then pocketed a wallet and a phone. But even lawful Brigadiers elicited complaints, presenting themselves as neighbors when they weren't, pushing their way in with the single-minded goal of a kitchen table sales pitch.

Lane had never seen a Welcome Brigade lady in real life before today. And she didn't want to see one now. This was a terrible time for a sales pitch. She was still unnerved from leaving Henry with Miss Fiske, who seemed to her to be completely unsympathetic. Except now that she thought about it, Henry hadn't seemed bothered by Miss Fiske at all. Doctor Bruce had been clear: Lane was supposed to follow Henry's lead. Doctor Bruce was always clear and his advice always sounded smart when she was with him. But sometimes after she left, it lost its stick.

"Hey neighbor," the Welcome Brigade lady called out.

Lane ignored her. The woman pressed on behind her up the fieldstone path. This was exactly what people complained about. An aggressive salesperson who wouldn't take the hint. Now the saleswoman was a hot breath away.

Lane fixed her attention on trying to get her key into the lock. It really wasn't helping to have someone breathing down her neck.

"The doorknob is the problem," the woman told her. "You have to jiggle it a little and then the key will go in."

Lane turned around. "I'm not interested. I don't use coupons or bumper stickers. I don't need any baskets." There were flowers on top of the basket, a clever bouquet that gave the illusion of having been freshly picked from a backyard garden.

The woman looked confused. "Oh. Okay. I just thought you should know, you have to jiggle the knob. That lock always gave Nathan a hard time. I'm surprised he didn't fix it. Here." She handed Lane the basket and moved over to jiggle the knob herself. The door groaned open. She took the basket back. "Do you at least want the flowers?" She lifted them out. Purple petals wept off the stem.

Now that Lane looked at it, there were no bumper stickers or coupons in the basket. There was just a green gingham tea towel folded lightly atop two loaves of what looked like homemade quick bread and next to them a small mason jar filled with jam. The basket was weighing heavily on the woman's arm. She looked tired. She looked like someone who'd been baking. "You're not a Welcome Brigade lady are you."

"I don't know what that is. I live next door."

"You're the dentist?"

"Rory's the dentist. She's on the other side. I'm Karin. The baker."

It took a cup of tea and a slice of what turned out to be very tasty zucchini bread before Karin accepted her apology.

"It was crazy how many complaints I got about the Welcome Brigade," Lane told her. "Sometimes it happens like that. Everyone's upset about the same thing. I got dozens of letters."

Karin nodded. She might have stayed annoyed at Lane if she hadn't been so delighted to discover the woman renting the house next door was Roxie. "I can't believe that *Roxie* lives next door to me. I can't wait to tell everyone."

"Do you have to? I'm really no good at giving advice in person. People always wind up disappointed when they find out I'm the one who writes the letters."

"I'm sure that's not true. You want me to lie?"

"No. Unless—is not telling the same as a lie?" Lane read Karin's face. Her neighbor was not buying the technicality. "You're right. Tell whoever you want. If anyone asks for advice, I'll just tell them I'm a disaster at giving advice in real life." She glanced at her watch.

Karin noticed. "Oh. You have to work. Sorry. Don't want to keep you from your fans."

"Thanks for stopping by." Lane wanted to mean it. "Your bread is amazing." She tried to sound like she meant it.

"Want the recipe? Practically everyone on the block has it."

"I don't bake," Lane admitted. "Probably for the best." She tapped her stomach. "Less bake, less belly."

"Oh. Do you not want the bread? If you don't want to eat it I can take the rest home."

"No. Of course I want it. Henry will love it."

Lane waved goodbye and closed the door and leaned against it. Why did she say things like that? Why tell someone who'd just baked her a bread that she was concerned about her weight? She shook off the question, letting it join all the other unanswered questions she enjoyed not thinking about and went upstairs to set up the soundproof back bedroom as her home office.

Over the next few weeks a parade of visitors rang her bell. Neighbors welcomed her with cookies and cupcakes. Teenagers stopped by to sell magazine subscriptions to support the field hockey team and oranges to support the band. Children rang the bell asking if Henry could come out to play. She always passed their invitations on to him but he never accepted. He preferred to stay in and draw. And how could she blame him? She hadn't accepted any of her invitations either. Not to the new-member coffees at the Jewish center and the Unitarian church or to the book group on her block or to the movies-in-the-morning club. The only invitation she didn't turn down was the one from her neighbor Dana, the real estate agent, who came over daily now in her capacity as property manager for the landlord.

In addition to the repairs Dana oversaw before Lane moved in—the installation of the second-floor window guards, even though no one else in the neighborhood had them, and the removal of the creeping vine from the tiny cracks in the grout of the Manhattan Schist—she was now handling a myriad of repairs. The boiler went on the fritz first and after that, the hot water heater failed to send hot water to the fixtures on the second floor. When the radiator in Lane's office had what the plumber called a valvular breakdown that resulted in a minor geyser that just missed destroying her laptop, Dana offered to host a dinner party in her honor to make up for her trouble.

"It's the least I could do," she said after Lane resisted. "It could be anything you want. A cocktail party for the whole block. Or a small dinner for . . ." She counted on her fingers. "I think there are eight kids Henry's age. How about I invite those kids and their moms to dinner? That way Henry can get to meet everyone at once. Sound fun?"

Lane pretended it did because what it sounded like was a good idea for Henry. Having a group of friends right here on the block could be just what he needed. Maybe, finally, after all the years of moves, she'd finally made a move that would work.

12

Henry didn't like it when people talked about slippery things. Slippery things were things that might be right to do, or might be wrong to do. It was hard to know.

One slippery thing was *Telling*. Sometimes it was wrong (tattle-telling). Sometimes it was right (safety first). Another slippery thing was *Lying*. It was Always Wrong to Lie except for when it was Allowed. The reason a lie was allowed was usually, *Because*. *Because* meant a thing you would understand when you got older.

Secrets were the most slippery things. Secrets could be good or bad, depending. When Henry asked his mom how he could tell the good ones from the bad ones her first answer was, *That's a question that could wake up a nest of hornets*. Her second answer was, *You can tell if a secret is bad if it makes your tummy hurt. You can tell if a secret is good if it makes your smile come out*. For an example of a good secret she told Henry to think about the time his class gave him surprise balloons on his last day at his old school. She did not tell him an example of a bad secret.

When Henry thought about slippery things for too long his head got confused. The best idea for not getting a confused head was don't. Don't Lie. Don't Tell. Don't Think About It.

What happened on the Blue Rabbit was a Don't Think About It. His bus was called the Blue Rabbit. All the buses at his school had names that were animals and colors. His friend Francesca's bus was the Red Rooster. Ezra and Beatrice, who went to Speech with him, were on the Green Squirrel. Henry didn't know why the buses had animal names but there were a lot of things he didn't know like why did they call it Speech when all he did was draw.

The way Henry knew he was on the right bus was if it had a blue sign with a rabbit picture pasted to the window. The blue sign on his bus was curled in at the corners. That was as much as he wanted to think about the Blue Rabbit.

Sometimes when his mom lay next to him in bed she could see through his eyelids into his feelings. So the night after What Happened on the Blue Rabbit, he decided to end the New Norman part where his mom slept in his bed.

He made it a good surprise. He made it about, he was growing up. He said, "I think tonight you should sleep in your room because I'm growing up." He closed his eyes extra tight. Sometimes if he closed his eyes extra tight she couldn't see in.

She said, "Okay." And then she got quiet. And then she said, "Are you sure?"

With his eyes closed he couldn't see her face but he could hear from her voice she was Worried. He nodded to make her unworried and she said, "Can you please use words?" Now her voice was Disappointed.

He made his voice very strict. "Yes. I'm sure."

She said, "Okay," again, and then she said, "Shove over. We're still going to have Tell Me That Story, aren't we?"

He shoved over and asked if she could tell a short one tonight and then he gave her an idea. "Maybe a story where someone wrote to you with a problem and you wrote back an answer that made them happy and then you got happy?"

"That's a good suggestion. Let me think of one." She thought for a long time.

His eyes got sleepy waiting, so he closed them. He heard her say, "Are you still awake?" but he was too tired to talk so he nodded and then crossed his fingers under the blanket that she wouldn't get mad that he didn't use words.

She didn't. "Okay buddy. Sleep tight." She kissed him good night and left the room.

As soon as she left he opened his eyes. Even though he was in bed and his eyes were facing the wall, he felt like he was still on the bus, inside the Blue Rabbit. He could see the blob of pink gum that was on the back of the red seat in front of him and he could see the mud stuck in the ridges on the floor mat and he could see the driver with sticky-out ears and no hair and the bus aide who had big ankles but her socks fell down anyway.

The boy on the Blue Rabbit who yanked Henry's hair was in fifth grade or fourth, regular size with fat hands and long sneaky arms that could reach over the top of the seat and grab hair without making any sound. His name was Sighless.

The first time Sighless yanked his hair, Henry thought he got an all-of-a-sudden headache. For a headache he was supposed to go to Miss Fiske and show her the note that said, NURSE. But Miss Fiske wasn't on the bus and the bus aide wasn't for helping with headaches.

The second time Sighless yanked his hair, Henry felt a pull and a sting. He was staring at the pink gum on the back of the seat in front of him when it happened, which made him think maybe there was gum on his seat too and that's what pulled his hair.

He turned around to look. No gum. Maybe the pull and the sting was his imagination. Mrs. Wexler, his teacher in his old school, said he had a very good imagination which was a blessing and a curse.

After he saw there was no gum, he saw Sighless sitting in the seat behind him not doing anything except looking out the window and smiling.

The third yank was the hardest. At the third yank, Henry's hand went, all by itself, to the back of his head to try and make whatever was yanking stop. He felt something pull away and he turned around fast as the wind but nothing was there. Just Sighless sitting behind him looking out the window. His smile was even bigger now.

The bus aide saw him turned around and yelled out, "Face front. Right now. Or I'll . . ." She didn't say anything else. She just closed her mouth and gave him a glarey look.

Henry wanted to tell her that he was turned around because his hair got yanked three times but his mouth wouldn't let him.

Doctor Bruce told him that most people didn't know it, but *Not Talking* was a Super Power. He said it was the same Super Power as *Invisible*. A person who didn't talk could be like a Fly on the Wall. Flies on the Wall could listen to what people were saying without the people knowing they were there. Doctor Bruce told him the tricky part about being *Invisible* was that it could be a lot of fun or it could be a lot of boring. The good part about being *Invisible* was if it got boring, all he had to do was go back to talking and poof! No more *Invisible*. So far his Super Power wasn't fun or boring.

He faced front for a minute with his hand guarding the back of his head in case another yank came. Then, very slowly, he got onto his knees and, very slowly, he turned his body around to check on whether someone was hiding behind him. Maybe a monster who slipped onto the bus when no one was looking. He knew his Super Power was work-ing because the bus aide didn't see him turn around.

No one was there. Just Sighless. He faced front.

The bus aide was looking at her phone, which had pictures of sneakers on it, when Sighless laughed. When Henry turned to see why his laugh was so loud he saw that Sighless was leaning forward in his seat so close to Henry's head that Henry could hear what he said next even though Sighless whispered it.

What he said was, "You're a weird dope."

Henry faced front and waited for another yank but nothing hap-pened. The game was over.

Except it wasn't over because now Henry felt something hot on his ear which turned out to be Sighless's mouth on purpose touching his ear while Sighless whispered, "All you have to do is say stop and I will."

Henry wanted to say *Stop*, but his mouth wouldn't listen. After a while Sighless got tired of waiting and he yanked Henry's hair again, three more times, yank, yank, yank. The last time he yanked so hard a noise came out of Henry's mouth and the bus aide looked up and Sighless said, "See? He can talk when he wants to."

It wasn't words that came out of his mouth, though. It was just a sound that meant, *He's hurting me.* But the bus aide didn't understand sounds so she shook her head because, *Boys, stop bothering me.* Then she went back to looking at sneakers on her phone.

Henry waited for something else to happen but nothing else did. When the bus turned onto the street where the school was, he snuck a peek at Sighless who was staring out the window with his hands folded on his lap like they were supposed to do during morning announce-ments. Sticking out of his hands was hair.

Henry didn't know for a hundred percent sure if the hair was his but it did have the same brown color and the same *curly-Q* and his head hurt worse than before so probably it was.

When Sighless saw Henry looking at the hair he said in a quiet voice that Henry wished he didn't hear, "If you tell anyone I pulled out your hair, I'll come to your house tonight while you're sleeping and I'll pull out the rest."

Henry wanted to say that he was very good at not telling but his mouth still wouldn't work.

Sometimes when he didn't talk people said, *Just try.* They didn't know trying didn't always show on the outside.

On the way home from school, Sighless didn't sit behind him. He sat in the back of the bus with the noisy boys. That night Henry didn't tell what happened. He wasn't sure how Sighless would know he didn't tell but he hoped he knew so he wouldn't come over to pull out the rest.

It was still dark out when the phone woke him up. Probably Aunt Shelley. Aunt Shelley was the only one who called before the sun came in the window. He didn't hear her words but he heard his mom's voice. Mad.

After her voice stopped and it got quiet, he heard feet walking down the hall and someone breathing in his room. He wanted to look sleeping but what if it was Sighless? He opened his eyes.

He didn't mean for his mom to see that his eyes were Sad but all the Sad from the day popped in at once. He could tell she saw because her eyes got Worried and she asked if everything was okay. He nodded but she still looked Worried so he told her he was okay, just a little lonely from sleeping by himself. The last part was true.

His mom said, "Scoot over," so he did and she climbed in next to him and touched his hair and by accident pulled on the spot where his hair had been yanked out but her eyes were closed so she didn't see him make an Ow face.

They both fell asleep after that. The alarm woke him up. The sun was in the window. His mom's eyes were open. He could tell by her eyebrows she was Sad. To make her happier he said, "I think today it would be better if I stayed home with you."

She laughed and said, "I wish."

After she got out of bed he crossed his arms over his chest and tried to get all the air out of his body so he would be completely flat because if he was completely flat, how could he sit on a bus?

His mom laughed and said, *Up and atom*, in a voice that meant she didn't have time for games today.

After she went downstairs to make breakfast he got dressed very, very, extra very slowly. When he put on his socks, he wiggled his toes in slowly, until he could see them poking at the very tippy end. When he pulled up his socks he stretched them slowly, as high as he could get them, until they almost touched his knees. He walked down the stairs slowly. He ate his cereal one Puffin at a time. He chewed the Puffins into a thin paste while he watched the hands on the clock. These hands didn't jerk ahead, one minute at a time, like the ones at school, but he could still see time move so he knew that he needed to be a little more slow. Just a little more slow so he could miss the bus and his mom would have to drive him to school and then he would never have to tell her anything that happened on the Blue Rabbit.

13

Lane glanced over at Henry. His spoon was in his mouth, the handle sticking out, but he wasn't chewing. He wasn't moving. He looked as if he'd fallen asleep sitting up. "Hey buddy," she said. "Better get going with that cereal or we'll miss the bus."

He took the spoon out of his mouth and started chewing. Slowly. He looked exhausted. It wasn't a mystery why. Her sister's call had woken him up and it had taken him forever to fall back asleep.

Lane briskly unloaded the few things left in the dishwasher, wiping the bottoms of the cups that weren't completely dry before putting them away, and thought about the call. She didn't usually let herself get mad at Shelley and when she did, she rarely let her sister know. But this time she had. Maybe it was because she wasn't fully awake. Or maybe it was because her once reliably steely self-control, which started to slip when Aaron died, was still not back in working order.

"What's wrong with you?" was what she said to Shelley. "I was sleeping. Next time you call me, look at the world clock on your phone first. If it says it's before six a.m. here, wait."

Shelley didn't react, which was odd. "I need to tell you something."

"No, you don't. You call when you want to call. If it's morning for you, you think it's morning for everyone."

"Wow. Someone woke up on the wrong side of the bed."

"Wow. Someone woke me up before dawn." They were both silent. "Can you please not call before six? I'm not getting enough sleep as it is."

"Okay. Sorry."

"Thank you. What did you want to tell me?"

"Nothing."

"You just said you needed to tell me something. What is it?"

There was a pause, an intake of breath, a sigh, and then, "Do you have any idea how hard it is to manage Mom and Dad from a distance?"

Lane was unable to stifle her laugh. Probably because she'd hardly slept. "You're kidding, right?"

"No. I called because Mom asked me to. She wants to visit you."

"You must have misheard. Mom never visits me." Lane thought about it. It was possible. Anything was possible. "Okay, so, if she wants to visit me, why doesn't she call *me*? If you wanted to visit me, would you call her? Don't answer that," she said unnecessarily. "It doesn't matter. Visiting is a terrible idea. Henry's still adjusting to a new school and a new house."

"Adjusting to a new house is the one thing Mom's good at."

"No, it isn't. If she mentions it again, tell her not to come. Can you do that?" She waited. "Please?" She sat with her sister's silence. It really was impossible to tell Shelley what to do. Her ears pricked up at a sound from across the hall. She waited. It came again, louder. A cough. "Great. Henry's awake. I told you it was too early to call. I have to go."

When she got to his room, Henry was pretending to be asleep, but his lightly fluttering eyelids gave him away. "Scoot over, buddy."

He did. She climbed into bed and they both stared, silent, out the window at the ash-colored sky. Henry was unusually fidgety. He turned toward the wall, toward the door, facedown, faceup. Finally, on his back, chest lit by moonlight, his breathing slowed. She waited a few moments, to be sure he was asleep. It was as she was gently rearranging herself, to slip out of bed, that she noticed the streaks on his face. Dried streaks of tears. It took her breath away, thinking about how he'd tossed and turned and fidgeted, and all the while he'd been silently crying.

The last of the dishes put away, Lane looked over and saw that Henry had moved his bowl aside so he could lay his head down on the table. She felt his forehead. It wasn't warm. He wasn't sick. He was tired, because her sister had woken them up early for no good reason.

It took what felt like forever for Henry to finish his breakfast and to put on his shoes and his coat. He trailed behind her as they walked. "Run," she called. "I hear the bus."

Instead, he crept. By the time he reached the corner, the bus was rattling down the street without them.

"It's okay," Henry said as if she needed consoling. "I don't mind. You can drive me."

She did the math in her head as they hurried home; Henry's school was twenty minutes away, which meant twenty minutes there, twenty minutes to find a spot to park and walk him from the car to the school, twenty minutes back. Her day, already too short for what needed to get done, was now even shorter.

"I think I know the bus route," she told him. "Let's get in the car. If we hurry, I can catch it."

"Hurry in the car?"

She stopped. The last time someone in his family had hurried in the car it was his dad and that hadn't ended well. "You're right. No hurrying in the car. Safety first. I'll stick to the speed limit on the way to school. I'll stick to the speed limit always. Deal?"

"Deal."

॰॰

Mrs. Lindsey, the resource room teacher, was standing guard at the door where the walkers came in. She agreed to let Lane walk Henry to his class just this once. "They don't like parents in the halls," she explained. "Security."

"That's fine," Lane said. "I'm sorry. I'll go."

"It's okay," Mrs. Lindsey said. "You didn't know. Go ahead. You can take him."

The door to the classroom was open as children filed in. Henry allowed her to kiss the top of his head and then disappeared into the scrum of classmates at the cubbies. She breathed in the smells of his room—apple juice, old lunch boxes, markers—and watched him stuff his coat into his narrow cubby. From there he walked to a large attendance book that lay open on a table. With great care he wrote in his name. His tongue poked out from the corner of his mouth; he was concentrating hard.

"Come on in," Miss Fiske called over.

Lane was about to enter when the teacher met her eyes and shook her head. She wasn't talking to her. "Francesca," the teacher called. "Come on in."

Lane turned and realized she was blocking the doorway. "Sorry," she told the little girl and stepped aside so the child—Francesca—could scoot past.

"Be good," a woman called out from behind her. The woman stopped next to Lane. "Francesca," she called to her daughter. "I said be good."

"I'm being good." Francesca ran over to her teacher. "I'm here, Miss Fiske," she yelled.

"Inside voice, please," said Miss Fiske as she walked to the door, nodded to the two mothers, and shut it.

໑

Lane was halfway down the hall when she realized the other mother was calling her.

"Roxie!" The woman accelerated and caught up. "I'm Claudine. The class mom. Francesca's mom. You're Roxie, right? From the column?"

That got around fast. "I'm Lane. I write as Roxie. There was a Roxie before me and there will be a Roxie after me."

"Really? I didn't know. I adore Roxie. I guess that means I adore *you*."

"Thank you."

"Want to know a secret? I used to wish I had a little Roxie in my pocket. That way, whenever I had a question, which is pretty much every second of every day, she could tell me—you could tell me—what to do." She laughed. "I still wish it. My life is such a mess. I'm sure you've heard."

"Mmm," Lane said and kept walking.

Claudine picked up her pace to keep up. "Sorry about what happened on the bus."

Lane gave a pleasant smile and accelerated.

"They really need to do something about that boy."

"Mmm." Lane pushed open the heavy steel doors and walked out into a blaze of light.

"Is Henry still upset? I don't blame him if he is. He really is an awful boy."

That got through. "Pardon?"

"I'm talking about Silas. The wild child. Makes trouble wherever he goes. I'd be furious if I were you. Is that why you came in? To talk to Miss Fiske? She's no use, by the way. You might as well talk to the wind. I always tell parents, if something's wrong you have to go to the principal. If something big is wrong, you have to make your husband go. Miss Oppido is an expert at tuning out moms, but she's terrified of dads. Oh no. I forgot. I'm so sorry. My condolences."

"Thank you." So news about Aaron had gotten around too.

"Just so you know, Francesca wanted to tell Miss Fiske, but Henry begged her not to so she didn't. Out of respect for his wishes."

"He begged her? Henry talks to Francesca?"

"He doesn't exactly talk. It's more he whispers to her and she shouts out what he said."

Lane was vaguely aware that Claudine was still talking but she stopped listening; instead she imagined it: Henry leaning over to cup his hand on the little girl's ear. A second later, the little girl shouting out what he'd said. Picturing it, she felt a pain in her chest, as if a bit of her heart had literally chipped off.

"You're surprised he picked her, of all people. I get it. I hear it all the time. People say it to my face, a little Francesca goes a long way. She doesn't mean to be difficult."

"That's an awful thing for people to say. I think Francesca has spunk. She seems like a great kid to me."

"I know. And look-it, Henry could have picked anyone in the class to talk to, but he picked her. So she can't be all bad."

"She's zero bad," Lane said.

"She's very upset about what happened to Henry."

"What exactly happened to him?"

"He didn't tell you? Oh she's going to kill me. I promised not to tell anyone, but I figured you already knew. I thought Henry spoke at home. At least that's what Miss Fiske told us."

Lane quickly triaged the information. Miss Fiske had told the parents that Henry didn't speak except at home. How had she told them? In an email blast? Was this information passed along on a phone chain? Miss Fiske should have discussed it with her first. They should have made a plan together.

No. This wasn't on Miss Fiske. It was on her. She should have brought it up with Miss Fiske. She should have asked Doctor Bruce for advice on how best to introduce Henry to his new class. The problem was whenever she asked those kinds of questions, Doctor Bruce always said the same thing. After she organized support services for Henry, her job was to treat him as if the next moment would be the one when he would speak. Because eventually—he told her this every time—he would. She had to have faith. Doctor Bruce talked a lot about faith. He talked about it as if it was something a person could just decide to have.

Part of the problem was that it was hard to see Doctor Bruce regularly now. She really needed to find someone closer because— She stopped. Something had happened to Henry. On the bus. She felt her cheeks get hot. "What did the boy—what did Silas do to Henry?"

"I don't know for sure it was Silas. It's just, if anyone is going to pull out hair, that's who I think it would be."

"Silas pulled Henry's hair," she said aloud and then let out a sigh of relief. Kids pulled hair. It wasn't fun but it wasn't the worst thing.

"Pulled out," Claudine corrected her and then mimed a yank.

Lane's hand reflexively went to the back of her head. This morning, when she got into bed with Henry after Shelley's call, she touched his head and he jumped.

"—and then to threaten to pull out the rest if Henry told," Claudine was saying. "Awful!"

Lane sat down on the cool concrete steps.

Claudine sat next to her. "Don't worry. None of the other mean kids are mean to Henry. They like him. It's Francesca they don't like. Because face it, she can be annoying. Henry's not annoying. He's quiet. No one minds a quiet kid."

"Apparently Silas does."

"Here's some good news: Silas is moving. Which is a relief. Believe me, Henry isn't the only one he bothers. I know because I volunteer at lunch on my days off. You should volunteer at lunch. Everything happens at lunch. I was there yesterday. Which is how I know Henry isn't mean to anyone. The mean kids—not Silas but the other ones, the regular mean kids—they ignore him. I wish they'd ignore Francesca.

They might if she'd just toughen up. She's so thin-skinned. Everything bothers her. Literally everything. If I don't cut the labels off her clothes, she's beside herself. You know how many times I've accidentally cut holes in brand-new clothes because I was trying to remove a label that no other kid would even notice?"

Lane felt the label on her own shirt start to tickle at her neck. "That must be hard for her."

"Well it's no picnic for me, I can tell you that." Claudine got quiet.

Lane seized the moment. "I have to go. I have to get to work. Thank you so much for telling me what happened with Silas. Will you thank Francesca for me? Can you tell her how much I appreciate her being a good friend to Henry?"

"No. I can't do that. I promised her I wouldn't say anything about Silas."

"But I have to tell Henry you told me. I'm sure you can understand."

Claudine begrudgingly agreed that she did. "You realize what's going to happen is Henry's going to be mad at Francesca and Francesca's going to be furious at me. But okay. I get it. I'll give her a heads-up that Henry's going to dump her. Soften the blow."

"He's not going to dump her. He's not that way. I bet she'll understand why you told me. Francesca seems like a smart kid."

Lane ignored that Claudine did not look convinced and thanked her again. She was hustling to her car when someone tapped her shoulder. She swung around.

It was Claudine. "Sorry. I didn't mean to scare you. I just forgot I need to ask you a favor. I hate asking for favors but given my situation . . ." She paused to give Lane a chance to ask what her situation was. When no question came, she went on. "Could you take Francesca with you tonight? Unless you have a full car. If you have a full car, I'll try and find someone else. Which won't be easy. I have to give Miss Fiske credit for putting Henry in Francesca's group. Don't worry," she said. "I wasn't a big fan of the idea either. I mean a book group for first graders? That's insane. You should have seen us all at back-to-school night when she announced it. No one said anything but you could see it on everyone's face. The horror! Turns out it's not as bad as we thought. We alternate houses. We eat pizza. We talk about the book for five seconds. The kids play for an hour." She eyed Lane. "Did Henry not tell you about book group?"

No way Lane was going to admit that. "It's tonight?"

"Oh no. Are you not on the book group email yet? Can you go? I can't. I'm on call. Hospice nurse. Don't look so impressed. I'm not a saint. I'm comfortable with bodily fluids and death is all. Probably no one will die tonight, but you never know. I get that it's a 'parent-child' book group but should Francesca be penalized because I'm on call in case someone dies? Unless—do you think Henry won't want her to come with you because she squealed about Silas?"

As a general rule, Lane was not a fan of favors. She found the culture of reciprocation more nuanced than people admitted. But saying no to taking Henry's new friend—a girl who'd been fretting over what happened to him on the bus, a girl about whom people said, *a little goes a long way*—she would not say no to that. "Of course I'll take her. I'm sure Henry won't mind."

"Thank goodness." Claudine dug out a tiny notebook from her purse, wrote down her address and ripped out the page. "I knew I was going to like you. I liked you before I met you. Honestly, I think I might be Roxie's biggest fan!"

Lane smiled and tucked the paper in her pocket. For a moment she considered telling Claudine she was wrong about her, that the person she liked lived only on the page. But she didn't bother. Like everyone else, Claudine would soon find out for herself.

As Lane walked toward her car, she heard Claudine call out, "Roxie rules!" So she raised her hand, gave a backward wave, and hurried on her way.

14

Lane's conversation with Henry did not go the way she expected. For one thing, he wasn't mad at anyone. Not at Francesca for telling her mom, not at Claudine for telling Lane, not even at Silas who, it turned out, had confided to Francesca that the reason he'd yanked Henry's hair was to stop Henry from giving him the silent treatment.

"She sounds like a real peacemaker," Lane told Henry after he recounted the details of his friend's classroom mediation. First Francesca told Silas not to take Henry's silence personally, because he gave everyone the silent treatment except for her. Then she told Henry that Silas terrorized people on the bus because he was mad that no one would sit next to him. The reason for that—Francesca again—was he smelled like his dog. According to Francesca, Silas had a very large and slobbery dog.

"I never smelled dog on Silas," Henry admitted to Lane. "But I should have sat next to him on the bus. And I shouldn't have told Francesca what happened. I didn't know it would make her upset."

This was not the takeaway Lane wanted. "You did everything exactly right. You were brave with Silas and you were brave to tell Francesca." She waited a moment. "How come you didn't tell me?"

"Silas made me promise not to. And a promise has to stick or else. Do we have anything special for snack?"

Sometimes Lane saw bits of herself in Henry that she liked and sometimes she saw bits of herself that she didn't. This was a bit that she didn't. At six, Henry was already an expert at changing the subject.

They were running ten minutes late when Lane pulled up across the street from Francesca's house. She parked quickly, at a slant that gave the car an abandoned look. Henry stayed in the car while she ran across the street and up the steps. She rang the bell and while she waited, went through a list of possible apologies for why they were late. Halfway through the list she stopped; did she need to apologize? They weren't that late. Or were they? Lane wasn't sure what a normal amount of late was. Roxie would know. What would Roxie say?

Roxie said, *Stop worrying.* Lane shook off the worry and rang the bell again. Okay. No one was home. They were very late. So late, Francesca called her mother and told her the lady never came. So late, Claudine called another mother, a more reliable mother, who'd quickly snatched up Francesca and zoomed off to book group. This was no way to win friends.

Okay. Not everyone needed friends.

The front door opened a crack, revealing a sliver of a woman's face, one anxious eye, half an anxious mouth. The mouth stayed firmly shut.

"Hi. I'm here to pick up Francesca for book group."

The sliver turned around so that now Lane was looking at a shaft of dark-brown hair and a piece of an off-kilter tortoiseshell barrette. "Francesca?" the woman called. She closed the door but Lane could still hear her. "Francesca." She sounded angry.

A minute passed, then two. How many minutes was a person supposed to wait? Ringing again would definitely be ringing too much. Maybe she should knock. She knocked. Should she go in?

She flashed back to the *Roxie* letter about the big, unfriendly dad who never came in the house when he picked up his daughter. The man who stood outside on the front steps looking threatening. There was certainly nothing threatening about Lane. She was more like a bird than a bear. But unfriendly? She had no problem imagining people thinking that. She considered what a normal person would do. A normal, friendly person. Probably they would check to see if the door was unlocked. She tried the knob. Bad luck, it turned. Should she open the door and walk inside? That might be what was expected, that she open the door and go inside and wait there. She really had no idea.

This was what her readers didn't understand. In print Roxie always knew exactly the right thing to do. In real life Lane was flummoxed by the most elemental codes of conduct.

The door swung open. Francesca smiled. "I'm here!" She slammed the door behind her, put her skinny arms around Lane and gave her a tight hug.

"Aw thank you," Lane said. Francesca looked up and smiled but didn't let go. "Did you say goodbye to—"

"My aunt." Francesca peeled herself off and rolled her eyes. "She's mean. I have two aunts. A nice aunt and a mean aunt. Where's Henry?"

Lane pointed to the car.

Francesca let out a high-pitched scream. When she was done she said, "That means I'm excited." She skipped down the steps and raced to the sidewalk. Lane raced after her to keep up. When they reached the curb Francesca practically toppled into the street and then, regaining her balance, started to dart across, oblivious to the car that had just turned the corner and was now heading toward her.

Lane sprinted, caught Francesca by the arm and pulled her back, just in time. Francesca tried to squirm out of her grip but Lane held her tight.

The car passed slowly; the driver, a heavyset woman wearing thick glasses that made her eyes look huge, glared.

"Sorry," Lane called to the woman as the car drove off. "Francesca sweetie," Lane said. "You need to hold my hand when we cross the street, okay? And we always have to look both ways."

"Okay." Francesca held Lane's hand and looked both ways, many times, back and forth, with every step they walked, until they reached the curb. When she stepped onto the sidewalk, she looked up at Lane and beamed.

"Good job," Lane said.

Francesca's smile widened. "Thanks." She tried to yank the back door open and when she couldn't, she banged on it and screamed. She turned to Lane and calmly said, "It's locked."

"I know. Hold on."

A dance of bad timing followed, Francesca pulling on the handle a second before and then, again, a second after, Lane clicked the electronic key.

"Let me in," Francesca yelled.

Lane stayed calm. "Wait for the click, Francesca. Not yet." And finally, "Freeze."

The girl froze. Lane double-clicked. Francesca yanked the handle. When she opened the door she shrieked again, then stopped. "That means I'm happy." She slid in, gave Henry a hug and buckled up.

As Lane got in the car she saw Henry moving his hands away from his ears. Francesca's hands were now neatly folded in her lap. She had a big voice but tiny hands. A child's hands. Lane thought of Claudine's words, *A little Francesca goes a long way.* She winced at the thought that someone would say such a thing about a child.

As soon as Lane pulled away, Francesca settled down and began chatting with Henry, completely unfazed by his refusal to hold up his side of the conversation. When Lane next glanced in the rearview mirror, what she saw in the back seat was a bubbly, high-spirited girl entertaining a totally silent boy.

℘

The mothers were in the living room when they arrived. Lane quickly took in the scene: the stack of closed pizza boxes on the dining room table. The pile of paper plates. The roll of paper towels. Two short towers of plastic cups. The book group had waited for them to arrive before eating. A large Brita water pitcher sat beside five bottles of white wine. Two bottles of wine were empty. The book group hadn't waited for them to arrive before drinking.

Next to the boxes of pizza were half a dozen plates covered by mounds of aluminum foil. Cookies, Lane guessed. Claudine hadn't told her anything about bringing dessert and she hadn't thought to ask.

The host mother guided them into the living room. The rest of the mothers got up and gathered round to welcome them. Children were called up from the basement. Pizza was doled out. More drinks were poured. Henry's classmates conducted a conversation in animal voices for reasons not apparent to Lane, which didn't seem to bother Henry.

Quacking, braying, clucking and mooing children wolfed down their slices, while Henry ate and watched the barnyard cacophony play out, as if he were in the audience.

Among the women, the conversation seemed stuck on the topic of the unseasonably warm weather. There was no way for Lane to know if this was the usual pre-book-talk chitchat but her suspicion was, it was not. Instead it had the feel of something one might choose to discuss in front of a newcomer who was not yet—and might never be—one of *us*.

As Claudine predicted, discussion of the book didn't last long. The children were succinct in expressing their strongly felt opinions. *I didn't like it. I didn't read it. My mom forgot to get it.* The host mother tried various methods of imposing order and extending the discussion but once it was clear she failed in both regards, she quickly moved on to the business of picking the book they'd read next. Luckily for Henry the voting process was thumbs up, thumbs down.

Francesca complained this wasn't fair. "My thumbs don't work right."
Across the room Lane noticed a woman roll her eyes.

"What about if Francesca votes with her toes?" Lane suggested.

The room got quiet. A mother whose name Lane had already forgotten asked Francesca to explain what she meant by that, her thumbs not working right.

Francesca replied by rolling her tongue. "I can roll my tongue." She rolled it again. "Can you? Not everyone can. Same thing with thumbs."

This prompted the children to investigate first, whether or not they could roll their tongues and then, whether or not their thumbs worked right. To move things along the host mother announced, "Okay. My house. My rules. Francesca can vote however she wants. Toes instead of thumbs is fine."

A boy piped up to say this wasn't fair; he wanted to vote with his toes too. The rest of the children immediately echoed his objection.

"Okay," the host mother said. "Toe votes for all."

The room filled with the sound of Velcro and pleas for help with laces and stubborn socks. One boy, who had been the first to remove his shoes, misunderstood the delay and asked for help in getting his shoes back on. The vote was delayed further by a communal fascination with how some second toes were longer than the big toe. An earnest discussion ensued about whether in those cases, the second toe should be called the *big* toe. This was all to say, book group, which started late, ended later.

What Lane was thinking as she turned onto Francesca's street was whether or not she should call Dana to report that this morning, when she took a shower, the pipes had whined so loudly it sounded like they were about to burst. The reason for her hesitation was that Dana had been popping by nearly every day to check on whether anything new had gone wrong and Lane did not want to encourage the habit. She also did not want any pipes to burst. Francesca's voice broke through her debate.

"What's happening?"

The scene in front of her snapped into focus. Through the disorienting flash of emergency vehicle lights, she counted the police cruisers—one in a driveway, two in front of a house. "I'm not sure." As she got closer she saw what she feared: the driveway was Francesca's. Lights were on in every room of Francesca's house. A crowd was assembled on her lawn.

"Did someone die?" Henry whispered in a voice so quiet at first Lane thought she had imagined it.

"Your dad died," Francesca reminded him. She looked out her open window. "Why is there a police car in my driveway?"

At the sound of her voice a man on the lawn turned and started yelling. It was gibberish, guttural, tinged with fury. He sounded unhinged. Was that why the police were here? Because a madman was on the loose? The madman met Lane's eyes and raced toward her car.

"Don't worry," she said as she raised the windows and locked the doors. "He can't get in."

Despite the old man's age and girth, he moved quickly. He was now so close, Lane could see comb marks on his slicked-back hair. He pounded on the door, startling her, and bellowed nonsense, his voice a growl. She made out words—"get you," "get her"—as he pulled on the handle. Francesca screamed.

Lane kept her voice steady as she reminded Francesca that the doors were locked. "You're safe. He can't get in." She turned toward the wild man now banging his fist on the window and yelled, "It's locked. You're not getting in. Do you hear me? Go away."

"She locked the door," the old man shouted.

"You bet I did," Lane snapped back.

The man tugged on the handle again, this time with so much force he fell over backward when he let go. A policeman ran over. Finally.

Lane turned to the children. "You're safe. The policeman's here. He'll take the man away. The man will get the help he needs."

But the policeman wasn't taking him away. He was helping him up, gently, even though now the man hissed—Lane could hear him through the closed window—"She's a devil."

"Miss Fiske is here," Francesca said.

Lane turned and saw the teacher. Why was their teacher here?

The man was back at the window. Spit was coming out of his mouth. His eyes were filled with fury.

Lane yelled to the policeman, "Please get him to stop."

"Why is he crying?" Francesca wailed.

The old man yelled back, "Get out, Francesca! Unlock the door and get out."

Lane was struggling to understand what was happening when she heard a knock on her window. Startled, she turned to see a policeman motioning for her to lower it. He looked exactly like the policeman who'd come to her apartment to tell her Aaron died. She felt her stomach drop and for a brief moment she wondered if she had fallen through a portal into a time warp, if the policeman from back then had come here now to tell her she'd been right all along. That it wasn't Aaron who died. That the person who died had stolen Aaron's car. To her surprise, when she imagined this, she felt relief.

"Ma'am?" He was knocking harder now.

She was in shock. Of course he was not the same policeman. He didn't look anything like that policeman. Of course Aaron was not alive. She'd identified his body and buried him. She pressed the button and her window retracted.

"Ma'am, unlock the door and let the girl out." His voice was calm but Lane noticed his hand was resting on his gun.

She pointed to the old man. "He's threatening us." But now, she saw, he wasn't. She could hear the old man pleading with *his* policeman to do something about *her*.

"Your granddaughter's okay," his policeman was saying. "See? She's okay."

"Ma'am." All courtesy was gone from *her* policeman's voice. "Unlock her door."

Numb, she pressed the button and the lock clicked. The old man swung the door open and yelled for Francesca to hurry up and get out. He struggled to pull her free.

"I'm stuck, Grandpa. That hurts."

Through a haze of confusion Lane told Francesca, "You have to unbuckle." She told the old man, "Her seat belt is buckled." She told the cop, "She can't get out. She's still buckled."

There was a rush of fabric, shirt struggling against seat belt, and Francesca was free. Her arms were wrapped around her grandfather's neck. As he ran she asked him, "Why are you crying? Grandpa, don't cry. It makes me cry when you cry."

The crowd split apart to allow them across the lawn. The man, Francesca's grandfather, clambered up the steps and stumbled, clumsy as a bear. The crowd gasped. A policeman ran over and ushered grandfather and granddaughter to the house. A door yawned open to receive them. Several people hurried in. The door closed.

"Miss Fiske went inside," Henry whispered to Lane. "With Mrs. Abramowitz."

She tried to take this in, that someone had called the school counselor because Francesca was missing. That someone had called Miss Fiske.

An ambulance careened onto the block. Competing strobes from the emergency vehicles cut through the dark of the night, turning it red, then blue, then white.

The policeman at Lane's door left to talk to a team of paramedics.

"Can we go?" Henry whispered.

Lane flicked on her blinker and pulled away from the curb. She could not afford to look in the rearview mirror because she knew if she saw Henry's frightened face now she might fall apart, right here, driving the car. She sat up straight and focused on the road, which was why she had no idea until she turned onto her block, until sirens pierced the quiet of the night, that two police cruisers had followed her.

She saw the rest as if watching from above. The first squad car pulled close to her rear bumper. The second one pulled ahead and then backed up until that fender was kissing hers too. Her car was sandwiched in, as if they were worried she might try and escape.

It was a different policeman at her window now, one with a granite face and slits for eyes. "Do you know why we pulled you over?"

She shook her head.

"Why did you flee the scene?"

"What scene?" she asked but another siren tore through the night, drowning out her voice. A third squad car turned onto her street. Three sets of cherry lights flashed. House lights flicked on next door and then across the street and then spread, like a virus, up and down the block. The new policeman conferred with the ones who were already there.

The granite cop came back and stood at Lane's car door, pointing his flashlight toward the back seat. Henry lifted up his arm to shield his eyes. "Ma'am, who's the boy?"

"My son."

"Can you please ask your son to roll down his window? What's his name?"

"Henry. He won't speak to you. He doesn't speak to anyone—"

"Ma'am. Window. Down."

She saw Henry fumbling with the buttons on his door panel to lower his window and realized with a start that he had never raised or lowered his own car window before. His parents controlled his windows. *His parent,* she corrected herself. She pressed the button on her door panel and his window slowly lowered.

The granite policeman moved a few steps back. "Henry, right?" Henry nodded. The policeman shined his flashlight on Lane. "Can you tell me who this is?" He waited a moment and then asked again. "Son, who's sitting behind the wheel of the car?"

"Hey buddy," Lane said. "I know this is hard for you, but can you try—" Lane saw his eyes fill. Another piece of her heart chipped off. Henry tried. He always tried. "He can't answer a question like that," she told the granite policeman. "He can't speak to strangers even if he wants to." She could feel her anger surging. It wasn't going to help this situation if she was in a rage. She paused, took in a breath, let it out. "He can understand you and he can nod and shake his head. If you ask him a yes-or-no question, he can answer." She turned back to Henry. "Don't be scared, buddy. He's just trying to find out if I'm—"

"Ma'am. I need you to be quiet now." The hard surface of the policeman's face was interrupted by a line where his mouth was supposed to be. When he turned back to her son nothing softened. "Son, I need you to tell me who is driving this car."

"I told you," Lane snapped. She stopped. It would not help to yell. She took another breath. "He cannot answer that kind of question."

Two cops hurried over, hands on holsters. Granite cop stepped away. The three cops huddled. Even as they discussed how to proceed, granite cop's eyes remained fixed on Lane. When they split up, it was a different cop who came to the car. A younger cop, whose face hadn't turned to stone.

"How you doing?" he asked Henry. Henry didn't move. "Not so good, huh? Me neither. I'm going home soon, though. I got a son your age at home. You're seven, right?" Henry shook his head.

Lane watched through the mirror, hands clenched on the wheel.

"My mistake," the cop said. "Eight?" Henry shook his head again, this time with more conviction. "Don't tell me you're six. You're too big to be six. Are you six?" Henry nodded. The policeman pointed to Lane. "You know this lady?" Henry nodded. "She a neighbor?" Henry shook his head. "Friend?" Henry shook his head. "Relative?"

"He wants to know if we're from the same family," Lane explained. Henry nodded.

"Is she your aunt?" the cop asked. Henry shook his head. "Is she your mom?" Henry nodded.

Lane didn't realize she'd been holding her breath. It came out in a rush. "Why are you questioning him? What's going on?"

Granite cop was back. "Because of the girl. The one you locked in your car."

"Francesca?" This made no sense. "Her mother asked me to take her to book group." Her voice got louder. "As a favor. She asked me to take her and I took her and I brought her home."

For a moment both cops, granite and young, stood still. They looked as confused as she felt. When they stepped away to join the third cop for a conference, she felt her heart racing. Her eyes took in the small crowd that had gathered across the street. The old woman from the corner house—she met her the first time she picked up Henry at the bus—was standing in her bathrobe next to her neighbor, the man Dana told her lived alone with his five daughters. There were other neighbors, neighbors she'd never seen before, all of them standing with mouths agape, watching the drama unfold as if this was their own personal episode of *Law & Order*.

A walkie-talkie broke the silence. Two of the cops peeled off to respond, their squad car squealing as they raced to the next emergency. Only granite cop and not-yet-granite cop remained. They stood close, granite cop glancing over his shoulder at intermittent intervals to make sure Lane had not fled again while not-yet-granite cop spoke on his phone.

When not-yet-granite cop was done with his call he returned to the car. "Appears there's been a misunderstanding. I apologize. I'm sure you can understand that when we get a report about a crime in progress we have to check it out." He turned to Henry. "Sorry if we frightened you, sport."

"What kind of crime?" Lane asked.

"Abduction. We got more than one call."

"I abducted Francesca? Her mother asked me to take her to book group. I told her aunt that's where we were going. Did you talk to her mother? Did you talk to the aunt? Francesca told me her aunt was mean. What did her aunt say?"

"We've been in contact with the mother. She's embarrassed. There were complicating factors. It was a confusing situation. I apologize. But when a call comes in—and in this case it was more than one—that a woman grabbed a child off the sidewalk, we have no choice but to respond."

Lane thought about the car that drove down Francesca's street, the one that would have hit the girl if Lane hadn't pulled her out of harm's way. Was that who called? The glaring driver with the big eyes? Or was it the mean aunt with the tortoiseshell clip who wouldn't open the door more than a crack? "Something is not right in that house," Lane said. "Instead of questioning me you should look into that."

"It's an unfortunate misunderstanding."

"Are you going to explain that to my neighbors?" She gestured to where they stood, watching. "Are you going to report that to my son's teacher?" She didn't mean to be shouting. She wasn't a shouter.

"Ma'am. I understand. And I apologize. Are you okay?"

She had to be okay. Henry was watching her closely. She took a deep breath. "I'm fine. I'll be fine if we can go inside. We both want to go inside."

The cop opened the door. "You know what I think?" he asked Henry. "I think you deserve an extra cookie tonight. What do you say, Mom?"

"Yes." Lane got out of the car. She could feel her neighbors watching, hungry for details. Should she go over to them to tell them what happened? She started toward them, but Henry tugged at her sleeve so she stopped. He wanted to go in the house. So inside they went.

They were there just long enough for her to find—to her relief—that there was a box of cookies in the cupboard, when the bell to the side door rang. Henry stood up, ready to bolt.

"Hang on, buddy. I'm sure it's just a neighbor checking to see if we're okay. Will you stay with me? You don't have to talk."

He nodded.

She didn't recognize the man at the door, even after he introduced himself.

"Nathan," he said. "Nathan Knapp. Silent *K*." He waited. "Your landlord."

"Oh. Of course. I'm sorry. Come in."

"I'm the one who should be sorry," he said as he walked into the kitchen. "Dana's been telling me about all the things that have gone wrong here. I apologize. I had no idea. I thought I kept the house in great shape." He noticed Henry and smiled. "Hey pal."

Henry moved behind her. Lane moved her hand behind her back and Henry held on to it.

"Sorry to intrude," Nathan said. "But when the police called, I figured I better come over."

"They called you?"

"Not exactly. The monitoring company called the house. When no one answered here, they called Dana's cell. That's the first number on their list. Dana's out of town—overnight, I don't know where—so she told the monitoring company to call the police. Then she called me. She told me she's going to call the monitoring company tomorrow to get your cell added to the list." He saw her confusion. "The alarm went off. Dana tried your cell. You didn't pick up."

Lane pulled out her phone and saw the long list of missed calls.

"Everything's fine," Nathan told Henry. "No intruder," he told Lane. "The alarm company says something went kerflooey in the electric panel." He saw something in Lane's face that he couldn't read. "You okay?"

And just like that the events of the night hit her; she felt unsteady on her feet. She gently moved Henry so that she could sit down on the closest chair. Henry sat down beside her. "I'm fine," she told her landlord. She turned and saw Henry was studying her face. "I'm fine, buddy," she told him and then leaned over to give him a hug.

"I apologize," Nathan said, "for all the stuff that's gone wrong with the house. I swear I thought it was in great shape. I asked my contractor if he ever heard of a house all of a sudden going bad. He said sometimes it happens with an old house. But it's nothing fatal. It's like a phase. It will pass. Everything can be fixed. I wouldn't set the alarm tonight, though. Are you okay with that? They're coming tomorrow between noon and two to check it out. I can let them in, if you can't be here. I'm really sorry."

"It's not a problem. I'll be here." It really was the least of her problems. Henry looked up at her and leaned over and rubbed her arm and she gave him another gentle hug, this time longer.

Later Nathan told her it was that moment, seeing Henry gently rub her arm, seeing her lean over to give him that tender hug, when he had the surprising thought: *Could a woman like this ever be with a man like me?* He knew right away the answer was no. This woman had the world ahead of her and he was like his house, in a bad phase, except with him the phase was probably not going to pass.

What Lane remembered about meeting Nathan that night was thinking, *This man, watching this sweet domestic scene, he really has no idea.*

May 15, 2017

Ask Roxie!

Roxie Reader Good News Alert! Our poll deadline has
been extended!

Are you excited for Roxie's Live-Chat Wednesdays?

Would you be even more excited if a Roxie podcast
started soon?

Click here to enter the Roxie Sweepstakes Poll and let
us know!

Be one of five lucky readers to win a free one-year
subscription to Guild-Plus!

Dear Roxie,

Something is weighing on me and though I've tried for
some time to navigate the best way forward, I finally

realized this is not something I can figure out myself. I need your help.

Here's my question: When is the right time for a parent to reveal themselves to their child? I'm talking about their deep down true self. The person they started out wanting to be before certain things happened, the way things do, that turned their life's path into a dead end.

Some days I think it's best to do this early on. Share your story when your children are young. If that's correct, it's too late for me. Other days I think a person should wait until their children are grown, with children of their own. If that's the case, the time for me to tell is now. Some days I think the answer is never. Some things are never okay to share. Some days I think the most loving thing a parent can do is to die with their story untold.

This comes up now because it's just occurred to me that my children don't know me at all. Not really. At least not the person I started out to be, before my life took a turn.

Sadly, I've been through this once before, with my mother. When she was alive, we were close. People were jealous of how close we were. They'd say so all the time. But after my mother passed away, I learned I only knew a fraction of who she was. I was only a fraction of her story.

Now I'm on the other side of that equation. I'm not like my mother. I don't have spells or episodes like she did.

Episodes of what? I have no idea. She never said. I only knew a fraction.

Now all I can think about is: How much do I tell? Can my grown children handle hearing the things that happened to me before they were born? Things about which they have no idea. I made sure of that—that they'd have no idea.

I know they see me as diminished. To them I'm like a bottle of old wine gone bad, cloudy with dregs rising. They're not entirely wrong. I am slipping away. What they've got wrong is the reason why. They assume it's age. It's not. It's because of the life I've lived, the choices I've made. Choices that don't make me proud.

I think the reason I feel an urgency to tell them now is because I want them to know it doesn't have to be this way. I'm worried that if I don't tell them why I turned out like this, if I don't tell them the story of my life, it may end up being their story too.

Have you ever had the experience of looking at the face of your grown child and seeing everything all at once, like a pentimento. You see them as a baby wiping their nose on your shirt, and as a kid with dirt under their fingernails and Band-Aids on both knees, and as a teenager spitting mad as they slam the door in your face, and as a young adult packing their bags and moving away for good. Everything in that one vulnerable face.

Do all mothers have X-ray eyes that can see into their child's core no matter how old the child? I do. I see their core and in it I see reflected back their disappointment their mother is not the mother they wished they'd had. When is it the right time to tell our children the story of our lives? Am I too late? Am I there now? Or is the answer never?

Yours,
Cloudy with Dregs Rising

Dear Cloudy,

May I share that your letter broke my heart twice? First when I read it through the lens of a mother's eyes and again when I read it through the lens of a daughter's?

If you're a regular reader of my column you know when it comes to our most intimate relationships I'm a big believer in honesty. But honestly, you didn't share a single clue as to what it is you've spent your life protecting your children from. Which makes it very hard for me to comment on whether or not disclosure would help them, or cause them harm.

Are there situations where the truth is so dreadful it might harm a grown child to know? Yes. Does that apply to your situation? I have no idea.

Notice that I used the word *might*. I chose that word because it's something we can never know for sure.

Yes, parents ought to do their best to avoid hurting their children even when those children are grown. But does withholding information accomplish that? Not necessarily.

Have you ever noticed that children are excellent observers? If you haven't, find a way to spend some time with a baby and you'll see. They stare. They study. They imitate the melody of our voices long before they understand our words. They copy our smiles and twitches, even when we're not aware we're smiling and twitching. What they can't do is interpret. Children need us to help them make sense of it all. Left alone, they can be very inventive and completely wrong.

This is why a sick parent who decides to keep their illness from their child might end up bereft to discover their child felt the withdrawal and misconstrued it as a sign that the parent is angry with them. This is why a child whose parent has been violent in the home might decide the anger is because of something they did or neglected to do. It's not that they *can't* make sense of it, without context or information. It's that they can make the *wrong* sense of it.

To be clear: I'm not advocating telling difficult truths to young children. But when children reach adulthood, that's a different story. You're right about this: they might need to hear your difficult truth in order to keep their own lives from careening out of control.

The reason you haven't found an easy answer to your question is because there is no easy answer. But there are some things you should know:

For sure, now is the time to let your children know you are not cloudy with dregs rising. For sure, now is the time to tell them that you've lived a life with wonder and grace and disappointments. For sure, now is the time to let them know you've made choices you regret. This will be a gift to them so that when they encounter life's disappointments and regrets, as they most surely will if they have not already, they'll know in a deep way, it's all part of the mix of life.

You talk about seeing the vulnerability on your children's faces. Here's the good news: their faces are where you'll find your answer. Watch their faces when you talk to them and listen to what they say. The answers will be in the gaze of their eyes, in how they hold their mouths, in the plane of their shoulders. In those small ways you'll hear: *go on I want to know more* or *please stop and let the past stay blurry.*

As for the incorrect assumptions that they've made about you, I say rise high and forgive them. They can only know you as much as you've allowed them to.

Sending wishes for courage and love.

Yours forever, or at least for now,
Roxie

15

Working out the after-school logistics for Henry was a good distraction from worrying about why Sam had asked her to come in for a late-afternoon meeting. The brief email from his assistant, Chloe, had offered no explanation for why he'd cut short his Guild-Europe trip, but Lane doubted he would have come back for anything less than an emergency.

Henry agreed to aftercare without complaint, probably because—luck of the draw—today was his resource room teacher Mrs. Lindsey's turn to be in charge. As for the plumber coming over to fix the whining pipes, who hadn't arrived by the time Lane had to leave, Dana offered to meet him at the house and handle that.

As soon as Lane stepped into Sam's office for her meeting, half an hour early because Sam thought on time was late, she smelled trouble in the air. Mentho-Lyptus.

A moment later Bert strode in. "Okay. Let's get started."

A well-groomed young woman skittered in after him and sat down in the guest chair next to Lane. Bert took the seat behind Sam's desk.

"Shouldn't we wait for Sam?" Lane gestured to include the well-groomed young woman. "We can come back."

"In three months? Sam's away building Guild-Europe. This can't wait."

Lane did the calculation. Three months meant Sam would be back mid-August, which meant for three months— She stopped. "But Sam asked me to come in today, for this meeting."

"No. Chloe asked you to come in."

She took out her phone and found Chloe's email. Bert was right. Chloe hadn't said anything about Sam's being in the meeting. It was Lane's assumption that if Sam's assistant was setting up a meeting, it would be with Sam. Another wrong assumption.

Bert pulled in his lips. When he released them, they made a popping noise. "Here's the plan. We're going to nip this in the bud. Correct course now. Before you sink."

"Pardon?"

"This is three days' worth." He tapped the folder in front of him. "Email. You really pissed people off with that Dear Queasy letter."

Dear Queasy. The woman who was worried because her daughter's friend had a scary father. "Okay. So? I thought you liked disagreement. I thought the more conflict the better."

"You thought right. Disagreement is good for eyeballs. Conflict is good for clicks." He tapped the folder again. "There's no conflict here. These people agree. Your answer was out of control." He opened the folder and riffled through until he found what he wanted. "Here we go." He cleared his throat and read, "Roxie says we're not allowed to call people weird anymore. All of a sudden weird is against the law. If I listened to Roxie I'd have to cover my mouth with duct tape and never say another word. Well guess what? Roxie is not the only game in town. As of today, I am officially a fan of *Dear Prudie.*" Bert met Lane's eyes. "You understand what this reader is saying? She's left the Guild for *Slate.*"

"I never said you're not allowed to call people weird. I agree with that, but I didn't say it. Anyway, that's one letter. From a crank. Why do you care? Let her go have at it, over at *Slate*."

"You don't like that one? Okay. How about this one?" He found another. "How dare she! Who does Roxie think she is, telling a woman to call Child Services on a neighbor just because she didn't like how he chewed his food at dinner!"

"Chewed his food? That person didn't read my answer. Fine. It doesn't matter. People complain. It's human nature. Not every reader has to love every letter. Aren't you happy they clicked and commented? Clickety clickety?"

He picked up the file. "Do you hear any clicking?" He held it in the air and waited for her to admit she did not. "You don't. Because there is no clicking. Because these aren't comments. They're emails. To me. From ex-readers. Pissed off former *paying* Guild-Plus readers. Readers who were so angry they skipped over clicking and quit." His hand made a gimme-gimme motion to the well-groomed young woman. "The other one." She handed him the other folder that had been sitting on her lap. He dropped it on the desk. "These are complaints about the letter from the lady wondering should she or shouldn't she tell her children the story of her life. These people, like me, have no idea what any of what she said, or what you said, meant." He pointed to the first folder. "Annoyed ex–Guild-Plus members." He pointed to the second folder. "Bored ex–Guild-Plus members. See a trend?" In case she didn't, he helped her. "All of them. Ex. Guild. Plus."

The young woman lifted up her hand, as if to be called on, and then spoke so softly Lane had to strain to hear her. "I think—we think—it's because of the national mood. You know. Depressed."

"I'm sorry. Who are you?"

"I'm Summer. I'm . . ." She looked at Bert as if she wasn't sure it was okay to say.

"Summer's your new producer. She's smart. She's young. She's hungry. And she's yours. You're welcome." He smiled at Summer, who smiled back. "Summer is going to bring your column back to life. She's going to help you figure out your thing."

"What's my thing?"

"Exactly. What is your thing? A column needs a thing. Like . . ." He snapped his fingers as if to summon a thing to appear. "Sex. Sex is a thing. Or getting rich or getting healthy. Those are things. You used to have a thing. Snark. Now? Your column is one long blah blah blah. Blah blah blah is not a thing. But Summer is here to fix this. She will help you get your snark back. So it sticks. So we can market it across platforms. Column, online chat, podcast—"

"I'm not doing a podcast. Sam and I—"

Bert squinted. "I don't get you. A lot of people would sell their soul to do a podcast." He shrugged. "Doesn't matter. This is not a debate. Podcasts are no longer the future. They're the present. The present is not negotiable. Relax. This will not be painful. Summer's entire job is to make it fun. Why do I care if you have fun? I don't, except—Summer, you tell her."

Summer's smile came out slowly, like the sun sliding from behind a cloud. "If you have fun, your readers will have fun?"

Bert tapped his head. "She's a smart one, right?" He folded his hands on his desk. Mission accomplished.

Lane felt her spine stiffen. She had a mission too. To keep her job. She proceeded with care. "Summer is smart." She smiled at the eager young woman who, having been praised, was now radiating goodwill and joy. "The thing I wonder is, is it smart for a column to be snarky *all* the time? Life can be tough. Some readers write letters filled with pain. Don't you think they deserve answers that are compassionate?"

"Yes. No argument here. Totally agree. Knock yourself out with compassion. On your time. On my time?" Bert knocked on the desk. "Snark."

"But Sam agreed—"

"Where is Sam?" Bert looked around. "I don't see Sam. I just see you and me and Summer. Here's the deal: I've got an IT guy working out a way for Roxie's letters to go directly to Summer. Once that's in place, you'll only see letters that fit the model. Perfect, right? You'll have zero temptation to answer letters from people wallowing in pathetic problems that—let's be honest here—you can't solve."

"Summer screening my letters won't work. No offense," Lane told the well-groomed, grinning, extremely young woman now sitting at the edge of her seat.

"You know," Bert said, "some people might wonder if this attitude problem of yours is because of something going on in your personal life. I don't wonder because"—he leaned closer—"I don't care about your personal life." He leaned back. "It's going to be great. We'll have the new *Roxie* team up and running by early fall."

Lane took that in: the new *Roxie* team.

"Podcast target start date is October one. Soon as we get a publicist on board, we'll fine-tune the brand. Still undecided about a voice coach." He looked confused by her expression. "Because . . ." He gestured in the general direction of her mouth.

Okay. Bert thought something was wrong with her voice. She disagreed. She had a perfectly good voice for someone who was definitely not going to do a podcast.

"Just to be clear," Summer said, her smile glimmering back on, "I'm only here to help." She tucked several strands of her silky hair behind her adorably small ear. Was she even twenty? "And nothing is locked in. Everything's fluid so if there's any—"

"Nothing is fluid." Bert stood up and gestured toward the door. "Thank you." The meeting was over. Summer left.

Lane did not. "Did Sam agree to this? Did he buy into Summer screening my letters? I mean she seems like a lovely young woman but—"

"The only person who needs to buy in is you." He sat down. "Should I be worried about you, Lane-Roxie-Lane?"

She'd heard stories about Bert from Jem. About his mercurial temper, his lack of loyalty, his questionable ethical core. But he'd always been civil to Lane. Now she wondered, had his hands-off attitude toward her been a courtesy in deference to Sam? Sam who was going to be away for the next three months. She needed to keep her job. She took a breath.

"I'm good," she told Bert. "We're good."

"Good." Bert slipped a Mentho-Lyptus out of its wrapper and popped it in his mouth. He offered one to Lane.

She opened her palm. He dropped it in. She closed her hand around it. "Thanks. Saving it for later. For when I'm writing. With clarity."

He smiled and pointed at her with his two-finger gun. "Clickety click?"

She nodded and pointed back. "Clickety clickety."

"Howdy, stranger!" Hugo, who had not been at his desk when she arrived, quickly pelted her with questions. "Were you just with Bert? Did he say anything about Sam? Did you hear about Jem?"

Lane's basset-hound-eyed seatmate had already told her the news that Jem had been laid off, for reasons that sounded suspiciously vague. She'd called Jem right after she heard, to offer the name of one of the attorneys she consulted for her column, the one who specialized in workplace discrimination. "I'm not saying you have a reason to sue," Lane explained. "But why not talk it through with a lawyer to be sure?" Jem had agreed. As for what Hugo was referring to when he asked about Sam, Lane had no idea. "I thought Sam was away working on Guild-Europe. Unless—is there something I don't know?"

"Just rumors"—he lowered his voice—"that he might not be coming back."

That was an alarming thought. "Don't listen to rumors," she told Hugo and herself.

"The thing is . . ." He looked around to make sure they were alone. "Bert without Sam is a nightmare. People are starting to bolt. Do you think I should leave? Or should I wait it out? I mean it's awful here, but at least I have time. To write." He whispered the next. "I'm working on a play." He lifted up his phone to show her. "If I start a new job, I won't be able to—"

The double doors whooshed open. "Hugo." It was Bert. "I need you. Now."

"Don't wait it out," Lane advised under her breath.

Hugo pasted on a smile and jogged over to where Bert was waiting. "How can I help?"

There were delays on the A, C, B, and D lines. By the time a train finally came there were no seats left. Lane snagged a leaning spot at the door at the rear of the car. A team of buskers boarded and brushed by doing backflips and spins around the poles. Everyone's dead eyes stayed stuck on their phones. When they finished and walked the car with their hats out for money, Lane thought about how Aaron would have put in a dollar. She thought about how often his dollar made the people around him reach into their pockets. She didn't have any dollars on her so like everyone else she stared at her phone, half reading an article she'd clicked through from the Guild home page. Your Child Is Stressed: The News Could Be Good.

A muffled announcement came over the speaker. She turned to a woman standing near her. "What did she say?"

"Who knows?" The woman shrugged. "Guess we're going express. Next stop, 137th Street."

Lane peered out the window as the train accelerated past the 96th Street station and struggled to accept the fact that in her haste she'd gotten on the right train in the wrong direction. She pulled out her phone and called the school but there was no service between stations so she had to make do with reminding herself Henry was safe. The aftercare teacher would stay with him no matter when she picked him up. Hopefully he'd be happily drawing and wouldn't even notice she was late. Unless he was watching the clock. Henry liked to draw clocks, different kinds, different shapes. If he was drawing clocks . . . She shook off the thought but she couldn't shake off the feeling that she was failing him again.

If she were a person who wept, that's what she'd do now. She'd weep. But she wasn't a person who wept and anyway, what would weeping do? She checked her watch. Sprinting. That's what was called for. Good thing she was wearing flat shoes. Sprinting was more useful than weeping. With luck, when she got out at Times Square, if the sidewalk wasn't clogged with gangs of Elmos smoking cigarettes or people walking four abreast while taking selfies, she might get to the Port Authority in time to make her bus.

She was a fast runner. The flat shoes were a help. But she missed the bus anyway. When she got to the aftercare room, Henry was the only one there. As soon as she walked in, he looked up at her and his face lit up. She walked over and saw, with relief, that today his drawings were not of clocks. They were of buses. The Red Rooster. The Green Squirrel.

Mrs. Lindsey called over a hello and then motioned for her to come to where she was sitting, at the desk. She stopped Lane midapology. "I get it. Stuff happens. But you should know there's a strict two-strikes-you're-out policy here for late pickup. Personally I think it should be three. Two seems severe. But no one asked me. Anyway it's different for me. I live alone with a cat. Most teachers here have to get home and make dinner for their families. They have kids waiting for them. We can't leave until the last child is picked up."

"I'm so sorry," Lane told her. "It won't happen again." In the car, she apologized to Henry. "I'm sorry you had to wait, buddy."

He was looking out the window when he answered. "I wasn't waiting. I was drawing." Then he met her eyes in the rearview mirror. "How come you were late?"

"I got on the wrong subway. Can you believe it?" Henry nodded and she smiled. Then she took a breath and told him what she'd forgotten to tell him in the morning. "We're invited to a dinner at Dana's house tonight. She's making a party for us. A little party. With kids your age."

His eyes locked on hers. "Will they try and make me talk?"

"Absolutely not." Like a child she crossed her fingers; like a mother she crossed them at the bottom of the steering wheel where Henry couldn't see.

Agreeing to come to the dinner was a mistake. While none of the women in Dana's bumped-out family room seemed interested in making Henry speak, they were unanimous in their opinion that he would have a much better time if he went downstairs, where the other children were gathered under the supervision of Dana's son, Eric.

"In human years he's sixteen but he acts like he's eight," Dana said. "Kids always love him. You'll love him too," she told Henry. "Plus they have some really good food."

A peal of laughter came from the direction of the basement. Henry's head swiveled toward the stairs.

"There's red velvet cupcakes down there." It was Karin, the baker from next door. "I'm famous for them. I made biscotti for us," she told Lane.

"Up to you," Lane said quietly. "Want to have a quick cupcake and then we'll go?" He nodded and she excused herself to take him down.

The basement, which had the same layout as Lane's, was crammed with a timeline of clutter. Bins of wood blocks, stacks of kits and, against the wall, standing sports equipment: hockey and lacrosse sticks, baseball bats and shin guards, a paddle with the name of a summer camp etched on it.

In the center of the room Eric sat surrounded by children who had dug into what appeared to be an open and nearly empty dress-up trunk. So far Eric was wearing what looked like part of a hamburger costume, one clown shoe, one skeleton-hand glove, and a hula skirt. Two children stood next to him painting his hair with green glitter glue. He smiled when he noticed Henry. "Hey there. Who are you?"

"This is Henry," Lane said.

"The new kid. Cool. Hey, everybody," Eric called out. "Say hey to Henry."

Commingled voices shouted greetings and then everyone went back to what they were doing. A girl opened a Sharpie. A boy pulled the stuffing out of a sock puppet.

"Don't worry," Eric told Lane. "I'm not letting anybody do anything even remotely dangerous. But if they want to pull out some stuffing or paint my hair?" He shrugged. "Cool with me. I get a hundred bucks if everyone stays down here tonight. One person goes up, I get zero."

A boy came and asked Henry if he wanted to help him knock down a block tower. Henry looked up at Lane for permission.

"Want me to stay down here?"

"He'll be fine," Eric said.

Henry confirmed this by running with the boy toward a high tower of precariously arranged wood blocks.

"He doesn't speak," Lane told Eric quietly.

"Cool," Eric said.

"If he needs me, I'm right upstairs."

"Got it."

She hesitated. Henry noticed and waved goodbye.

"Fabbo," Dana said, when Lane returned upstairs alone. "I made you a plate." She handed it over. "I knew Henry would love Eric. Everyone loves Eric. Come sit."

Lane returned to her seat and balanced her plate on her lap. She tried to think of something to say but came up blank. She was always a failure at small talk.

"So." Rory the dentist sat next to her. Lane felt herself relax. The conversational reins had been picked up. "What happened that night all those cops came?"

Of course. Word had gotten around. Everyone was wondering. "There was a mix-up," she said and then stopped. Best to leave it at that.

A woman whose name eluded her sat down in a chair across from her. "I heard it was Francesca." The woman turned to the crowd. "Francesca went missing. And the cops came. And a bunch of teachers went over to help. Mrs. Abramowitz told me," she confessed. "She was there. Francesca's teacher was there too. And the gym teacher, I heard."

"I just love this town," Dana said. "Something goes wrong, everybody pitches in to help."

"It was a mix-up," Lane said again. "Her mother asked me to take her to book group and when we got back to her house the cops were there. They thought she'd been kidnapped. I don't really know what happened. Francesca's aunt was there when I picked her up. I told her aunt we were going to book group."

"Weird," Karin said. "What did Claudine say?"

"I never heard from her."

Karin looked puzzled. "You didn't call her?"

Now everyone looked puzzled.

"No. Claudine asked me to take Francesca to book group," Lane said. "And then the police accused me of kidnapping. I thought it was on Claudine to call me."

"On Claudine?" a woman repeated.

"On the aunt, maybe," Rory said.

"I know the aunt," Karin said. "She's definitely weird."

"All's well that ends well," Dana said. "If you think about it, the way we all rush around from one thing to another it's a miracle there aren't more mix-ups like that. You know what I'm upset about?" She turned to Lane. "Your house. I honestly cannot believe all the things that have gone wrong in there. And it's not like Nathan didn't take care of it. He did."

"Just the surface," Karin muttered. "Remember when his driveway cracked? Right down the middle? He never got it repaved. He threw on some tar and called it a day. He's a patch-it-up guy is what he is."

"Karin's got a problem with Nathan," Rory said.

"I'm not the only one," Karin said.

Lane wasn't sure what she was supposed to say so she said, "Mmm."

A shouted curse rocketed up the basement stairs. Footsteps followed. Henry bolted over to Lane.

Eric was right behind him. "You cost me a hundred bucks, you little snot."

"Eric," Dana warned.

Henry looked pale. Lane pulled him closer. She heard the zoop of a text and watched as all hands moved to phones, except for hers. Right now there was nothing that would take her away from holding Henry.

"Mine," Dana announced. Everyone set their phones down. "Actually it's for you." She handed her phone to Lane. "Nathan," she told the crowd.

All eyes on her, she took Dana's phone and read the text. "My alarm went off again," she said. "Sorry. My phone must have been on silent. We need to go. I have to organize a time for the electrician to come over." She hoped Dana wouldn't challenge her. The text said her alarm went off again, but it didn't say anything about her needing to go home right now. But Dana was otherwise occupied, putting out dessert.

"Before you go . . ." Karin hurried over to the buffet and returned with a paper plate. "Sea salt and caramel biscotti. My first try at making them. Let me know what you think."

"I once lost a tooth eating caramel," a depressed-sounding woman was telling the crowd as Lane and Henry headed toward the door.

According to Henry, the problem in the basement was that he didn't have a hundred dollars.

"They have a *toe*," he explained.

"What do you mean?"

"A *toe*. Like the kind you pay when you go over a bridge or in a tunnel."

"You mean a toll?"

He nodded. "Eric said if anyone wanted to use the stairs before it was time to leave, they had to pay him a hundred dollars. But I didn't have any dollars. So I had to wait for you to know I wanted to leave. But you didn't."

"I'm sorry." She laid a hand on Henry's head and gently twirled one of his curls around her finger. "But you left anyway. You didn't listen to Eric. That was brave."

"I listened until he went to the bathroom and then I stopped listening. I tried to make my feet *tread lightly* on the stairs, like in Grandma Sylvie's Rule Number Four. But it didn't work. They have a squeaky step. Probably so no one leaves without paying the *toe*."

Tread Lightly So You Don't Leave Tracks. Another rule Lane didn't remember sharing.

"You know what, buddy? What Eric told you about the toll—he made that up. He said that because his mom promised to give him a hundred dollars if no one went upstairs. I'm really proud that you left anyway. If you feel uncomfortable somewhere, you leave."

"Like when we felt uncomfortable in the apartment and we left? Rule Number Two?"

Move Forward and Never Look Back. It was unnerving, Henry knowing so many of her mother's rules. Had he overheard her discussing them with Shelley? Where was Shelley? They hadn't spoken in days.

"Do we have rules like Grandma Sylvie's?" Henry asked.

"No. I don't think her rules work very well." She stopped. She was supposed to listen carefully to Henry. "Do you want rules? Would you feel better if we made some rules?"

"I would feel better if I went to bed."

For Tell Me That Story, Henry asked for one about the time they went camping, which was another story Aaron often told him.

"We all slept in a big tent," she said to start.

"Medium-size," Henry corrected her. "And the door zipper got stuck. And the flaps got stuck. And the screens that were supposed to keep the bugs out didn't. And every time you heard a bug, Dad made a buzzing noise and said, 'No, that's just me. I'm the biggest bug here.'"

That was true. He did do that, back when things were good. She laughed remembering it.

"What else happened in that story?" Henry asked her.

Lane thought about it. "The campground was at the edge of a lake. And we had kayaks."

"Canoes," Henry said.

"Canoes. And no one else was camping there. It was quiet. Peaceful."

"Except when the loons came out," Henry said. "At night."

"Right. And they started to cry. That mournful cry. And it woke us up."

"Except not Dad," Henry said. "He stayed asleep. Even when the loons stopped crying and started laughing. And then we started laughing like loons." Henry did an imitation of his loon laugh. "And you had a laughing fit. Which made your arm hit the pole. Which made the tent come down. Which made Dad wake up. Which made him think a bear was trying to get in."

Lane laughed and then Henry laughed and soon they were both laughing, hard—Henry so hard tears started coming out of his eyes. And then he was crying.

"You miss your dad, don't you?" He nodded. Lane nodded and held him closer. "I miss him too." She didn't admit that this was the first time she'd felt this way since Aaron died, that until this moment she'd actually forgotten how much she loved him.

When Henry asked if they could go back to the Old New Normal, Lane said, "Of course," and Henry scooted over so there'd be room for her, just for tonight, in his bed.

16

The next morning Lane toggled between a phone conference with a lawyer—his advice was that her reader try to work with her homeowners' association rather than continuing to confront the cigar smoker next door—and emails with the social worker who was putting together a list of patients' rights for her reader who was fighting the hospital she believed was discharging her mother too soon. She finished her last call and headed to the gym. Today's swimming goal wasn't big; she just wanted to get in a half hour before she met Henry at the bus. The new gym was less than a mile away, but she still hadn't found time to swim since the day she joined.

The gym had no bells and whistles, which was fine with her. She briefly stretched her calves at the wall—a prevention tip for cramps she'd read about on a swimming blog—and lowered herself into the water. The temperature was a little warm, but it would do.

On the first lap she thought about the house in East Aurora, which surprised her. They didn't live in that house for very long. Several breaths later she realized why the memory had come. This pool, with its overchlorinated water and temperature a few degrees past the edge of too warm, reminded her of the pool where she'd taken lessons when they lived in East Aurora. She did the calculation; she was ten at the time.

Another memory came. There was a problem in East Aurora. Something with the neighbors. Something with Uncle Albie. Yes, now she remembered. Uncle Albie had a bad bout of the blahs in East Aurora. So bad that he had to stay in the hospital overnight. And then—what? There was some kind of mix-up when he came back. Right—when he came back, he somehow ended up at the wrong house, and the people who lived in that house weren't pleased.

Second lap. East Aurora was also where there was that Christmas cookie swap on their block, which her mother refused to join. Or maybe it was that they didn't invite her mother to join. Either way, what she remembered was that people kept coming to the door. Ringing the bell and banging on the door. And there were phone calls. Lots of phone calls at all hours. Shelley would probably know more. Maybe next time Shelley called—

Ow. The cramp came without warning. Lane stopped swimming and grabbed her foot to straighten out her curling toes.

A lady in a pink swim cap bobbed over. "This is a no-treading zone."

Lane glanced at the clock on the wall, a large LED timer used at swim meets and by people trying to improve their personal bests. She was nowhere near completing her half-hour goal.

The lady in the pink cap was now bemoaning a general decline in etiquette, not just in pools but everywhere. "It used to be that swimmers cared what other swimmers—"

"Mmm," Lane said and then, "Sorry. Got to go." She turned and, breathing through the pain, did a quick sidestroke to the edge and hoisted herself out.

Her cramp was gone and forgotten, her foot fine, by the time she met Henry's bus but Henry didn't seem fine. And it wasn't because of Silas. Just as Claudine had predicted, Silas had moved away a week after he'd bothered Henry on the bus.

"You okay?" she asked as they walked home.

He nodded but seemed subdued.

"Something happen on the bus?" He shook his head. "Something happen at school?" He shook his head again, but this time in a way that let her know her questions were annoying him so she stopped.

As soon as they got home, Henry asked if there was anything special for snack. There wasn't, so Lane offered what there was: two chocolate chip cookies, the last in the box.

Henry nibbled slowly. A mouse could have finished the cookies quicker. When he was done he scrunched up his napkin into a ball and said, "Mabel isn't allowed in our car."

"Why not?" And then, "Who's Mabel?"

"She sits behind me. It's because she asked Francesca if it was true that you kidnapped her and Francesca said yes." He wiped his eyes with his sleeve. "I wanted to tell Mabel that Francesca wasn't saying the story right because the police explained it was a big *mix-understanding*. But my mouth wouldn't listen to me so I couldn't."

Lane took a breath. "That sounds like it must have been hard."

Henry nodded. "Did you ever fake kidnap me? Mabel said she heard you once did that."

"I don't even know what that means."

"Fake kidnapping is when someone pretends to kidnap you so they can get money. That's what Mabel said she heard you did. Francesca said she heard it too. She's not allowed in our car either."

"Francesca isn't allowed in our car? Since when?"

Henry shrugged his shoulders and closed his eyes and when he opened them again they were wet and full. "I tried to whisper to Francesca that you never kidnapped anybody and that what happened with her was a big *mix-understanding*. But she put her hands over her ears and screamed and then Miss Fiske ran over. Miss Fiske was really mad. She told Francesca to take her hands off her ears *right now*. So she did. Then she told Miss Fiske she was only holding her hands on her ears so I wouldn't whisper in them anymore. She doesn't like it when I do that."

Lane took Henry's hand. "I'm so sorry, buddy." His hand was damp from wiping his eyes.

"Mabel asked Miss Fiske if she knew that Francesca got kidnapped by you and Miss Fiske reminded her that in our class we have a rule that no one can talk about something if they weren't there when it happened. She said, 'If you weren't there it's called gossip and there is no gossip allowed in my room.'"

Lane forced herself to breathe. "That sounds like a good rule."

"It is but it didn't work because Francesca said she *was* there the night you kidnapped her so it's not gossip when she talks about it."

"What did Miss Fiske say to that?"

"She said a lot of people were there that night and that's beside the point because the point is a new point, which is adding." He stopped and nibbled his cookie.

"What does that mean?"

"You know. Adding. She clapped her hands five times to get everyone's attention and asked, 'Who here knows how to add numbers in your head?'"

Lane nodded. "Sounds like a tough afternoon. You know what, buddy? I'm going to email Miss Fiske. I think we need to have a talk about this. And Mrs. Lindsey. And Francesca's mother."

"I don't think that's a good idea. Francesca's mom is mad at me. Everyone is mad at me. I think I should go draw."

Lane started to protest but Henry had decided what he wanted so she said, "Okay buddy. Good idea. Go ahead and draw."

He retreated to the living room. He liked to draw there in the late afternoon because of the way the light came in through the back window. He stayed drawing quietly until the doorbell rang. At the sound of that, he grabbed his sketch pad.

As Lane went to answer the door Henry, sketch pad close to his chest, ran upstairs. She felt another chip break off her heart. When she opened the door, there was Nathan, with the contractor who'd come to check on the electrical panel.

In the basement, the contractor identified the problem right away. "This here's your culprit." He pointed to the wire stapled around the periphery of the electrical box. "See this white part? Rust. Copper pipes rust green. Steel rusts red. White rust? Aluminum. With a house this age that means someone took out your copper wires and put in aluminum. Which is cheaper. But rusty aluminum wiring?" He shook his head. "Not a good thing. If it were me, I'd replace it. Fast."

"Okay." Nathan turned to Lane. "You can't stay here. I'll book you a room in a hotel. I'll help find you another house. A safe house."

"This is not an emergency situation," the contractor told Nathan. "You guys don't need to move," he told Lane. "You need to replace the wires. Probably the box too, now that I'm looking. I mean if you want a bigger house, a bigger yard, a warmer climate, be my guest. Move. But you'll still have to fix this. Rusty wiring is going to be a problem for inspection."

"Oh, we're not—" Lane started.

"Together," Nathan finished. "I'm not that lucky. I'm just the landlord."

"I'm just the contractor telling you, you got a problem. It's wear and tear. Nothing fatal."

"Story of my life," Lane said.

Nathan offered a lopsided smile. "I'm really sorry."

The thought popped into her head that someone at Dana's house didn't like him. One of the neighbors. Maybe more than one. Why? It didn't matter. "You didn't know."

"He couldn't know," the contractor said. "It's an old house. With a house like this, it's all about what's behind the walls. You can't know anything until you open up the walls. Old walls can hide cracks, corrosion—"

"Be nice." Nathan grinned. "You think you'll be young forever? A hundred and twelve years from now when you're my age you'll be relieved if the worst you are is corroded."

Lane laughed and Nathan told the contractor how he wanted to proceed. "To make it safe, to do it right, how long will it take?"

The contractor smiled. "I always tell my wife, I got two kinds of customers. The ones who want to know how much and the ones who want to know how long. He's a good one," he told Lane. "Let me take a look around. But I won't know anything for sure until—"

"You open up the walls," Lane and Nathan said together.

The contractor left to see what he could see.

"Come out to dinner with me," Nathan said. "You and Henry. An apology dinner. For my house falling apart on you."

"Thank you but Henry doesn't like restaurants. He doesn't like to talk to strangers." She stopped to consider about how much more she needed to share.

"Perfect. I know just the place."

Which is how Lane, Henry and Nathan ended up at a small café where Henry got to pick out his dinner from a well-stocked wall of grab and go shelves. It was the perfect choice for him. The café had the feel of a large family kitchen with walls filled with shelves of cookbooks and a center island that held tin trays for people to use to carry stoneware ceramic plates and vintage flatware to their table. Sturdy glasses sat beside help-yourself jugs of water, lemonade and iced tea. No interaction required.

It was over dinner that Nathan told Henry about his job doing voices for video games. "Only evil ones," Nathan shared. "Can you believe it? In real life I'm a good guy but in video games I'm evil all the time. Want to hear?"

Henry nodded.

Nathan cleared his throat. "*Lock him in the dungeon and drop that key into the moat.* That's my evil king. I also have an evil emperor and a bunch of evil knights. *Scottish knight. French knight. Knight from the planet Vlargh.*" He add a snarl to that one. Henry laughed. Nathan met Lane's eyes and smiled.

She felt herself blush and smiled back. She really knew nothing about this man except that he had a gentle way with Henry, which was pretty much all she needed to know.

"I really want to play a hero," Nathan told them. "I keep asking my boss and he keeps saying no. Does that seem fair to you?"

Henry smiled and shook his head and Lane said, "Not at all."

"I know. But I don't complain. Because—" He leaned forward to whisper his secret. "The evil guys get the best lines. Besides, what can I do? I was born with a good voice for evil. You were born with a knack for drawing."

Lane expected Henry, who'd spent a good part of dinner quietly drawing, to close his sketch pad but instead he beamed.

"You probably have a knack for a lot of things," Nathan said. "I bet you could do evil voices if you wanted. It's all in the throat. You retract your chin, you compress your neck, you get a little phlegm going on." Nathan adjusted his chin, made some phlegmy noises and growled, "*If you've done nothing wrong you shall not be punished.* Want to give it a try?"

Henry laughed and shook his head.

"I think Henry prefers to draw," Lane said. It was a hard habit to break, speaking for him.

It was after dinner, in the car on their way back to the house, that Nathan gave them a heads-up. "Just a warning: this probably won't happen, but if we bump into each other on the street tomorrow and I look like I don't know who you are, it's because I'm a little face blind." He looked at Henry in the rearview mirror. "You know what that is?" Henry shook his head. "It's when you have a hard time recognizing faces. Some people have it really bad. They can't even recognize their own face." Henry looked wide-eyed. "I don't have it like that. But it has happened that I've run into people who I know who recognize me and I have no idea who they are. Apparently, from what people tell me, it's extremely annoying. It's better than it used to be. I've developed some tricks that help. I'm good at recognizing voices, for one. And smiles." He directed the next to Henry. "I always recognize kids. No problems there. I have no idea why."

Henry looked relieved to hear it.

Back at the house the electrician was gone and an envelope with an estimate was poking out of the mail slot. Nathan took it, thanked Lane again for being understanding about the repairs, and said good night.

When he turned to leave he looked up and stopped. "Check out that moon. Looks like a fingernail in the sky."

Henry looked up. He held out his arm and pointed his finger at the moon to compare.

"Wow," Nathan said. "You and the moon. Perfect match."

Seeing how much Henry liked Nathan, Lane could feel herself being drawn to him too. For Henry it was probably all about missing his dad. But for her—she had no idea. She hadn't felt anything for anyone in a long while.

"I should go," Nathan said. "School night, right?"

Lane nodded. "Come on, buddy. Time to go in."

Henry shuffled, slowly, toward the house. He started to unzip his jacket and slowed even more. He seemed to be unzipping one zipper tooth at a time. He was moving in the right direction but his steps were getting smaller and smaller until he stopped. At first Lane thought it was a ploy to delay going in. Then she noticed he was yanking the zipper, hard. It was stuck.

"Can I help?" she offered.

With a curt shake of his head, he ran over to Nathan, lifted his chin in the air and pointed to the pull.

"Do you mind?" Nathan asked Lane. She told him she didn't. Nathan tried to yank the zipper, first up, then down, but it wouldn't budge. "Can you wriggle out?" he asked.

Henry tried. He got his jacket over his head and wormed it up as far as his ears but he couldn't get it any farther than that. Arms up, head covered, he stomped around the lawn like Frankenstein's monster and walked into a tree.

"You okay?" Lane called to him.

The jacket nodded.

"May I give it one more try?" Nathan asked. The jacket nodded again. As Nathan worked on the zipper he ran through the voices of his characters: Evil queen. Evil warlord. Evil jacket manufacturer. *"I will make zippers that no one can remove."*

The jacket laughed hard and continued laughing right up until the moment the zipper budged and then caught. Henry howled. Lane ran over and saw the zipper was gripping a tiny bit of the skin on Henry's neck. He howled again as Lane tried to move it.

"Stop that!"

She turned and saw her neighbor, Karin, standing at the edge of her lawn.

"What are you doing to him?"

"Trying to get his coat off," Lane said. "His zipper's jammed. I think we need to cut it off, buddy." She turned to Karin. "Do you have a pair of scissors I could borrow?"

Karin raced into her house and didn't come back out.

Nathan asked Lane where she kept her scissors and then ran into her house and found them. By the time she was finished releasing

Henry, remnants of his coat were scattered across the lawn: strips of fleece, pieces of hood, two sides of a defanged zipper.

"What is wrong with her?" Lane said, eyeing her neighbor's house while she gathered the torn pieces of Henry's coat.

"She's not crazy about me," Nathan said.

"Right. So I heard. Because she's friends with your ex."

"Correct. You know how divorces go. Maybe you don't. Let's just say it didn't end well. Karin was not thrilled when I moved in next door. Probably popped open a bottle of champagne when I moved out." He shrugged. "Life."

Lane shrugged. "People."

Nathan smiled and turned to Henry. "Methinks," he said, and turned his voice into a growl, *"the lady next door gives off the stench of anger something fierce. Do you not smell it, my liege?"*

Henry smiled while he rubbed his throat.

"We better go in," Lane told him and then watched in astonishment as he ran over to Nathan and gave him a hug.

They both watched Henry run inside.

"He's not just shy, right?" Nathan asked. "He doesn't talk."

"Only to me," Lane admitted. "Only when we're alone. Just since my husband died. January. According to the professionals I'm not supposed to worry. It's usually self-resolving. Grieving takes time."

"Sounds hard. If there's anything I can do—"

"Thanks," Lane said. "We're good. Totally good." She hurried inside in case Nathan could tell from the expression on her face that she wasn't as sure as she sounded.

As soon as Lane got back from the bus stop the next morning, she sent an email to the resource room teacher requesting a conference. After she pressed *Send*, she glanced at her phone and saw that she'd missed a call. She listened to the message.

"See?" It was Shelley. "This is why I don't call you at a normal time. You don't pick up. We need to talk. Call me."

Her sister must have called during the hubbub of bus stop good-byes, the parents herding their children onto the bus with last-minute instructions: *Have fun. Don't forget to hand in your permission slip. Tell your teacher she needs to help you find your hat.*

She quickly dialed her sister's number but the call went directly to voice mail. Did Shelley do this on purpose? Tell her to call right back and then not pick up? She left her a message. "Sorry I missed your call. I was getting Henry off to school. I'm here now. Call me." She took a breath, switched her focus to her laptop and opened the folder of curated *Ask Roxie* letters that had just arrived from Summer. She scrolled down the list.

Dear Roxie, This country is going down the toilet.

Dear Roxie, My neighbor says I'm praying to the wrong god.

Dear Roxie, My mother never asks me what I want for dinner.

It was amazing how thoroughly Summer had ignored her directions. Lane had only requested a few things, having sensed early on that Summer was one of those people who was allergic to negativity and ter-rified of screwing up. In the end all she'd asked was for her to remember the three kinds of letters Roxie would not answer: letters about politics, letters about religion, letters that were boring. Yet that's exactly what Summer had sent. Lane deleted them all.

And why had Summer bothered to ask her for a list of pet topics? Lane didn't have pet topics, at least not that she was aware of, but she had dutifully given it some thought and sent Summer a short list: mar-ginalized children, difficult parents, toxic gossip. Yet Summer had not sent her a single letter that addressed any of that.

An email floated by the top of her screen. Summer again. A sec-ond folder of vetted letters. Lane opened the folder and skimmed the contents. Again, she deleted them all. She trashed the next email too, from the media trainer Bert hired to help her with the podcast she wasn't going to do. The email after that one was from Bert. She noted the all-caps subject line: WHY AREN'T YOU ON EEZE?

She skimmed the email and forwarded it to Sam along with a note: *Can we speak? Today if possible?* Seconds after sending it, her email bounced back with a *delivery failure* notice in the subject line. Was the rumor Hugo told her true? Was it possible that Sam left the Guild? If he had, what did it mean for her?

What it meant was she needed to get better at managing Bert and she needed to get better at mentoring Summer. Most of all she needed to keep her job. The realization hit her like a punch to the gut. She would have had options, if she were a different person, the kind of person who'd kept up with the editors who used to give her work, the kind of person who'd meet them for lunch or drinks, who'd email now and then to see how they were, who'd post birthday wishes on Facebook and like their Instagram feeds, who'd send over flowers for promotions and weddings and funerals. But she did none of those things. She'd let all her precious contacts drift away, even those who'd made a deliberate effort to reach out and keep in touch.

Now what? There were not many places for someone like her, an advice columnist with a well-earned reputation for being uncomfortable in person. She couldn't afford to add to that a reputation for being difficult at work.

Her phone rang and she relaxed immediately. She always felt better talking to Shelley. But it wasn't Shelley.

"This is Arlene," the voice said. "Principal Oppido's assistant. Don't worry. Nothing's wrong. But Miss Oppido would like to talk to you. Can you come in?"

Lane looked at her calendar. "Sure. Next week is pretty open. What day is good?"

"Today," Arlene said. "Today is good. Can you come in now?"

17

Lane had just finished reading the secretary's desk plate, No need to repeat yourself. I ignored you fine the first time, and moved on to reading the sign framed on the wall behind the desk, I can only help one person a day. Today is not your day. Tomorrow doesn't look good either, when a short heavyset woman walked out of a large supply cabinet, dropped a pile of folders on the desk and plopped into the chair. Her cheeks dimpled as she smiled. "You are?"

"Lane. Lane Meckler. Arlene?"

"Yes. Great. Please." She gestured toward the three metal folding chairs that sat against the pale-green wall. "Have a seat."

The door to the principal's office swung open. A set of parents gushed out. "Thank you," the man said and the woman echoed, "Thank you so much."

"Don't thank me," Miss Oppido replied. She was tall and spindly with thin gray hair pulled tight off her face. "You are the heroes who made her."

Lane hadn't realized her shoulders had lifted toward her ears until she felt them drop. Apparently not every meeting with the principal was about a problem. Maybe today the principal wanted to share good news about Henry.

But when Arlene called out Lane's name, Miss Oppido's expression turned businesslike. Two teachers peeled away from a group that had been chatting in a huddle near the mailboxes. None of them looked happy to be here.

Okay. The news was not going to be good.

Miss Oppido's desk chair appeared to have been adjusted so that she was perched at a higher elevation than everyone else. Lane was wondering whether that was intentional—or could the chair's instruction booklet have been poorly translated from another language?—when she realized introductions had begun.

She tried to catch up. She'd missed the name of the teacher from the district child study team but she recognized the other teacher, Mrs. Abramowitz, the school counselor who'd been at Francesca's the night of the book group fiasco. Lane wondered if anyone had told Mrs. Abramowitz that what happened that night was not her fault.

"Mrs. Lindsey couldn't join us today," Miss Oppido told Lane. "She's filling in over at the high school. She's very fond of Henry, you know. We all are," she quickly added. "We're sympathetic to what he's been through. That being said, things have progressed—"

Lane sat up straighter. Progress was a good thing, but Miss Oppido was not pleased.

"To more troubling behavior," she concluded.

The door opened and Miss Fiske hurried in. "Sorry. Couldn't find anyone to cover for me. I asked Madame," she told the principal. "She got all huffy. She said language teachers don't cover but she'd make an exception this one time. I mean . . . really?"

Miss Oppido scribbled on a pad. "I'll have a word with her."

"What do you mean by troubling behavior?" Lane asked.

Miss Fiske raised her hand. Miss Oppido seemed happy to cede the floor. "Touching behavior," Miss Fiske said and then quickly added,

"Not that way. I mean hugging. Lots of hugging. Tight hugging. Mostly Francesca. Who doesn't like it." Lane heard the rest as if through a scrim. ". . . to make sure there's nothing happening at home that we don't . . . We have many resources we can offer once we're sure that . . ."

The door opened again. This time, the nurse. Henry didn't like the nurse and the nurse didn't like him back. Her main complaint—she'd said those words to Lane, *my main complaint*—was that Henry refused to tell her what was hurting when he came to see her.

Lane had met with the nurse the week Henry started school. She'd given her suggestions for how to handle Henry's silence, even though they were things she thought the nurse should already know. Instead of asking open-ended questions like how do you feel, ask questions that could be answered with a nod or a shake of the head. "Or you could ask Henry to draw how he feels," she'd said.

The nurse had bristled. "I don't go for that kind of tomfoolery."

Miss Oppido was saying something again. Lane was having a hard time staying focused.

". . . mind telling Henry's mom what you saw?"

"Of course." The nurse turned to Lane. "This morning I saw a bruise." She put two fingers on a spot between her collarbones. "On Henry's jugular notch."

It took a moment for Lane to figure out what the nurse was referring to. "That? Oh, that's from his zipper. Last night it got stuck. And then it got caught on his skin. Pinched his throat. I had to cut his coat off."

"That's from a zipper?" The nurse's fingers hadn't moved from her throat.

"Yes?" Was this an intervention? "What did you think it was from?"

"I asked Henry," the nurse reported. "He wouldn't say."

"Well now we know," Miss Oppido said. "It's from his zipper." She thanked the nurse, who left, looking skeptical. "Zipper aside, we have concerns about Henry's behavior."

"It's because the hugging is something new," Mrs. Abramowitz added. "New behaviors can be a sign of a new problem. Maybe something at home?"

"He's fine at home," Lane said. "It's at school that he's anxious."

The child study consultant nodded. "Exactly. That's the problem. Anxiety."

"I've gotten calls," Miss Oppido said.

Calls. Plural. "What kind of calls?"

"Complaints." She took off her glasses. "From Francesca's mom. Multiple complaints."

Suddenly the room felt hot. Lane turned to Miss Fiske. "You realize Claudine is the person responsible for the mix-up after book group. I don't know who called the police that night but I know that Claudine forgot that she asked me to take Francesca with us. She asked *me*."

Miss Fiske nodded. "I see that you're upset. Maybe that's the problem. You're still upset about something that happened weeks ago. Maybe Henry's picking up on that."

Lane shook her head. "What Henry's picking up on is that Francesca keeps telling people I kidnapped her. Look, I'm not saying anything against Francesca. She's a child. But I think she has some issues. She's the one who needs the intervention. Not punishment. Help." All eyes were on her now, none of them friendly.

The principal spoke first. "Francesca's issues are not why we asked you to come in. We're here to talk about Henry."

"Okay." Lane leaned back in her chair. "What do you recommend?"

What they recommended came in a packet that Mrs. Abramowitz presented to her. There were pamphlets to read, assessment forms to fill out and instructions for how to set up a follow-up meeting using the parent portal.

Miss Oppido stood up. "I'm confident this can be resolved. So long as we work together." She reached out her hand and Lane shook it.

As she walked out of the principal's office she riffled through the packets. CHILDREN AND PERSONAL SPACE. STRATEGIES FOR MANAGING ANGER. WHO DOES STRESS HURT MOST? When she passed Arlene, she met her eyes.

"I don't make the problems," Arlene said. "I just make the appointments."

Lane felt her throat tighten and a strange sensation came to her eyes. No. She was not someone who cried, but even if she was, she most certainly would not cry here, in front of Arlene, who'd just taped up a new sign: NO COFFEE, NO WORKEE.

A bell rang. Lane looked up at the large clock. The minute hand jigged to the next number. It was ten minutes till dismissal.

"I'm going to get Henry," Lane said.

Arlene shrugged. "I'm not stopping you."

When Lane got to Henry's classroom, she saw Madame, the covering teacher, sitting at the desk reading a novel. The title was in French. She had no idea how long Madame had been reading—or how she managed to concentrate on her book—while the class devolved into a *Lord of the Flies* situation. To Lane's relief, Henry did not appear to be a character in this particular drama. He was in the back of the room, in the small free-play area, building a fort of blocks.

The main event, as far as Lane could tell, involved Francesca and a girl who was teasing her. Francesca, Lane saw, was crying. The girl teasing her, small, with delicate features and a shrill voice, was surrounded by a troop of what looked like eager and obedient sidekicks.

"You're not allowed to play with us," the shrill girl told Francesca. Several of her minions began repeating her words in a loop without pause. Lane wondered if the girl had made up this rule, or if she was repeating something her teacher had said. Francesca could be difficult, but that was no excuse for anyone, especially a teacher, to make a rule of exclusion.

She glanced at Henry, who remained focused on his fort. Judging by its height, she guessed he'd been at it for some time. She wondered whether this was a good thing, her son diligently locking himself in behind a tall wall. She didn't dwell on it because Francesca's crying now turned into sobs. She sounded bereft. She waved her hand in the air, as if she were desperate for Madame, who was still reading, to call on her.

Once again Lane was reminded how despite all the noise that came out of Francesca's mouth, she had tiny hands; the hands of a child. She was a child. A child being teased so hard, she was turning into a puddle of misery.

Lane called out, "Francesca, are you okay?"

At the sound of her voice the children froze, except for Henry, who hearing his mother speak in a classroom where mothers were not allowed, stood up so suddenly his fort collapsed around him. Several children laughed at the sight of Henry surrounded by tumbled blocks.

Francesca's small hands turned into hard fists and she let out a scream. The children blithely put their fingers in their ears and waited for it to pass.

Madame looked alarmed. Apparently she didn't know Francesca. Perhaps Francesca took another language. Spanish or Chinese.

"Arrête!" Madame shouted, bolting up from her trance. She noticed Lane in the doorway. "Who are you?"

It was then that Miss Oppido walked in, with Miss Fiske hurrying behind. Lane saw the two of them take in the scene: Madame screaming, "Arrête!" Francesca shrieking full blast. Henry ashen-faced in the middle of his collapsed fort. Children with fingers plugged in their ears. Lane frozen in the doorway.

Miss Oppido clapped her hands. "What on earth is going on here?"

Francesca stopped screaming.

Madame walked over to where the principal was standing. "One minute the children were playing quietly. The next minute a girl was screaming and this woman was standing in the doorway, yelling."

Miss Oppido turned to Lane. "Why are you here?"

"To pick up Henry."

"You can't do that," Miss Fiske chided her. "Just show up and take your child. We have rules about pickup at dismissal."

Miss Oppido swiveled on her pumps. "Follow me."

Lane followed the principal down the hall and out the double doors of the school to the bullpen where the parents whose children didn't take the bus waited. Lane scanned the crowd of people she didn't know and people she'd briefly met whose names she'd already forgotten.

For a moment, conversations stopped, the parents taking note of the mom being escorted out of the building by the principal. Then it started up again. It seemed to Lane that everyone was engaged in animated conversation with a dismissal-time buddy. Everyone but her.

They were both quiet in the car on the way home, but as soon as they got inside Henry asked, "Do you need to cry? If you need to cry, you should. Otherwise you'll get stopped up, right?"

He paid such close attention to everything. "I don't need to cry. But thank you for asking. That's sweet. I have a question for you." She touched his head, felt his curls, felt his warmth and asked, "Have you been hugging Francesca?"

Henry looked at his shoes. "Yes."

She nodded. "So, hugging is a great thing when both people want to hug. But if one person does and the other person doesn't, it's not okay."

"I know," Henry said. "I don't like it when people hug me. Unless it's you."

"Exactly. I love when you hug me and I love to hug you. You can hug me anytime you want. But today I learned that Francesca doesn't like it when you hug her. So you have to stop."

"I don't want to hug her. I only hug her because she told me to."

"What do you mean?"

"She told me that she'd stop telling Mabel you kidnapped her if I hugged her. So I did. Then I heard her tell Jasmine you kidnapped her, so I ran over and hugged her again, harder, since the first time I hugged her it didn't work. Then she got mad and she told Miss Fiske. Miss Fiske gave me a talk about, Do I Know What Personal Space Is and Do I Know Hugging Francesca is Inappropriate."

She took in how he slowly said the word, *Inappropriate*, making sure he got every syllable right. "Did you tell Miss Fiske that you hugged Francesca because she asked you to?"

"I wanted to but my mouth didn't work." Henry studied his feet for a moment and then asked if he could go draw.

Lane blinked her dry eyes. "Want to do something together? Maybe bake cookies." She suddenly realized they didn't have ingredients to make cookies. "We'll have to go to the store first but that could be fun. Or we could go for a bike ride." She suddenly remembered she didn't have a bike. "You could go for a bike ride while I run beside you. Or we could drive to the nature preserve. Want to go for a hike?" She wished she had hiking shoes, or a bike, or ingredients for cookies.

"No thank you. I'd like to draw."

"Can I draw with you?"

"I think today I'd like to draw alone."

"Of course. Have fun." She watched as Henry disappeared to draw in the living room. Watching him go, her body felt heavy. Heavyhearted. She found her phone and called the only person she had to whom she would share that feeling but Shelley didn't pick up. She checked the time. Of course she didn't pick up. In England it was the middle of the night. Who was she kidding? Even if it were the middle of the day, Shelley never picked up.

After dinner Henry asked, "Do we have anything special for dessert?"

Another regret. She should have stocked up on snacks and desserts. There was nothing. She was not keeping up. She was just getting by, getting through her day, meeting Henry's bus on time, giving Summer enough of what she needed so that she would have nothing negative to report. But things were falling through the cracks. And it wasn't just special snacks and desserts and ingredients for cookies. Earlier in the day she noticed they were down to the last package of toilet tissue. Except for one pair of socks with a heel so thin it was transparent, all of Henry's socks and underwear were sitting in the laundry room sorter, waiting for her to do a wash. There was now only enough milk in the refrigerator for a single bowl of cereal. Tomorrow Lane would have to make do with drinking her coffee black.

Maybe there was something for dessert she'd missed. She opened the freezer hoping for a forgotten pint of ice cream but they hadn't been in the house long enough for ice cream to be forgotten. "Sorry, buddy. We're all out. There's nothing for dessert."

"Wait." Henry ran over to the counter and found a paper plate covered with foil. "What about this?"

Lane had forgotten about her neighbor Karin's biscotti. "Would you like one? Do you like caramel?" Henry nodded and took one and Lane did the same.

"I like it," she said. She wasn't totally lying. She liked the salty caramel flavor. But the biscotti was stale. Still, better than nothing, she thought, until her last bite when her tooth broke.

Unlike Lane's sister, Rory the dentist always answered her phone. "Come on over. I'll take a look."

It didn't take long for Rory to assess the situation. "It's an avulsion. But don't worry. I can take care of it. Want to come in my car? Or we could meet at the office. It's just ten minutes away."

"You mean now?" Lane asked and Rory nodded. "It can wait till morning. I'm not—"

"If you want to save that tooth, don't wait. It's really not a big deal. I end up at my office one night a week at least. Sometimes two. You'd be surprised how often people have dental emergencies."

Lane drove to Rory's office so she could have more time to convince Henry that just because he'd come up with the idea of having biscotti for dessert, it didn't mean it was his fault that her tooth broke. "That tooth's been bothering me for months," she told him. "I shouldn't have ignored it. That's on me, not you. Okay?" His nod was not convincing.

She'd failed him again. She failed him every day. Every day in a different way. Today because she'd bitten down on a biscotti with a tooth she'd been neglecting. Now, instead of getting into pajamas and listening to a Tell Me That Story he was being schlepped to the dentist.

The tooth was not the problem. The problem was there wasn't a single person she felt comfortable calling to ask to stay with Henry for an hour while she took care of a dental emergency. Her shoulders sank. She'd lived with this fact her whole life. Everyone in her family knew it. She did not know how to have friends. Which was fine when Lane was single and fine when Lane was married to the friendliest person she'd ever met and fine when Henry was born and Aaron was there to pick up the slack. But Aaron was gone and it wasn't fine anymore.

She looked in the rearview mirror. Henry, gazing out the window. No matter how many times she failed him, he never complained.

After they got out of the car, she noticed Henry didn't have his sketch pad. "Did you leave your sketch pad at home? We can go back and get it." She was wondering how much Rory would mind the delay when Henry interrupted her thoughts.

"It's not at home. I don't have it anymore."

"What do you mean?"

Before Henry could answer, the front door of the single-story office building swung open.

"Welcome to my world," Rory said. She motioned for them to come in.

Henry entered first, Lane close behind, both of them following Rory to her waiting room. Spotlights illuminated a wall covered with photographs of children's faces, rows of stapled Polaroids memorializing first-visit smiles, joyous and expansive, bashful and forced.

"There's some books over there," Rory told Henry. "And LEGOs over there. Believe me, you'll have more fun playing here than watching your mom's tooth get drilled. Or pulled. Hopefully not pulled. Ready?" she asked Lane.

"You want to come in with me?" Lane asked Henry. "Or play out here?"

Henry sat down at the box of LEGOs, making his choice clear. He looked forlorn. Lane pressed her lips together and forced herself to follow Rory into the exam room.

Between the sound of the drill and the noise of the instrument hooked over the side of her mouth to suck out her spit, Lane didn't realize Rory was speaking through her mask at first. It was only when she dropped her mask that Lane understood she'd just been asked a question.

The Novocain made it hard to speak. *"Pahdon?"*

"Do you think it could have anything to do with the video?"

"Pahdon?" Her body felt heavy with regret. It had taken so long for the Novocain to work—"Very sensitive nerves," Rory concluded—that

Lane's reserve of neutral conversation had been exhausted. Still, she regretted sharing that she was upset about her visit to the principal and unnerved by the teachers' complaint that Henry was hugging too much.

"I'm just guessing," Rory said. "I don't really know . . ." She went back to drilling. When the drill stopped she finished her thought. "But it just seems like maybe it could be connected to the video. I know everyone has to be super careful right now. Which is good. But for a little hug to get blown up like that. All I'm saying is, maybe the teachers saw the video and it made them think, okay, maybe Henry hugging is not a one-off thing. You know?"

Lane didn't know. She had no idea what Rory was talking about. But before she could admit that, Rory's mask was back up and her foot was tapping a pedal Lane couldn't see. The drill shrieked on. The room filled with the smell of burned tooth. Lane closed her eyes and tried to concentrate on remembering to breathe.

"Spit."

Lane spit and watched her blood-tinged spittle circle down the small drain.

"Here." Rory handed her a tissue so she could blot her mouth dry. "Could it be that the teachers think hugging is a problem for the family? Like, in some families people drink too much and in some families people hug too much? I'm just thinking out loud."

Before the drill started up again Lane touched Rory's arm. *"Wha oo you mean?"*

Rory had no trouble understanding. "I mean, is it possible Henry's teachers saw the video of you on YouTube and connected the dots? Connected them wrong."

"I ohn't oh wha you mean."

Rory laughed. "Okay. After I get this tooth fixed up, I'll show you what I mean."

When they were done, Rory shepherded Lane into the small office where she discussed root canals and suspicious growths on the phone with endodontists and throat surgeons. It took her about a minute to find what she was looking for on her computer. It took longer than that for the video to load. "Here we go." She swiveled the screen toward Lane.

It took a moment for Lane to understand what she was seeing: a video taken by one of her parents' neighbors in Florida, one of the people who'd held up their phones to capture the moment when she'd embraced the driver of the recycling truck. She could hear it in the background, people chanting, "Hug. Hug. Hug."

"How did you find this?" The thought hit her hard. "Did you google me?"

Rory laughed. "I wish I had time to google people." She stopped to think about it. "I guess someone googled you. Who first showed this to me?" she wondered aloud.

First showed it to her. More than one person, then.

Doctor Bruce was booked solid for the next few days but he offered to squeeze her in for a short video chat. Before the call, Lane sat quietly at the desk in her home office, repeating, *Do Not Sound Defensive. Do Not Sound Defensive.* The last thing she needed was for Doctor Bruce to take the school's side. Doctor Bruce told her there was only one side. Henry's side. A lot of people said that, but it never felt like any of them meant it.

The therapist didn't bother with small talk. "What's going on?"

"There's been a problem at school."

"What kind of problem?"

Being careful to sound concerned but not angry, she recounted the meeting with the principal. She described the atmosphere in the room at the meeting as hostile. She told him the nurse was alarmed by the wound that Henry got when his zipper caught on his throat. She shared what Henry had told her about Francesca asking him to hug her and how the school reported that behavior as troubling. She admitted her discomfort at her discovery that someone had googled her and shared with her neighbors a video of her hugging the recycling truck driver in Florida. Finally she reported what Henry told her when they got home from the dentist, that his teacher had taken away his sketch pad.

The doctor had been sitting perfectly still until she said that. He shifted and his eyes narrowed. "Why would she do that?"

"She said it's become a distraction. That all the children are demanding a sketch pad now. That it was out of control and it has to stop."

"That must have made Henry very upset."

"More resigned than upset."

He took that in. "Okay. The good news here? Henry's been using his drawing to communicate. You should encourage that however you can. Make sure there's always paper and art supplies available. Make sure he has access to a space at home where he can draw whenever he wants. And remember what I told you: it doesn't matter what he draws. Ask to see his drawings but don't insist. If he shows them to you, admire them no matter what. You can always ask questions and be curious. But never be critical. Prepare yourself to love the drawings equally, no matter what. This is nothing new. This is all about following his lead. Sound like something you can do?"

"Of course." She waited and then asked the question on her mind. "So that's the good news. What's the bad news?"

"How much time does he have left in the school year?"

"A few weeks."

"Okay. Here's what I recommend. Call the school and tell them you need to take Henry out for the remaining weeks of the term. Tell them you're going to homeschool him. Personal reasons, if they ask. None of their business, if they press. There'll be paperwork to fill out. Packets for him to do. There's a procedure is what I'm saying. They won't have to invent this."

Lane was confused. "Homeschooling? For three weeks? Why?"

"Structure is important for Henry. But it isn't worth destroying him. A teacher who takes away his notebook like that—without discussing it with you—that's dangerous to his well-being. If it were earlier in the school year, I'd say get him into another class. I would help you navigate it. But for three weeks? That kind of change isn't worth it. Best thing for him is to get him out of that class. Get him out as fast as you can."

18

Two seconds into the Live-Chat and already Lane was burning up, boiling-hot mad. Roxie's first ever online Live-Chat Wednesday was turning out to be exactly what she'd feared, the disaster she'd imagined from the moment Bert said it was a green-light nonnegotiable go.

"A hot-green go," were his exact words. "No opt-out option. Don't worry," he'd added. "It's going to be great. Have fun with it, Lane-Roxie-Lane. Summer will be a clickety click away. She's going to make it as easy as taking a bath."

A cold bath, maybe. Within the first two seconds she knew it wasn't working because within the first two seconds Summer had revised her intro so that now it sounded nothing like Roxie. At least not Lane's version of Roxie. The voice was wrong. The first word was wrong. *Guys!* All the words were wrong. *Guys! It's finally here! Roxie's First Ever and Most Awesome Live-Chat!*

It got worse. *Guys! I'm not kidding! We're doing it! Right now! For a whole hour! I'm here just hanging out and waiting for whatever you got! This is it, guys! Ask me anything!*

If Lane were to ask a question herself it would be, *Who are you and what have you done with Roxie?*

And where was the first question? Nothing was coming in. Nothing! What would happen if one of Bert's coveted Guild-Plus subscribers logged in now and saw nothing? Not a single question. This was a disaster.

Okay. She knew what she had to do. She had to give up on her Eeze boycott and reach out to Summer. It took a couple of tries before she logged on and was able to send Summer a message. It was the first message Lane had ever written in all caps.

WHY ARE THERE NO LETTERS?

Zoop. As if a reader had heard her complaint, a letter arrived.

Hey Roxie!

This is so cool! I do kinda feel like we're hanging out together.

So, here's my question: Paper or plastic?

LOL! Just kidding! My question is actually serious. I mean, like, super serious. Like the most serious possible. My question is: Do you have any tips for how I should tell my mom I'm pregnant? And before you get all, how old are you? I'm old enough. I'm nineteen. Which is old enough! Except not to my mom. Who is going to freak. Because I've always been a total Goody Two-shoes. I'm sure she's sure I'm a virgin. ¯_(ツ)_/¯

Before you ask, yes, the father of the baby knows and, no, he's not interested in having anything to do with it. But no biggie. He's not that great. I mean he was great for one night but not for, like, an entire life. I'm not just saying that either. I'm super excited to do this on my own. I've never done anything on my own. I don't have any regrets. I'm totally psyched. I'm going to be the coolest mom ever. So much cooler than my mom. Who I'm scared to tell. Because she's going to hate me. She's irritating beyond description, but I love her. I don't want her to hate me.

Easy one, right? LOL! Any tips?

Yours,
Baby Bump

Exhibit A. The perfect example of why a Live-Chat was a terrible idea. What was she supposed to tell this person who sounded like she was twelve? What if she was twelve? What if this was a joke? It was a joke. A joke on Roxie. And on Lane. Because she agreed to this. Roxie was live. Okay. She took a breath and typed.

Dear Baby Bump,

That was a start. Now what? She knew what she wanted to say. She wanted to say:

Dear Baby Bump, Are you out of your mind? Do you understand that once you have a child you

will need to put that child's well-being above
everything else for the rest of your life?

Or she could take the alternate route and say:

Dear Baby Bump, Are you kidding me? Is this
some kind of practical joke?

Or she could cut to the chase and straight-out ask:

Dear Baby Bump, What year were you born?

She didn't write any of that. She sat with her fingers hovering
above the keyboard until—what was happening? The cursor started to
move. She watched as her comma was deleted and an exclamation mark
arrived. Two exclamation marks. Three.

Dear Baby Bump!!!

What was happening? She'd agreed to Bert's suggestion that the
Live-Chat would be on a one-minute delay but the way Bert explained,
it was for her benefit only. A safety valve so that if she got stuck—really
stuck—Summer would rescue her. The delay was not put in place so
that Summer could insert words and punctuation marks that made her
sound like a teenager.

Roxie would never say, Dear Baby Bump!!!

She clicked on Eeze again and typed a second message to Summer.
I am DELETING all exclamation points. Do not add any more.

She eliminated the exclamation points and proceeded to type.

Dear Baby Bump,

> Congratulations! Having a child is one of the most
> wondrous experiences in the world and I'm with
> you all the way.

Ugh. *Wondrous experience? With you all the way?* Delete, delete, delete. She started again.

> Dear Baby Bump,
>
> Congratulations! What great news! I'm so happy
> for you! Being a mother is a privilege and an
> honor and it sounds like you are clearly all aboard.

All aboard? What was she, a train conductor? Delete, delete, delete.

> Dear Baby Bump,
>
> Congratulations!

And . . . what? She had nothing. Nothing. She rubbed her hands together and blew on them like she was about to toss out a pair of lucky dice. But she had no dice and she had no luck.

Okay, if she were answering this letter *not* in real time, what would she say? Nothing. Because she would never choose this letter. It was a giant pothole, a sinkhole, of a letter.

Okay, if Bert forced her to answer this letter—*not* in real time—if Bert said, *You must answer this letter or you're fired*, what would she do? She'd call on her resources. She'd talk it through with a psychologist and a social worker. She'd do a little digging into the issues a nineteen-year-old would face raising a baby alone in the year 2017.

But on the spot? What could she responsibly tell this young woman, who in her gut she still suspected might be twelve years old? Either way, twelve or nineteen, she sounded clueless.

Honestly, the letter raised more questions the longer she thought about it. How pregnant was she? Had she gotten any prenatal care? Could Lane ask? She had to ask.

> Dear Baby Bump,
>
> Congratulations! I'm so happy for you. I'm curious, though. Do you live with your parents or do you live on your own? Are you working or still in school? What's your financial situation? Have you been to the doctor yet?

No. Not right. Wrong tone. Delete. Delete. Delete.

> Dear Baby Bump,
>
> Congratulations!

Delete.

> Dear Baby Bump,
>
> Congratulations!

Delete.

She had nothing. This was exactly what she'd feared. *Roxie Live* was like *Lane Live*. She had no idea what to say. Her mind was blank. It wasn't that she wasn't trying. She was trying hard—trying to find the right words and to say the right thing. But her mind was not cooperating. It was as if her mind had gone on strike.

Henry. This sounded exactly like how Henry described what happened when he wanted to talk and his mouth wouldn't cooperate. *It was as if his mouth was on strike.* Here, now, it was the same with her. She wanted to think, but her mind wouldn't cooperate.

That wasn't exactly true. She could still think. She could think about Henry. She could always think about Henry. What she couldn't think about was an answer for this *Roxie* letter.

Okay. Focus. The letter. The letter was about . . . What? A baby. A woman, a girl, was having a baby. A girl who was afraid to tell her mom she was going to have a baby. Okay. Roxie should advise the girl that . . . Nothing. Blank.

Her mind went blank at the worst times. She'd been like this for as long as she could remember. Maybe she'd always been like this. No. Not always. It was only since—blank. The thought was gone. What was left was blank. She seemed to have no control of her mind at all. Did other people ever feel like this? She'd never met anyone who admitted they did.

Something on the screen caught her eye. The cursor was moving again. How long had that been going on? Words were appearing. Streams of words. Sentences forming on the screen. But her hands were not moving. These were not her words.

Dear Baby Bump!

Congratulations!!! You are going to be an awesome mom! I mean, look how super concerned you are about finding the perfect way to tell your mom about your baby! Too bad there's no such thing as a Preg-posal! Like a Prom-posal but for pregnancy? Wouldn't that be awesome? Maybe you should do

that. You could get all your friends together and
they could help you figure out a really fun way to
tell your mom you're pregnant and then they could
film it while you did it and you'd have it forever!
How awesome would that be?

Lane stared at her hands. Still not moving. She stared at the screen.
Words still coming.

If you don't want to go with the Preg-posal idea,
that's cool. You can always sit your mom down with
a big glass of vodka and say, Congrats Granny!!!

Roxie would never say that. No one would ever say that. A Preg-
posal was a ridiculous idea that sounded like something a high school
student would come up with. Was Summer in high school? Had a high
school intern taken over her Live-Chat?

Just make sure she's sitting down when you tell
her so she doesn't faint. LOL!

Never ever would Lane write LOL. Her eyes skipped to the top of
her screen. Eeze messages were floating by.

Summer: Are you there? Are you there? Are you there?

Bert: Take it over, Summer. You're on. Right now. Go.

Summer: Awesome!!!

Having a mind that went blank under pressure was the exact opposite of awesome. It was an incontrovertible truth: her mind went blank
when she needed it most and had done so for as long as she could
remember.

Her mother used to tell her it was for the best. "Nothing to be
gained from ruminating," Sylvie said.

Why had her mother said that? What did she have to ruminate about then?

She stared at the screen. It was too late to save the chat. The one-minute delay was ten minutes too short. She shut her laptop, went to the kitchen and made herself a cup of tea. As she drank it she let her mind go as blank as the screen on a dead computer.

19

Lane made the proposal over the phone. The principal immediately agreed. "I totally understand," Miss Oppido said. "I want what's best for Henry too. There's three weeks left to the term. We'll call it an independent study."

Lane kept her tone neutral. "What is an independent study for a first grader?"

"Packets," Miss Oppido said, as Doctor Bruce had predicted. "Miss Fiske will put some together. Worksheets. Mostly review. There is a year-end culminating activity he'll miss. But I don't imagine that will be a problem. He's a bright boy. He's ready for second grade. You'll need to fill out some forms. Arlene will call you when she's got everything ready."

The school situation settled, Lane turned her attention to the parade of contractors marching through the house. This was the week repairs had begun in earnest. Workers had fanned out, measuring doorways, opening walls, threading wires, laying pipes. There were so many contractors coming in and out, Henry stopped bothering to run upstairs every time the bell rang. Or maybe, Lane thought, he stopped running because he was already feeling less anxious, now that he knew he could complete the rest of the school term at home.

With Henry less anxious, Lane felt lighter too. Now she was able to laugh with the workers who, having overheard that she was looking for a new place to live, were making a game of offering suggestions. The electrician said she should move to Lake George. The plumber's assistant advocated for Hawaii, the dry side of the Big Island. If she moved there, he told her, he'd be happy to come fix her plumbing for free in exchange for a room.

Nathan had come along with the army of contractors. She assumed he was there in the capacity of general contractor until an actual general contractor showed up. Later, when she overheard him telling the man replacing the window sensors for the new alarm system to check with him first before going into a room where the boy was, she wondered if that was why he'd come—to run interference between the subcontractors and Henry.

His daily offerings were what made her finally understand, he was coming because he wanted to make amends. He took it personally that the house was in disrepair, despite every worker assuring him no one could have known what was happening behind the walls. He came anyway, with prepared food on the day the water was turned off, with flowers on the day the house smelled of wet plaster.

She tried to make him understand that she didn't blame him for the failings of the old house. She assured him working in the middle of chaos was not a problem for her; she had a highly honed ability to tune things out. What she didn't admit—what she was embarrassed to even think about—was that she had come to look forward to his visits. On the one day he didn't come by—because he had to work—she felt the sting of disappointment.

But the gifts were unnecessary. "You don't need to bring something every time you come," she told him the day he brought the flowers.

"It's as much for me as it is for you." He saw her puzzled look. "If I tell you why, you'll think I'm an idiot."

"I doubt that."

He shrugged. "Okay. There's this thing I do. It's like a personal daily goal. You're going to laugh."

"I won't. I promise."

Nathan cocked his head. He wasn't sure he believed her. He told her anyway. "I try to do three things every day. Three good things. Bringing you flowers to brighten up a construction site . . ." He gestured toward the bouquet of yellow roses that Lane had temporarily placed in the sink. "That counts as one. So for today, I only have two left. See? It's for me. Selfish."

As promised, Lane didn't laugh. "Not selfish. Sweet." She thanked him and hoped he wouldn't notice that she had left the bouquet gently resting upright in her sink because she didn't own a vase. And why would she? A person who never bought or received flowers didn't need a vase.

Nathan did notice, though, and while he didn't say anything about it, the next day he came, his gift was a vase, a tall glass cylinder with small etchings of birds flying up one side. "One good deed down," he told her. "Two to go."

The day he arrived with a gift of art supplies for Henry, she insisted he stay for dinner. He accepted and then gave her a quick preview of the gift, a sketch pad of cold-press artist-quality paper, a plastic sleeve of short-handled brushes, a sample palette of watercolor paints.

Lane opened the palette and looked at the half-inch dots. "Ultramarine violet, PV-fifteen," she read. "Lightfastness one."

"Transparent and nonstaining." Nathan pointed to where it said that. "Professional quality. Which he deserves."

"Thank you. He'll love it."

"Hope so. I wanted to get him something special. To make up for all the people stomping around. Don't worry, I didn't go overboard.

The sample palettes are cheap. And there's a lot more paint on those dots than you'd think. Artists need samples. Pigment changes from one company to the next. No one should commit to a tube before they know what they're getting. Like that yellow ochre there. Some yellow ochre's opaque, some's transparent. Ochre is a prehistoric color. Did you know that?"

"Were you an artist in a previous life?"

"No. I was a lot of things in a previous life, but never an artist." He looked sheepish. "It's possible I spent more hours than I'd like to admit watching videos of watercolor artists last night."

"For Henry?"

He nodded. "And for you." He shook his head. "That came out wrong. I don't mean—"

"Of course," Lane said. "I didn't think you did. I'm not in a place where—"

"Me neither," Nathan said. He took a breath. "Let's start over. What I meant to say was, I'm here for you and Henry, as a friend." He nodded as if he was happy to have gotten that out of the way.

"I'm glad you are." Lane smiled and in the quiet that followed, thought about how she and Nathan had at least that in common. Neither of them wanted a relationship and neither of them wanted to say why.

"Hey Henry," Nathan said. "How's it going?" Lane turned and saw Henry standing at the threshold of the kitchen. "I got you some watercolor paints. Want to see?"

Henry nodded.

"It will be half an hour till dinner's ready," Lane said. "If you two want to go into the living room and try out those paints, there's time."

"You're allowed to paint in the living room?" Nathan asked as he followed Henry out of the kitchen. He whistled. "You are one lucky duck."

At Nathan's request, Lane brought them two glasses of water for their brushes. She stopped to watch for a moment while they settled in at the small art table near the back window of the living room.

"Check this out," Nathan told Henry. "If you move your brush through the water in a figure eight, it comes up clean. See? Amazing, right?"

Henry, eyes bright, smile wide, nodded.

"Okay, my liege," Nathan said in the voice of one of his knights. *"What dost thou think about these blues?"* Henry smiled and Nathan switched back to his own voice. "Hmm. I want a blue sky, a night sky. So I can make stars. I watched someone do that on a video. She painted a dark-blue sky and then she cleaned her brush—figure eights—and then she dipped her brush in white paint and flicked it. Like this." He tapped his dry brush to show what he meant. "Tiny white spots sprinkled all over the paper. Stars. Think I should try it?"

Henry nodded, and checked to see if his mother was nodding too, which she was.

"So which blue?" Nathan asked. "Cobalt or ultramarine?"

Henry pointed at one of the dots.

"I agree," Nathan said. "Ultramarine is perfect."

Over dinner Lane told Nathan what Henry already knew. Their move out of the house—the newest problem, a crack in the waste pipe, meant demo in the foundation, which meant it was going to be a construction site for months—was not going to be temporary. Lane decided, with Henry's agreement, that it was time for a fresh start. The problem was where.

"Are you open to a crazy idea?" Nathan asked them. "Maybe it's more a seize-the-day idea. A try-something-radical idea."

Henry was vigorously nodding his head so Lane said, "Sure."

"I have a place. A summer place. I haven't been there in years. Long story why. Doesn't matter. Point is, I'm going this summer. For a good-bye summer. To get the place ready to sell. It's way past time to sell." Nathan stopped, took a breath, and continued. "You should come. I'll be in the main house but there's also a little guest house. Nothing fancy. But perfect for two. It's on a pond. My opinion? Most beautiful spot in the world. Spectacle Pond. On Martha's Vineyard. Ever been there?"

Lane and Henry shook their heads.

"We used to spend summers there. Well, technically only my ex and my son did. I'd come in August for two weeks, if I was lucky." His face shifted. "Leo, my son—he just turned twenty-five—spent . . ." Nathan closed his eyes and did the calculation. "Fifteen summers of his life on that pond. Best fifteen years I ever had."

This was the first Lane had heard of a son. She was about to ask Nathan where his son was now, where did he live, what did he do—but she stopped herself. If he hadn't mentioned his son, there was a reason. If he wanted to share the reason, he would.

"The pond is like a secret. Totally tucked away. Lots of people on the Island don't even know it's there. My ex wasn't crazy about the location. It was too rustic for her. She wanted to be where the fancy lawn parties were, not where the injured birds of the world came to nest."

Lane saw that Henry was confused. She imagined him picturing a pond filled with injured birds. "Did your wife mean actual injured birds?"

Nathan shook his head and smiled. "She meant a certain kind of person. People who went through tough times and came out the other end wanting a different kind of life. A quieter life. Ruth was a very stiff-upper-lip type, not one to complain, but she let me know life was too slow for her there. She'd see one amazing sunset and think, *Okay. Who needs to see another?* I suspect you'd feel differently."

"Maybe," Lane said.

"The guest house is right on the water. Like I said, it's small. The rent would be less than what you're paying here. It's kind of perfect. You could stay the whole summer. Take your time figuring things out. You ever swim in a pond so clear you could see to the bottom?"

Eyes wide, Henry shook his head.

"You should try it sometime," Nathan said. "Why not go? Figure out your next move there. Who knows? You might fall in love with the Island. You wouldn't be the first one. More I think about it, more I think the crazy thing would be to not go."

"I don't know," Lane said. "Moving to a place I've never even seen a picture of? Sounds pretty crazy."

"You're right. I'll bring you a picture. I'll bring you a box of pictures. Pictures of the pond and the house and the Rec Center. There's about a dozen houses around the pond. There's a day camp for kids at the Rec Center. There's a farm at the end of the road where you can get fresh eggs every day, if you get down there early enough before they're all gone. Okay, maybe it's a little crazy. But maybe a little crazy isn't that crazy."

Lane agreed to look at the pictures and left it at that.

The crazy continued the next afternoon when Dana showed up at the door, unannounced. "Hear me out before you say no." She bustled in with shopping bags. "I just got off the phone with Nathan. I told him I'm sending you two out for dinner on me. He said you won't go. He said you'd rather stay home with Henry. I told him I didn't think he should speak for you."

"He shouldn't," Lane said, following Dana to the dining room, "but he's right."

Dana hoisted the two shopping bags onto the table and started emptying them. "These books are for Henry. Have you been to the bookstore yet? It's the best bookstore in the world and I'm not exaggerating. They picked these out. All I told them was Henry is six and adorable and brilliant and that's all they needed to know. Listen," Dana said. "Nathan told me you're moving and I feel awful about it. I mean it's not my house, but I am the one who talked you into living here. Least I could do is treat you to a dinner out with Nathan. You'll have more fun with him than with me. Anyway I'm going to have dinner here, with Henry. Look what I got for him from the art store. Have you been there yet? I have no idea how she stays in business." She lifted out a box of markers from one of the bags. "Monica—who owns the art store—she says kids love these." She read from the box. "Ninety-six markers. Dual-tip brush. Blend pad for mixing." She put the box down. "Monica said when she was Henry's age, she would have fainted from joy to get a box of markers like this."

Lane turned and saw Henry peering into the dining room, trying to see what was on the table.

"Perfect timing," Dana said. "Come look at what Auntie Dana brought you."

Henry inched closer.

"Is Henry allowed to draw while he eats dinner?" Dana asked.

"If he wants," Lane said. She watched as Henry moved closer to survey the supplies.

"Great," Dana said. "Henry, do you think you could make a drawing using every one of these ninety-six markers? Wouldn't that be cool? A drawing with ninety-six colors in it?" She turned to Lane and winked. "I'll be right back. Dinner's in the car. My life is in my car."

As soon as Dana flew out of the house, Lane turned to Henry. "Don't worry. I'm not going out. I'll be very polite. I'll just explain to Dana that I'd rather stay home and have dinner with you. She can go out with Nathan. They'll have a great time. So will we. She can take back the markers. I'll get you a box of our own."

In response, Henry emptied all ninety-six markers onto the table and began sorting them by shade. Pine green. Moss green. Sage. He looked over his shoulder to make sure they were still alone. "You should go out," he told his mother. "I'll stay with Dana and draw."

"Who's got macaroni and cheese?" Dana sang out as she walked back in. "Henry, bring your markers in the kitchen. Keep me company while I heat this up."

Craziest of all, that's exactly what he did.

In the restaurant, Lane looked at all the photographs Nathan brought with him and then told him the problem with his idea. "I'm not saying it doesn't look beautiful. It does. But I keep jumping from one bad decision to the next. It's not fair to Henry."

"I get that. What I don't get is, how is this a bad decision? You're taking him out of school, right? Staying in the house here makes no sense; it's a construction site. You haven't found another place to go." He shrugged. "I'm not usually one to boast but I feel like I came up with a pretty amazing solution."

"You did," Lane said. "I appreciate your generosity."

"What generosity? I rented you a house that turns out to be unlivable. I owe it to you to make it right." He picked up the stack of photographs and found the one of the guest house. "Look how perfect this is. I'll never be able to make this offer again." He found another photo and held it up. "Look at the pond. Look how pristine. You love to swim, right? Imagine swimming in that pond every day; imagine sometimes you'll have it all to yourself."

He had her attention, that was for sure.

"And the day camp? If Henry wants to go? It's great. Leo loved it." He got quiet and then shook off a thought. "They hold it in this big Rec Center. Like one of those old-style Adirondack camp buildings. The counselors are all former campers. They know every inch of the pond and the Island. They take the kids kayaking, fishing, clamming. And they do arts and crafts. If Henry wants to draw all day long, he can do it. No one will mind. It's totally laid-back."

A laid-back camp where Henry could fish or draw. A pond where she could swim alone. They did have to go somewhere. Maybe the crazy thing would be to say no.

"Only hitch," Nathan said, "if you want to go, you should go soon. So you're there when camp starts. Day one is when kids make friends. After that, it gets harder."

"When does camp start?"

"Right after the Fourth. I wish I'd thought of this sooner. It's crazy fast, to pack up and move by the Fourth."

"That's not a problem," Lane said. "I can move fast." She was a Meckler, after all; the Mecklers could move at any speed. It was staying that was the problem.

20

Marshall stood at the bottom of the stairs and called out, "Sylvie?" No answer. He walked to the door of the basement and opened it wide. "Sylvie?" Nothing. He forced open the sticky door to the backyard. This time when he called, it wasn't a question. "Sylvie." Muttering, he tromped across the carpet and stopped at the side window, the narrow one they used only when they wanted to peek out at the driveway.

The car was there. Sylvie was not. Where was she? She never went anywhere without telling him. "This is why you have to be careful what you wish for," he announced to the empty room. Among the wishes that often came to him in flashes, and that he immediately ignored, was that Sylvie would stop reporting every little move she was about to make. *I'm going to the bathroom. I'm going to the laundry room. I'm getting a box of tissues from the pantry.* It made him want to scream, although he never would. And now, she was gone without a word.

He tried to think of where else to look and came up blank. Deflated, he moved to the love seat and sat down, alone. He looked at the TV. An old stooped man, sitting on a couch much like his, looked back, slack-jawed. With a start, he realized the TV was off and the old stooped man was him. He gestured at the man to get lost. The man gestured back. They both slumped.

"I shouldn't have said I wanted him dead," he told his dim reflection. He thought about other things he wanted that he shouldn't have said. That time could be reversed was the main one. "Oh Sylvie," he said. His voice sounded odd. Old.

No thank you. He was not going to sit around and have a pity party. He lurched up and got his phone. He had to try four times before Shelley picked up. "Hah!" he said when she did.

"What's up, Dad?" When he told her she wasn't pleased. "I'm sure she's fine. Maybe she went for a walk. Maybe she's visiting a neighbor."

"Your mother does not voluntarily talk to the neighbors. And it's a hundred degrees outside. No one here goes for a walk. I'm telling you, something happened. Your mother doesn't blow her nose without letting me know she's about to do it first."

"So call the police."

"This isn't a matter for the police."

"When's the last time you saw her?"

"I don't know." He looked at his watch. "Two hours ago."

"Mom's gone for two hours and you want to call the police?"

"I *don't* want to call the police. It's lunchtime, by the way. Lunchtime and nothing's prepared." He could hear in Shelley's sigh that she had lost whatever tiny speck of patience she'd ever had. "Where could she be?" He heard how he sounded. Weary.

"I don't know. Why don't you call Turtle? Maybe Mom told *her* where she was going." There was a moment of silence and Shelley added, "Mom told me she was going to call her. To tell her about Uncle Albie."

"Why would she do that?"

"Why wouldn't she? When someone dies in your family, you tell them. Turtle isn't a child anymore. Call her. She might be able to help you. Bonus point: she's on the same continent as you and in the same time zone. I'm not either of those things, in case you forgot."

"I didn't forget. That brings up something I've been meaning to talk to you about. We want to visit. Your mother and I. You know we couldn't travel before. Now we can."

Shelley took a moment to respond. "You—come here? You're kidding me, right?"

How did he end up with these daughters? "Forget it. We're not coming. We can't come. Your mother's vanished. Not that you care."

Another sigh. "Did she leave you a note? Did you even look?"

Marshall looked around. "No note."

"Have you checked the log on Alexa?"

"What log? I don't know what you're talking about. I never use that thing. I don't even know why we have it."

"I got it for Mom. Hold on. Melinda," Shelley called. "Come tell Gramps how to use Alexa." There was a whispering and then the phone was handed over.

"Hello, Gramps." As always, Melinda spoke fast and sounded unnecessarily jolly. "Are you ready? All right then. First things first, you have to go to settings. Do you know where the settings are? Are you writing this down?"

"Yes," he told her. "And slow down. Or do you have a train to catch?"

"A train? Why would I have to go on a train?"

When he got off the phone, he followed her directions and somehow it worked.

At 9:09 a.m. Sylvie asked: "Alexa, what day is it?"

Alexa answered: "Today is Tuesday, June 20th, 2017."

At 9:15 a.m. Sylvie asked: "Alexa, what should I do?"

Alexa answered: "Learn about the world and universe."

At 10:21 a.m. Sylvie asked: "Alexa, can I tell you a secret?"

Alexa answered: "Tell me anything you're comfortable with me knowing."

At 10:23 a.m. Sylvie said: "Alexa, was it my fault?"

Alexa answered: "Sorry, I don't know that."

At 10:25 a.m. Sylvie said: "Alexa, do you think Turtle will ever forgive me?"

Alexa answered: "I'm sorry, I can't see into the future."

He called back to tell Shelley that was no help. But this time she didn't pick up, even after eight rings. The answering machine didn't pick up either. Annoyed, he gave up and dialed Lane. Of course she was surprised. He never called her. As soon as she answered he remembered why. She had that thing in her voice. Some people called it shy or reserved. He heard it for what he knew it was. Fear. There was so much she was afraid to know.

"Hey Dad. Everything okay?"

What a mistake. He needed to get this over with fast. "Yes. How are you and the boy?"

"We're fine." There was a pause. "What's wrong?"

"Nothing. Why do you have to make a big megillah over a phone call? Your mother and I wanted to know how you were. Now I know. You're fine."

"Can I talk to Mom?"

A totally terrible idea. "It's lunchtime. You know your mother. No talking on the phone during meals. She's fine," he added quickly. "She's fine and I'm fine."

There was a moment of silence and then Lane said, "Okay. I'm glad you called. I wanted to let you and Mom know that we're going to be moving again."

"Okay."

"I'll let you know the details once we're settled."

"Okay."

"Don't you want to know where we're moving to?"

"Okay."

"Martha's Vineyard. Is something wrong?"

"No."

Hanging up on Lane felt different from hanging up on Shelley, probably because he hung up on Shelley several times a week, sometimes twice in a day. Shelley was tough as nails. She could take it.

He rested his head in his hands, then decided he had to stay strong and sat up. He glanced across the room at the electronic device. "Alexa," he shouted. "Where's Sylvie?"

"I'm sorry, I didn't understand that."

He got up and pushed the thing to the floor and then, before he even knew what he was doing, picked it up and apologized. What was happening to him? It wasn't the machine's fault. It wasn't Sylvie's fault. It wasn't his fault.

The problem was, all those years she paid attention to one person. The wrong person. The problem was, they let things go on too long. The problem was, where was she?

He stood up and called out in the empty house. His voice was hoarse and low. "I'm sorry, Sylvie. I'm sorry I wasn't better to your brother. Please come home."

He was so tired. Deep in his bones tired. Maybe he needed to lie down. He grunted out a laugh. That was a good one, that now it was his turn to lie down.

As soon as he walked into their bedroom, he saw the yellow note on his pillow. As notes went, it wasn't much. A sticky with barely any stick left.

"You're old," he told the sticky.

What it said back was everything he needed to know. Flight UA 2221 departing from SRQ at 12:15 p.m., landing at EWR at 3:06.

He looked at his watch. "Oh Sylvie. What have you done now?"

21

The day she went to pick up the packets and sign what Arlene called the independent study contract, Lane had asked Henry if he wanted to come along. Maybe it would feel good, she'd suggested, to stop in his classroom and say goodbye to his friends. It wasn't a surprise that his answer was no. What was a surprise was that even though they were alone when she asked—a rare moment when there were no workers in the house, no Dana and no Nathan—his *no* was wordless. With a slow shaking of his head, and a mouth tightly closed, he made his feelings clear. He was done with that school.

Later that day, when he asked what school he'd be going to in the fall, Lane answered honestly. She didn't know yet, but she promised that was something they'd figure out together. When she said the word *together*, it was as if a cloud finally passed. He smiled. A small smile, but still, a smile.

The morning after she picked up his packets was when Lane found an envelope on their front step. She opened it as she walked into the house. Inside was a note from Miss Fiske apologizing for forgetting to give this to her the day before, when she stopped by. The note was clipped to a stack of letters. There were twenty-five letters, goodbye letters to Henry. Every student in the class had written one. A class assignment, Lane guessed, with the instruction to say one thing about Henry they'd miss.

They sat on the couch in the living room and looked at the letters together. Some children wrote with such perfect careful penmanship. Some wrote with bubble letters, and dotted the *i*'s with hearts. Some pages were covered with cross-outs. Some were torn by overzealous erasing. Some had colorful illustrations to go with their notes. Others were annotated with stick figures. One letter was written in an adult hand.

"He doesn't know how to write yet," Henry said about that one. "So his aide writes for him."

Lane nodded and asked Henry if he wanted to try and read the letters himself or if he wanted her to read them aloud. He chose her reading aloud. She read slowly—so that Henry could take it all in—and watched carefully for cues, the slight movement of a finger or his head, to indicate when she should move from one to the next.

"I liked the way he drawed," said the first one.

"I liked that he wasn't bossy," said another.

"I liked how when he drew me he made my head look like the sun."

"I liked the way his hair had curls."

"I liked that Henry never talked too much."

"I liked that his smile was in his drawings."

The last one Lane read was from Francesca: "I liked when he used to whisper his ideas to me and I wish I never said that I didn't."

Roxie Classics was an idea Lane came up with right after Henry was born, as a way to extend her maternity leave for two additional months. Sam had given it his immediate approval. The rubric for what made a *Roxie* letter a classic was simple and unscientific. A classic was any letter Lane liked that had gotten a lot of readers' comments when first published.

The suggestion to publish *Roxie Classics* now was Sam's. She still hadn't spoken to him yet—they were playing a very long game of phone tag. But in his most recent email, the same email where he told her he'd be back for the first Monday meeting after Labor Day if she could just hold on till then, he suggested she consider resurrecting *Roxie Classics* for the summer. She reread his words—*if she could just hold on*. Okay. If Sam wanted her to hold on, she would.

"I'll sell Bert on *Roxie Classics*," Sam wrote. "And I'll let him know I'm approving your working remotely for the rest of the summer. We'll catch up when I'm back. First Monday after Labor Day. I'll shoot you an email once I've spoken to Bert. You should reach out to him after that. Let's keep him at least feeling like he's in the loop."

That gave her pause. She looked at Sam's address. He was still using his personal email. Something was going on, behind the scenes. She sat up a little straighter. She could deal with it, whatever it was, so long as Sam prevailed.

She entered the date for Sam's return on her phone and then began to search for a letter to kick off the *Ask Roxie, Classics Collection, Summer Edition*. When she finally found one she liked, she drafted an email to Bert to send as soon as Sam confirmed he'd connected with him. In the email she acknowledged, without apologizing, that the Live-Chat had not turned out the way either of them hoped and added that she was eager to sit down with him and Sam in September to work out a plan for *Roxie* that all of them could get behind, moving forward.

Once that was done, she emailed Shelley again. She'd already called twice and sent a text without hearing back. This time she wrote, NEW ADDRESS, in the subject line and in the body of the email she wrote, I'm moving. Where are you?

Her family was getting more exasperating by the day. Earlier, she'd had the oddest phone call with her father. Something had been bothering him but he wouldn't— She felt a presence and turned to find Henry in the hall, waiting for her to notice him. He looked like he'd been waiting for a while. "Hey buddy. Everything okay?"

He walked in and whispered, "Someone's at the door."

Lane stood up. "Nathan?" Henry shook his head. "A contractor?" He shook his head again. "Someone you don't know?"

He shook his head again and leaned in close to whisper in her ear.

"Is she alone?" Lane asked she headed toward the stairs.

Henry shrugged but didn't follow.

When Lane got to the door, her mother was standing outside on the top step, her suitcase beside her.

"I have something to tell you," Sylvie said.

"What's wrong? What happened? Come in."

Sylvie came in and turned around in a circle, slowly taking in everything. With a start Lane realized that in all these years her mother had never visited her anywhere she'd lived. Even when Henry was born, she didn't come—another ill-timed bad bout of the blahs for Uncle Albie.

"What happened?" Lane asked again now. Her mother seemed frozen. "Come. Let's sit down." She led her mother to the living room couch and practically had to force her to sit. When she did, it was with her purse in front of her, like a shield. Still she said nothing.

"Do you want something to drink?" Her mother shook her head. "A glass of water?" Another shake. "Okay. What is it? Whatever it is, just tell me."

Her mother's face went slack. "I'm sorry."

PART THREE
WEST TISBURY, MASSACHUSETTS
SUMMER 2017

July 1, 2017

Ask Roxie, Classics Collection!

Roxie Classics are selected by readers like you!

Help grow the collection by Voting Now!

Thumbs Up! Thumbs Down! Your Choice!

Dear Roxie,

As happens with a woman of a certain age, I have accumulated a lot of experience sitting with friends grieving all kinds of losses. Sometimes a pet, sometimes a spouse, sometimes a parent, sometimes a friend, in the worst times, a child. In my crowd I've become the go-to gal for grieving. I'm not saying I'm good at everything. I can't cook or sing or knit. But I know how to listen. I don't mind tears. I'm comfortable with silence.

The problem is I have a friend who won't admit she's grieving. A month ago she lost her husband of fifty years yet she insists on acting like nothing happened.

In the thirty days since her husband's passing she hasn't cried once. She acts what could best be described as cheerful.

We're worried about her. Worried that she's stuck in the first stage of grieving, denial. Worried that she's on her way to being stuck in the fourth stage, depression.

She's already started to withdraw. She won't answer my calls. She won't answer any of our calls. It's confusing because she's not an uneducated person. Why is she refusing our help?

Can you help me help her heal?

Yours,
Helpful Healer

Dear Helpful,

I applaud your big heart and unusual capacity to sit with sadness. How comforting that must be for some of your friends. But, yikes!!! Who died and made you head of the Grief Police?

Sorry to break it to you, dear helpful one, but we're not all copies spewed out of a printer. The Kübler-Ross "stages of grief" model, which you quote like it's the bible, is not the only way to grieve. There is no *one* way when it comes to how people react to loss.

Before you try to heal your friend, consider this: Do you know for sure that she needs healing? Has she ever shared her true feelings about her late husband? I know you think you know how she felt, but is it possible you're wrong? Assumptions can be so tricky.

But okay, say your friend adored her husband like you think she did. It's possible she adored him so much that living without him now is a challenge. It's possible her strategy for getting through the day, with a wound so deep and fresh, is to minimize her feelings for a while, until she gets stronger. If that's the case, let her be. What she needs is what she'll get: time.

But you know what else is possible? She didn't adore her late husband. What you saw was a mask. In the privacy of their home he wasn't so great. It's possible he was a control freak or an abuser or a liar or a drunk or all of the above. It's possible your friend is not so much cheerful as relieved.

Here's what we can know about someone else's marriage: nothing. We can never know for sure what goes on behind the closed doors of other people's homes.

I commend your heartfelt desire to help your friend. You just need to make a slight adjustment. Your assumption is that what you're offering—a shoulder to cry on, an ear to listen—is what she needs. The facts disagree. The choice your friend has made is to carry on. Your mission is to support that choice.

Helping is not as easy as one might think for the simple reason that we cannot read minds. For every grieving person who appreciates someone taking in their wash, there's another who finds doing laundry therapeutic. A freezer meal is not helping someone who's lost their appetite. What is a friend to do? Ask. Simple as that.

Yes, as a woman of a certain age you've experienced a lot of loss. But you haven't experienced everything.

At the risk of sounding like a broken record: Less judging. More loving.

Yours forever, or at least for now,
Roxie

22

There was no traffic until the approach to the Bourne Bridge but still the drive felt long. Lane, in the back middle seat, Henry's head resting on her shoulder as he dozed, tried to let her mind go blank.

Sylvie sat in the front where Nathan was making a valiant effort to engage her in conversation. "Ever been on the Island?"

"Not really," Sylvie said.

His eyes widened at the strangeness of the response but when he met Lane's eyes in the mirror, she just pressed her lips together and shrugged. Her mother being unintelligibly vague was nothing new to her.

Before they left, Lane shared with Nathan what she'd learned since her mother's arrival the week before. There wasn't much to share. Her father was in a mood, was the first thing she'd gotten out of her mother. He needed some time to himself. It was almost as an afterthought that she added, "Your uncle passed."

"What? When? How?"

"A few weeks ago. Sorry I waited to tell you. I couldn't bring myself to say it over the phone." She met Lane's eyes. "It wasn't what you think.

It was very peaceful. In his sleep. May his memory be a blessing. Oh well." She looked around. "Which room is mine?"

Lane had felt a familiar fog descend, the same numbness that often came over her when she was with her family. She felt it when she walked upstairs and showed her mother to the guest room and she felt it as she watched her mother unroll the clothes from her suitcase, meticulously folding them into tiny packages that she laid out on the dresser top.

"You don't mind if I leave them here until I find a proper place to put everything, do you?" she asked.

Dumbstruck, Lane said she didn't mind and then excused herself. She closed the door to her bedroom and called her sister three times, their Bat-Signal for catastrophe.

Shelley picked up on the third try. "I'm afraid to ask. Who is it? Who died?"

"Uncle Albie."

Shelley let out a sound of relief. "Oh. You scared me. That's not exactly hot-off-the-press news. Who told you?"

"Mom. Just now. She's here. Was there a funeral? Did you go?" It amazed her to think that this was something she could imagine, that her sister went to the funeral while she didn't even know about the death.

"There was something," Shelley told her. "Maybe just a burial. I forget. I didn't go. I don't think they went."

It never got less bewildering, how her family seemed to decide, as a unit, that it wasn't necessary for her to know things. But no good would come from thinking about it. Better that she take care of what needed to be done now. There was a lot to do. She needed to help get Henry started on his first worksheet. She needed to reach out to Summer to make sure Bert was going to run her July *Roxie Classics* letters. She needed to pack up the house.

"Let me do that," Sylvie said when she came upon Lane in the kitchen, cabinet doors open, looking overwhelmed. "You know I'm an excellent packer."

Lane agreed because the alternative—that she did the packing while her mother watched with a critical eye—was not worth it.

As it turned out, there was an advantage to having her mother around that Lane had not anticipated. Henry hadn't accumulated a lifetime of grudges against his grandmother, so being with her wasn't hard. In fact, because Sylvie took up so little space in a room, it was easy for Henry to forget she was even there. Lane watched it happen, Henry slowly relaxing in his grandmother's presence until—first tentatively, then more boldly—he started to show her his drawings. Sylvie's response was a perfect mix of muted admiration and no questions. Her mother didn't interrogate Lane about Henry, either. The day Lane explained to her that Henry had a problem speaking, her mother took it in, nodded slowly, and left it at that.

What remained a puzzle for Lane in the days that followed was why her mother had come. Was it to tell her about Uncle Albie in person? Was it because her father was in a mood? Had they had a fight? And hadn't Shelley mentioned that her mother was thinking about coming? So it was something she'd been mulling over. But why?

Equally up in the air was the question of how long she was staying. Lane had tried gently prodding to find this out but after sending up several conversational flares that were returned with the usual, "Oh well," she changed her approach and told her mother her own plans—their moving date—so that her mother could accommodate her.

Lane prepared, coming downstairs with a list of flights to Florida spread over several days before their move. Information in hand, she approached her mother as she sat in a corner of the living room couch, reading an Agatha Christie novel.

Her mother looked up, smiled vaguely, and went back to reading.

Lane took a breath. "Hey Mom. I wanted to remind you that next Friday is when we're moving to the Vineyard. I looked for some flights—"

"We're flying?" her mother interrupted. "I thought we were driving."

You're coming? Lane thought. "You're right," she said. "We're driving. With Nathan."

"Can we fit everything in his car?" she asked. Lane was still digesting the news that her mother seemed to have no leave date when her mother added in a whisper, "Is Nathan someone special?"

"Just a friend." Lane felt a fog descend. "I hired a mover. They'll follow in a few days. I'm putting stuff in storage. I'm not sure where Henry and I are going after the summer." She paused and then—maybe it was the numbness that made her risk a question—asked, "Don't you want to get back home to Dad?"

"Oh well." Her mother got up and busied herself examining a carton shoved against the wall. "Don't forget Rule Number Five: If You Didn't Unpack It in the Old House, Don't Bring It to the New One."

It wasn't until Lane got out of the car in Woods Hole, to use the restroom before getting on the ferry, that she felt her fog lift. The sky, she noticed with a start, was a shade of blue she'd never seen before. And there was something about the air. What was it? The air felt light. Clean. Curative. She parted her lips and tasted salt. She glanced over and saw Henry watching the snaking line of cars, and then enormous trucks, that had just begun to drive into the wide belly of the ferry. She heard her name and saw Nathan motioning for her to get back in the car. He followed the ferry staffer's directions and drove on board.

"Lucky day," he told them. "The luggage cart is at the back of our lane. That means we'll be first off the boat."

While he hadn't been on the Island for over a decade, he moved about the boat like he belonged, hurrying them to a particular stairwell and then up three flights and out onto the packed upper deck. The large crowd, he explained, was partly because it was Saturday—turnover day for rentals—and partly because July Fourth was only days away. He ushered them to the less populated side of the ferry.

"Soon as we pull out and turn," he said, "we'll be in the shade. Best seats on the boat."

Lane sat and closed her eyes, feeling the breeze blow her hair as families, small, extended and chosen, negotiated what to bring to their beach barbecues and whether they would go to the parade this year and if they should go by shuttle bus to see the sunset in Menemsha or take their chances with finding parking.

Other people's families always looked so happy, Lane thought, from a distance.

She turned and saw her mother rubbing her arms. Despite the mild breeze, goose bumps had risen on her pale, freckled skin. She dug around in her bag, found the shawl she'd tucked inside and draped it lightly over her mother's bony shoulders.

"Wrinkled," her mother said, and drew it closer.

When the ferry gently bumped and then settled into the dock, Nathan stood up. "This way." He guided them back down the stairs to the vehicle hold, where they walked, single file, through the narrow space between the parked cars.

"Don't worry," he told Lane after holding the door open for her mother to slide inside. "The pond has a way with people."

Lane wasn't sure about that, but her mother, she'd noticed, had quickly warmed to Nathan. He had a way with people too.

Henry seemed to fall under the spell of the pond on the drive there. Like a happy puppy, he tipped his head as far out the window as his seat belt allowed and opened his mouth to drink in the salty air while the breeze made a party of his curls.

Nathan rolled down his window and opened his mouth to the air too. "Do you know what they say?" he called out to be heard over the sound of the wind. Everyone shook their heads. "Every day you breathe in Island air adds a day to your life. I think it's been scientifi-cally proven."

Her mother smiled. Henry closed his mouth and sat back. Lane imagined him wondering how things might have gone if his father had tried that, drinking Island air instead of city bourbon.

After he pulled into the parking spot at the back of the guest house, Nathan asked Lane and her family to wait in the car for a minute. When he came back, he got in, turned the engine on, and headed up the hill to the main house. "Change of plans. It's too small. We're switching. I'm staying at the guest house." He followed the road around a bend and there it was, the clean lines of a large house with gray weather-beaten shingles and hydrangea-blue trim. "It's too small," he said again. The wheels crackled over the oyster-shell driveway. Nathan turned off the car. "You stay here. I'll stay there. There's no point in arguing about it. That's what makes sense."

"No." Lane shook her head. "Absolutely not. We don't need a lot of space. We'll be fine in the guest house."

Nathan sat for a moment and then gave up. He restarted the car and drove back down the hill. "See for yourself."

She did. To call it cozy would be an exaggeration. In theory, it would be fine. It was charming, perched on a small rise at the edge of the pond. Magical even, like a tree house, with two bedrooms, which sounded like enough until Lane saw them: the first was a sleeping loft accessible by a narrow staircase that would be too treacherous for her mother; the second was a tiny room, a closet really, with nothing in it but a set of bunk beds.

Nathan was waiting for her in the narrow kitchen. "I remembered it wrong. Everything is so small. The bedrooms. The bathroom. The refrigerator. I didn't even realize they made two-burner stoves. I guess we never cooked down here." He let out a stream of disappointed air. "Look, if it was just you and Henry maybe it would be passably okay. But with your mom? No way. It won't work. We're switching. It makes sense." Lane said no several more times. Nathan continued to press his case.

Finally Lane gave in. "We'll switch for tonight. I'll look for a place to rent in the morning. I'm sure I'll be able to find something." She tried to sound sure. She wanted to be sure. But she wasn't. "It's not right for you to stay down here."

"I want to," he told her. "I love this place. I have so many good memories of staying here. Leo and I used to come down for sleepovers." He smiled thinking about it. "Not much sleeping happened those nights. Leo was quite the talker. If I drifted off for a second, he'd give me an elbow. I used to beg him, *Please, Leo, I got to sleep.*" He shook his head and smiled, which did nothing to disguise the scrim of sadness that had descended over his face.

Henry saw it too; he ran over and gave Nathan a tight hug.

Chip went another piece of Lane's heart.

In the end, Lane took Nathan at his word; he preferred staying down at the guest house. She couldn't argue his other point: the bigger house, with its four bedrooms, three bathrooms and two decks, was a better fit for a family. What she didn't share with him was that the main house, set up for renters, underfurnished, and aside from a well-stocked shelf of board games, free of knickknacks, almost made her feel at home.

When Nathan finished explaining the house's temperamental details—a window shade that would be lopsided if the double strings weren't pulled at exactly the same time; a sliding door that tended to stick if you didn't give it a hard shove—he said, "Okay. I guess that's it. I'll leave you all to settle in."

He was halfway out the back door when he stopped and, with a touch of shyness, asked Lane if she and her family might consider joining him on Monday at the Rec Center for Opening Party.

"It's an annual thing," he said. "I haven't been for so long, people are going to be shocked to see me. They're all going to want to meet you," he added. "Even if they don't know it yet. Will you come?"

To her surprise, she agreed. Maybe the pond was already working its magic. How else to explain that Lane Meckler had voluntarily agreed to attend a party?

That Sylvie opted out of going to Opening Party was not a surprise. That Henry decided to join them, was. Nathan had sold him on the idea with the simple statement that it could make his first day of camp easier. Although camp would start the day after the Fourth, the campers traditionally came to Opening Party to have their own reunion, in the supervised back room of the Rec.

As they walked down the dirt path, Nathan filled them in on who they were about to meet. Details didn't stick—who was a first-generation ponder, who was second-generation, but what was clear to Lane was that he spoke about these people as if they were relatives he rarely saw, but remained fond of.

"The Rec Center is run like a co-op," he said as he bushwhacked some of the branches that had encroached on the path over the winter. "People take on different jobs depending on what they want to do. I used to be in charge of checking bacteria levels. Don't laugh," he said after Lane did. "Me and Leo did it together. We were like a couple of mad scientists, collecting samples in test tubes. It was fun. Everything was fun. Utopia on the pond. Until it wasn't." He didn't offer details and Lane didn't ask. They shared that, a high tolerance for silence.

"First to arrive," Nathan said when they reached the building. "Did I mention there's no electricity?" He pushed open the swollen door. "By unanimous vote. It's in the DNA of the place. The more rustic the better. Pretend pioneers. Here we go." He pointed to a line of lanterns that stood against the far wall, like soldiers at attention. "That's our solution to no electricity." He reached inside his pocket and scooped out a handful of double-A batteries, which he offered to Henry. "Want to help me put in new ones? Back in the day, people were forever forgetting to turn the lanterns off. Beginning of the season, they were always dead. I doubt that's changed."

Henry opened his hands to receive the batteries and under Nathan's light supervision, replaced the batteries in all the floor lanterns. Nathan found a stepladder in a storage closet, which he used so he could change the batteries of the Chinese-style paper lanterns strung across the ceiling. When all the lanterns were on, the main room glowed.

"At least something is like I remembered," he said. "Magical."

They turned at the sound of branches cracking under feet, followed by bursts of laughter.

"Here they come." Nathan reached for Lane's hand and immediately pulled away. "I'm sorry. I don't know why I did that."

She didn't know why either. The doors flung open. A crowd swarmed in. Lane could hear the news traveling.

"Nathan's here." "Nathan's back." "I thought Nathan was dead." "Who's Nathan?"

"There you have it," Nathan whispered to her. "Old gang thought I was dead. New gang never heard of me." A man was fast approaching. "I have no idea who this is."

"Nathan Knapp," the man said.

"Hey," Nathan replied.

"I knew you'd come back. People said you wouldn't, but I knew you would." He let out a hearty laugh and Lane could see it on Nathan's face. The laugh had told him who this was.

"It's great to be back, Stretch," Nathan said. "It's great to see you looking so well."

"I'm still alive, I'll admit that. Who have we here? Wife Number Two?"

Nathan laughed. "No. I'm not that lucky. This is my friend Lane. She's renting the house for the summer. I'm camping out down at the cottage. Last hurrah and all. That's my friend Henry."

"Nice to meet you." Stretch offered a hand to Lane and then to Henry. "How old are you, son? Nine? Sixteen? I'm not good with numbers."

"He's six," Lane said.

"Six," Stretch said. "Great age. Great age." He called to someone who'd just walked in. "Brian, look who's back. Hey—do we actually have all the originals here tonight? Well, first wives excluded. And Aggie." He looked around. "Aggie's not here, is she?"

A woman giving Nathan a welcome-back hug stepped aside and said, "I hope not."

The door continued to creak open and bang shut, letting in the scent of bug spray and pie. Exclamations continued. "Wow!" "I didn't think I'd see the day!" "Now the party can begin!"

Nathan had peeled away from the well-wishers long enough to point Lane to where the kids were gathering. She held Henry's hand as they walked into the back room. The first to spot them was a little girl, who tugged the boy standing next to her and then pulled him along so he'd skip over with her.

The girl spoke first. "Are you new? I'm Esther. We're seven. This is Russell. He's my brother. We're twins. Who are you?"

Lane started counting back from ten, which was what Doctor Bruce told her to do so that Henry would have a chance to answer if he chose to. Waiting was harder than people might think. She only got to seven. "This is Henry."

"This is Henry," Esther trumpeted to the crowd. "Come on, Hen," she said. "We're making seaweed note cards."

Lane followed Henry, who followed Esther and Russell, to a long table, on top of which sat several basins filled with water. A dozen children were standing around the table. A woman on a stool was explaining the art project.

"The main thing you have to do is stare," the woman said. "Just stand and stare for a good long while. Who knows how to stare?"

The children showed off their best efforts at unblinking stares. To Lane's surprise, Henry joined in, making his eyes go bug-eyed wide. She laughed out loud and then apologized.

The woman flashed Lane a smile. "No matter how much fun you have fishing for seaweed here," she told the children, "you'll have more fun in the sea. This is for argument's sake."

"I'm not arguing," a boy yelled.

The woman smiled. "Good. Now keep staring until a clump of seaweed speaks to you."

"How does seaweed speak?" Esther asked, and Russell added, "What does it say?"

"It's going to say, *Pick me,*" the woman told them. "It's going to say, *I'm the perfect one for you.* Don't listen here." She tapped her ear. "Listen here." She pointed to her heart.

Several children exchanged doubtful looks. Henry looked captivated.

"Once you hear the seaweed talking to you, scoop it up." She plunged her arm into the water and swiftly pulled out a clump. "That's step one. Catching it and laying it out on your blank card. But try to take a picture in your mind of how it looked in the water because that's the shape you're going to try to stretch it back to. With a gentle touch. You don't want it to break. Who wants to try?" She pointed to Henry. "You?"

Lane opened her mouth to decline on his behalf, but before she could, Henry stepped forward and dipped his hand into the water.

"Excellent choice," the woman said when Henry pulled out a dripping seaweed bouquet.

"Lane?" She turned to see Nathan in the doorway. He motioned her over. "Want to come meet some neighbors?"

She looked at Henry, who waved. She walked over and took him aside. "I'm going to have a quick word with the art counselor, okay? To let her know that you might not feel like talking tonight and that's okay."

Henry shook his head.

"I won't make a big deal about it."

He shook it again.

"Are you sure?"

Henry let out an exasperated sigh and folded his arms across his chest. He was unequivocally sure. He did not want her to say anything to the counselor.

"Got it." She smiled. "Message received."

Back in the main room, Nathan filled her in on the few people he recognized. "I wish I understood why some people I recognize and others I don't. It's unpredictable." He nodded toward a couple standing at the drinks table. "That's Erica and Mitchell Roth over there. I used to rent my house to them until Teddy Peabody died. The Peabody house is right across from mine. The Roths made an offer on it before the funeral. They wanted it that bad." A laugh exploded from across the room. "Ah. Harvey Schwartz. Here's all you have to know about Harvey: he once caught a four-hundred-and-thirty-six-pound tuna. All the times I've heard him tell that story, he's never once rounded it down to four hundred and thirty-*five*. I think it takes him longer to tell the story than it took him to catch the fish."

"Is that Nathan?" A woman, hands on hips, shook her head. "You haven't aged a day."

"Hey," Nathan said. "This is Lane Meckler. She's renting my house."

"Nice to meet you," the woman said. "I'm Wren. I live in the house next door." She gave Nathan an affectionate punch on the arm. "I haven't decided if I've forgiven you yet. Don't trust this guy," she warned Lane. "He'll tell you he's your best friend one day and the next day, he'll walk past you on the street like he's never seen you before. Not to mention out of the blue, he'll pack up his bags and disappear for—how long has it been?"

"Ten years," Nathan admitted.

"Unbelievable. Simon," she called across the room. "My husband," she told Lane. "Simon, come here and tell this lovely newcomer why Nathan is the worst."

Wren's husband joined them and Lane watched as they did an awkward dance, Simon going in for a hug, Nathan extending his hand, both of them missing, then switching, so out of sync it almost looked choreographed.

"For god's sake," Wren said. "Just kiss each other on the lips and get it over with."

Simon seemed to take the suggestion literally, but Nathan laughed it off.

A woman rang a bell and called out, "Meeting time. Take a seat, please."

Wren and Simon stepped away and Nathan's smile slipped off his face, replaced by what Lane thought looked like regret.

It seemed to Lane that on the surface the activity was to go around the circle and catch everyone up on all the good news that had happened over the winter. But if there were any events that were not celebratory, they were not being shared. The news was all good. The smiles were all bright. Still, Lane felt an undercurrent of tension. She stopped listening to the updates and watched the faces instead.

A moment later all the faces turned, as one, to the sound of a disturbance. She turned too, and saw Henry charging out of the back room. He looked distraught. The twins came running behind him, followed by Amanda, who introduced herself as one of the counselors.

Henry raced into Lane's arms. "What happened?" she asked. She moved her ear close to his mouth to hear his answer, but he stayed silent.

"He got scared," the counselor said. "I'm really sorry."

"It was because of Griffin," Esther piped up.

"He was outside the window," her brother added. "He looked like this." He opened his mouth and panted like a dog to demonstrate.

"He's not dangerous," Amanda said. "His bark is worse than his bite."

This was something new. Henry had never been afraid of dogs before. She leaned close and asked if he wanted to go home. He didn't speak or nod but she felt a slight shift in his weight. He wanted to go.

The circle talk started again. Across the room a woman began describing how many dumpsters it took to clear out her house over the spring. "We downsized," she said, "but we did not down*grade*. I have pictures. Want to see?" She handed her phone to the person next to her.

Lane leaned over and quietly told Nathan they were going to leave. He nodded and started to stand up. She put a hand on his shoulder to stop him. "Stay. Catch up with your old friends. We'll be fine. I can retrace our steps. Turn left at the T and follow the path to the house. That right?" It was. She turned to Henry. "Ready, buddy?"

He nodded and—was it her imagination? Or did he say a very quiet, *Yes?*

Maybe the pond did have a way with people.

23

Henry learned about Okay Days from Doctor Bruce. The first time Doctor Bruce asked him if he was having an Okay Day, Henry gave him a shrug. He learned about shrugs from his mom. She told him a shrug was a good thing to do if someone asked him a question he couldn't answer. She said if he didn't answer at all, they'd probably keep asking more questions. If he gave a shrug, they'd probably nod and not ask anything else.

When Henry answered Doctor Bruce's Okay Day question with a shrug, Doctor Bruce didn't nod. He put on his serious face and explained all the kinds of days a person could have. He said, "Bad Days are days with mostly bad parts. Good Days are days with mostly good parts. Okay Days have some parts good and some parts bad." He also told him about the fourth kind of day, which was Super Bad Worst Possible Thing Happened Day. Doctor Bruce said most people didn't get more than one or two of those in their whole life and most six-year-olds didn't get any.

That made a lot of questions come into Henry's head. One question was, if people only get one or two Super Bad Worst Possible Thing

Happened Days, was he going to get another one? Would he get it soon? Another question was, if most six-year-olds didn't get any, why did *he* get one? He didn't ask any of the questions, though, because his mouth still wasn't ready to talk.

After he learned about all the kinds of days a person could have, Henry started paying attention to his days so he would know what kind of day he was having the next time Doctor Bruce asked. He kept track of the days on the back of his sketch pad. First he wrote the day—Monday—then he wrote the kind of day, *Good, Bad, Okay* or *SBWP*. *SBWP* was short for *Super Bad Worst Possible*.

The day they got to their new house was a Bad Day because there was so much driving and no one was talking in the car and then on the ferry Grandma Sylvie started shivering even though the sun was hot and when they got to the house where they were supposed to stay, it wasn't good and his mom tried to sound like she didn't care, but he could tell she did. Her face was Disappointed.

The next day started out Okay. They went shopping at a farm stand where there were small green baskets of tiny strawberries that smelled like candy and vegetables that were purple, like a bruise, and yellow, like the sun. After the farm stand they went to the General Store where they got beach chairs and art supplies and bug spray and sponges. The sponges were for Grandma Sylvie, who told his mom, *New house, new sponge*. When they got home he got to draw so the day ended Good.

The third day was the day he went to the Rec Center. He thought it was going to be a Good Day because he liked the part where he got to play with seaweed, but then it turned into a Bad Day because of Griffin in the window.

The fourth day was the Fourth of July and they drove into town and sat on the curb in front of a house that had big American flags in front and a picket fence completely covered with more American flags. They watched a long parade with soldiers and old cars and men wearing skirts and farm trucks with kids in the back and a float with a lighthouse on it and a bus with Alice in Wonderland on it, and people walking llamas and a tiny, tiny horse. The people on the parade floats threw out candy and his mom said he could run and get some so he added a new kind of day to his list: Very Very Good Day.

Now it was the fifth day, which was the day he was starting camp. He didn't know yet if it would be Good, Bad, Okay, SBWP or Very Very Good. He never knew for sure until nighttime, when the day was all over, except for the day that was SBWP. The SBWP day went bad in the morning. For real, it was the night before when it went bad, but he didn't find out that night. For him, morning.

So far today was Okay. To wake him up his mom touched his cheek, which made his eyes pop open. Then she touched his hair, which made him smile. Then she kissed his forehead and said, "Good morning sleepyhead. I love you so much. Time to get up," which made him get up.

While his mom was making waffles downstairs, he pulled out the box in the hiding place under his bed. The box had his baseball in it and his flashlights. He looked at the baseball and tried to decide if—Yes or No—he should bring it to camp for Show and Tell. The *Yes* would be because at school they always had Show and Tell on the first day and if you didn't have something to show, it felt Bad. The *No* would be if they didn't have Show and Tell at camp and if you brought something to show, it felt Embarrassed.

Why he hid the box under his bed was because he shouldn't have sneaked it into his moving carton. It was against Grandma Sylvie's rule, which he heard her tell his mom, "Rule Number Five: If You Didn't Unpack It in the Old House, Don't Bring It to the New One."

He put down the baseball and looked at the three flashlights in the box. He had two regular and one constellation flashlight. The constellation one was his favorite. It came with twenty-four caps so you could shine twenty-four different constellations on the ceiling or, if he made a tent under his blanket, twenty-four constellations on his sheet. It was his dad's idea to shine them under his blanket. His dad said it would be a good idea for his mom not to see constellations on the ceiling. When he asked why, his dad said, *Because* and then he said, *Sorry buddy. Some questions are too hard to answer.*

The day after his dad said that, Henry wondered if maybe the reason his mom wouldn't like constellations on the ceiling was because she was worried they might leave marks. He decided to ask his dad about that when his dad got home that night. But his dad never got home that night or any other night, so no questions. No answers.

To decide whether or not to take the baseball to camp for Show and Tell, he did Eeny, Meeny, Miny, Moe. He got as far as Catch a Tiger by the Toe when he remembered how Show and Tell worked. The Show part was fine. He could pass around the baseball and people could ooh and ahh or not. But the Tell part meant he would have to say something about the baseball out loud, so, No. No Show. No Tell.

He put the baseball back in the box and took out the *This Is For Real Hank Aaron's Baseball* letter that came with it. When his dad read him the letter, his voice was the most happy possible. Henry used to think the reason Hank Aaron was his dad's favorite was because they both had Aarons in their name. But one night at Tell Me That Story, he found out the real reason. When Hank Aaron tried to win Best-Ever at home runs, everyone got mad at him. The reason they got mad was they liked the person who'd already won it more. The surprise ending to the Hank Aaron story was that people being mad at him made him work even harder. He worked so hard, he finally won Best-Ever. The happy ending to the story was that people ended up liking him after all. That was a Never-Give-Up story. His dad had a lot of Hank Aaron stories. Another one was about how Hank Aaron learned to play baseball with bottle caps and sticks, because he didn't have enough money to get a baseball and bat. That was another Never-Give-Up story.

One time he asked his mom why his dad told so many Never-Give-Up stories and she said, *Gee. I don't know. Oh well.* One time his mom told him that Grandma Sylvie said, *Oh well*, when she didn't know what else to say so probably that's why his mom said it too.

Not every story his dad told him had a secret special meaning. How he knew a story had a secret special meaning was that his dad's voice got very slow and very quiet. Now his dad didn't have any voice.

When his mom first read the *This Is For Real Hank Aaron's Baseball* letter she told him, *Fifty-fifty chance that letter is real. Fifty-fifty* she told him later, was the same as Maybe Yes / Maybe No. She said either way, he should play with it if he wanted because baseball was a very good game. He wasn't sure if that meant his mom wanted him to play baseball instead of drawing or if she wanted him to play baseball and keep drawing. He'd have to Wait and Sea.

Miss Mary was the one who taught him about Wait and Sea. She said Wait and Sea was a good way to figure things out. His mom liked to figure things out by Let's Dream on It. They used Let's Dream on It when they had to decide big things, like move to New Jersey now or never, or visit Florida now or never, or invite his dad's brother over now or never so Henry could at least meet him for Goodness Ache.

Sometimes Let's Dream on It meant they would talk about it again in the morning. Sometimes it meant they would talk about it again never.

The Bad part of the first day at camp started when he got to the bottom of the box and saw that underneath the Hank Aaron letter and the twenty-four constellation caps there was another letter, from his dad to his mom. He knew it was to his mom because it said *Dear Lane*. He knew it was from his dad because his dad did scribble writing that was hard to read. Sometimes his mom and dad fought about the scribble writing but his dad kept doing it anyway.

Henry tried to imagine what his mom's face would look like if he told her he found a letter from his dad. To help figure it out he drew her face all the ways it might look. The faces he drew were: Mad, Sad, Disappointed, Happy. He counted three Bad faces, one Good. So, probably not a good idea to show it. He crumpled up the drawing and put it in the garbage underneath the drawings he made yesterday, which his mom said were Good but not Good Enough to Keep.

Henry imagined what his mom's face would look like if she found out he found the letter and didn't give it to her. To help figure that out, he made more faces. This time the faces he drew were: Mad, Sad and Disappointed. Three Bad, no Good. He crumpled that paper into a small ball and put it in the tippy-tippy bottom of the garbage.

He still wasn't sure which to do, show or not show, so he decided to Dream on It.

Grandma Sylvie wasn't at breakfast yet, so Henry decided to ask his mom a question he'd been worrying about which was: would she be Very Mad or Just a Little Mad if she found out he accidentally broke Rule Number Five, Don't Move Things to a New House That You Didn't Unpack in the Old One. His mom said, *Forget all those silly rules,* and then her face turned red and when he turned around he saw Grandma Sylvie standing there.

Grandma Sylvie's nose looked crinkly, like she smelled something she didn't like, but the only smells in the kitchen were waffles and coffee so probably her crinkly nose meant, Sad.

Miss Mary said he was a good guesser because he noticed clues. The clues he usually saw on Grandma Sylvie's face were a mouth in a straight line and sighs. Grandma Sylvie never used her yelling voice, not even in Florida, but she used a lot of sighs.

One time when he was Sad, his mom held his hand and his Sad went away, so he decided to try and see if that would work with Grandma Sylvie. He reached over to hold her hand, but he only got three fingers. His mom was busy making waffles so she didn't see that when he touched Grandma Sylvie's fingers her hand jumped, like it was

Surprised. Her hand was very soft, especially the parts that had bumpity veins. Grandma Sylvie's eyes looked like they wanted to smile but her mouth didn't agree. Her mouth won. She pulled her hand away but not speedy fast. Maybe she did it slow so he wouldn't notice.

He didn't tell his mom anything about the letter from his dad at breakfast because sometimes Dream on It took more than one night. Also his grandma Sylvie was there so he couldn't talk. When Doctor Bruce first told him that not talking was his Super Power and that Invisible could feel very boring, he forgot to tell him it could also feel very Sad.

Usually his mom acted regular around his Super Power but today it was making her twitchy. To get less twitchy, she filled up the room with questions. They were Yes-or-No questions, the kind he could answer, but she asked them fast, all in row. Did he like swimming in the pond and drawing with Nathan and sitting on the deck with Grandma Sylvie?

He couldn't answer about swimming in the pond because he hadn't done it yet, so he didn't know if it had a slime bottom or a sand bottom. If it was slime, the answer was going to be No. He could answer about drawing with Nathan. He liked drawing with Nathan because one, Nathan never tried to make him talk and two, he always liked his drawings, no matter what they were of. Sometimes he liked them so much he asked if he could have them.

He wasn't sure how to answer, *Did he like sitting with Grandma Sylvie on the deck.* The answer was Yes, except when she shivered, but since she shivered most of the time the answer was also No.

It took him such a long time to decide which question was the best to answer that his mom got tired of waiting and asked a new question, *Are you excited about Camp Eclipse?* But before he could answer that one, Grandma Sylvie asked another. *Why do they call it that for Heaven's Ache?*

His mom told her that was how the camp worked, every year it got a new name. Last year it was Camp Shark and all the activities were about sharks including they had a visit from a real live shark scientist. This year it was called Camp Eclipse and all the activities would be about that.

Grandma Sylvie's mouth got so small it almost disappeared, but not so small that she couldn't talk. What she said was, *I do not like the sound of that one bit.*

Henry wasn't sure which bit she didn't like the sound of. Maybe it was the name Camp Shark because she was afraid of sharks. Maybe it was the name Camp Eclipse because she was afraid of the dark. Maybe it was his mom's voice, which was very strict when she explained about the camp. Maybe it was the sound of his fork accidentally hitting the edge of his plate. He didn't think it was that, but he stopped eating anyway, just in case.

The first person to say hello at camp was a counselor called Dylan. Henry remembered Dylan from Opening Party. That night Dylan was too busy talking to the other counselors to say hello. This time Dylan came right over and said, "I'm Dylan and I'm going to be your favorite counselor."

Henry did not know how Dylan could know that. So far all Dylan knew about Henry was he had round eyes, long eyelashes, and curly hair.

For getting oriented, Dylan told them about morning and afternoon activities. Morning activities were: projects or board games. Afternoon activities were: go in the pond. If it was raining or the pond had too much bacteria, it was morning activities all day. No Show and Tell.

Dylan told Henry he could sit at whichever activity table he wanted. All the activities were about the eclipse. The first table he showed them was finger painting on paper plates. That was for the littlest campers. They had two colors. Yellow for the sun. Black for the dark side of the moon. The next table was a teaching table, where they had constellation cards. Dylan started to explain about constellations but Henry's mom said, "He knows all about constellations. He studied them with his dad."

Henry was surprised to hear his mom say that. It made him wonder if maybe now she wouldn't mind him using his constellation flashlight on the ceiling. He wished he could ask his dad about it but, no dad.

His mom turned out to know a lot about constellations. She told Dylan that Orion was his favorite and that the Big Dipper used to be his dad's favorite.

Dylan said, "Cool," and then asked Henry what his dad's favorite constellation was now.

His mom's cheeks turned bright pink and she said, "What are the children over there doing?" Dylan looked where she pointed and forgot about Henry's dad, which was the point.

"They're making up constellations." He put his hand next to his mouth and said, "Kind of lame, right? The best table is that one, in the back. Pinhole boxes."

Henry glanced toward the table Dylan thought was lame. His mom noticed and said, "I think Henry would like to give a try at drawing at the table where they're making up their own constellations."

"Really? Okay, little man. But the pinhole boxes are way more awesome. Useful too. First you make it, then you use it to watch the eclipse. Without going blind. I don't want you to grow up regretting that because you didn't make a pinhole box, you weren't allowed go outside and see your first total solar. My dad still regrets that he wasn't allowed to go outside to see the last one. Want to know what happened?"

Henry guessed from his mom's face that she didn't, but Dylan was not a good guesser.

"The last time there was a total solar he was a teenager. Fifteen to be exact. And everyone back then was super worked up worried that all the kids, even teenagers, *especially* teenagers, would look out the window at the sun and go blind. So they closed his school and sent everyone home. He had to watch the eclipse on TV."

Henry's mom's forehead got crinkled—Worried—and she said, "Henry, you know you can go blind if you look at the eclipse without special glasses, right?" He nodded and his mom said, "Okay, good."

"That's why the pinhole boxes are super cool," Dylan said. "My dad makes the most awesome pinhole boxes. He's legit obsessed with them. All because he wasn't allowed to be outside the last time." Dylan turned to Henry's mom and asked if her school got closed too, and if she had to watch the eclipse on TV like his dad.

His mom shook her head and then she saw Amanda across the room and she called over to her and thanked her for helping the other night, when the scary dog came.

Henry didn't know what his mom meant by that and from how Amanda's and Dylan's faces looked, he guessed they didn't either.

His mom reminded her, "At Opening Party. The dog in the window? Griffin?"

Dylan laughed and Henry felt his mom's body get stricter and he guessed Dylan felt it too because Dylan stopped laughing and said, "I'm sorry, Mrs. Meckler. It's just Griffin isn't a dog. He's a person. No need to be scared of Griffin, little man. Me and Griffin were in school together. He's a couple of years older than me. He looks like a giant on the outside but inside he's still a little kid. He likes animals more than people. He doesn't mind people as long as they like animals. My favorite animal is a horse. Want to tell me your favorite animal, little man?"

What Henry wanted to tell him was that he did not like being called Little Man but he didn't say that or anything. He just shrugged and his mom said, "He likes all animals," and the counselor Amanda said, "Want to come draw animal constellations with me?" and he nodded.

The first constellation Henry drew was a cow. He drew it very fast so he would feel calm, which worked. Just as he was starting the second one, which was not going to be an animal, his mom came over to get a goodbye hug. After the hug, Amanda walked his mom to the door. They talked for a long time. He didn't hear everything but he did hear the last part, which was, *He'll be fine.*

The Bad part of the day came at the end while his mom was on the Kitchen Deck, barbecuing *Sword* steaks, and he was on the Looking at the Pond Deck, with Grandma Sylvie. Grandma Sylvie had a favorite spot on that deck, where she liked to sit and watch the paddlers go by. He liked it too, because it was quiet. Except now it wasn't quiet. Now something was buzzing. Something loud. Probably a bug. Probably a big one. When Grandma Sylvie heard the buzz, she started looking in her bag. Her bag was where she kept the round wooden frame with the cloth on it that had words in script, which he couldn't read. She carried her bag everywhere but hardly ever took the wooden frame out. Now he could tell that the buzzing was coming from inside the bag. He was in the middle of wondering how the big bug got in the bag and also, how it would get out, when his grandma pulled out a phone. At first he didn't realize it was a phone, because it was the flippy-up kind, but then he saw that it was the phone, her flippy-up phone, which was buzzing.

After Grandma Sylvie pushed a button and said, "What?" her mouth turned into the straightest line Henry ever saw. Henry heard a voice coming through the phone and recognized it. Aunt Shelley. He watched Grandma Sylvie's face go from Worried to Mad. She said, *Tell him I said he's being ridiculous.* And, *If you have to come you have to come.* And, *No. I do not want to see him.* And, *No, I'm not telling her. You tell her.* And, *Oh well.* She pressed the *Off* button and snapped the phone shut and put it in her bag and looked at Henry and said, "Of course they want me to break the news."

She didn't say what the news was but he figured it out. Aunt Shelley and Grandpa Marshall were coming. He didn't know what day they were coming, but he knew that was going to be a Bad Day for sure.

24

Routines. To Sylvie, they were like a religion. When Lane and Shelley were young, their mother made sure each of them stuck to one extracurricular routine, one activity they could do no matter where they moved. For Shelley, it was theater. In every town they lived, their mother found first a children's theater group, later one for teens. Her sister didn't especially enjoy performing in front of an audience, but she loved the rest of it. Being part of a troupe, after-rehearsal hangouts, postplay celebrations. For Lane, it was swimming. In every town they lived in, their mother would find a pool and sign her up, first for lessons, later on a team. Lane never liked being on a team, but she loved the feel of being in the water. Submerged, she felt free.

As for her own routines, Sylvie had a few, but the main one was walking. Unlike Lane's relationship with swimming, though—the main goal of which was to lose herself—Sylvie always walked as if she were on a mission, her face set not in dreamy reflection, but in a hard and focused stare.

But so far, on the island, Sylvie hadn't walked anywhere. She seemed reluctant to leave the house at all. To Lane it seemed as if her mother was acting like a person in recovery. As to what she was recovering from, she didn't yet have enough information to speculate. All she could do was observe her mother sinking, every day, further into herself.

On their very first day, Nathan had asked Lane to join him on a walk around the pond and after Lane agreed, she invited her mother and Henry to join them. They both declined. When Lane got back, she excitedly reported what she'd seen: frogs croaking on lily pads in the pond, dive-bombing hummingbirds. "You'll love walking here," she told her mother. "The air smells like pine. So many birds trilling in so many trees."

Her mother was unmoved, so Lane began to take a daily walk herself. In part this was to get some exercise; ever since their arrival, Spectacle Pond had been closed to swimming because of high levels of bacteria. Not uncommon, Nathan told her, after a rainy spell. This was why they always had a pond volunteer checking on water quality and why the results of those tests were posted on the whiteboard outside the entrance to the Rec. The sign, which also included announcements of camper birthdays, holiday greetings and the day's weather, listed the swimming conditions as either, hooray, we can swim, with a smiley face, or boo, no swimming today, with a frown. So far, the sign had been, frowny face, no swimming today, every day.

The other reason Lane walked was the hope that if she kept doing it, her mother would join her. So far, no luck. Since their arrival, Lane had walked the pond every day, alone.

She didn't mind. The pond was so quiet in the morning, her only company was hummingbirds and dragonflies. She used the walk the same way she used her swimming time, to work through the things that were weighing on her. There were a lot of candidates.

Work was one. Summer's texts, for starters. The last few had been filled with emojis that Lane didn't understand. Each time she got a new one, she googled it to parse out the meaning. But even googling didn't help. There was no unanimity on the internet about the meaning of the emoji that looked like a whistling face, or was it a face blowing a kiss? Googling did nothing to explain what the woman dancing in the red dress had to do with her. So she texted Summer and asked her to please use words, that emojis were not effective for communicating. Summer replied with an upside-down smile.

Sam was another worry. To her surprise and joy, an email from him had arrived the night before, but the joy didn't last. His email said his return was up in the air, —but hang in there. I still have your back. That was not at all reassuring. It was also not from his Guild address. Why, she wondered, had he stopped using Guild email?

She picked up her pace and her thoughts switched to Shelley, whose phone calls, once again, had stopped without explanation. They hadn't spoken since Lane's arrival on the Island. Their last conversation was the one where Lane mentioned the news that Uncle Albie had died. Those two facts—her sharing the news about Albie and Shelley not calling again—were definitely connected. But how? She had no idea. Now she was engaged in the useless exercise of calling Shelley every day and leaving a message, which, no surprise, her sister was ignoring. Was Shelley— She stopped herself. Dwelling on her sister's phone habits was a waste of time. The path looped to the left and she followed it, the sun tracking her like a spotlight.

The light in her day was Henry. Things were going well for Henry. He'd even made friends. Camp friends who, like him, loved nothing better than drawing. Amanda, his counselor, had told her this at the end of the first week when she picked him up. While most of the campers complained about the pond being closed for swimming, Henry and his gang sat with smiles on their faces as they silently sketched their made-up constellations using charcoal or pastels or watercolors. Lane stopped herself and took a moment to revel in what she had just thought: Henry was part of a gang.

The other bright light in her day was Nathan. He stopped by the house almost every day, and just as he had in New Jersey, he frequently came bearing gifts. She suspected the gifts continued because his guilt continued. First it was because he'd rented her a falling-apart house in New Jersey. Now it was because the guest house had not turned out to be what he'd promised. Yesterday, her second Sunday on the island, when he showed up with arms full of freshly cut true-blue hydrangeas, heavy with bloom, she told him he didn't have anything to apologize for; she'd gotten the good end of the deal. She should be bringing flowers to him.

There was no one she would admit it to—she could barely admit it to herself—but it was becoming hard work, trying to see Nathan as just a friend.

Round and round her thoughts went, from work to Shelley to Henry to Nathan and—oh!—how the dappled light danced through the branches of the beetlebung trees. And—oh!—that brown-and-green leaf opened as if with wings because—oh!—it wasn't a leaf; it was a perfectly camouflaged butterfly. And—oh!—how strange to see a caterpillar hanging on an invisible silken thread so that it looked as if the tiny thing was actually dancing in the air. And—oh!—just as strange as the caterpillar dancing was Lane noticing that she, who usually rushed through life as if being chased, was standing still, watching the dance.

"You have to go for a walk," she told her mother when she got back to the house that morning. "I saw a dozen dragonflies and a dancing caterpillar. The wildflowers are huge. Or maybe they're weeds. It's impossible to tell what's a weed and what's a wildflower."

To her surprise, her mother agreed. Right then, in that very moment, she stood up, said she would go, and left the house. Left for her first walk around the pond from which she did not return. Not after one hour or two or three.

When her mother didn't return after three hours, Lane called the police. The man who answered the phone was kind. He came by ten minutes later. He carefully wrote down the description and then asked her mother's age before gently raising the question of dementia.

"She's of sound mind," Lane said. "More or less."

He nodded and told her he'd notify the other towns' police departments and discuss with his supervisor whether or not it was too early to put out a Silver Alert. "It's a judgment call with our elders," he explained. "We don't like to wait for a situation to become critical. But we don't want to embarrass people."

They were right to wait. Her main thought when Sylvie was finally home was how lucky they'd been that Henry had been at camp when it all happened. She wouldn't have wanted him to be there when the police came to take the description, or to watch the spectacle of her annoying conversation she had with Shelley, whom she'd called after the policeman left the house.

Shelley had picked up on the third call and sounded irritated that, once again, no one had died. "Mom taking a long walk is not an emergency," she said. "What's wrong with you people? The two of you. You and Dad both." She paused and then added, "I know you don't mean to, but the messages you leave are making Dad even more anxious."

That was how Lane learned the difficult-to-digest news that her stay-at-home father had somehow gotten himself to Shelley's house in England for a visit.

In the end the resolution was a happy one. Sylvie, it turned out, had been picked up by mistake by a memory care center van. It was a social worker from the center—Connie—who brought her home and explained what happened.

"She got lost on her walk and we picked her up by accident. It's nobody's fault."

Lane waited for her mother to comment but she said nothing. She just sat, cheeks flushed, staring into her lap while the social worker told the rest of what happened.

Connie didn't live on Spectacle Pond but she'd hiked in to kayak enough times to know the spot that tripped Sylvie up. "It's the split where Lower and Upper Spectacle divide. The trees all look the same. It's easy to get lost. Our van driver could tell she was lost. His mistake was thinking she was one of ours." Connie looked at Sylvie and beamed. "And now she is."

"Pardon?" Lane said.

"I convinced your mom to volunteer. We have lots of volunteers at the center who come in to do crafts or play guitar or sing. Your mom just sat with our clients. They love her. She's a very calming presence."

It wasn't how she thought of her mother—calming—but she had noticed her mother had the same effect on Henry. He was very relaxed with her. Maybe there was more to her mother than the sliver she saw.

After Connie left, Sylvie told her side of what happened. "When I got to the center they realized I was picked up by accident and they offered to bring me here. But I couldn't tell them where to go. I don't know the address here. All I could say was it's a house on the pond. Did you know there are something like sixty ponds on this island?"

"Why didn't you call me?"

"I didn't take my phone. They offered me theirs but that didn't help. I didn't know your number. Normally I press your name."

Normally, Lane thought, *you don't call.* By this point they were sitting on the couch, her mother tucked into the opposite corner, close enough for Lane to see her agitation. "But it all worked out fine, right? Better than fine. Sounds like you're the star of the memory center." Her mother's hands, she saw, were clasped tight. Her knuckles were white.

After a long silence her mother spoke. "I never understood."

"Understood what?" She watched as her mother struggled. She seemed to be weighing whether or not to say more. "Understood what?" she asked again.

Her mother drew a deep breath. When she let it out it was shaky. "Your uncle used to get lost. Terribly lost. Totally lost. And I would get so angry. So very angry. I couldn't understand how a person, a grown man, could get lost going for a walk. And now." She shook her head. "I did exactly that. And you're not mad at all." Her mouth was a flat line that broke only when she whispered, "I was awful."

Lane didn't know what to say so she said nothing. She drew the quietest possible breath and stayed completely still, save for her startled blinks. This was, as far as she could remember, the first time her mother had ever brought up the subject of her uncle. When it was clear her mother wasn't going to say anything more, Lane said, "I didn't know Uncle Albie got lost."

Sylvie met her eyes. "Well that's good. You were a child. Your father and I weren't sure what you knew. It was hard to know in all the commotion. There wasn't always commotion. Just when he got himself into trouble. He never meant to make trouble. It was the opposite. He was trying to stop trouble. Who could blame him? Well some people did. They didn't understand."

Again Lane waited and when nothing more came, she prodded, "What kind of trouble?"

"Oh," her mother said. She shook her head, remembering. "Sometimes he'd end up way on the other side of town at a park. Parks were the worst. Children on monkey bars would make him physically ill, he was so sure they would fall. Little things set him off too. He'd see a child outside alone and lose his mind. A small child, outside their own house, drawing with chalk on the sidewalk, would make him rave like a lunatic, yelling at them to get in the house. Of course they'd run inside, terrified because a lunatic had started yelling at them." Her eyes filled up. She shook her head again, sat up straighter and lifted her chin. "We tried. No one can say we didn't." She slumped. "Nothing worked. Nothing."

"What did you try?"

"Therapists. A new one in every town. Medicine. He tried so many pills. I could barely keep track of which ones he'd already tried. Amoxa-something. Trimipra-something. Fluoxa-something."

"Wait." Lane closed her eyes. She felt something niggling at the far recesses of her memory. She heard the tune first and then found the words. *Amoxapine and Trimipramine, you take them every day. Fluoxetine and Sertraline will send you on your way.*

"I don't know why you girls made up that horrid song about your uncle's medication."

"That song was about the drugs Dad sold."

Her mother laughed. "No, it was not. That song is a list of your uncle's medicine. His useless medicine." She shrugged. "I suppose there is no medicine for what he had."

"What did he have?"

Her mother slumped and waved the question away. She took a breath and straightened. "You know, Turtle, the van driver for the memory center, the one who picked me up today, he really could not have been nicer. Do you think I should send him a thank-you note?"

"What? Sure. Yes. Why not? We were talking about Uncle Albie."

"I know, but now I want to talk about the van driver. You probably can't understand how it happened but it took me some time before I realized he wasn't bringing me here. Of course eventually I figured it out. Suddenly we weren't in the woods anymore. We were on a road, going past the ocean. A beautiful road, with a pond on one side, and the ocean beyond that, and a pasture with herds of cows and sheep and goats. None of the other people on the bus said a peep. And then the van finally stopped and everyone stood up and shuffled off so I got off too. When I asked people where I was, they said, 'Have a cup of tea. Have a piece of cake.' They have very good cake."

Lane wasn't sure what a normal person in a normal family would do in this situation. She tried to imagine what Roxie would say to someone who wanted to get their mother to go back to talking about the past when she seemed nearly desperate to do anything but that.

Sit with her, is what Roxie would say. *Take what's offered with an open heart.*

So she did. She sat in silence for several minutes and when her mother finally met her eyes and said, "Oh well," Lane nodded and reached for her hand and her mother did not pull away.

25

It was on Wednesday, the second week of camp, when Henry's favorite counselor, Amanda, took Lane aside. "Dylan's been leaning hard on Henry," she said. "Trying to convince him to stop drawing and join the pinhole-box table. Henry told me he doesn't want to so—"

"Wait. Henry spoke to you?"

"Oh sorry." Amanda blushed. "He signed to me. I taught him a few words. I hope you don't mind. I've been a mother's helper for a deaf kid, for a couple of years. I'm not fluent or anything." She demonstrated as she spoke. "I just showed him *Yes*, *No*, *More*, and *Stop*. Should I have asked you first?"

"No. That's so lovely. What a great idea."

She shrugged off the compliment. "The thing is, I told Dylan that Henry does not want to switch tables and to leave him alone and let him draw. But Dylan doesn't listen to me. Or any of the counselors. He does listen to parents, so—"

Without thinking, Lane lurched forward and gave Amanda a hug. She immediately backed away. "Sorry," she said. "I didn't mean to overstep."

"That's totally fine," Amanda said. "Dylan's right over there if you want to talk to him."

As Lane headed to the table at the back of the room where Dylan was sitting, she thought about how there was always a Dylan. Always a Dylan and always a Silas. The Silas's took Henry's silence as a personal rejection. The Dylans took it as a challenge. From what she'd observed at camp drop-off and pickup, Dylan seemed fairly indifferent to the rest of the campers but he was determined to take Henry under his wing, regardless of whether his wing was a place Henry wanted to be.

Dylan's chair was tipped back, the front feet up in the air. Dangerously, Lane thought. "Can I have a word with you?" she asked. "In private." He followed her outside to the Rec's small front porch. "I think it would be best if you let Henry choose his own activities for now. If he wants to draw, let's let him draw."

"Okay, cool. It's just—like I explained to the little man—I don't want him to be left out and end up filled with regret. I don't know if you know this, but the kids won't be allowed to come outside to watch the eclipse at the end-of-camp party if they don't have a pinhole box."

Lane's stomach clenched at the words *pinhole box*. She had underestimated how hard attending an eclipse party was going to be. Probably because she had no choice; no matter the theme, Henry's end-of-camp celebration party was not something she would miss.

Dylan was still talking. "I'm sure you don't want the little man to grow up bitter like my dad. I mean, think about it. He's upset about something that happened in the nineteen hundreds."

"I think you mean the nineteen seventies," Lane said. Dylan looked wounded. That was not helpful. "I know your concern comes out of kindness. But Henry's not interested in that project. Does he know the rule that if he doesn't make a box he can't go outside during the eclipse?"

"I tell him every day."

"Okay. So no need to tell him anymore. He's made his choice. He's fine with not seeing the eclipse." She didn't say the rest. She was fine with it too. The counselor begrudgingly agreed. They both returned inside, Lane to say goodbye to Henry, Dylan to resume testing gravity with his chair.

She found Henry sitting with his new friends, all three of them concentrating hard on their drawings, today their fingers fisted around fat markers. As she headed toward him she heard an uptick in a voice behind her. Dylan had detoured to ask her one more question.

". . . probably why you're not bitter like my dad?" He was like a dog trying to get marrow out of a bone. "Because you got to see the eclipse. Right? So, goes to show, Henry should—"

She cut him off. "I appreciate your concern. But Henry wants to draw. So that's what he should do. Okay?"

"I guess." Dylan saw her expression shifting to a warning. "Okay."

Lane gave Henry a quick goodbye and made a hasty exit, waving another thank-you to Amanda as she left. Dylan eyed her, but stayed where he was. His voice came with her, though. She heard him as she walked down the narrow path to the water. *Probably you're not bitter because you got to see the eclipse.*

What she'd wanted to say was, *Stop talking.* What she'd wanted to say was, *You have no idea how I feel about that day.* But instead she'd cut him off. Now Dylan was a member in good standing of the crowded tribe of people who thought her rude.

The path stopped at the lake and offered up its choices. She picked the route to the left.

She hadn't meant to be rude to Dylan but she had no choice. Getting into a conversation about the last total eclipse of the sun with him was out of the question. And what would she say? She laughed out loud imagining it. *My school wasn't closed but my mother kept me home. Not because she'd feared all the children of the world would go blind at once but because we were getting a rare visit from her brother.*

That day was the second time Albie had come to see his nieces but Lane had no memory of the first time. She'd been too young. She felt like she knew him, though, in the way people felt as if they'd experienced things when family stories got told so often the lines between hearing them and living them became blurred.

"I adored my brother," her mother often said. "And he adored me back. He would have followed me off a cliff. Did I ever tell you we promised to live next door to each other when we grew up?" she'd ask, again and again. "Unless we lived in apartments. Then it could be next door, or above or below. Aunt Beadie put a kibosh on that promise," she'd tell them, over and over. "Good thing she doesn't know about the other promise."

Lane and Shelley always moved their lips slightly—just enough so they'd both know they were doing it—to mouth what their mother always said next. "Eclipse of the sun."

"We're going to watch the next total eclipse of the sun together. When the last one came we were little children. Uncle Albie was seven."

"Last time you told us, he was eight," Shelley would say, to be annoying.

"Maybe he was eight. I was ten. We were so excited. My father made us special glasses. Not like what they have today. It was just cut-up cardboard with lenses made out of film. My mother said it was a waste of film but he did it anyway. He woke us up early so we wouldn't miss it. But it never came where we lived. My grandmother saw it, though. She lived in Minneapolis. She called, all excited, to tell us how it came at sunrise. How one minute the birds were singing and the next they stopped. Poor Albie, he got so upset at that. He started crying. Sobbing. Because he wanted to hear the birds stop singing. So I promised him he'd get another chance. There'd be another eclipse. And he made me promise we'd watch it together. Which I did. I promised whenever the next eclipse came, he would come over to wherever I was, which would probably be right next door, or downstairs or upstairs, depending on where we lived, and we'd watch it together. He won't forget," she told Lane and Shelley more than once, sharply, as if they'd challenged her.

And they'd nod, to show they knew she was right. Their uncle would not forget.

He didn't. The day of the total solar eclipse their mother woke them up to tell them the good news. "He remembered! He's coming. With your cousin, Ivy. So we can all watch it together." Then, more good news. "You're staying home from school."

Shelley wasn't happy. She didn't want to miss school. She had her own plans to watch the eclipse with her friends. But their mother wouldn't budge. Friends were replaceable. Family was not.

That was why, while the rest of the world prepared for the marvel of a total solar eclipse, her mother prepared the house for the bigger marvel of the arrival of the beloved uncle her children couldn't remember meeting and the cousin they forgot they had.

Lane only remembered bits of the visit but those bits were vivid. Ten-year-old Shelley dancing into her room to share what their father had told her about Uncle Albie, that the reason they never saw him was that he was the black sheep of the family. Every family had a black sheep, she'd explained and then abruptly stopped speaking.

From the look on Shelley's face, Lane deduced what her sister wasn't saying: if every family had a black sheep, in their nuclear family, Lane was it.

Other things she remembered: Uncle Albie showed up like it was nothing special, like he and Ivy stopped by every day. There were neither hugs nor introductions. It was just, "Hey, kiddo," and a smile that showed off the wide space between his front teeth. He didn't seem self-conscious about the gap.

Lane could still see it in her mind's eye, her uncle's gap-toothed smile. Ivy had it too.

Another memory: her mother was not herself. On a regular day if the doorbell rang, Sylvie would grab the nearest daughter and push her toward the foyer with instructions to tell whoever it was to go away. But on that day Sylvie raced to the door and let out an odd laugh—delight or embarrassment, Lane couldn't tell the difference—before skipping, like a child, arm in arm with her brother to the living room.

That the TV was on was not unusual; that it was tuned to the news was. Until that moment, Lane had thought news was only on at night. She didn't watch the TV, though. Her eyes stayed fixed on her cousin with the gap-toothed smile and the braids on either side of her face. Ivy's face was as round as the moon and tipped, from the minute she arrived, toward Shelley.

When the broadcaster began describing exactly where in Oregon he was speaking from, Ivy announced she'd been to Oregon too, the previous summer, to visit her mother's parents.

"You went to Oregon?" Shelley said. "You're lucky. We never go anywhere."

Lane felt dizzy with confusion. Was her sister sick? Did she have a fever? Was it scarlet fever? Was that the one that affected the brain? Because something *had* affected her brain. Why else would she say, *We never go anywhere.* The Mecklers did nothing but go.

Maybe when Lane wasn't looking, Shelley had been hypnotized. She was acting hypnotized, complimenting Ivy on everything, even her braids. Shelley hated braids. Whenever their mother tried to braid Shelley's hair, she'd run out of the room and Sylvie would have to make do with braiding Lane's hair instead.

Why would anyone like Ivy's braids? They weren't neat or pulled tight like their mother made them. They had bits and pieces of tiny hair flying out every which way, like she'd been attacked by a jolt of static electricity.

But Shelley was seeing something else. "Can I touch your braids?" she asked.

"Sure," Ivy said. She tipped her head so Shelley didn't have to stretch to do it.

Lane wanted to barf; she wasn't sure why. Maybe it was because of Ivy's smile, which now took up half of her face, or maybe it was because of Shelley's voice, which was completely fake. Was this how Shelley made friends at school? Fake smile. Fake words. Fake nice.

Her sister seemed to have forgotten Lane existed.

At some point Shelley asked their mother to change the channel because it was boring. Ivy immediately piled on. "Boring. Boring. Boring me to death."

"It won't be boring when it happens," their mother said. "Maybe if it were a partial eclipse it would be boring. But not a total. They have no idea," Sylvie told her brother.

He agreed. "Not a clue."

The eclipse wasn't happening for a while, so Shelley asked, "Can Ivy and I go out and play?"

Ivy and I.

Their mother was the one who insisted she take Lane along. Shelley and Ivy made a face at that, with mirror-image eye rolls and two sets of lips curled up, but in unison—Ivy was a barely discernible millisecond behind—they both said, "Fine."

Outside Ivy asked Shelley why her house had a sad face.

Lane hadn't noticed it before but Ivy was right. "I see it," she said. "The second floor windows—with the shades halfway down—they look like droopy eyes. And the front-door window—it's like a frowny mouth."

"That's not it at all," Ivy said. "It's an upside-down face. The roof is the smile. See how the roof looks? Like a smile made out of rotten teeth."

Forever after, that was how Lane remembered that roof. A roof of rotten teeth.

Later, upstairs in Lane's room, when the sky darkened, Ivy and Shelley moved to the window, standing so close together it was as if they were a person and a shadow.

At some point Shelley called downstairs, "I think it's happening." Ivy repeated her words like an echo. The sky brightened, ignoring them both.

"False alarm," Lane said. "It was just a cloud."

Ivy wasn't sure but she took a step back. "We're not supposed to look out. We could go blind." She took another step back. Remembering her father's warnings had made her momentarily timid.

"Aw," Shelley said. "You're so cute. You don't have to worry. It's not the eclipse yet. You can still look. Too bad we don't have those glasses that let you look right at the sun. I asked my mom to get them but she didn't have time. I don't know why. She doesn't work like your mom."

Ivy nodded. "Someone's got to put food on the table."

It was taking forever for the eclipse to come.

"You're lucky," Shelley told Ivy. "Your mom works and your dad's nice."

Lane didn't know how to stop what was happening. "I don't think people are allowed to be best friends with their cousin," she announced.

Shelley snorted. "People are allowed to be best friends with anyone they want, except their sister." She turned her back and said to Ivy, "I love your shirt. I wish I had a shirt like that. I wish I had your hair."

Lane stared at her cousin's shirt. It was orange corduroy with snaps and a pocket, nothing to get excited about. As for Ivy's hair, Lane couldn't imagine why anyone would want hair the color of dead leaves.

"I always wanted blue eyes," her sister said next.

What about Lane's eyes? They were blue and her sister had never said a word about them. A sour taste came into her mouth as if something were percolating in her stomach. She moved closer to her sister and reached for her hand. With great economy—Ivy never noticed—Shelley flicked it away.

Ivy turned in a slow circle. "Whose room is this anyway?"

There were no clues. Except for Sylvie's embroidery, the Mecklers didn't put things on walls. Rule Number Six.

"Hers," Shelley said with a tip of her head. Now she wouldn't even say Lane's name. "Mine's down the hall. It's bigger. I always get to pick first because I'm older. We move a lot. Most of our houses are bigger than this one. In our last house I had an office next to my room with a desk and a chair. My dad lets me open his mail. My room has two closets. Want to see?"

They were heading out to see when Lane called over, "My room has a secret door."

Ivy stopped. "A what?"

Lane did not look at her sister. "It looks like a regular window but it's really a door." This was how logic looked when it was born out of desperation. "You can go outside through it. Onto the roof. Shelley likes to go out and sit on the roof to watch people. Sometimes I go with her."

"You do not. She does not."

Ivy whispered, "You're allowed on the roof?"

"Nope." Shelley shook her head. "But I go anyway. It's fun. I spy on people. If you stay perfectly still—" She froze. She unfroze. "No one even notices. I'm very good at staying still." She froze again.

"Wow." Ivy was impressed.

Well this had backfired.

"My parents don't know," Shelley said. "Cross your heart you won't tell?"

Lane needed to minimize the damage. "It's not dangerous. It's not really a roof. It's flat. Shelley would never go out on a pointy roof."

"It's not flat." Shelley pointed to the window. "See for yourself."

The danger of the eclipse temporarily forgotten, Ivy looked out the window. "Not flat."

Now there were teams. Two people on Shelley's. Just Lane on Lane's. Her eyes narrowed to slits. "If you're so brave, how come you're not going out there to watch the eclipse?"

"Too cold," Ivy said. "Plus she's afraid to go blind."

Lane saw her sister flinch at the word *afraid*. "Shelley's not afraid," Lane said. "You're the one who's a scaredy-cat." She turned to her sister. "Use my pinhole box. Over there." She tipped her head toward a carton in the corner of the room. "My teacher made us make them so no one in our class would go blind."

Shelley picked up the box and examined it. "You forgot to make a pinhole," she told Lane. "You're crazy if you think this would work."

"A total nuteroo," Ivy said.

Something flickered across her sister's face. Shelley didn't seem to like Ivy calling her a nuteroo.

"I'll go with you," Lane told her sister. "Without the box. Just us two."

"Your sister is a loony tune," Ivy sang out. "I wish I was your sister instead."

"We'll all go out." Shelley walked over and opened the window.

A bitter breeze blew apart the pleated curtains. From where she stood, Lane could make out a thin sheen of black ice on the roof.

"Who wants to go first?" Shelley asked. No one answered. "Okay. I will." She lifted a leg and straddled the sill, then poked her head out the window. She drew it back in and blew a cloud of vapor into the room. "I'm smoking. Who wants to smoke with me?"

Ivy laughed and puffed out invisible air. "I'm smoking too."

Shelley lowered herself onto the roof. "No one's outside." Her hand held tight to the sill. "I can see into everyone's house. They're all watching the eclipse on TV. It's starting."

The sun was strong and Lane was parched. She stopped for a water break on the small land bridge that gave Spectacle Pond its name. On the first day she walked the pond, with Nathan—he stopped often to pick up trash along the way, stuffing the trash in his pockets with a smile—he'd explained how along the right eye of the pond there were homes and around the left eye it was all undeveloped land owned by a public trust. The relationship between the eyes was not good.

"Riparian owners want to protect their privacy," Nathan had told her. "Trustees want public access and conservation. Such are the problems in paradise."

Now a sound broke through her thoughts. It was nothing she recognized. She scanned the pond through the trees as she walked, high grass sweeping her knees. She heard it again. Was it a bleat? Was it a goat?

At the edge of the left eye of the pond she saw it, a flutter of fabric. A shirttail, dark, the same color as the tree trunks—flapping in the wind. The sound, the bleat, repeated.

A voice, a woman's, called out, insistent. "Come on. Let's go." Another flutter of fabric. A woman was standing in the pond calling out, "Stop. Stop that right now."

Lane moved quickly, mud sucking at her sneakers, to help.

26

The woman—tall, spindly, her white hair loose in the wind—stood in the pond submerged to her thighs. "Okay," she said calmly. "Let's try this again. You want to kick me? Kick me."

Lane called over, "You okay?"

The woman turned and Lane caught a flash of her face. Skin, weathered. Eyes, electric blue. Her finger was at her lips. "Shh."

Now Lane saw why. There was a deer, a fawn, stuck in the mud. The woman turned to the deer but she spoke to Lane, keeping her voice steady and low. "I don't want to startle her. She's been trying to get out of this muck since yesterday. I'm afraid if she doesn't get out soon, she's going to die. Yesterday she was kicking hard. Now she's not. She's weak. Barely moved in an hour. It's okay," she cooed to the fawn. "You can do it."

"Can I help?"

The woman nodded. "Just move slow so you don't startle her. If the mud sucks at your shoes, use your arms to pull up your thighs. Quietly," she added in a whisper.

Lane did as she was told and moved, slow and steady, through the water. The muck grabbed her shoes so she lifted her thighs with her hands and took long steps until she was next to the woman.

"I'll take the rear," the woman said. "You hold her neck."

They worked together, gently pushing and pulling, rocking the deer back and forth until Lane heard the sharp sound of suction releasing, and the fawn leaped out of the water, legs spread wide, and took off. There was a racket of rustling, branches being broken as she ran, and then the fawn was gone; only her muddy prints remained.

The woman tilted her head back and laughed, and then called out to the vanished deer, "You're welcome." She wiped her muddy palms on her jeans and extended a hand. "Thank you."

"Thank you for letting me help. I'm sorry—I forget your name."

The woman hesitated. "Do I know you?"

"We met at Opening Party. I'm Lane Meckler. Henry's mom? I was with Nathan. I'm renting his house. I'm sorry. I'm terrible with names. I'm terrible at parties. Which is why I don't usually go to parties. I don't usually go anywhere."

"Neither do I. We've never met. I wasn't at the party. I'm Aggie. Griffin's mom." She saw a flicker of recognition on Lane's face. "Wow. Amazing how quickly people get caught up on who's who around here."

"No, I just—Henry, my son, he saw Griffin at the party and—"

"Ahh. He got scared. Don't worry. I'm not offended. Griffin scares people. He doesn't mean to. It's just he's big and he doesn't speak. Except to animals. He loves to talk to animals. Thanks for your help. Feel free to continue on your way."

"My son doesn't speak." Lane felt her cheeks heat up. She hadn't expected to share.

"Does he only talk to animals?"

"No. He only talks to me."

Aggie nodded. "Griffin talks to me too. Not much, but to be honest I don't talk much either. Mostly I talk to myself. When I'm home. And

314

sometimes when I'm walking in the woods. But not if I hear someone coming. Then I just try and blend in with the trees. I guess today I was so busy concentrating on our little deer friend, I forgot to hide. Well now you know. Aggie's tip: dress to disappear." She gestured at her clothes, a study in browns and greens, perfect camouflage, if it weren't for her shock of white hair. "It works by mutual agreement. I want to disappear and everyone else wants me to disappear too. Which eventually I will. And then what?" She laughed. "Oh boy. You're going to have a lot to tell the next time you go to the Rec. *The weird lady told me she's afraid of dying.* Don't say that, though. Don't say anything about me being afraid. That wouldn't go well for Griffin. Oh boy. You're going to be able to dine out on this for years."

Usually when people shared their suffering in person with Lane she just smiled as she looked for the nearest exit. But listening to this woman who sounded broken, she felt something shift. She was never any good at turning away from the wounded. "I worry about dying too," she said.

"You do? Why?"

Lane surprised herself by answering. "My husband died this year. Now my son will only speak to me. If I died today—he might never speak again." She took a breath. Her eyes felt wet. Was she about to cry? She couldn't remember the last time she cried. She quickly wiped her eyes and checked the back of her hand. Damp. "Okay. I guess now we can both dine out on each other's stories."

"I don't dine out. Anyway, how would that help either of us?"

They moved through the muck toward the trail and then walked on, side by side in silence.

Aggie broke it. "Did your son stop speaking because of what happened to your husband? Was he with him when it happened? Never mind. It's none of my business."

"That's okay. I don't mind." It was true. She didn't mind, which was strange. "He wasn't there. He stopped speaking because . . ." What was the right answer? There were so many choices. Because he was grieving over his father's death or because she'd waited too long to tell him his father died or because he'd been accidentally thrown away in a cardboard box. It was unsettling, tallying it all up. Who would want to speak, after all that? "I'm not sure why."

"He doesn't want to tell you," Aggie said, as if she were repeating something Lane had said.

But she hadn't said that. Henry had never offered a reason and she had never asked him. Because his therapist and everyone else kept saying her job was to act like nothing was wrong. Was it possible *they* were wrong? Was it possible Henry's silence was modeled after *hers*? She had to admit, she was an expert at not saying things.

". . . me for some tea?"

"Pardon?"

"Never mind. Don't know what I was thinking. Dumb idea."

"No, I'm sorry. I got carried away by a thought. Please—what did you say?"

"Just—that's my house." She pointed up the path. "So if you ever wanted to come over for tea, you could. You don't have to. It's fine if you don't."

"I'd love to," Lane said and then, "How's now?" surprising them both.

Seated on an Adirondack chair at the edge of Aggie's dock, Lane stared across the pond at the large building on the opposite shore. She counted a dozen kayaks, turned upside down. "Who lives there?" she asked when Aggie returned with their tea.

Aggie laughed. "That's the Rec. I spent more hours of my life in that building than I care to remember and now that I never step foot inside,

I get to stare at it all day. My destiny." She lifted her cup as if making a toast. "I wish it well. From far away."

"You don't like the Rec?"

"The Rec's a building. I have nothing against the building. Although—have you met Peggy Mellman yet?"

"Maybe." Lane was never sure who she'd met.

"She writes the *Pond Scribbler*. All the news unfit to print. The Kuritskys are just back from Peru. The MacGregors had a visit from their grandson. Peggy Mellman will want to do a story about you. Fresh blood. Don't worry. Peggy's harmless—but she has this theory that the Rec makes people do things they wouldn't otherwise do. Kind of a handy excuse, don't you think? The building made me do it?"

"I don't know what that means."

"I don't either. But I can tell you, every day there's a different drama in there. I don't mean little things either, although little things too. Someone gets a splinter, someone gets a stomach bug, someone gets a bug in the ear or a fly in the eye. I'm talking about big things. One year, Tim Stinton—he was ninety-two—lays down on the couch for a nap that seems to last forever. Turns out it was forever. I can't remember how long he was there before someone finally figured out he was dead. Heart attack. That same summer we came this close"—she pinched the air—"to having a birth. It was Louisa's, Stretch's first wife. Her water broke. Luckily the ambulance came in time. Hooray for paramedics. I think I heard she married the paramedic after the divorce, but I could be wrong. My ex was in charge of knowing things. I was always a bit of a wall hugger. Odd mother of the odd child."

Lane felt a chill. It was like talking to a version of her future self.

"Louisa and her baby disappeared after that summer, which happens on the pond. People disappear. I don't mean disappear in place, like me. I mean their time is up. Like poor old Tim Stinton dropping dead, or Louisa moving off after her divorce. Wren and Simon moved off for a while too after Nathan and Ruth split. I wasn't that fond of

Ruth but I've always liked Nathan." She took a long look at Lane. "I can see it now. You're his type. A little younger. But so what? Me and my ex were born a week apart and a lot of good that did us."

"We're not together. We're friends. New friends. I'm renting his house. He's been very kind to my son. I don't know anything about Ruth. I don't know much about Nathan's past. He doesn't talk about it." Lane felt something nagging at the edges of her consciousness. A vague sense of—what? She closed her eyes and tried to pull in the thought. Something about Roxie. A letter to Roxie. The letter from the woman worried about the scary father of her daughter's friend. The letter where Roxie told the woman, *When it comes to our kids, we can't afford to take chances.*

She met Aggie's eyes. "Should I be worried about Nathan? I'm very fond of him and my son adores him. But—is there a reason he never talks about his past?" She laughed, surprised by her question. "What am I saying? I don't talk about my past either." She shook her head. "Never mind. Not my business."

"No, I get it. You're a mama bear. We both are. Two mama bears. I don't really know much about Nathan. I know he got divorced. I gather it was messy. The main thing I know? He's always been kind to Griff. Which is not nothing. My opinion? You want to know who a person really is, watch how they treat someone who's different." She took a sip of her now lukewarm tea. "Pond looks so placid. Rec Center looks so welcoming. You'd never know it's a pressure cooker in there."

"How so?"

"The expectation is up here." She raised her hand to show a high bar. "The kids are supposed to be having the time of their lives. Summer friendships. Summer romances. They're supposed to fall in love there and marry each other in there and have kids and then their kids are supposed to do the same. If you didn't know, you'd think it was one big party. Swimming and bonfires on the beach. Underneath that, it's all hurry up or fall behind. Griffin has the pond in his DNA.

Third-generation ponder. And last. He was never going to make it with that crowd. Even when he was a little kid, I knew. Too quiet. More interesting, I told myself. Sweet, for a while. Never friendly. A loner."

Henry, Lane thought and then stopped. No. She was the loner. Henry was like his dad. The mayor of their building, until his silence shut that down.

"We moved here year-round when Griff turned thirteen. That's when he started saying no to things. No baseball. No homework. No showers. Kids at home were cruel."

"Was it better here?" Lane heard the eagerness in her question. She wanted the answer to be yes. She wanted Henry, who had started making friends at the Rec, to become mayor again.

"How old is Henry?" Aggie asked.

"Six."

She nodded. "It's a different story when they're little. No one was scared of Griff when he was a little boy. But now? He's twenty-four years old and people are terrified of him. It took me a while to take that in. I mean, he's my son. Who wants to think that about their son? I got an inkling when people started asking me—down at the newspaper tubes—if everything was okay. A casual question, right? I'd say fine and go on my way. Peggy Mellman was the one who finally came out and asked me if Griff was dangerous. Told me everyone was worried. That got my attention. *Everyone* was worried. I said, *Tell* everyone *not to worry. It's my life that's the nightmare.* Tactical error, saying that."

"Why?"

"My nightmare is Griff's future. What's going to happen when I'm gone? But Peggy heard something different. Next thing I know there's a rumor racing around the pond that I'm terrified of my son. That's when I got the offer. Ten families—out of eighteen—tried to buy me out. Nathan was not one of them. He called me when he heard. Asked if there was anything he could do. No matter what anyone says about him, I'll never forget that. I told the rest of them to go to hell. Did you meet Griffin?"

"No. Henry didn't meet him either. He saw him through the window of the Rec and he got . . ."

"Scared." Aggie nodded. "Don't feel bad. Griffin works out with weights in his room. That was my bad idea. At the time, I thought it was a brainstorm. Gave him something to do. Now I get it. When Griff walks he's silent. His gaze is straight ahead. His arms hang down like deadweight." She let out a long sigh. "Griffin thinks if he doesn't make eye contact, if he moves as little as possible when he walks, no one will notice him. I get that too." She shook her head. "People here should know better. They've known him since he was a speck." She took a final sip. "I told him to stop cleaning the Rec. I'm afraid it won't end well."

"Why does he clean the Rec?"

"Another brilliant bad idea. Started when he was fourteen, the summer after Nathan and Ruth left. Everyone was so busy being mad at Nathan and Ruth, they didn't notice. Nathan and Ruth were like the glue. When they split up, things fell apart. Wren and Simon split too, but they got back together. But there was that one summer when they were all gone. All the ringleaders gone. And everyone stopped going to the Rec. End of an era, people said. It was almost apocalyptic. The summer of storms. Trees came down. Branches broke through the Rec's windows. Animals started coming in. I watched it happen from right here. First the birds moved in, then barn owls nested. Stretch, next door, he was the one who told me a deer got stuck inside. Me and deer go back a long time. Griffin came with me to help me get her out. It was after we got the deer out that Griffin started going every day. To make sure no other animals were stuck. While he was there, he'd clean up. The next summer, after Wren and Simon patched things up and came back, things returned to how they were, except that Griffin was now cleaning the Rec. I was paying him. To give him something to do. I told him to get a job but no one would hire him to scoop ice cream, or be a camp counselor. They wanted him to stop cleaning the Rec. They still do. But nobody has the nerve to ask so . . ." She suddenly seemed self-conscious. "Sorry. It's been so long—years, maybe—since anyone's come by."

"Their loss."

Aggie smiled. "I know it's hard to have a son who's different. People tease them and gang up on them. It's the natural order. Peck or be pecked. But it's a different story when the boy becomes a man. Griffin is the same as he always was, to me. I still see the little boy. But other people? They see a scary man. You like to swim?"

"Yes."

"Here's a tip. If you go in the pond between the hours of nine and ten every day you'll practically be alone. That's when Griffin swims. Same time, rain or shine. Even when the bacteria level is high, he swims. I can't stop him. And he never gets sick. He's got the constitution of an ox. He swims right through the fall. Wears a wet suit when it's cold. That was another mistake I made—I guess I've made a lot—getting him a wet suit. He looks even scarier in that. Either way, in the wet suit or not, no one goes in that pond when Griff swims. That's why camp starts at nine thirty and the kids don't swim till ten."

"Because of Griffin?"

Aggie nodded. "He does a good job at the Rec. He works like his life depends on it. Washes the floor and the ceiling. Gets on his knees and pulls out every weed between every paving stone on the path. Got rid of all the poison ivy in the old outhouse one summer even though I told him no one uses it anymore." She raised her chin, defiant. "I'm proud of him."

"He's lucky to have you."

"Mom?"

And there he was. Despite Griffin's large size, he'd approached like a cat, without a sound. Against her will, Lane felt herself draw back. He was as Aggie described him. Big, with wide shoulders and muscular arms that hung straight down. Large hands curled into tight fists. Thick neck. Square chin. Dark hair hanging half over his eyes. Eyes pointed straight ahead.

"Mom? I think I have a tick. Do I have a tick? I hope I don't." His voice was deep but his words were those of a child. "What do I do if I have a tick?" He closed his eyes and stuck out his arm. "Can you look? Can you tell me? Is it a tick? I don't want a tick. Do I have one?"

Aggie got up and it was all business as she held on to his arm and examined every bit of him, narrating as she looked. "That's just a mole. That's a scrape from yesterday. That's a scar from when you fell out of the tire swing when you were little." The way she moved and spoke suggested this wasn't the first time he'd asked her to check. "Is this what you're worried about? I want you to look at it. This is a mosquito bite. It itches, right? That's because it's a mosquito bite, not a tick. You're good."

"Phew." Griffin pulled down his sleeves. Only then did he seem to notice Lane.

Lane stood and introduced herself.

"Griff," Aggie said. "You know what to do."

His eyes stayed straight ahead but he extended his arm and shook the proffered hand.

"Pleasure to meet you," Lane said.

"Griff? What do you say?"

Eyes on the ground now. "Thank you." His voice was deep but his words were the same ones Henry used when he felt self-conscious.

Used to use, she corrected herself. Back in the days when he spoke. Was Henry going to turn into Griffin? Was Aggie once like Lane? She stood up. "I have to go home. It's so nice to meet you both but I've got work to—"

"It's okay," Aggie said. "No need to make excuses."

"It's not an excuse. I do have work to do. But I'd love for you to come over sometime for tea. With Griffin. Griffin, I'd love for you to meet my son, Henry. You'd like each other. Do you like to draw?"

Griffin stared at his feet and nodded.

"Great. Henry does too. If you come over sometime, you can draw together."

Aggie smiled. "You're very kind." She looked over at Griffin, who was scratching his arm so hard it was leaving marks. "Come on, Griff." She put her hand on the small of his back. "Let's go inside and put some Benadryl on that bite." She turned and winked at Lane. Then she led her man-boy into the house.

27

At morning drop-off, Lane read the sign outside the Rec. It wished everyone a HAPPY BASTILLE DAY and said the weather would be two umbrellas and a lightning bolt in the morning, a smiling sun in the afternoon. In bubble letters at the bottom it announced the good news: HOORAY, WE CAN SWIM! Lane smiled back at the smiley face. Today she would finally get into the pond to do laps.

She walked briskly back to the house. When she got there, it was empty. Her mother had already been picked up; today was her day to volunteer at the memory center. With the house to herself, she brought her laptop outside and sat at the small table on the top deck. The gray pond was a perfect match to the steel-colored sky. The damp breeze held a mix of pine and honeysuckle. A murder of crows swooped and settled on a nearby cluster of drooping beetlebung branches and then, a moment later, they all flew off. Lane opened an email from Summer; the subject was *Podcast News!*

"Great news about our Roxie Podcast," Summer said. *"We finally figured out the format. It will be the two of us in conversation discussing the letter of the day! Awesome right? You'll speak as Roxie and I'll speak as me!!!*

Our working title is, Ask Roxie and Friends*!!! I'm the Friends! Awesome right? We're so excited. We think this is the perfect solution for keeping Roxie relevant across all age margins!!! So awesome!"* Summer ended with a series of emojis. Two women holding hands, a smiling juice box, a purple circle, a ringed planet, a diving mask.

Lane started to decipher it: *a team of happy juice box drinkers trying to circle the universe were saying let's dive in?*—and then decided her time was better spent concentrating on the words. First Summer's use of the words *we* and *our;* then her abundance of *awesomes;* finally *age margin.*

That was a Bert phrase. Bert was the architect of this news, Summer the messenger.

Lane found the number Sam gave her for his Guild-Europe phone. As usual, every time she tried it she got a fast busy signal and then the line went dead. She sent an email to his most recent address saying, Please call. I need your help. A moment after she sent it, a new message popped into her in-box. Her face brightened and then went dark. It wasn't an answer from Sam. It was Summer again.

> Hi again! Slight change of plans! *Roxie Classics* are not getting the clicks we'd hoped so we're going to have to switch direction. But no worries! The new direction is just the old direction. Attached are ten preapproved *Roxies*. Please answer and return at your earliest convenience. (You're going to love them. They're awesome. Some of them are totally—

Lane squinted at the emoji. Was it a banana? What did that mean? Some of them are totally bananas?

Things are super exciting around here! the email continued. Can't wait for you to get back! Awesome change is in the works! Summer signed off with an emoji of a smiling cat.

Lane considered deleting the email and attachment and pretending it never arrived. Things like that happened. Emails went awry. But if she pretended she never got it, Summer would just send it again, with more smiley faces added to her sign-off. So she opened Summer's folder and read through nine of the most boring Roxie letters she'd ever seen—letters no Roxie in her right mind would answer. The last one was a letter about aliens.

She reread Summer's email. *Awesome change is in the works?* What did that mean?

There weren't many people she could call to find out what was happening at the Guild. *Ask Roxie* was an island. A one-woman island. She had no colleagues and before Summer was thrust upon her, no staff. She had her experts—social workers, lawyers and shrinks—but they would be no help for this. She had her readers, but they couldn't tell her anything either. Jem had moved away. She couldn't call her basset-hound-eyed seatmate because she still didn't know his name. There was only one other choice.

"Color me surprised," Hugo said when he picked up the phone.

Lane got right to the point. "Summer told me awesome change is in the air. What's happening?"

"Ugh," Hugo said. "It's a nightmare. But I'm so glad you called." He lowered his voice. "Bert's after you. He wants you out. Alyssa told me."

"Who?"

"Alyssa. You helped her when she first started here. She loves you. You convinced her to go to the All Aboard party and she went and— you don't remember?"

"Right. The party. Yes."

"Alyssa is very good friends with Summer now, which is how she found out that Bert is trying to take down Sam and everyone on Sam's team. Which includes you." He paused to let her take in the news. "I've been wanting to call you and tell you what I heard but I didn't think you'd want to hear it, being that it's just a rumor and all. Do you?" She didn't, but said she did. He whispered the rest. "The rumor is Bert told Summer to steal a letter from the advice columnist at the *Times* to pass along to you. Not the current columnist. From the archives."

"What? Why?"

"It's a purge. Like I said, he's trying to get rid of all Sam's people. The rumor is this is exactly what he did to Roxie One. I don't know if that's true but— Hold on." Hugo shouted out a friendly hello. "Of course, Bert, I'll be right there." There was a moment of silence and then he got back on the phone. "Be careful, Lane. Don't trust Bert. And don't trust Summer."

"Where's Sam?" she asked him. "He's not answering my emails. The number he gave me for his Guild-Europe phone isn't working."

"He's not in Europe. He's in Asia. Guild-Europe is now Guild-Asia. I think it's going to end up Guild-Global. I don't think he has any idea what's going on here. Ugh. Hold on." Again, a change in tone. "Sure. Be there in a sec." He whispered to Lane: "Got to go. Watch your step."

Lane stared at her laptop, as if she could get Sam to answer her email through force of will. Instead an alert floated across the top of her screen. Another update from Summer. The subject this time: Roxie Alert! Second batch of most awesome letters ever!!!

Okay. There was no way for her to know for sure if the things Hugo told her were true. But she needed to proceed with caution until she could confirm what she'd heard with Sam. Proceeding with caution was something she knew how to do.

The second batch of letters was more dreadful than the first. An old man railing about the failings of millennials. A holier-than-thou neighbor complaining about the burden of a shared driveway. And then—was it even real?—a letter from a man in love with his bulldog.

It was like playing a game of advice column roulette. Any of the letters Summer sent could be the one that was purloined. Most likely suspect? The bulldog love letter. She copied and pasted a paragraph of the letter's text into Google and immediately squinted, afraid of what she'd see. It was nothing weird; just two pages of results about the care and temperament of bulldogs.

She tried the other letters, googling paragraphs of each one in turn. Again, no matches.

Did that mean anything? If a stolen letter had been slightly altered, would it come up in Google? She slumped. She couldn't risk publishing a stolen letter. She couldn't stand publishing a boring letter. She refused to publish a letter about a man in love with his dog. But no letter—that would make it easy for Bert to get rid of her.

She checked her email. Nothing from Sam. She refreshed it and checked again. Still nothing there.

A third read through of Summer's letters did not improve them. She needed new letters. But per Bert's instructions, the IT department's reconfiguration of her email meant all new *Roxie* letters went to Summer. Why had she agreed to that?

She'd agreed to that because her mailbox had become so overfilled with *Roxie* letters she couldn't keep up. She'd agreed because by the time she finished sorting one bunch, a new bunch would arrive. She'd agreed because she was spending too much time dragging letters in and out of Sooner, Later, Never, Now.

No. That wasn't it. Those weren't the reasons. She'd agreed because she didn't have the mental space to say no. She'd agreed because she was grieving. She closed her eyes and repeated the sentence to herself: *She was grieving.* For the past six months she'd fooled herself into thinking she felt nothing after Aaron's death. It wasn't true. She pinched her eyes tight against the tears she could feel rising. She could not afford to fall apart now. If she fell apart now—if she let herself feel her grief for

Aaron—it wouldn't stop there. She opened her eyes, took a deep breath, blinked away the wetness, glanced at her desktop. The folders came into focus. Sooner. Later. Never. Now.

That was it. She had folders filled with letters that weren't new to her, but they would be new to her readers. And some of them were good. There was one letter she still thought about regularly. Where was that one? She opened all four folders at once and started searching. It was a letter she debated answering several times, before deciding the answer was no. It was too short, was her final reason. Too short to publish. But something about the letter haunted her. There. She found it. In the Never folder. Never say never. Never was now.

> Dear Roxie,
>
> She doesn't know. She doesn't know what it was like before. She doesn't know how hard it's been. She doesn't know it's not her fault. She doesn't know I love her. I don't know what to do.
>
> Yours,
> Anguished
>
> Dear Anguished,
>
> I don't know either. I don't know what it was like before or how hard it is now. I don't know who she is or why she thinks it was her fault. I don't know who you are, because I only see your shadow. All that's clear is your anguish. But your anguish speaks of love.
>
> Is it possible you haven't told her because too much time has passed? If so, we have something in common.

That's exactly how I felt about your letter. As you know—and now all my readers know—your letter did not just arrive. It's been sitting on my desktop for a long time, in a folder of letters unfit for publication.

What makes a letter unfit for publication? Sometimes it's because it feels too intimate. Sometimes it's because it feels concocted. How do I decide what's too intimate and what's concocted? It's not easy.

If you're a regular reader of this column you know that I'm a big believer in listening to your gut. Here's what you don't know: I have as much trouble trusting my gut as you. But I have recently found that if I let myself get very quiet, totally quiet, if I allow myself to just sit, I can hear it.

The reason your letter, dear Anguished, was filed away, was that I thought it was too short. But it has stayed with me, haunting me, for over a year. Haunting me, much like whatever it is that happened to you is haunting you.

So may I respectfully suggest that you follow my lead and seize the day? Make today the day and now the time that you call or visit the person whom you believe you've harmed. Tell that person what's in your heart, be it love, regret, fear, shame, sorrow, anger, hope, or all of it, all the feelings all at once.

Better late than never is a corny proverb, but corny proverbs sometimes hold the truth. And as another corny proverb says, *The truth will set you free.*

Be well. Be brave. Be free.

Yours forever, or at least for now,
Roxie

After rereading the letter several times and making minor changes, Lane attached it to an email to Summer and copied Bert. She kept the email brief and friendly. No point making trouble, yet.

Hi, Summer! Thanks for sending on those emails but I decided to answer this old chestnut, which I could not get out of my head. I originally thought it was too short to answer but short and sweet feels right today. Thanks for your help. Cheers!

She pressed *Send* and snapped her laptop closed. Through the open screen door, she heard a noise inside the house. She found her in the kitchen, making tea.

Her mother glanced up. "You look unwell."

"I'm fine," Lane said.

"No need to be snippy. I'm just describing how you look. Unwell." Sylvie dipped her tea bag three times into the steaming water and then wrapped the string around the spoon and pressed the bag against the side of the cup. A rivulet of dark liquid ran down the side. "Tonight is movie night at the center. They invited me to stay. Maybe I should go back." She carried her cup to the table and sat down. "They have pizza first and then a movie. It's—" She stopped and studied Lane's face. "What happened? Did your sister call? Is it your father? Is he all right?"

Lane opened her mouth to speak and then closed it again. Where to start? "No one called," she said. "I have no idea how Dad is. Why did he go to Shelley's? What made you decide to visit me now?" Her mother blew on her tea and said nothing. Lane sat with the silence, just as she'd instructed her reader to do. The next question she asked was one she'd been holding on to for what seemed like her entire life. "What happened to us?"

"That's awfully vague. One question at a time is the rule and for good reason. More than one at a time is actually quite irritating."

Lane thought about how Henry kept questioning her mother's rules and then she thought about how Henry was unable to speak to anyone but her. The thought of his silence—the thought that it was, in part, because of her, because of what she did or didn't do or say—made her chest feel tight. Having a heavy heart, she'd learned lately, was a real thing.

She looked at her mother. "Have you ever felt like you've messed things up so badly you didn't know if you could fix it?"

Her mother looked startled. "Yes." Her eyes readjusted to a stern stare. "Nothing good comes from picking off scabs." She gazed out the kitchen window toward the pond. "The light is so lovely at this time of day. Everything is lovely here."

"It is," Lane said on automatic pilot although she wasn't looking at the light and she wasn't feeling at all lovely. In the silence she felt a quiet rage slowly grow. Rage about silence. So much silence about so many things. "I need to understand what happened to our family. I need to know why we don't speak to each other. It's because of Uncle Albie, isn't it? Because of Ivy." She said the next slowly. "Because of what happened to Ivy." She expected to feel the usual wave of regret at having spoken but instead she felt a shift, a weight lifting.

"You're a touchy one, Turtle. Always been a touchy one. So sensitive. We never could predict how you'd take things. It's best to let things be. It is what it is."

"I don't know what that means."

The startled look was back. "It means things happen. And not everyone understands why. And time passes and more things happen. And people say things. And then they regret the things they said, or they don't regret them, but they can't unsay them. And one day, there's nothing left to say." She met Lane's baffled look with cold eyes. "Your sister called. They're coming here. I'm not up to it, Turtle. Since Albie passed, your father and I— We don't know what to do."

"If you tell me what happened, I can help you figure out what to do." Seeing her mother's distress, she felt herself soften. "Lots of people think I'm good at that. Figuring out what to do."

"Not in real life." Her mother stood up. "You've said it yourself. Don't look so bereft, Turtle. It's not your fault." With that, Sylvie Meckler got up and went to bed.

28

Heaviness. Lane felt it upon wakening. She tried to puzzle out why, before she got out of bed. She didn't want to bring the heaviness with her when she woke up Henry. It took several moments and then came to her. It was disappointment. She felt let down. She'd made a mistake, letting herself believe the crusty wall that cocooned her mother was coming down.

In the two weeks since they'd spoken about her uncle, their conversations had returned to the safety of small talk. About the weather. About the condition of the pond. About what new outing Nathan had proposed that Lane rejected.

He'd made a lot of proposals. Birding at Felix Neck. Hiking at Cedar Tree. Cycling to the bike ferry in Menemsha and then, across the water to Aquinnah. Lane was as good as anyone she knew at saying no, but Nathan was better than anyone she'd ever met at being persistent. It was a gentle persistence and it wore her down until, finally, she agreed. Today they would go clamming.

"You probably won't want to," was how he started, readying himself for his daily rejection. "Which is fine. It's just, I bumped into an old friend of mine yesterday who's got a great house on the bay, in Katama. He was heading off-island when I saw him. He leaves every August because he hates the crowds. He goes to Maine. He could make a lot of money if he rented but he doesn't want to rent. He hates renters. He hates day-trippers. He hates a lot of things. What he likes is letting friends use his house when he's away. As home base to go clamming. You can walk right into the water from his backyard. I know you're busy, but if we time it right, with the tides, we can get a bucket of clams in an hour. What do you say? I'm not suggesting we make a day of it. It will be more like we're shopping for dinner. The bay will be our fish store. What do you say? No? Maybe? Yes?"

His yes sounded so full of hope and kindness that Lane said yes right back.

He led the way back behind his friend's house, down the lawn that sloped to the bay, to a path that wound through wild grass and pink rose mallow to the water. The water was cool. The sun beat down. They weren't alone. A couple was clamming to their left, though they seemed to be doing more canoodling than clamming. To their right was a large group of mixed ages, an extended family Lane guessed, maybe a reunion. They seemed to be doing more splashing than digging.

Nathan continued on, toward the far shore where dunes separated the bay from the ocean. Here were the solo clammers, heads tipped down toward the water, the sun turning them into silhouettes. Though they worked separately, from afar they moved as if in a coordinated dance. One bending down to scoop their catch, another standing up to deposit their catch in a floating basket, a third raking slowly, reach and pull, reach and pull, reach and pull.

Nathan pointed toward the dunes. "The clams are there."

They sloshed across the bay—at its deepest it was at their waist—passing clammers whose bobbing baskets were all empty, half empty, nearly full, until they reached an unoccupied swath of water.

"Here," Nathan said and stopped. "Perfect." As if to prove his point, he bent down in the knee-deep water, dug around with his hand and pulled up a quahog. "Success!" He took a clam gauge out of his pocket and Lane watched as the clam slipped through the center. "Too small," he said. "Got to let the babies grow." His face darkened.

"Everything okay?"

"Yes." He smiled. "Sorry. It's just, last time I was here it was with Leo." He shrugged off the mood. "Good with the bad, right? Can't be greedy. Beautiful day. Beautiful bay." He gestured toward the seagrass waving in the wind. "Waves breaking on the other side of the dunes." He stopped and they both listened. "All things considered, I'm a pretty lucky guy." He shook off his mood. "Okay. What you have to do is listen while you rake. It's a tiny sound when you hit a clam. A little ping. Not everyone hears it. Some people who don't hear it, feel it. The rake catching on something. Main thing is, you have to pay attention. You listen. You feel. You find. You measure."

Lane lifted her rake and put it back down. She had paid attention. She had heard the grief in Nathan's voice. "What happened to Leo?"

"Nothing happened. Nothing like that. He's fine. Me and Leo, not so much." He winced. "I'm not sure I'm ready to talk about it. It's pretty painful. You can understand, right? I feel like you could."

"I can." Lane started raking and immediately heard a ping. "I hit something."

"Let's take a look."

She lifted her rake out of the water and saw a giant gob of seaweed clogging the rake's teeth. Tangled inside the middle, she found a clam and carefully removed it. Nathan watched as she tried to put the clam through the center of the gauge. "It doesn't fit."

"Hurrah!" Nathan called out. "We get to keep it. You're a natural! You sure you never did this before?"

Lane heard the echo of the same encouraging tone he used with Henry when he admired his artwork. He was so good with Henry. Sometimes when he'd ask Henry a question, Lane found herself holding her breath, wondering if this would be the moment Henry would finally speak. It never was, but Nathan never seemed to mind.

Aggie's words came to her out of nowhere: *You want to know who a person really is, watch how they treat someone who's different.*

Nathan called to her. "I hit the mother lode!" He held up a pile of seaweed with half a dozen clams nestled within the clump. Lane saw that he didn't need to measure to know which ones to throw back, which ones to drop into the bucket that floated beside them.

After that haul, both of them had several false alarms, pings that turned out to be knots of deteriorating plastic. Pings that were broken shells. Pings that were clumps of seaweed mixed with particles of crab.

Lane didn't mind the false alarms. The sun was still warm and the breeze was still cool and the basket was filling up and the family clamming in the distance was sending out echoes of laughter that sounded like bells.

They were walking back to shore when Lane said, "What a perfect day." She hadn't meant to say it aloud. "I'm not used to days like this." She hadn't meant to say that either. "I can't remember how long it's been since I've relaxed." She laughed and felt a hand on her shoulder.

When she turned, Nathan was staring at her. As if it were happening without her will, she felt her chin rise toward him. He blinked, surprised. His eyes, the color of the sea, were not happy. It wasn't going to be that kind of a day.

That was a relief. She hadn't wanted it to go that way. But still, why sad? "What's wrong?" she asked.

He shook his head. "I'm not worth it."

"Not worth what?" she asked. "Not worth being my friend?" She tried to sound sure about this, that to her, the day had been about nothing more than two friends shopping for dinner in the sea. She brightened her voice. "I think we have enough for dinner, don't you?"

Nathan peered into the bucket and counted. "I believe we do." He smiled. "Perfect number of clams. Perfect day of clamming with a friend." He held on to the end of the lanyard attached to the basket and pulled it behind them as they walked to the shore.

Despite their attempts at reassuring each other that friendship was all they were looking for, both of them were silent as Nathan transferred the clams from the wire basket into a cooler of ice in the car, silent on the drive home, silent as they carried the cooler inside, silent in the kitchen as Nathan put the clams into a large bowl and then poured in seawater from a container he'd filled at the bay.

"Now they have to soak," he said. "Takes a few hours to purge the grit." He slid the bowl onto the bottom shelf of her refrigerator and closed the door. He looked at the floor and then the ceiling and then met Lane's eyes. "I've got to talk to you about something."

"No you don't. We had a lovely day. We have a lovely friendship—"

"It's not about that. There's something I need to show you. I'll get it. It's in my car."

Nathan put the stack of papers he'd brought in from his car on the kitchen table. They were drawings, she saw when she looked closer. Henry's drawings.

"Where did you find these?"

"Henry gave them to me. First he showed them to me. Then after I looked at them and admired them, I asked if he'd shown them to you. He said no, so—" He stopped and quickly clarified, "He shook his head no, so I asked if I could have them. I thought you should see them. Maybe you think that was wrong. Dishonest. Taking them so I could show you." Lane didn't know what to think, yet. "They're beautiful drawings," Nathan said. "But why I think you should see them is they tell a story. Which I don't understand." He tapped a small figure in the picture that was on top. "This is Henry, right? Curly hair's the giveaway."

Lane moved closer. The figure was Henry. He was standing beside a hole, holding a shovel. An upside-down shovel. "Oh. Yes. At his father's gravesite. Someone offered him the shovel. Someone I didn't know. And Henry spun around and buried his head in my coat." Lane could feel the anger she hadn't let herself feel that day because on that day if she let herself feel anything, she would have fallen apart and she'd needed to stay strong, for Henry. She had no idea who it was who offered him the shovel. She forgot about it almost immediately. She was good at that, forgetting things.

But Henry hadn't. He'd memorialized it in this drawing, with changes. In the drawing he actually did take the shovel and then held it upside down so that it was raining dirt, small specks of dirt, a gentle rain of dirt, into the hole that was the grave where his father lay. Except— what were those crossed-out lines in the grave?

"Oh." She took a step back. The dirt was piled on top of a head. Henry had drawn a rough sketch of his father's head; he drew it as if Aaron had been buried standing straight up, the top of his head poking out of the hole like a too-tall Alice in Wonderland, stuck in a tiny house.

"Oh," she said a third time. She touched the eyes of a person standing beside Henry. "That's me."

"Do you know who this is?" Nathan pointed to a roughly sketched man standing in the distance, body turned toward the grave, head facing front.

There wasn't much detail on the face, but Lane saw the pencil mark on the man's cheek and knew it was Aaron; Henry had drawn his father as a guest at his own funeral. "That's Aaron. He had a dimple on his right cheek. He used to tell Henry that was where he kept his personality. Then one day Henry asked why he didn't have a personality—since he didn't have a dimple. So Aaron told him his personality was in his curls." Her finger traced over Aaron's face.

"There's two more," Nathan said after a moment. He slipped the drawing on top to the bottom of the pile, so Lane could see the next one.

In the next drawing, the boy, Henry, was standing beside a woman, Lane, on a small patch of grass under a cluster of trees.

"That's outside his old school," Lane said. "Where parents wait at dismissal time. He's got the balloon." She'd forgotten about that, how his teacher had called her to say the children voted on a going-away present for Henry and a balloon won. Except the school had a rule against balloons, because of a student in another grade who had a latex allergy. "His teacher asked if I would buy a balloon for the children to give to Henry outside at pickup time. The children planned everything. Mainly Milo. Henry's best friend." She stopped for a moment. It seemed so far away, a time when Henry had a best friend named Milo. A time when Aaron was alive and Henry was still speaking. No one at that school had made a fuss about his silence. Why had they moved? She looked back at the drawing. "The kids were so sweet that day. When school got out, Milo raced over and took the balloon from me and raced back to where Henry was standing and presented it to him. And then all the children circled around Henry and started singing. It was a clapping song." She sang, remembering it, her voice quiet and slightly off-key. "Goodbye old friend. Come back again. Goodbye old friend, dear Henry." She wiped at her eyes.

"So you see a happy moment?" He studied her face as she nodded and then seemed to measure his words. "Okay, well. What I see is this." He put his finger on the string that came out of the balloon. "See where it goes?"

Lane traced the string with her finger, starting at the spot where it began at the bottom of the balloon high above Henry's head, and following it down to his hand, to his torso, out the other side of his torso, into her. She placed her hand over her chest. "It goes into my heart."

Nathan nodded. "Here's the last one."

She wiped at her eyes again and looked at the last drawing, a jumble of scratchy lines.

"When I asked Henry if I could have the pictures, he didn't want to give me this one. So I told him it was my favorite, that I loved the way it captured action. Like frames in an animated movie. He gave me the others and kept this one, until the next day. It was almost like he needed time to think about whether it was a good idea to give this one to me."

"He needed to dream on it," Lane said.

Nathan didn't ask what she meant. "I felt bad telling him it was my favorite. I have a strict policy about lying. I don't lie. Been there. Done with that."

"It's okay," Lane told him. "Not all lies are the same. I'm an expert on lies. I became an expert for my column. There's a whole vocabulary about lying. What *you* did, that's a noble lie." Nathan looked dubious. "It is. A noble lie is when you tell a lie for a greater good. You told that lie to help Henry." She looked back at the drawing. "I don't understand this."

Nathan pointed to the figure farthest away from the action. "That's Henry."

"Right. Standing on the doormat. In the hall, outside our apartment. In the city. And inside are . . ." She counted. "Six people."

"No. It's two people. You have to look at this as three panels of action with the same people in every panel. Same man—see how he's wearing the same striped blue shirt in every panel?—and same woman."

Lane looked closer. Like the man, the woman wore the same shirt in all three frames. A patterned shirt. "He took his time with this. All the little red boats. All the tiny white sails." She looked at the man and took a sharp breath when she noticed his mouth. His only feature was a wide-open mouth with sharp pointy teeth. "He's terrifying." Her gaze returned to the boy. "Henry has no mouth."

"Henry is crossed out."

How had she not noticed that? She took it in, the monster man in her apartment, arm raised in every frame except for the last frame where the woman was on the floor, as if she'd just been hit. While Henry stood outside on the sisal doormat. Henry, intentionally crossed out with a firm *X*. She looked at Nathan. "Aaron never hit me. He never threatened to hit me."

"I don't think she's you." He pointed to a figure she hadn't noticed. "I think that's you."

She looked at the figure she'd missed, a woman in the upper-left corner of the page, far from the action. A woman sitting at a desk. "Yes. That's me. I'm working. Henry's in the hallway. Aaron's in the apartment hitting someone. Brielle? I feel sick." She hurried to the bathroom and closed the door and stood, hand against the wall, waiting for her stomach to quiet. When it did, she returned to the kitchen. "I have to tell Henry you showed these to me."

"Of course," Nathan said.

"He might be angry that you showed them to me."

"I know." Nathan stood up. "I'm going off-island tomorrow for a week. With luck, by the time I get back, he'll be ready to forgive me. If not, that's okay. You *have* to talk to him about this. It's not a choice. If Henry's upset I showed them to you, so be it. I'll take one for the team."

It was only after he left that Lane wondered, when had they become a team?

29

After Nathan came back with his favorite recipe for spaghetti and clams, after they cooked and ate and talked about their days, Sylvie retreated to a chair by the window to watch the darkening sky and Henry drew, with Nathan doodling beside him, at the dining room table. At the sink, as Lane scraped food off plates and scrubbed the pots, her mind remained stuck on how best to approach Henry about the drawings temporarily hidden in the top drawer of her bedroom dresser.

The problem was that when she had time to really examine them, she thought they had the feel of dreamscapes. The settings were real: gravesite, school-dismissal spot, hallway outside their apartment. But the rest, the action, felt exaggerated, as if the drawings were renderings of dreams. Did she—did anyone?—have the right to demand that Henry explain his dreams? Or did she have an obligation to ask? Roxie had told people more than once, *When it comes to our children, we can't afford to take chances.* But Lane now wondered, what if the opposite was true? What if her fretting was hurting Henry? What if her taking a chance was what he needed? The question felt urgent.

She stepped away from the sink and, closing the door gently behind her, went outside to the deck where she pressed Doctor Bruce's number. A recording answered. *Doctor Bruce is unavailable. If this is an emergency, hang up and dial 911.*

As she hung up she whispered, "You shouldn't have left us," and then laughed that now, after months of hating him, she was finally missing Aaron. She knew exactly why. Even when they were barely speaking, even when everything he did was irritating, even when they disagreed on minor details of child-rearing—should they or shouldn't they arrange for Henry to go on a late-over?—Aaron was her partner. His love for Henry—and for her—had been fierce. But okay, Aaron wasn't here. Doctor Bruce wasn't here. She was on her own. As usual.

Except she wasn't alone. She had Roxie. She *was* Roxie. And she could hear Roxie now, telling her, *You've got this. You can navigate through this, for Henry. You always do. No matter how much doubt or fear or guilt or grief—yes, grief—you have, you find your way. Maybe you don't always take the most direct route. Maybe you take jug handles and detours. But you get there. Because you've got a North Star and his name is Henry. Follow that and your gut won't let you down. Now off you go.*

Her first Tell Me That Story offering was about her afternoon clamming expedition with Nathan.

"Yes," Henry said. "I want that one. Tell me that story."

She was careful to include lots of details about the clamming part. How the bottom of the bay felt so sandy and smooth. How she'd gripped the rake so hard she felt the beginnings of blisters on her palm. How a shellfish constable had sloshed over to check that they had their license. Henry was particularly interested in that part, that they needed a license to get clams. She described what the constable wore. "Rubber overalls that started on his feet and went straight up, like boots that stretched from his toes to his shoulders."

Henry had laughed at that and then stopped. He studied her face. "Did someone die?"

"What? No."

"I can tell something Bad happened. Because your Tell Me That Story is about how you got clams for dinner but your face is about, Something Bad happened. Maybe something Super Worst Possible kind of bad. And your teeth are making a noise. Are you Sad? I don't want you to be Sad."

Now she could hear it too. She was making little tapping noises, biting down on her teeth. He noticed everything. "I'm not sad. I didn't know I was tapping my teeth." She paused. "But it might be because . . ." Henry closed his eyes. "Are you up for a talk right now? There's something I'd like to talk to you about, if you are."

"Can I be up for a listen? With my eyes closed?" She told him he could. He rolled away and turned onto his side. "Okay. You can start now. I'm listening."

When Lane imagined how this would go, she pictured presenting the drawings to Henry, one at a time. It would be much easier letting the drawings speak for themselves. "You know what, buddy? I'm going to run to my room for a second. There's something I want to show you. Okay?" She waited. "Henry?" No answer. "You awake?" She stroked his curly hair and gently kissed his head, but he didn't stir. He was asleep.

She quietly slipped out of the bed and went to her room and took out the drawings and stared at them. It felt to her as if Henry knew exactly what she wanted to discuss. Knew and didn't want to know. He was his mother's son. She heard her teeth clicking again, chattering as if against the cold. Following Henry's lead was not always as easy as it sounded.

Downstairs, she tried her sister again. Would Shelley ever pick up? The machine clicked on and Lane left a message. "Mom told me you and Dad are coming. Is that true? Call me." She hung up and waited, fooled for a moment into convincing herself her sister would actually call right back. Some wishes were hard to quit.

She found relief in her laptop, in a letter from the SOONER file. A veterinary technician ranting about people who brought their dogs in to have their nails clipped. *I am not a groomer,* the technician complained. *I'm a caregiver for animals. Every minute I spend clipping the overgrown nails of a lazy owner's dog is one less minute I have to spend with a sick animal who needs my care. Maybe a person who can't clip their own dog's nails shouldn't have a dog.* And it was off to the races, Lane disappearing into the world of someone else's problems.

The next morning, she found her mother at the kitchen table. She eyed the single slice of dry toast on her mother's plate. "Are you feeling okay?"

"I'm a bit under the weather."

Under the weather. Like Uncle Albie. "What's wrong?" Lane asked.

"I told you. I'm under the weather."

Henry walked in, rubbing his eyes. "What are we having for breakfast?"

"You're having waffles," Lane said. "I'm eating later, after I swim."

Her mother smiled at Henry and Henry smiled at her and they all continued on in their fake tableau of domestic peace.

When she got back from dropping Henry off, her mother wasn't in any of her usual perches, not in the kitchen, not out on the deck, not in the reading chair in the living room. When she went upstairs and saw the guest room door was shut, she knocked.

Her mother called out, "Can't a person have some rest?"

"Sorry." Lane slipped into her bedroom and put on her bathing suit. As she crossed the lawn to the edge of the pond, she tried to put everything—her mother, her father, her sister, Aaron's dimple, Henry's drawings, Sam, Bert, Summer, summer—out of her mind. The water was cool. She waded in up to her knees, splashed her legs and arms and dived in.

Her first lap started slow. Summer popped in, first in line in her mind. Last night Summer had sent two emails that sounded different. Her chirpiness was gone. She sounded almost gloomy. What was happening with her? What was going on with Sam?

Shelley joined her next. Why wasn't her sister sharing her plans? If her mother hadn't mentioned she was coming, Lane would never have known. When was Shelley coming and why? The temperature dropped. She was approaching the middle of the pond where the water was deeper.

Her father popped up next. That he had gone to London to see Shelley was completely confounding. Had her parents negotiated these trips, one going to Lane, the other to Shelley? Had they decided to divide and conquer? Why would they do that? Her mother continued to avoid answering the question of whether she was on a prolonged visit or staying for good. If she was staying, there were things they needed to talk about first. There was no way she could just—

She lurched forward, her pace quickening as suddenly as if someone had pushed her to hurry her along. But no one was pushing her. She accelerated on her own and her mind responded to her quickened pace by quieting.

The sound of her breathing matched the rhythm of her stroke. Her body calmed. Her shoulders felt loose. Her limbs felt fluid. And then— a sudden spasm, her foot, an unexpected cramp. She opened her mouth in surprise and gulped water and then had a fit of spitting and coughing. It took a moment of flailing before she regained her equilibrium.

Embarrassed, she treaded water and looked around. With relief, she saw she was alone. She continued to tread for a moment, concentrating on slowing her racing heart and then—another spasm, this one worse. The cramp that started with the toes on her left foot traveled down to her sole and then up her calf. She bent down and grabbed her foot to fight the curled toes, treading with one leg as best she could.

She took a breath—the main thing was to stay calm—and assessed the situation. The last time this happened, in New Jersey, she'd side-stroked to the nearby edge of the pool. But there was no nearby edge here. She flipped onto her back into a dead man's float. The cramp returned, spreading up into the muscles of her calf. How long did these cramps last? She had no idea. She hadn't paid attention to that in the pool because it didn't matter. In the pool she could swim to the edge and heave herself out. Maybe it would only last a minute. A minute could feel long but it was just a minute. She could float for a minute and then swim. She could float for five minutes and then swim.

The pain sharpened. Now her entire leg was in a clench. She forced herself to open her eyes and concentrate on the clouds above. The sky was gray, the same gray as the sky on the day Shelley and Ivy climbed onto the roof. The cramp released.

She flipped to her side but after a single stroke the cramp was back. She looked toward the shore—too far—and toward the house—same distance. She was in the middle. The median. The mode. She forced herself to take several long strokes, muscling her way through the pain. Her chest tightened. Panic.

Okay. Panic was not helpful. She needed to keep her focus on making it to the shore. She could backstroke her way to the shore. Henry wanted to teach Uncle Albie the backstroke when they were in Florida. There was so much her mother didn't say in Florida. And what she did say was not true. The story about Uncle Albie on vacation? Why had Lane believed that? Of course he wasn't on vacation. He was probably in a hospital for—what did her mother used to call it?—a tune-up.

Her toes curled again. She could swim through this pain, for Henry. She just had to breathe. That's what she told readers who wrote about panic attacks. Her readers had lots of panic attacks. They had them on planes and in cars, while giving presentations and planning weddings, while dealing with divorce and death.

After Ivy fell out the window, Lane had ended up on the floor in a dead faint. Her mother told her later she'd fainted because she stopped breathing. *Breathe,* her mother said then. *Breathe,* she wrote to her readers. *Breathe,* she told herself now.

Slow breath in. Think of Henry. Slow breath out. Think of Henry.

The cramp moved upward. Now it was in her stomach. She tried to make her body go limp to see if that would release the pain. She let herself sink, let go of all tension, all thoughts, except one: *Breathe.*

It happened fast. First there was a shadow, something big, too big to be a fish and then there was a body, a body at her side. The body lifted her. The body was a man with strong arms and hair slicked back. The body was Griffin, holding her with one arm as he swam through the water. She let herself become a fish, fluid and boneless, as he carried her to the shore.

When he finally rose, dark eyes blinking, sunlight catching the water at the edges of his lashes, he held her in his arms and walked out of the pond like he was the creature from the Black Lagoon, and she his bride.

Someone must have seen her in the water because by the time Griffin placed her, gently, on her dock there were several people waiting. She recognized Aggie first, who ran as she called out to her son. "Griff. Are you okay? Good," she said with relief, after he nodded.

"Everything's fine," Lane said to the small crowd as she slowly rose. She saw that her mother's face was lined with worry. "I'm fine," she told her. "I had a cramp. That's all." Her mother's hand was over her mouth as she eyed Griffin.

"Did he come after you?" The woman speaking looked unfamiliar. "I've heard he does that. Just rears up out of the water to scare people."

"No," Lane told her. "He was trying to help me. To save me." She looked toward where Aggie had been standing but now she was gone. She and Griffin were both gone, vanished into the woods as if they'd never been there at all.

30

Henry was painting a mural for Eclipse Day called *Oh Henry's Galaxy*. His mom didn't know about it because it was a secret. The good kind of secret. The Surprise kind. Everyone at camp was making a Surprise for their mom to see at the end-of-camp party. Or for their mom and dad. His was just for his mom. He was pretty sure his Surprise would make her happy, but it was hard to know. He didn't understand all the rules of Happy.

Esther and Russell's Surprise was a play called *Esther and Russell*. The play was about a brother and sister trying to figure out what happened to the Gemini constellation. In the play, the Gemini constellation falls out of the sky and no one can find it. Esther and Russell like the Gemini constellation best because it means twins, which they are. Jonah and Penelope's Surprise was a concert they made up on the piano. Dylan told them not to do that Surprise because the piano was Out of Tunes but he was wrong. Penelope and Jonah found lots of tunes on the piano.

Because his mural was big, Henry was painting it in the room called the Back Office, to keep it a surprise. His drawing friends were helping him. At first Dylan told them they couldn't help because, "It's called *Oh Henry's Galaxy* for a reason. Only Henry can paint it."

Someone told Amanda what Dylan said so she asked Henry if he wanted to paint with his friends, Yes or No, and he said, Yes. He didn't say that in out-loud words, though. He said it in sign language. Every time he used sign language, it made Amanda's smile Extra Happy.

His friends helped paint the planets and the sky but they let Henry paint all the constellations by himself.

The counselors put a countdown on the easel next to the door to show how many days were left until the Eclipse Party. Before the countdown, what the easel said was the weather, and if it was a holiday like National Merry-Go-Round Day, and if they could Swim in the Pond, HOORAY or NO, and the name of everyone who saw the Snapping Turtle under the Dock. He saw the turtle the first time he went in the lake, but he couldn't tell anyone so his name didn't make the list.

The first day of the eclipse countdown it said, TEN DAYS AND COUNTING. The day it said, FIVE DAYS AND COUNTING, was the day Henry forgot to wash the constellation paint off his hands at the end of camp. He didn't notice until he was home in the kitchen with his mom, who started making dinner and asking questions about his day like, "Did you have a good day?"

Even though he hid his hands behind his back, his mom saw them and wanted to know why they had paint on them. He tried to look surprised that his hands had paint on them because he did not want to tell his mom about the mural. If he told her, it wouldn't be a Surprise and he'd have to make up a new Surprise because the rule at camp was Everybody Has to Have a Surprise for Eclipse Day. Henry didn't think he could come up with another Surprise he liked as much as a mural of *Oh Henry's Galaxy*.

The paint on his hands made his mom's face look Worried. But she had looked Worried for a lot of days in a row so maybe it wasn't because of the paint. Her Worried face started on the night she asked if she could talk to him about something and he pretended to be asleep so she didn't. He wasn't sure what she wanted to talk about, but the look on her face didn't match I Have Something I Want to Talk About. It looked more like, I Have Something I Do Not Want to Talk About.

While he was looking at his painted hands he got an idea about what she might be Worried about. His idea was, maybe she found the letter from his dad that was in the box under his bed. That letter might make her say she wanted to talk while her face said something else.

He waited till she was doing dishes and then ran upstairs fast and pulled out the box to check and, phew. The letter was still there. He was shoving it back under his bed when his mom came in for Tell Me That Story. Now her face looked Worried and Disappointed.

He picked the story but instead of listening to her tell it he thought about, if he gave her the letter from his dad now, would her eyebrows go Unslanty or More Slanty? Even though he was a good guesser, he couldn't guess the answer to that.

He was still trying to decide whether he should show it or not show it when he noticed his mom had stopped talking. Her eyes were closed. Not resting closed. Sleeping closed. Probably sleeping. He put his hand under her nose to make sure she was breathing. She was. Breathing and sleeping. Falling asleep in the middle of Tell Me That Story used to happen Never. Then it happened Sometimes. Now it happened A Lot.

On the day when the eclipse was THREE DAYS AND COUNTING, Henry asked his mom if instead of Tell Me That Story they could have Show and Tell. She said, Yes. Then he asked if it was okay to do Show and Tell if the Show part might make the other person sad.

His mom's face got Very Serious. "What a good question. I would say sometimes that might not be okay. But with me, it's fine. You can share anything with me." She said, *Anything*, a second time and then, "Okay?"

He nodded and asked if she wanted to go first or second. She said he should go first because she hadn't figured out what to show him yet. He reminded her that she had something to Show him and then he reminded her about the night they ate clams, when her teeth were clicking and she was going to Show him something and then she forgot.

Her face got Surprised. "Aw buddy. I didn't forget. I thought you didn't want to talk about it. And I didn't want to force you to talk about something you didn't want to."

"Oh," he said. "What is it?"

Her eyes looked like they were itchy. She rubbed hard on the itch and then gave him a squeezy hug and said, "That will be my Show and Tell. You go first."

He pulled the box out from under his bed and told his mom he was sorry he broke Rule Number Five. "I didn't unpack this in New Jersey so it should have stayed in New Jersey."

She wrapped her finger around one of his *curly-Qs*. "I'm starting to think Grandma Sylvie's rules aren't really right for us," she said. "What do you think?"

He wasn't sure what he thought so he said, "Thank you." Then he pulled the letter out from underneath the flashlights. Seven constellation caps flew onto the floor. He scooped them up fast so she wouldn't get Mad. Her face stayed Waiting.

He handed her the envelope and pointed to her name. "For you. From Dad. I know it's from Dad because . . ." He pointed. "Crunchy handwriting." She didn't say anything. "My guess is he put it in the box so he could save it for the right time to give it to you. But then he ran out of time. You can read it later."

At first nothing moved on her face and then her mouth moved and she said, "Thank you." And then her eyes moved, Blinky and Sad.

That made him feel sad so he changed the subject to, "Where's your Show and Tell?"

Her eyes stopped being Blinky but they stayed Sad. "I'll get it. Be right back."

❦

He didn't notice that his mom didn't come back right away at first because he was thinking about the constellations in his mural. Some things in the mural were from the Real Sky and some things were from his Imagination Sky. The constellations were from his Imagination Sky.

The first constellation he made for his mural was the Hank Aaron constellation. He thought of it the day his counselor Amanda asked if he was named after Hank Aaron. She asked him if he knew that Hank was a nickname for Henry and he shook his head. No one ever told him that.

That made him wonder. Was he named for Hank Aaron? His mom would know but he wasn't sure if it was an okay thing to ask her. It might make her Sad. Sometimes he guessed right about what made her Sad but not always. He really didn't like when she was Sad.

Thinking about her being Sad made him realize, she hadn't come back yet with her Show and Tell. He didn't have a clock in his room so he didn't know what time it was, but it felt like longer than, *Be Right Back*.

Maybe she was busy reading the letter from his dad. Except the letter from his dad was short and his mom always said she was the fastest reader in town.

He called out, "Mom?" but she didn't answer. He tried to think of all the reasons why she wouldn't answer and then he tried to only think about the reasons that weren't scary. One reason that wasn't scary was that she went on her computer and forgot to listen with one ear while she was working. Another answer was he was too quiet when he called. He tried again, louder. "Mom?" Still no answer.

One time his mom told him the way to get his brain to not think about scary things was to give it something else to think about. He tried it now, but it didn't work. All he could think about were scary things. The most scary thing. Was she dead?

He opened the door. She wasn't dead in the hall. She wasn't dead on the toilet. He held his breath while he pulled back the shower curtain. She wasn't dead in the tub.

Grandma Sylvie's door was open wide so he could see his mom wasn't dead in there unless she was dead in the closet. Sometimes at night he hid in his closet but his mom didn't know, which was good because that was a thing that would definitely make her face Disappointed.

After his dad died a lot of people told him he was Brave. He didn't know why they said that. If it was true that he was Brave, he would be able to look in Grandma Sylvie's closet now. The closet door was only a little bit open so he closed his eyes and pushed it open more. He opened his eyes so they were tiny slits. No one was inside, dead or not dead. So, true. He was Brave.

When he walked out of Grandma Sylvie's room he heard people talking downstairs, one voice loud—his mom's—one voice quiet, probably Grandma Sylvie since no one else lived with them.

He stopped at the top of the stairs and closed his eyes to try and decide what his mom would want him to do: Go Down Now and Remind Her She Forgot about Her Show and Tell, or Stay Where He Was and Wait Until She Remembered. The problem with Wait Until She Remembered was what if she never remembered? The problem with Go Down Now and Remind Her She Forgot was what if she felt so bad about forgetting that she had to hold her breath to keep her tears in, like the day she told him What Happened to his dad?

He thought about going back to his room and getting in his bed and going to sleep and Dreaming on It. But his eyes were Poppy-Open Wide Awake and his heart was Thumping Loud in His Ears. So he decided to Wait and Sea.

31

Lane gently touched her mother's hair; as always, it was pinned up in a bun of carefully coiled concentric circles. The length of her hair was just one more mystery she and Shelley used to guess about. No matter what time their mother got up or where she was going, her fine dark-blonde hair was up, anchored in a nest of bobby pins. But now, it was coming undone. Her mother was undone.

What had brought Lane downstairs was a sound—a long, quivering exhale that she heard when she came out of her bedroom, right after discovering that Henry's drawings weren't where she'd left them. Neither were they in any of the places she checked where she might have mindlessly put them. She was heading toward her workspace to see if she'd left them on her desk when she heard it. A sound of distress from the living room. The sound of grief from her mother.

Her mother was sitting at the very edge of the couch. At the sound of Lane coming down the stairs she quickly sank back. Her arms were left splayed out at an awkward angle, giving her the look of an injured bird.

It took Lane a long moment to realize her mother was crying. Her mother, like Lane, never cried. None of them cried, or at least none of them had in a very long while.

She seemed to be distressed about her crying, and quickly wiped her eyes with her sleeve. She seemed agitated. Everything was agitating her. Now it was the damp spot on her shirt that bothered her. Lane watched as she pulled a tissue from her sleeve and started rubbing the spot, then pressing the tissue against it. She looked desperate to make the spot disappear.

"It's just tears," Lane told her. "They'll dry." But her mother kept rubbing. "What's wrong?"

Her mother shook her head and then said something so quietly Lane wasn't sure whether it was, *I know*, or, *I'll go*. She gave up rubbing her shirt and laid the damp tissue on the coffee table. "Oh no," she said. "Now look what I've done." She moved the tissue off—*there they were*—Henry's drawings. Her mother saw her notice them and reclaimed her tissue and started blotting her sleeve again, and then her eyes, and then her sleeve.

"It's okay," Lane told her mother. "The drawings are fine. Nothing happened to them."

Her mother gave a sharp shake of her head. She wasn't upset that she ruined the drawings.

Lane looked at them again. The drawing on the top was the one of the woman getting hit. "Don't worry about that picture," Lane said. "That's not me."

Another quick shake of her head. More blotting of her sleeve with the tissue.

Lane went to the kitchen and got her a paper towel. "Here," she said when she came back. "Let me." She pressed the towel onto the sleeve. She could not imagine why her mother was distraught about her sleeve. But like her father said, she wasn't an expert on everything. Maybe tears did stain. And it was her mother's favorite shirt. She'd arrived with a suitcase full of shirts but this was the one she kept wearing and washing and wearing again. What she loved about it, Lane had no idea. Maybe the patriotic colors. Maybe the abstract pattern, which, she saw now, as she pressed the paper towel, were small simple geometric shapes.

And then she saw it; they weren't simple shapes at all. The white triangles were sails. The red semicircles were boats. The blue background was the sea. She hadn't noticed it, but Henry had because Henry noticed everything, including that the pattern on his grandmother's favorite shirt was made up of sailboats. The woman he drew in the apartment with his father was her mother. She held her mother's arm and asked, "Did Aaron hit you?"

"Why would you say such a thing?"

Lane looked at the drawing again, this time at the man. The man did not have a pencil slash of a dimple on his cheek. "That's not Aaron." She scanned the picture again and noticed, for the first time, the room had a roof. The room wasn't in an apartment; it was in a house. A house with a roof that looked exactly like the roof on her parents' house in Florida. "That's Dad."

Her mother pulled in her lips until they disappeared and her face turned into an inscrutable mask and the mask turned toward the stairs and her gaze shifted and she smiled and said, "Hello dear."

Henry was standing at the bottom of the stairs.

"Hey buddy," Lane said and then remembered, with a start. "You were waiting for me." He nodded. "I'm so sorry. I was talking to Grandma and I guess time got away from me."

He was crying, she now saw. "Oh buddy." She opened her arms and he ran into them. "There there," she said, and stroked his soft curls. "There there," she said again.

It was only when Henry stopped crying that she realized her mother had disappeared up the stairs, as silent as a ghost.

She gently wiped the tears off Henry's face with her hand and then twirled her finger around one of his curls. "I'm sorry. I was looking for your drawings. That was what my Show and Tell was going to be. I wanted to talk to you about them. But they weren't where I left them and when I came downstairs I saw they were here, with Grandma."

Henry straightened up and saw the drawings on the table. "How did they get here?"

"Nathan gave them to me," she said. "Because he thought it was important that I see them. And he was right. That's what I wanted to talk to you about." She pulled Henry close and held him while she asked, "Can you tell me about the picture on the table?"

He pulled away. Now it was Henry's lips that disappeared. He shook his head and didn't stop for what felt like a minute. When he did stop, he closed his eyes. He sat, completely still. He was shutting down.

"Want to dream on it, before we talk about it?"

His head moved, a tiny nod. "Okay. Dream on it tonight. We'll talk about it tomorrow?"

He opened his eyes and nodded again.

"Okay, good."

As Henry got ready for bed, he slowly seemed to return to himself. When Lane asked him if he wanted to be tucked in, "snug as a bug in a rug," he smiled and said, "Yes." When she offered three Tell Me That Story choices, he asked for the one about the day his parents met.

"Dad's roommate in college was my study partner—"

"I know this part. He told Dad he should marry you because you were smart and beautiful and kind and a good listener. And he shouldn't let you be the one who got away."

"Dad told you that?"

He nodded. "And Dad told him, maybe he should meet you before he proposed."

Lane laughed. "I never heard that before." Her eyes filled for the second time that day. "What else did Dad tell you about that?"

"He said you were the last girl he met in college and that he saved the Best for Last. And that the biggest thing he learned in college was, The Best Things in Life Are Worth Waiting For. Why are you crying?"

"I guess because I miss your dad."

Henry touched her tears with his finger and then tasted them. "Salty." Then he tasted his own. "Salty." They lay, side by side, silent for several minutes. Then Henry asked, "Want me to tell you what happens next in the story of how you met Dad?" She nodded and he did.

Hearing Henry's version felt to Lane like listening to a familiar fairy tale where all the unpleasant parts had been carefully erased, leaving only the good and the sweet.

32

Emergencies, Lane thought as she called her sister the required three times in a row, were really in the eye of the beholder. To her eye, this was one. Henry had drawn a picture of her father striking her mother, which meant Henry had seen her father striking her mother, which meant she needed to talk to Shelley and her father on the phone now, all of them now, at once, if possible—before anyone visited.

It was her niece, Melinda, who answered. "Is it Nan?" she asked. "Or is it Gramps? It can't be Gramps because he's with Mum unless— collywobbles, is it Mum? Say it fast. Who died?"

"No one died," Lane said.

"Oh well that's a relief, isn't it? I thought Mum told me that was the rule. I thought she said, 'If Auntie Lane rings the home phone three times in a row, it means someone died and you have to pick up.' Less than three times, means you just want to have an ordinary chat and it's fine if I let the call go through to the machine. Did I not get that right?"

"You got it right. No one died. I just need to talk to your mom. I tried her cell three times but the calls keep dropping so I can't leave a message. Maybe her phone died."

"Could be. I wouldn't know. She's visiting Florida. With Gramps. What a relief. I probably wasn't meant to say that. Don't tell Mum I said that. Doesn't take much for her to go all argy on me these days."

"Florida? When did they go to Florida?"

"Two days ago? Three? Let's see. How many days in a row have I had Pot Noodles for dinner? Three. They've been gone three days."

After Lane got off the phone, she went to Henry's room and stood for a moment, watching him sleep. Asleep he looked so peaceful. She checked the time—so much for peace—and stroked his forehead. "Rise and Shine." His eyelids fluttered open and then closed. "Five more minutes, okay? I'm going down to get breakfast started." He nodded.

She found her mother in the kitchen, watching the toaster. There'd been a chill between them, over the past few days, her mother and Henry equally intent on avoiding all discussion of his drawings. She'd broached the subject with Henry three times and each time he reacted the same way, by lowering his gaze and pulling in his cheeks. Each time, Lane backed off. With her mother, she'd broached the subject twice. Both times her mother mumbled, "It's not what you think," and then changed the subject to the weather. It seemed now they did nothing but discuss the weather. The heat index. The low pressure. The risk of high wind and possibly hail.

Lane had only so much to say about the weather, even hail. She was tempted to turn silent, but while it was okay to be silent as she passed her mother in the hall, it was not okay to be silent in front of Henry. So in the night, during one of her usual hours of sleeplessness, she resolved that today would be different. Whatever problems she and her mother had needed to be set aside. Today was Henry's end-of-camp celebration. Eclipse day. Lane's second dreaded eclipse of the sun; her mother's third.

"Guess what," she said, to break the kitchen chill. "I just spoke to Melinda." Her mother turned around. She looked even more pale than usual. "She told me Dad and Shelley are in Florida. Why do you think they would go there?"

"No idea." Sylvie's toast popped. She picked the slices out of the slats and carried her plate to the table. Another day, another jailhouse breakfast of dry toast and black tea. She sat with her back to Lane, so Lane moved and sat down in the chair facing her.

"Look," Lane said gently. "I know today's going to be hard for both of us."

"Not for me," her mother said. She broke off little bits of toast and began moving them around on her plate. "I'll be fine." She met Lane's eyes. "We know how to do that, be fine."

Henry padded in and came over to see what his grandmother was eating. He looked confused and pointed to the little pieces of bread. Then he made a frowny face. Lane hadn't noticed it, but he was right; the pieces of toast her mother had been playing with were assembled into a frown. She wasn't sure her mother knew she'd done that either, but now that Henry pointed it out, she quickly put several of the little pieces in her mouth. She offered the last piece of the frown to Henry and he ate it.

"Henry dear," she said after he swallowed. "Would you mind terribly if I didn't come to your camp party today? They need me at the memory center. They're having a party too. And they're short-staffed. If you mind terribly, I'll come of course."

Henry looked at his mother for help. Even if he could speak, her mother's question was full of potholes. Should he mind if she couldn't come? What did it mean to mind terribly? He looked sad. He looked like he wanted his grandmother to be at his camp celebration.

"Please come," Lane said. "Henry's been working on a surprise for us. You don't want to miss that, do you?"

Sylvie thought about it and said, "No. I don't. You win."

"Yay," Lane said. "I win."

Family and guests were invited to come at eleven. At a quarter to, Lane and Sylvie started down the path to the Rec.

Her mother seemed nearly electric, humming as she walked, arms skittering about as if she were having an extended and agitated conversation with herself in her head. A year ago, a month ago, a week ago, Lane might have ignored this. But she had grown so weary of ignoring things. She stopped walking. "I can see you're upset."

Her mother looked startled. "Not at all."

Lane ignored the denial. "It's understandable. If I had my way? There would never be another eclipse of the sun. There would never be any more eclipses of any kind. But I don't get to choose what happens in the galaxy and neither do you. All we get to choose is what we do in our family. And I don't think we've been choosing very well."

"Don't do this now. Not today."

"I agree. Not today. Today is supposed to be a happy day for Henry. It's his big end-of-camp celebration. Let's try and enjoy it, for him. And tomorrow, we can talk." Her mother's eyes held a question. "About everything."

Sylvie started walking.

"Just pretend," Lane called to the back of her mother's head. "Pretend to enjoy Henry's surprise. Pretend for once it's a regular day." The back of her mother's head nodded briskly. Of course her mother could do that. She was an excellent pretender.

As Lane expected, Sylvie had no problem pretending it was a regular day. During the short play about the hunt for the Gemini constellation, she leaned over and told Lane she thought the children had done an excellent job of learning their lines. During the song and piano recital, she ignored the lyrics about the sun and the moon and complimented the melody. As they walked past the paper-plate mobiles, she appeared oblivious that the plates were in simulated orbit and instead admired the thick brushstrokes that decorated them. As for the pinhole boxes on display, she kept her distance from those.

Henry seemed very proud, as if he'd had something to do with every part of it. And maybe he had. It was only when he took Lane's hand to lead her and his grandmother to the back room where his mural was waiting, that she felt his grip tighten and his mood shift.

"You okay, buddy?" she asked him.

He nodded and stopped. Lane turned toward the mural and read the title displayed above it, on the wall: *Oh Henry's Galaxy*.

She recognized some elements right away: the Earth, the Sun, the planets. It took her a moment to recognize the constellations. Henry had invented them all. So creative, she thought and the next thought surprised her; it was exactly what his father would have done.

Henry took her hand and led her to the legend that was posted on the wall, next to the mural. She could feel him studying her face as she read it aloud.

- Constellation Number 1: Aaron the Hunter
- Constellation Number 2: Aaron the Eagle
- Constellation Number 3: Aaron Major
- Constellation Number 4: Aaron Minor
- Constellation Number 5: Hank Aaron the Big Dipper
- Constellation Number 6: Nathan the Winged Horse

Henry was still watching her when she felt a hand on her back. A firm hand, thin fingers, gentle pressure. Her mother's hand gently pushing her. Prompting her. Lane understood.

"Oh Henry," she said. "This is spectacular."

"Take a picture," Sylvie urged her. "You should send it to a magazine. You should send it to the Guild. They should do a story about Henry and his galaxy. Such an imagination."

Henry beamed and let out a long breath; it made Lane's eyes fill to realize he'd been worried about her reaction to his mural.

As for the actual eclipse itself, Dylan announced to the visitors partway through the celebration that the view on the Island was going to be a C-minus at best.

"More like a D," he admitted a few minutes later. And then finally, "It's an F. But don't feel bad. I have a great solution." He proceeded to invite everyone to join him in a viewing party via video chat, with his dad. "He's in Nashville. He's been racing all over the place trying to find the best spot to view the path of totality. It's going to be epic."

Sylvie, Lane and Henry opted to make origami cranes instead. Lane was helping her mother fix the folds in her paper when she heard Dylan grumbling about how the spotty cell service in the Rec was totally ruining his day. The crowd around him dispersed.

Some people moved to listen to a talk about eclipses and the sea, by a mom who was a scientist. Some went to participate in an eclipse poetry slam, run by a dad who was a poet. Lane, Sylvie and Henry continued to work on their cranes. They had just finished when Nathan arrived.

"No way in the universe I was going to miss this," he told Henry. He followed them to the back room, to see Henry's mural. "Wow. That is the most amazing painting I've seen in my life. And I've lived a long time and seen a lot of paintings."

When Henry walked him over to the legend on the wall and pointed to the Nathan constellation, Nathan bowed and in his best Good-Guy Knight of the Round Table voice announced, *"I am honored and forever in your service, my talented liege."*

Henry smiled and in a very quiet, clear voice said, "Thank you."

Lane grabbed him in a tight hug and immediately excused herself to hurry out of the room before Henry could see that she was weeping.

They were walking home, Lane and Nathan ahead, Henry and Sylvie lagging behind, when Nathan asked Lane if they could have dinner.

"Of course," Lane said. "We were talking about getting lobster." She noticed his reaction. "You meant just me?"

Embarrassed, Nathan nodded. "Is it a terrible idea? I thought maybe Sylvie or Amanda could watch Henry. Forget it. You're right. It's the worst idea I've ever had. I take it back."

"It's not the worst idea," she told him. "It's just, I'm not sure my mom is up to watching Henry. Not today. And it would probably make her feel awkward having a babysitter around. And the lobsters were to celebrate Henry's mural." She didn't notice that while she was running through her list of reasons to decline, Henry and Sylvie had caught up and were listening too.

"Why don't you pick us up some lobsters and then go out?" Sylvie suggested. "Henry and I can have ourselves a lobster dinner party on the deck. What do you say, Henry?"

Henry gave her two thumbs up. He turned to his mom and waited. It was her call.

33

"Nathan!" The greeter at the restaurant gave Nathan a hug. "So great to have you back."

"Great to be back." As soon as they were seated and alone, at the last available table on the porch, Nathan apologized. "Sorry I didn't introduce you. I have no idea who that was. I have no idea how he could remember me after all these years. It's like we're two different species."

"Maybe he's just a fan," Lane said.

"I don't think so. I don't have a lot of fans."

"Why do you say that?" Her question surprised him. She understood why. While they had never discussed it, there seemed to be an unspoken agreement between them that the less shared the better. But it wasn't working for her anymore.

"If it were just me," she told Nathan now, "if it was just us, trying to figure out whether or not we're going to be friends, or something else . . ." She saw his face brighten. He hadn't expected this. "It would be different. But it's not just us." She looked out at the pond where storm clouds were gathering. "It's you and me and Henry."

"He's mad I showed you the pictures. I'm not surprised. I figured that was—"

She cut him off. "It's not about that."

"Okay." Nathan looked confused. He waited.

"Henry adores you. And for good reason. You're so patient with him and encouraging. But when I hear you say things like you don't have a lot of fans, a warning bell goes off."

"Have we decided?" The server took their orders and then opened the café umbrella that stood beside their table. "Precautionary," she told them. "Storm isn't supposed to hit until after midnight. But you know how predictions are."

Lane looked out at the bifurcated sky. Above was a high canopy of clouds, below was the setting sun. Gulls swooped out of the light and then disappeared into darkness. Across the lagoon, the houses were bathed in a golden glow.

"Just so you know," the server said, "if you have to make a run for it, no problem. I'm the fastest to-go bagger on the Island." She moved on to put up the umbrella at the next table.

"Henry deserves better," Nathan said. "You're right. He deserves the best, which he's got, with you. I'm not in that league. I shouldn't have imposed on your night."

"You're doing it again." Lane stared at the pond and tried to sort out her feelings. The Nathan she knew was kind and sweet. But she'd met people who were wary of him. And he seemed wary of himself. "Why?" She hadn't meant to say it out loud. "What don't I know about you?"

"Hmm." Nathan thought about it. "There's a list. You want it all?" She nodded. "Okay. First off, I'm not going to lie. Henry reminds me of Leo. When I'm with him, it's like I'm time traveling back to when Leo was a kid. Except with Henry, I get to do things different. I get to be better than I was the first time round."

"I'm sure you're a great dad."

"No. Okay was as good as I got. Now I'm not much of a dad at all. So there's that."

"See? You're doing it again. You drop a hint. You change the subject." As soon as she said it she realized, he wasn't the only one. Her mother did it. Her sister did it. She did it.

But Nathan didn't know about any of that. "Sorry," he said. "Habit." He rubbed his forehead. "Here's what you don't know. I fail everyone I love. I failed my ex-wife. I failed my son. I can't recognize the faces of my friends, not to mention the guy who showed us to our table. I've lost count of all the people who've lost patience with me. Your old neighbors, Rory, Karin—that bunch. They all think I'm the rudest person in the world. Except for Dana. She never got insulted. I don't know why."

"Because Dana could talk to a statue." Lane smiled. Nathan struck a pose. *The Thinker.* Lane got serious. "What happened with your son?"

"Nothing you haven't heard before. Collateral damage from the marriage. I was absent. I had a big job. I was a banker. Which is not an excuse. It's just I was out of town more than I was home. But even when I was home, I wasn't there. The only place I was ever present was right here. On this island. For two measly weeks in August. Leo's friend Artie would come with us too. The three of us—me, Leo and Artie—we had some great adventures. Artie didn't have a dad and he drove his mom crazy playing video games all day long so she loved it when he came with us. I got him out of the house and into the water. Swimming. Fishing. Clamming. He had the last laugh, Artie did."

"How so?"

"Right out of college he started a gaming company. He's my boss. The one who hired me to play his evil voices." He smiled. "Life can be strange." Lane nodded. "Leo and Artie's favorite thing? We'd go to Cuttyhunk. I'd charter a boat. Bring sleeping bags. We'd sleep under the pitch-black sky. Just us and a million stars. We had great times here. For two weeks. Two out of fifty-two. Back home, I'd take off again.

Always on the move. Going, going, gone. It was inevitable. I had no right to be surprised when Ruth gave me the ultimatum: join the family or leave. I told her it didn't work like that. I didn't have a job where I got to choose where I went or for how long. She said, *Get a new job*. I didn't know how to be the person she wanted me to be. Second time she gave me an ultimatum, stay or go, I left." He met Lane's eyes. "Moved into the house where you ended up with Henry. Decided—this was completely delusional—it was for the best. That I wasn't meant to be a full-time dad. That I would be the best part-time dad there ever was." He laughed. "You probably never heard anything as dumb as that."

"I've heard everything," she reminded him.

He nodded. "Then you won't be surprised to hear that Leo didn't agree with my assessment. He wanted nothing to do with a part-time dad. Ruth called and told me. She said, *Leo doesn't want to see you anymore*. I tried to get him to change his mind. I quit my job. Got a new job, fewer hours, no travel. Called Ruth. Told her I changed. She said, *Sorry. Too late*. Neither of them wanted anything to do with me. Ruth remarried, not long after that. Leo calls her husband *Dad*."

The server put down a plate in front of Lane. "Swordfish for you." She put the other plate in front of Nathan. "And the lamb. Enjoy."

"Here's the thing," Nathan said, when the server was gone. "Artie— the kid I used to take fishing, the kid who's now my boss—he told me Leo asked about me the other day. Out of nowhere. Asked how I was doing. I asked him to give Leo a message, to tell him I would meet him anywhere, call him anytime, do anything it takes to make things right. Artie sent him a text." Nathan shook his head. "No response. Crickets." He shrugged. "My son is not interested in forgiving me. Maybe some things are beyond forgiveness. What do you think?"

"Are you asking me or are you asking Roxie?"

Nathan looked surprised. "Same thing, no?"

Now it was Lane's turn to be surprised. "Most people say I'm nothing like Roxie."

He shrugged. "You seem the same to me." He looked out at the gathering clouds. "Before I met you, I thought I had come to terms with my life being what it is. Treading water. Trying to do no harm. Doing a dot of good a day."

"Three good things," Lane said, remembering what he told her.

Nathan nodded and then laughed. "Put that way, it sounds kind of selfish. Doing good things so I'll feel better. See? I don't deserve forgiveness. Henry deserves better than me. Both of you do. Sorry. This isn't the dinner conversation you were expecting. This must be your worst nightmare. An *Ask Roxie* letter, the worst you could imagine, come to life in front of you."

Lane laughed. "I've gotten this letter already. From you and from your ex-wife."

"You got a letter from Ruth?"

"From someone *like* Ruth. Someone *like* you." She thought about it for a moment and then explained, "I used to think the letters were a rotation of agonies. But now I think there's just one. One agony. The agony of letting ourselves down. We want to do better but we don't know how. There's so much suffering."

"Maybe people who hurt people should suffer. I hurt Leo. I don't deserve happiness."

"I don't see it that way. Sounds to me like Leo doesn't either. Sounds to me like he's ready to give you another chance. He's just working out whether he can trust that this time you'll be there for him. I think you and Leo are going to end up okay."

"I like the way that sounds. Thanks, Lane. You're pretty good at your job." He smiled. "Okay, your turn. What is it I don't know about you?"

Right. This was why she never asked people about their problems in real life. The interaction called for reciprocity. How much to share, was the question. "My husband was a drunk."

"I gathered."

"When he died, it was at a moment when we'd both forgotten we ever loved each other." Was that true? "Or maybe it was just me who forgot." Nathan nodded without judgment. She took a breath. "It's possible it was my fault he drank the way he did."

"I don't think it works that way." Nathan smiled and she smiled back at his kindness. "But even if it did, I can't imagine you doing something to him that would drive him to drink."

"I didn't do anything to *him*. But I told him what I did to someone else." She closed her eyes against the memory of it. Sitting on the pullout couch with Aaron the night they moved into their second apartment, the one that would be Henry's first home. Feeling so safe and tucked away, on the eleventh floor; she'd chalked it up to that, the odd sensation of feeling safe. That and the wine and the candles and the takeout pizza they swore was the best either of them had ever tasted. Aaron shared first. She already knew some of it; the part about losing his second parent as a teenager, about moving in with his aunt and uncle. What she hadn't known was the rest, that Aaron felt a constant pressure to entertain his aunt and uncle and cousins. Though no one had explicitly told him, he felt it as clearly as if they had: the cost of shelter in that home was to keep the household laughing. After Aaron's disclosure, it was Lane's turn to share her own never-told story. The memory switched. Aaron and the pullout were gone. In their place was Ivy.

She opened her eyes. Nathan was smiling, waiting, patient as always, for her to say more. There wasn't much more she was willing to say. "I told him a story he found unsettling. Disorienting, was how he put it. Not too long after that, he started drinking. So, connect the dots." She left it there.

Nathan nodded. She assumed he was wondering what she told Aaron that had so derailed him, but he didn't ask. She weighed the risk of telling it again. She and Nathan hadn't yet declared any feelings for each other. Theirs was a friendship tentatively leaning toward the possibility of something else. What would she lose if she shared? What would she lose if she didn't? Her phone buzzed. A text.

i'm here with henry. at the house. where are you? you need to get here now.

"My sister," she said as her fingers moved quickly, texting back, what's wrong? She pressed *Send*. "I knew she was coming but I didn't know it was tonight." She watched as the status line moved and then stopped halfway, stuck. A moment later an exclamation mark appeared. An alert: **Message Not Sent!** "I just lost service."

Nathan checked his phone. "I don't have any either." He looked at the sky. "Must be because of the storm."

At the first crack of thunder, they jumped. As the skies opened, they ran inside. By the time they settled the check, they were soaked. Nathan's arm draped around her shoulder, they raced to the car while their food, neatly packed up in a to-go bag next to the cash register, stayed behind.

The deluge had turned to a drizzle by the time they reached the house. Lane quickly counted half a dozen emergency vehicles parked at strange angles, three on the road before the turn, two in the driveway, one resting at a slight incline on the grass. As they pulled up, an ambulance marked OAK BLUFFS turned around and took off into the night. A pickup with a WEST TISBURY EMS sticker above the bumper beeped as it backed up.

Lane caught a glimpse of the face of the passenger as the truck raced off. "Aggie." She got out of the car and ran to the house. It took several minutes for her to register what she saw inside: her parents, mother and father, sitting side by side on the couch, talking to two policemen.

Sylvie looked up. "Henry's okay. He's upstairs. With your sister."

34

". . . told them that it was a big *mix-understanding*," Henry explained to Lane from his perch on Shelley's lap. To someone who knew nothing of how things had been, it might look like an unremarkable moment: a boy, in his room, sitting on his aunt's lap, speaking—in a calm, strong and unselfconscious voice. It had happened just as Doctor Bruce predicted, without warning or fanfare. One moment Henry wasn't speaking, then there was a quiet *thank you*, now he was chattering in sentences and paragraphs. What struck her was how unprepared she was; she had somehow neglected to think this through. When Henry uttered his quiet *thank you* in the Rec Center, she'd run out of the room to hide her tears. Was that right? Should the milestone pass unmarked? The thought flashed through her head that surely this was something Doctor Bruce should have prepared her for. She didn't linger on the thought. Instead, she followed her chipped heart, scooped Henry up in a tight hug and told him she loved him.

"Why are you crying?" he asked her when she let go.

"I'm happy. I don't know why sometimes people cry when they're happy." He stared at her face, which she knew did not look one bit happy. "I'm relieved," she admitted. "I'm happy and relieved that you're okay."

Shelley, who'd been waiting for her turn, opened her arms. "Hey you." Lane walked into her embrace and Shelley held her close.

After a moment, Lane stepped back, wiped her cheek and asked why there were police downstairs. "I saw an ambulance pull away when we got here. What happened?" Before Shelley could answer, she added, "Why did you come?"

"I know," Shelley said. "I know. I know. I know. I swore I would never come back." She cleared her throat. "But I also swore I'd finally have this conversation with you."

"What conversation?"

"Griffin broke his toe," Henry piped up. Shelley nodded. "Grandpa maybe broke his toe, but we don't know because he won't let anyone look at it. He feels bad that the chair fell over the railing and broke in half. He said he'll replace it. Don't be mad. He didn't know."

Lane sat on the floor and gave Henry her total attention. "What didn't he know?"

Shelley sat down next to Lane. "Dad thought that man was an intruder."

"His name is Griffin," Henry told his aunt. "He's just a boy. He came over to play with me. Mom invited him to." He turned to Lane. "Did you? Griffin's mom said you did."

Lane felt like she was underwater. The facts were coming in a fast current. She tried to keep track of all the things she didn't yet understand. Her father and mother were in the living room talking to the police. Her sister was in Henry's room. Henry wanted confirmation that she'd invited Griffin over to play with him. Had she? She had. She'd invited him to come over when she was sitting on Aggie's dock. "Yes," she told Henry. "I did. What happened?"

"I think Grandpa didn't realize Griffin was a boy who stayed a boy, even when he got big. He probably never saw a kid that size before. I didn't know Griffin was a kid either the first time I saw him. But now I know. He's a giant-size kid. He likes to swim, like Mom," he told his aunt. "And draw, like me," he told his mom. "We were out on the deck drawing when Aunt Shelley came. We were drawing the storm sky. Grandma Sylvie wasn't sure it was safe for us to sit outside when a storm was coming so Griffin's mom checked with Griffin to make sure he knew what you do if it *lighteninged*. Griffin knew. He said, *If it lightenings, we'll run in at the first bolt, faster than the wind*. Then Grandma said she'd make Griffin's mom some tea if she wanted. I think that's what they were doing when Aunt Shelley came with Grandpa. They came to surprise us, but instead Griffin surprised them and everything got in a mess."

"It looked like no one was home when we came in," Shelley told Lane. "I went to the kitchen to see if anyone was there. Dad saw Henry out on the deck. He went out to say hello and saw Griffin and—"

"Griffin wouldn't talk to him," Henry interrupted. "Even when Grandpa asked his name in his angry voice, Griffin wouldn't talk."

"He told me Griffin wouldn't look at him," Shelley told Lane. "I think they spooked each other. Dad decided Griffin wasn't supposed to be here, and he started yelling at him to leave."

"Which made Griffin scared, which is why he stood up really fast, which is how the chair hit Grandpa, which was an accident. But Grandpa didn't know it was an accident and he picked up the chair and threw it at Griffin, and Griffin ducked and the chair went over the railing. Which made Grandpa yell more, which made Griffin walk backward to get away from him. And then Griffin got close to where the stairs start and the deck stops, and I didn't want him to fall off like cousin Ivy."

Shelley opened her mouth and then closed it.

"Because the stairs aren't as high up as a window, but they're high up. So I screamed loud. Like Francesca screams when people don't listen to her."

Lane took his hand and kissed it.

"And then Grandpa grabbed Griffin and they both fell down and the table crashed and Griffin started yelling, 'Ow, ow, ow,' and his mom came out to see what happened. And then there was a lot of yelling and then there were sirens and then a woman came and said, 'May I check your foot,' and then she said, 'I think it's broken.' And then Grandma Sylvie said she should check Grandpa's foot and Grandpa yelled, 'Don't touch me.' And everybody got tangled up and then untangled. And they went to the living room except for me and Aunt Shelley. We came up here. And here we are."

"And then—" Shelley said, urging him on.

"And then Aunt Shelley and I had a big talk. And she asked me some questions and I told her some answers and she said she was glad she came and I said I was glad she came and I asked her if she could live with us and she said, 'I wish.' Is Grandpa going to be mad at me forever?"

"Why would he be mad at *you*?" Lane asked and Henry shrugged.

"We should go down and check on them," Shelley said. She turned to her nephew. "Want to stay up here or come?"

"Stay here." Henry reached for his sketch pad and grabbed a pencil and started drawing.

Shelley filled Lane in as they walked down the stairs.

They found their parents in the kitchen, sitting at the table chatting, as if it were any old day. The police were gone.

Marshall was the first to see them. "I'll replace the chair and the table. With something sturdier than particleboard. That stuff is flimsy." Lane said nothing. "It's because I didn't know who that fellow was. And Henry looked scared. Come on, Turtle. No harm no foul?"

"Please don't call me Turtle. Henry was scared because of *you*."

"Okay. I see how this is going." He turned to his wife. "Shelley and I got us a couple of rooms at a motel. Nothing fancy, but clean. Shelley, are you coming? Or am I calling a taxi?"

"Before you go . . ." Lane sat down next to him. "Did you tell Henry not to speak?"

"Why would I say something like that?"

"He didn't mean anything by it," Sylvie told Lane. She tapped Marshall's arm. "You didn't mean anything by it. These things happen." She looked down into her lap for a moment and then met Lane's eyes. "I've told you before. Things happen. We can't always say why. Sometimes it's no one's fault."

"Tell Lane what happened when she came to visit you with Henry," Shelley said. Her parents sat frozen in place and said nothing. "Okay. I'll tell her." She turned to her sister. "One night when you were fast asleep like a turtle in a shell—this is obviously according to Dad . . ."

Marshall stared at his feet. Sylvie's arms were crossed over her chest.

"Henry got up to go to the bathroom but he got lost. And by accident"—she turned to her parents and repeated that—"*by accident*, he opened the door to Uncle Albie's room. And Dad heard him. And he came running out. And when he saw Henry in the hallway, he yelled for him to stop spying."

"I never said spying," Marshall corrected her.

"Spying is what Henry heard. Henry told me you yelled at him to stop spying. And he said he wasn't spying. And you wouldn't believe him. You said, 'Why would someone peek into a room that wasn't theirs if they weren't spying?'"

"Good point," Marshall said.

"It's because you didn't get a new bulb when the night-light burned out," Sylvie told Marshall. "Henry got lost because it was too dark in that hall." She was quiet for a moment and when she spoke again, her voice was steely. "You did get angry with him, Marshall. And it made him very upset." She turned to Lane. "He wet the carpet. He didn't mean to. I wasn't angry. But you know how your father can be when he's agitated."

Chip. Another bit of Lane's heart fell away.

"I didn't yell," Marshall grumbled. "I purposely didn't yell because that might have woken up Turtle. Lane," he corrected himself, and turned to her. "If I yelled and you woke up, you would have turned the whole thing into a big megillah. I didn't yell."

"A person doesn't have to yell to sound angry," Sylvie said. "You were angry. So angry. You were practically growling. 'Get out of the hall. Get in here right now.' It's really no wonder he was terrified." She whispered the next to Lane. "I swear I've never hit him before. Not once."

Lane's eyes widened. "You hit Henry?"

"No. I would never do that. I hit your father. It really was more of a push. A shove, to get him to stop. To get him to snap out of it. Which he did. He snapped out of it and he fell down. I'm quite sure it was because he wasn't expecting me to push him. Poor Henry just stood there. He didn't know what to do. I told him, 'Forget this. Forget everything you saw. Nothing happened. The carpet is fine. Your grandfather is fine. I'm fine. We will all continue to tiptoe around as if nothing happened.' And then you . . ." She turned to Marshall.

"What did I do now?"

"You told Henry he mustn't tell, no matter what. You told him his mother couldn't take it if one more thing happened. You made him promise. You said a promise has to stick or else. Then you just . . ." She mimed the rest: closed her mouth, locked her mouth, threw away the key.

Shelley nodded. "That's exactly what Henry told me. He made a promise that he wouldn't talk. And a promise has to stick or else. He's been worrying a lot about the *or else* part. He's not sure what that means, but he knows it isn't good."

Lane took it all in. "But he did speak. He never stopped speaking to me."

"I know," Shelley said. "He tried. But it didn't work. He could stay quiet with everyone but you. So he made a deal with himself. He just wouldn't talk to you about the part where Grandpa got mad and Grandma fell down."

"He got it all mixed up," Sylvie said. "I saw that in his drawing. It was the other way around. I hit your father. Not hard. It wasn't a real fall."

"She caught me off guard," Marshall said. "I didn't expect her to shove me."

"It's because it's been so hard." Sylvie patted Marshall's arm. "For such a long time."

Marshall's eyes went from one daughter to the other and then stopped at Lane. "He's a good boy, your son. I didn't mean to frighten him. I regret that. I regret a lot of things. But I regret that most of all. I'm tired." He sighed. "So very tired."

They heard it at the same time: Henry, who'd been sitting on the bottom step listening, was now running up the stairs. He came back a moment later, with a pillow and a blanket, which he handed to his grandfather. "You should take a nap. Then you won't be tired. You can sleep on the couch. Or you can take a nap in my bed. We don't have rules about that anymore."

Later, after Henry was in bed and her parents were downstairs waiting for their taxi, Lane and Shelley went to put fresh sheets on the bed in the room in which her mother had been sleeping.

Shelley jammed a pillow into a case and asked, "When did you tell Henry about Ivy?"

The question was not unexpected. "It's because I put up window guards. In the house in New Jersey. And he wanted to know why. So I told him. Not all of it." She sat down on the freshly made bed. "Why are they so uncomfortable around me?" Shelley shrugged. Lane went on. "Mom's been here the whole summer and she still gets all fluttery if she thinks I'm going to ask her a question. She gets fluttery and then she leaves the room. Dad won't even risk hearing a question; he avoids being alone with me altogether. You do the same thing on the phone."

"You're right." She placed the pillow on the bed. "This is the conversation I was talking about. The one we need to have. You must know what it is that everyone's avoiding." She studied Lane's face. "You don't know." She sat down next to her. "Do you remember what it was like in the house, after Ivy's accident?"

"Yes. Mom and Dad fought all the time. When they weren't fighting, either Mom or Uncle Albie was crying."

"It was everything at once," Shelley said. "Mom and Dad would be yelling and Mom and Uncle Albie would be sobbing. Remember what you did?" Lane shook her head. She had no idea. "You stopped talking. You marched into the living room one night and announced, 'I'm never going to speak again until you stop.' It was like you went on strike. You wouldn't even talk to me. It lasted about a week. You were totally silent. Mealtime. Bedtime. At school. And it worked. Mom and Dad pulled themselves together and they shut everything down. There were no more fights. There was no more crying. Dad must have read the riot act to Uncle Albie because after that is when he started taking his meals in his room. The next time we sat down for dinner, you said something, 'Please pass the chicken' or 'Can I have some salt?' and that was that. We were back to normal. Meckler normal. You don't remember?"

Lane didn't remember, but she knew what Shelley said was right. She could feel the truth of it. And more truth: from that day till now her family had withdrawn from her.

A thought occurred to her. If Henry did something by accident, something awful, she would never withdraw from him. She would hold him tight and love him harder. Because he was only a child. She'd been only a child. "How could they blame a child for an accident?"

"Oh, Lanie. No one blamed you. It wasn't your fault." Shelley lay down on the bed and patted the pillow next to her so Lane would lie down too. "Remember when I came to Florida, when Henry was a wee little thing?" Lane nodded. "Didn't you wonder why?" Lane told her she did. "I came because it was eating at me, what you thought. I wanted to talk to you about it. But Dad kept following me around the house like an old dog. I think he knew. He knew what I wanted to say and he didn't want me to say it."

"What did you want to say?"

Shelley took a breath and stared at the ceiling. "It was hate at first sight with you and Ivy. But that doesn't mean what happened was your fault."

"I was so jealous. I didn't even know what jealous was then, but I felt it. I couldn't bear for you to go out on the roof with her. I got so mad. So I—"

"No. You've got it wrong. You remember it wrong. I didn't go out on the roof. The roof had a skin of ice; I wasn't stupid. But Ivy didn't care about the ice. She was pushing me to go out. She was getting on my nerves." They lay in silence for a moment and then Shelley turned to Lane. "I wasn't there when it happened. After I told Ivy I wasn't going to go out and she asked you to go, I left. I ran downstairs and asked Mom if it was okay for Ivy to go out on the roof. I knew what Mom would do. And she did it. She raced upstairs and—" She stopped. "It wasn't your fault."

Lane closed her eyes. What was she missing? Her memory was clear to a point and then it stopped. "You just said you weren't there. You don't know."

"I know because you told me. Before you went on strike. Right after it happened. Right after Uncle Albie started wailing about how he couldn't call Aunt Beadie and Mom said, okay, she'd make the call. And Dad walked in with his suitcase, from a business trip. Talk about timing."

Lane remembered that. "Then the ambulance came. And they went to the hospital."

"And we stayed home. And I went to the basement to find something to do. And I came back with Operation. I guess I thought that was a good idea. That it would make us feel like we were at the hospital with them if we played Operation. Only you were no good at it. You were shaking too much. You couldn't remove a single organ without the buzzer going off."

Lane could hear it. The buzzer going off again and again. "And then they came back and told us Ivy didn't make it. I don't remember who told us."

Shelley did. "It was Dad. And then Uncle Albie made that sound."

Their mother's voice cut through their reverie. "Turtle? Shelley? The taxi's going to be here in a minute."

Shelley went downstairs, but Lane didn't move. She was hearing it now, as if Uncle Albie were there with her, keening in despair. "What happened?" she asked the empty room.

She closed her eyes as images flickered by. Ivy climbing up onto the sill. The roof glistening with its sheen of ice. Ivy asking Lane to get her pinhole box so they could watch the eclipse without going blind.

It was Shelley who noticed there was no hole in the box. "It won't work," she told Lane. "You made a no-hole pinhole box. It doesn't matter. We're not going out there."

Then Lane said she could fix it. And Ivy asked if she would come out on the roof with her. And Lane nodded. And Ivy said, "See. Lane's not a scaredy-cat." And Shelley ran downstairs.

Lane remembered how that felt, everything switching, Ivy suddenly deciding Lane was who she wanted to be with. Ivy urging her to hurry. Lane grabbing a thumbtack from her bulletin board. The box resisted. It was too thick.

"It's happening," Ivy called to her. "The eclipse is happening. Hurry. Give me the box."

Lane could see it, Ivy with one hand on the windowsill, lowering herself out so that she was half in, half out, waiting, impatiently, for Lane to make the hole in the box. She could feel it, how the pushpin resisted and then all of a sudden, went through. She stood up and took a step toward Ivy but before she could give her the box there were hands on her back, her mother's hands, pushing her out of the way so she could get to where Ivy was and pull her back inside.

Except when her mother pushed her out of the way, Lane's body went limp at her touch and her limp body flew forward and the box she was handing to Ivy flew forward and Ivy, on the other side of the box, flew forward, and out and down, sliding down the roof. The incline was gentle, but primed with ice it was angled enough to act like a giant slick slide.

"Turtle. Lane." Her mother stood in the threshold of the guest room of the pond house. She met Lane's eyes. "It was not your fault. It was *my* fault. All of it. Lanie, I'm sorry."

She flew into her mother's arms and they held each other tight, tears commingling.

PART FOUR

HOME

SUMMER 2018

35

From Global Guild International, this is *Problem Child* with Lane Meckler.

Phone call recording, Cody: My name is Cody. I'm ten years old and I live in Pittsburgh, Pennsylvania. My mom took me to hear your talk when you came to my school.

Lane Meckler: It happens more than you'd think. I'm only able to do a few school events a year but when I do them, there are always kids with questions, waiting at the end. At some point the facilitator moves to shut things down, so I tell the kids, the *Problem Child* podcast is for grown-ups but if you have a question and your parents give permission, you're welcome to call in to the show.

Phone call recording, Cody: My parents don't live together anymore. I live in my mom's house for one part of the week, and in my dad's house for the other part. Which is okay most of the time. But sometimes I want to switch houses, because my friends in the neighborhood where I'm not are doing something fun. My babysitter doesn't drive. Last time it happened, I asked my mom if I could switch houses for a day and she cried and said, *Ask your dad.* When I asked my dad, he didn't answer because he was busy being mad that my mom cried. That night I got a stomachache and forgot to do my homework. The next day, when my teacher walked around the room to collect homework, I told her I didn't do it and I told her why. She said I should ask my mom if I could tell my problem to Lane Meckler. Which is what I'm doing. What do you think I should do?

Lane Meckler: The first person I spoke to when I got the call was my son. He just turned seven. Here's what he had to say about Cody's problem.

Lane Meckler's son: I think Cody should ask his mom and dad if they could both move closer. Maybe on the same block or around the block. That way Cody could be with his friends any day he wants and his mom's feelings wouldn't get hurt and his dad wouldn't get mad about it. Living in two places sounds hard. Also, I think Cody's dad should try not to care when Cody's mom cries. Sometimes people have to cry so they don't get their feelings stopped up. Maybe his dad could do something to help him be less mad. Maybe take a walk. Also the babysitter should learn to drive.

Lane Meckler: There you have it. The wisdom of kids. Today on *Problem Child*, we're going to talk about the difficulty of coparenting after divorce with a woman who's spent her career listening to kids. Mary Arthur, student assistant counselor at the Lanapi School, welcome to *Problem Child*.

Mary Arthur: Thank you, Lane. It's great to talk to you again.

Lane told Henry he could pick anything he wanted to celebrate their move back into the pond house. They'd both enjoyed their winter rental house in Vineyard Haven. They liked being able to walk to the bookstore and the library, and to sit by the sea and watch the ferries come and go. But they visited the pond house often, sometimes several times in a week after Henry got out of school.

The crew putting in the new heating system—the old one was fine for a summer place but was not made for winter use—had adopted Henry. When they stopped by the house, there was always a special snack waiting—peanut-butter fudge from Murdick's, or a couple of apple fritters from Back Door Donuts—and they always invited him to help, either by passing them tools or holding a flashlight to shine on hard-to-see spaces.

Nathan was usually there too, busy outfitting the spare bedroom with the recording studio equipment he'd brought over from his New Jersey house for Lane to use for the podcast. Sam had been quick to approve the idea of Lane doing the podcast remotely, probably, Lane thought, because he was not only relieved she agreed to do a podcast, but happy that she'd come up with an idea that was simultaneously on-brand for her and also something new.

Summer took the news that she was not going to be Lane's cohost surprisingly well. While the gossip Hugo had shared was correct—Summer was directed by Bert to pass along a purloined letter to Lane—she'd never followed through. And Alyssa wasn't the only one she told. Upon Sam's return, Summer shared the details of everything Bert had been up to. She was very young—twenty-two, as Lane learned—but her sense of justice was as strong as her positive attitude.

It was Sam's idea to put Summer's positive attitude to use in the new Guild position of chief happiness officer. Summer's first project was already underway. A Wall of Win was now up in the reception area. On it were framed Guild and Guild-Plus reader emails that praised employees who'd been especially helpful, along with a variety of framed awards in categories Summer had created for staff members to earn.

Lane suspected that Hugo was going to be happily surprised when he saw the wall, upon his return from his leave of absence. It was just a summer leave, which he'd arranged immediately after learning that his play—the one he'd been writing on his phone, a musical about an abusive boss—had won first prize in a first-time playwright's contest. The prize, which included a small monetary award, meant that his play would be workshopped at the Williamstown Theater in Massachusetts.

Bert would not have liked the Wall of Win. There was not a single place to click on it. But Bert was no longer at the Guild. Last Lane heard, he was now CFO of a new digital addiction center in Arizona.

As for *Problem Child*, Lane assumed the appetite for podcasts would go away, just as everything else did, replaced by something no one had thought of yet. But in the meantime, she was relieved to have stumbled upon the idea for it. The best part was that she had filed away enough *Roxie* letters from children over the years, letters tucked away in the NEVER folder since Roxie never answered letters from children, that she was able to get a quick start. And to her great surprise, doing the *Problem Child* podcast turned out to be a joy.

It was the *Ask Roxie* readers who were having the toughest transition. They'd been slow to adjust to the new tone of the column, written by Lane's replacement, her friend Jem, now known as Roxie Three. Lane was quick to reassure her friend that the readers would come around; they always did. She also shared the good news—which Sam had shared with her—that *Ask Roxie*, as written by Jem, was attracting new readers, who skewed younger. This was great for the Guild. And with Sam back in charge and Bert gone and replaced, what was good for the Guild was good for Lane.

As for how to celebrate the move back into the pond house, Henry didn't hesitate. "First the carousel. Then donuts."

By the end of his first autumn on the island, Henry was a frequent rider on the Flying Carousel in Oak Bluffs. He even had a favorite, a gray horse named Moshup. He hadn't yet managed to grab one of the brass rings that would win him a free ride. But on this cool night, on the cusp of the summer season when the carousel was still only open on weekends, he seemed confident things were going to go his way.

While Henry waited in line, Lane and Nathan stopped to see Zoltar, the mechanical fortune-teller. Nathan fed a dollar into the slot; Zoltar's eyes moved and settled on Lane's.

"You are most beloved," Zoltar proclaimed, "when you are happy."

"Sorry to disagree with you," Nathan said, "but she is beloved, no matter what."

They got to the carousel just as Henry boarded. As soon as the Wurlitzer began, Henry stood up in the stirrups and put one of his knees on the horse.

"What is he doing?" she asked. "He's going to fall off." She opened her mouth to call to him but Nathan put his hand on her arm to stop her.

"He won't fall off." Nathan looked sheepish and admitted he told Henry to do that. "At his size, that's the only way he's going to reach the brass ring. He has to put up a knee and lean. It's a trick I learned from Leo. He's holding on tight. See?"

It took some work for her not to call out a warning. At one point she had to close her eyes and silently repeat, *He won't fall off, he won't fall off, he's not in danger of falling off.* Then Henry's voice cut through her thoughts.

"Mom!"

Her eyes snapped open.

"Look! I got it!" He held up a brass ring.

Lane applauded. Nathan gave a high five to the air.

Henry caught it, put it in his imaginary pocket, and deposited his brass ring on the spoke between the horse's ears. He got the brass ring three times that night. At one point, Lane asked Nathan if he'd paid someone off, because what were the odds?

Nathan laughed. "I think he's just having a lucky day."

After the third win, Henry got off the carousel. He walked over and asked Lane if she wanted to see his last brass ring up close.

"Don't you have to hand it in for a free ride?"

He looked at Nathan, who said, "He'll get his free ride in a minute. Take a look."

There was something odd in Nathan's tone that she couldn't place. She ignored it and told Henry, "Okay. Let me see it."

Henry peeled open his hand and Lane stared, confused. It wasn't a brass ring. It was an engagement ring.

Nathan kneeled down and took her hand. After she said yes, he asked Henry to help him slip the ring on his mother's finger.

After Henry washed up that night, he came into his room and saw his mom on his bed. In her lap was a box.

"I ordered this months ago," she told him and handed it over. "For you."

Henry traced the carving on top, a large tree with many branches and no leaves. At the bottom were the initials *A. D.* He thought about it for a moment and then said, "Aaron Dash?"

She nodded.

"What is it?"

"It's called a memory box. If you want, you can use it for memories about Dad. You could put in things Dad gave you, like your flashlights. Or you could use it for stories. We could write down some of your favorite Dad stories. You could illustrate them."

"We could both illustrate them," Henry said. "I could show you how to use the watercolor dots Nathan gave me. They're really easy to use. Would you like to do that?"

"I would love to do that."

Henry nodded. Then his face shifted. "Can I ask you a question you might not like?"

"Of course. We decided that, remember? You can ask anything, anytime."

"Okay." He seemed to relax. "Do you want to put your letter inside? The one Dad wrote to you? Unless you didn't keep it. Because you didn't like it. Or because you didn't want to move with it. Rule Number Five."

Lane smiled. "I don't believe in those rules anymore. And thank you for thinking of it. I did keep it. At first I couldn't find it, which made me upset. That's how I realized how much I wanted to keep it."

"Where was it?"

"In the back of my night table drawer. Exactly where I put it when you gave it to me."

"Is it a Happy letter? Or a Never-Give-Up letter? Or a Sad letter? You don't have to say."

Lane thought about how to answer. The letter, which Aaron had written only weeks before his death, was short. Four sentences that she had read enough times to know by heart. In it, Aaron apologized for his drinking and then explained that Brielle was getting him information about a rehab clinic that had helped several of their friends from AA. That was the most surprising part of the letter, that Aaron had been going to AA. In the letter he declared his intention to go to the clinic and get sober. Then he declared his love for her and Henry. Short and bittersweet.

"I'd say yes, it's a never-give-up letter," she told Henry. "Happy and sad, both at once."

"Can I read it?"

"Yes. When you're older."

"Will it make me Sad?"

"Probably. But you know how sad goes. It doesn't last forever."

"Is that a rule? Do we have any rules?"

Lane twirled one of Henry's curls. "We have safety rules. Always wear your helmet on your bike. Always buckle your seat belt."

"Don't look at an eclipse without special glasses," he added. "Never go out on a roof." He looked at her. "Is that okay to say?"

"Everything is okay to say. Those are all good rules. No looking at an eclipse without glasses. No going out on a roof."

"I have another one," Henry said. "But it's not about safety."

"What's it about?"

"It's about, never go to bed without a good-night kiss."

"Perfect. That will be our main family rule." Her phone buzzed. She checked to see who it was. "Good. I have a surprise for you."

"A good one?"

"I think so. Want to come and see?"

They got downstairs just as Nathan walked in. "Sorry I'm late. I got stuck in ferry traffic." He kneeled down and let loose the small puppy that had been pawing at his arms. "I'd say this little guy is pretty eager to meet you, Henry."

"The puppy's for me? For real?"

"For real," Lane told him.

Later, while Nathan was downstairs getting the training crate open and filling up the water and food bowls, Lane lay down next to Henry in his bed and answered a slowly petering-out round of questions.

"When Grandpa Marshall and Grandma Sylvie come for Thanksgiving, will they want to play with the puppy?"

"Yes."

"Do they like puppies?"

"I hope so. But if they don't, that's okay. Not everybody has to like our puppy. You know who definitely likes puppies? Cousin Melinda. Aunt Shelley told me she can't wait to play with him. Now all you have to do is figure out his name."

"I have two ideas but I can't decide which one to pick."

"What are they?"

"The puppy's name is either New Norman or Old Norman."

"That's a tough one. Those are both great names. You could just call him plain Norman."

"Okay," Henry said. "That's his name. *Plane* Norman." He rolled on his side. "Can Plane Norman sleep with me tonight?"

"He's not quite ready for that yet," Lane said. "But soon." She turned off the light and said good night.

"Wait—remember the rule?"

Lane came back and kissed Henry's head.

Then he kissed hers. "Love you, Mom. Forever, or at least for now."

"Love you, Henry. Now and forever."

ACKNOWLEDGMENTS

The author is grateful to all who offered support during the years of writing this novel. It takes a village. In particular:

To the beloved former Dear Prudie advice columnist, Emily Yoffe, who agreed to talk to a writer in her early days of conjuring a novel, my eternal gratitude. Lane Meckler is an invented character who lives only in this novel, and in the imagination of this novel's readers, but her good heart and best intentions were inspired in no small part by Emily's kindness, compassion, wisdom, and good humor.

For sharing other expertise, thank-yous go to: Debbie Miller, Barbara Lennon, and Fran Legman. I am also grateful to a brilliant early reader with a great critical eye and a keen sense of humor, who sadly is no longer around to read these thanks: the luminous Debbie Jurkowitz, who left too soon.

To my fellow scribes in the Montclair Writers' Group, who are as rich in talent and fortitude as they are in kindness, my heartfelt grati-tude. For acts of heroism above and beyond what any writer should dare expect, thank you Alice Dark, Lisa Gornick, Dale Russakoff, Christina

Baker Kline, Laura Schenone, Jill Smolowe, Cindy Handler. Thanks also to Marlene Adelstein, Jayne Pliner and Susan Dalsimer.

To Margot Sage-El, guardian angel of Montclair writers: thank you for your friendship and enduring support. Thanks also go to your dedicated colleagues, who help make Watchung Booksellers a sanctuary for readers and writers alike.

To my wonderful agent, Elizabeth Winick Rubinstein, and to the lovely Zoe Bodzas, thank you for your spot-on counsel and unwavering support. To the great editor Jodi Warshaw, thank you for continuing to be a writer's dream, devoted to doing whatever you can to make a book better. Thanks also go to the Lake Union team, including Danielle Marshall, Gabrielle Dumpit, Dennell Catlett, Rosanna Brockley, Nicole Pomeroy and their hardworking dedicated colleagues.

To Silvia Olarté, a kind soul with a brilliant mind and a life-size editorial eye: I am forever grateful.

I am so lucky to have the abundant good fortune of sharing my life with the huge-hearted lovelies who make up my family. To Izzy and their partner Raquel, to Lizzy, Peter and sweet Jonah and Penelope: no one could invent a more wonderful home-team than you.

Finally to my husband, Larry—soul mate, first reader, first critic, best champion, bread-baker and all around stalwart force of good, you know it is not hyperbole to say this: I could have done it without you, but I wouldn't want to.

ABOUT THE AUTHOR

Photo 2019 © Leslie Dumke

Nancy Star is the author of the bestselling novel *Sisters One, Two, Three*, a *Publishers Weekly* top ten print book and Amazon Kindle bestseller of 2016. Her previous novels, which have been translated into several languages, include *Carpool Diem*, *Up Next*, *Now This*, and *Buried Lives*. Her essays have appeared in the *Washington Post*, the *New York Times*, *Money*, and *Family Circle*. Before turning to writing fiction full-time, Nancy worked for over a decade as a movie executive at the Samuel Goldwyn Company and the Ladd Company, dividing her time between New York and London. She now lives in New Jersey and Martha's Vineyard with her husband. For more information, visit www.nancystarauthor.com.